SHORT-SIGHTED

Bishop Lukin of the Tribunal gestured sharply to Brother Giles, who produced a short length of rope with two crude knots in it. Giles fitted the knots over Sutter's eyes, then took the ends of the rope and wound them around a wooden, cross-shaped lever. He gave it a twist. As the rope tightened, it pressed the knots hard against the tender flesh of the prisoner's eyes.

"You'll see precious little in that vision sphere of yours without any eyes, my friend," Bishop Lukin told him. "What good will your magic do you then?"

"Please," Sutter begged. "I told you. I left Athaya." Then the words spewed out from the imprisoned man in a frightened stream, and the scribe snatched parchment and scrambled to take down everything the prisoner said.

"But I can lead you there," Sutter told them. "To Athaya's camp. With me to show you the way, you could take them all. I don't care what happens to her, to any of them. Please, just leave my eyes."

By Julie Dean Smith
Published by Ballantine Books:

A Caithan Crusade
   CALL OF MADNESS
   MISSION OF MAGIC
   SAGE OF SARE

SAGE
OF
SARE

Julie Dean Smith

A Del Rey Book

BALLANTINE BOOKS • NEW YORK

A Del Rey Book
Published by Ballantine Books

Copyright © 1992 by Julie Dean Smith

All rights reserved under International and Pan-American Copyright Conventions. Published in the United States of America by Ballantine Books, a division of Random House, Inc., New York, and simultaneously in Canada by Random House of Canada Limited, Toronto.

Library of Congress Catalog Card Number: 92-90614

ISBN 0-345-37154-2

Manufactured in the United States of America

First Edition: December 1992

Cover Art by Michael Herring

To my mother,
a sage of sorts . . .

And God granted His chosen people a measure of His grace; thus, as He is the master of men in heaven, so shall magicians be the masters of men on earth.

—Dameronne of Crewe
The first Sage of Sare

CHAPTER 1

※

S ISTER KATHERINE DARTED OUT OF THE TINY CELL AND
slammed the door behind her only an instant before an
earthenware goblet shattered into violent fragments on the
other side.

"And *stay* out, you bloodthirsty hypocrite!" a high-pitched
voice shrieked from inside the cell. The iron-banded door shuddered as another piece of crockery was dashed against it and
rendered into splinters. "Stay out and leave me alone!"

Assuming a mask of bravery, Katherine tipped up her chin
and let out a crisp puff of breath, sending aloft a wisp of honey-
blond hair that had escaped the confines of her wimple. Delicate
nostrils flared in a show of exasperation. "Delighted to oblige,"
she retorted, but the effect of her defiant words was ruined by
an unsteady voice. The young nun lingered at the door only long
enough to slide the dead bolt into place, locking the cell's enraged occupant securely inside.

That done, Sister Katherine cast a fleeting glance skyward.
"Lend me strength, Lord." She hid her slender, shaking fingers
inside voluminous sleeves and hurried down the corridor of the
convent's guest cloister, the skirts of her somber gray habit
whipping up behind her like churning waters.

"Oh!"

Katherine emitted a startled cry as she rounded the corner,
her hands flying up to her cheeks as she narrowly avoided a

1

collision with the two women silently approaching from the other direction. The first was a stout, stern-looking matriarch of middle years who held up a sagging chin with regal dignity and the second was an elderly wisp of a woman, shadow thin and humpbacked, whose face was as hard and pitted as the convent's limestone walls. Both were clad in the unadorned gray robes and starched white wimples traditional to their order; only the charcoal-colored stole draped over the younger woman's shoulders served to mark her as the highest-ranking resident of Saint Gillian's.

Sister Katherine placed one hand over her heart to steady its beating and then remembered herself and dutifully inclined her head to her superiors. "Good morning, Mother Abbess. Good morning, Sister Edwina."

Abbess Mary Helene nodded a wordless greeting, quickly discerning the look of distress on the young nun's face. Pursing her lips in distaste, she flicked her eyes briefly down the corridor from which Katherine had come. There could be no doubt as to what—or rather, who—had driven the young nun to such a nervous state.

"How is she this morning?" the abbess asked.

"Worse than usual, I'm afraid," Katherine replied. Wearily, she tucked the stray lock of hair back inside her wimple. "She was quiet enough yesterday, but today—" The nun bit down on her lower lip to keep it from trembling, but her frustration had grown too potent to suppress; her next words erupted like poison from a lanced boil. "Saint Gillian forgive me, but there are times when I think I'd rather have the Devil himself in my charge!"

"Katherine!" The abbess regarded her sharply, brown eyes flashing. "Do not cast such words about idly. The Devil has ears in Caithe and he might well grant you such a wish for your imprudence."

The nun lowered her oval face in contrition and sniffled softly. "I am sorry," she murmured. "I ought to have shown more compassion."

Abbess Helene cocked an ear at the faint sound of singing now drifting down the corridor, the eldritch music randomly broken by fits of shrill laughter. Her features shifted just then, growing darker and more condemning.

"We owe compassion to all God's creatures, Sister Katherine," she observed with cool deliberation. "Princess Athaya, however, is not among them." Then the abbess offered the younger nun a forgiving smile. "I only meant that you should not wish the Devil into our house. The Devil's Child is proving to be bad enough."

The abbess turned to the old woman at her side. "Come, Edwina. Let us see for ourselves how her Highness is faring today."

The elderly nun scowled up in displeasure, her face puckering like a piece of dried fruit. "And it had been such a pleasant morning ere now," she mumbled under her breath.

"With respect, Mother Abbess," Katherine ventured, anxiously wringing her hands, "I don't think that would be wise—"

"Now, now, Katherine . . . you are overwrought! It has only been ten days since I last saw her. How much worse can she be?"

Katherine's eyes grew desperate. "Please, I beg you—"

Her superior's austere glare quickly silenced any further objections. "You may go and change into another robe, Sister Katherine," the abbess said in brusque dismissal. "Yours appears to be stained."

The young nun glanced down at the streaks of grease striping the front of her habit—evidence of the butter dish that Athaya had thrown at her earlier—and flushed bright red. "Yes, ma'am," she replied. She dropped a brief curtsy and scurried out of the cloister, visibly glad to be gone.

Another fragment of tuneless music floated down the corridor, and the abbess absently adjusted her stole as she listened to the princess' voice echoing off the stones like the wail of a ghost engaged in a fine morning's haunting.

"P-perhaps Sister Katherine is right," Edwina said. She touched her withered fingers to the abbess' arm, suddenly discomfited by the idea of entering Athaya's cell without a pair of well-armed men at her back. "The king may have promised us that his sister's magic is beyond her reach, but I still fear what she might do."

"Nonsense," the abbess assured her, raising her chin up to its customary position. "Without her spells, Athaya Trelane is nothing more than a common madwoman. Erratic, yes, but she can do little worse than throw insults and crockery at us and *that* she's done several times before." The abbess set off down the corridor with unruffled confidence, and Edwina grudgingly followed in her wake, limping slightly.

Abbess Helene, however, was not as composed as she wished her subordinates to believe. The princess was getting worse, and at a more rapid rate than before. Fewer were the days when she remembered where she was or recalled the names of the sisters who tended her. And more frequent were the days she lapsed into nonsensical babbling, carrying on fragments of conversation with herself; the days when one misspoken word pitched her into a fit of violence and compelled her to smash every dish within her reach. The abbess knew that something would have to be done soon, not only for Athaya's sake, but for the sake— and sanity—of every nun at Saint Gillian's.

It had not been so bad at first. Three months ago, when King Durek delivered his recalcitrant sister to Saint Gillian's, Athaya was in excellent health, seemingly unaffected by any sort of malady. Granted, she was sullen and troublesome, but according to his Majesty, that had been her usual state for the whole of her twenty-one years. She was lucid and sane—as sane as a Lorngeld ever is, the abbess amended hastily—and conversed normally, when she deigned to speak at all, with the nuns attending her. And since the king had made no mention of sickness, physical or otherwise, the abbess was certain that Athaya's sudden and rapid plunge into madness was indeed God's retribution for her sins.

And what a shocking array of sins! Few women could account for so many at such a young age, and already Athaya had been charged with her father's murder, arrested for heresy against the Church, accused of treason against her country, and found guilty of a host of lesser crimes. And all of it because she refused to believe the simple fact that her sorcerous powers were evil, and worse, that she insisted on spreading her heresy throughout all of Caithe, teaching unsuspecting folk the art of magic and thereby luring them away from the word of God and into the foul grip of the Devil's devices.

Magic a gift from the *Lord*? A sign of divine *favor*? The abbess felt her flesh grow cold at the very idea. These Lorngeld could grow dangerous indeed if they actually came to believe such things.

And they were dangerous enough already.

Abbess Helene and Sister Edwina halted before an iron-banded oak door bordered by blocks of sandstone. The echoes of singing and laughter were gone now, replaced by a deep and resonant silence.

"His Majesty was sure her powers can't escape?" Edwina asked, breaking the silence by nervously working her swollen finger joints until they cracked.

"Now, Edwina, how many times have we gone over that?" the abbess chided gently. "No, the king was quite certain on that point. The wizard who cast this spell on Athaya—a 'sealing spell' I think his Majesty called it—told the king that there was no release from it other than by another spell. A spell that, apparently, only a very few wizards in the world know how to cast. And since the wizard who did this to the princess is now dead, I'd say that Athaya is quite secure in her prison."

Both of them, the abbess added inwardly. Granted, the convent's official records claimed that Athaya had come of her own free will—imprisonment in religious houses was strictly against canon law—but the abbess, Edwina, Katherine, and every sister of Saint Gillian's knew that the princess was no less a prisoner here than any poor wretch rotting in the dungeons beneath the king's own castle in Delfarham. Athaya was most certainly not here to atone for her sins as King Durek would have his people believe, but as punishment for disobeying him. His Majesty had ordered her to recant her beliefs in the divinity of magic or face death by burning, but when he had taken her to the city square in Kaiburn—the heart of her infant rebellion—Athaya had shocked the masses gathered there by ignoring his command and using the public forum as one final attempt to spread her pernicious doctrine. But rather than risk making a martyr of her, the king secreted her away in Saint Gillian's, where she could spend her remaining years pondering the error of her sorcerous ways and begging God's forgiveness.

Thus far, however, Athaya had done neither, and the abbess was growing impatient.

"Now let us see if her Highness is being as onerous as Katherine claims," the abbess said with forced levity. Sister Edwina cowered behind the safety of her superior's bulk while Abbess Helene braced herself with a lungful of air, snapped back the dead bolt, and pushed open the cell door.

She had not taken a single step before her body—and her soul—recoiled in horror. One hand flew to her mouth as the abbess stifled a gasp of shock at the small-scale wreckage before her: the carnage wrought by caged evil straining against its bindings.

The floor of the cell was littered with a treacherous carpet of crockery fragments, and a straw broom, no doubt discarded by Sister Katherine only moments ago, lay abandoned in the center of the floor amid the remains of numerous plates, bowls, and cups. A savage wind roared in from a pair of open windows, casting the princess' few possessions about the room like flotsam from a shipwreck. Countless sheets of paper swirled about the abbess' head like autumn leaves, alternatively settling to the floor and hurling themselves up again with each new gust. The wind had blown the bedcovers into a rumpled pile in the corner and had overturned a half-empty jug of wine long enough ago so that the dark red pool on the flagstone floor had grown sticky, like old blood.

But if the chamber itself was in chaos, its occupant was infinitely more so.

Athaya Trelane, only daughter of his late Majesty King Kelwyn and sister to the reigning King Durek, stood braced before the open windows as if trying to hold back the winds by sheer force of will. Her pose was defiant: bare feet spread apart, head flung back, and arms crossed tightly over her chest as if clutching a precious keepsake to her breast. But despite this commanding posture, Athaya herself looked appallingly weak. Her skin was white as flour paste from a summer without sun, and the nun's robe she wore, which had fit her snugly enough three months ago, now hung loosely on her frame, the wind catching the loose folds and snapping them viciously around her arms and ankles. Her hair, once tightly braided, was fast coming undone; one meager strand trailed down her back like a frayed rope about to snap while the rest scattered in thick, black tangles about her face. Only her eyes exuded strength of any kind, though of an odd, unearthly kind, and there was the hint of a smile about her lips as she spoke in silent incantation—to what, or to whom, the abbess did not venture to guess.

"Saints in heaven preserve us," Edwina whispered, her voice quavering as she clutched at the abbess' sleeve for support. "She's mad . . . utterly mad."

The abbess did not disagree. Athaya's wits were shattered, as useless as the shards of crockery at her feet.

"Your Highness?"

Unconcerned—or unaware—that she was no longer alone,

Athaya did not reply. Her lips continued to move in wordless incantation; by no stretch of the imagination would the abbess dare to call it prayer.

Abbess Helene walked past her to the open windows, giving the princess a wide berth, and glanced down with a frown as she spied another pile of broken crockery peppering the weed-covered rocks far below. Pursing her lips, she glared at Athaya as if wishing that she would toss herself out of the window instead of the costly dishes, but soon repented the wicked thought with a perfunctory gesture of forgiveness.

The abbess set her hands on her hips, unnerved by the princess' manner but equally unwilling to let it intimidate her. "You shan't be brought another breakfast, your Highness. You'll grow hungry by midday."

Athaya stared right through her, seeming to look past the abbess' eyes and into the mind behind them. Then, stepping neatly around the abbess, Athaya returned her unblinking gaze to the white-capped waves that rushed in to dash themselves to pieces on the shore.

"And we'll be forced to restrain you if you keep throwing plates and goblets out of the window. *And* at Sister Katherine," the abbess added irritably.

Again, Athaya said nothing. She watched the waves for another moment, and then smiled contentedly as if they had just whispered something she had long been waiting to hear. "Credony, lord of the first Circle," she responded in a lilting voice. Athaya picked up the skirt of her plain gray robe and danced a bit, as if to music. "Sidra, lord of the second—"

"Your Highness?"

The abbess pitched her voice louder this time. For the first time, Athaya perceived that she had visitors and abruptly stopped her silent dance. Her face grew wary.

Before the abbess could speak again, a powerful blast of wind ripped into the chamber and sent her veil snapping across her face, temporarily blinding her. Athaya laughed merrily, while the abbess muttered her displeasure at the indignity and glared at the open window as if to scold the winds for their lack of courtesy. Then she furrowed her brows, noticing how quickly the color of the sky was changing. Less than an hour ago, the shoreline of the Isle of Sare had been clearly visible across the channel; now, heavy gray clouds blanketed the horizon and cloaked the nearby island from sight. The air had grown markedly colder, and a greenish glow from the west warned of an approaching storm—a common enough occurrence in northwest Caithe during August, but potentially deadly all the same.

"Come, let me close these shutters," the abbess said placatingly, as if addressing a rebellious child. "There's a storm blowing in."

Her fingers had barely touched the shutter when Athaya's arm whipped out and viciously slapped them back. "No!" she shouted, baring teeth. "The wind . . . it speaks to me in its howling. It tells me I'm alive."

The abbess opened her mouth to protest, but hastily clamped it shut again upon seeing the murderous look in Athaya's eyes. Nothing would be gained by forcing a confrontation. Retreating a few steps, the abbess folded her hands inside her sleeves and regarded Athaya intently, and with more than a little dread. The princess was impossible to read at times like this; each of her words and gestures was like a flash of lightning without an ensuing roll of thunder to warn how close the danger was, lending no clue as to whether the storm was approaching or receding.

"Are you in pain today, your Highness?"

The question took Athaya by surprise. Her angry facade wavered, blue eyes pleading in silent supplication. *Yes . . . such pain! Make it stop . . . please, help me make it stop!*

"There's no need to hide it from us, Athaya," the abbess went on, careful to make no sudden movements toward her skittish charge. "We know that you are in great agony. We have known it for some time. But we also know how to relieve you, if you would only allow it."

Yes, anything—

Athaya blinked, and that fleeting glimpse of surrender was gone as soon as it had come, devoured by raw hostility; amid all her warped and tortured thoughts, Athaya had not forgotten that the nuns were her adversaries—that they would only end her pain by ending her life.

The abbess took a step back, worried that Athaya might lash out in anger, but to her surprise, the princess merely brushed a tangle of hair from her face and turned now-vacant eyes back to the sea. "It will get out one day," she said with a flat, dead voice, staring at the increasingly turbulent waves. "It's trying now. Trying so very hard . . ." A flash of mortal fear illuminated her face, and she quickly shut her eyes against the salty winds as if hoping they would blow her fears aside.

Sister Edwina inched closer to the abbess, new wrinkles of bewilderment breaking out across her face like fissures in stone. "What is she talking about?"

The abbess lifted her hands in a gesture of helplessness. "I have no—"

"But it can't," Athaya interrupted, tipping her head to one side. "Not now."

Abbess Helene snorted impatiently; the princess' manner was rubbing her nerves raw. "Princess Athaya, what *are* you—"

"I'd explode, you see. Everywhere. Just like he did." Athaya paused and laughed shrilly, not from amusement, but from soul-deep hysteria. "Just like Rhodri."

She squeezed her eyes closed against the memory, then relaxed as she began her oft-recited litany. "Credony, lord of the first Circle . . . oh, what are the years? Sidra, lord of the second . . . but the years? The years? The third Circle . . . what was the lord of the third Circle? Master Malcon!" she cried out, snapping her eyes back open with exhilaration. "Now the next . . . who was the *next*? And for how *long*?"

As Athaya continued to mutter to herself, the abbess backed away. Her foot caught the edge of a leather-bound book that lay abandoned in the middle of the floor, its cover splayed open like the arms of a dying man. Upon closer inspection, she realized that the sheets of paper hurling themselves about in the wind were pages that had been ripped from its broken binding. Abbess Helene picked up the ruined book, clicking her tongue at such perverse destruction. Penned by Adriel of Delfarham, the holy man to whom God had revealed the manner whereby wizards could be relieved of their curse, the *Essays on the Nature of Magic* was among the most sacred of scriptures. This had been one of the convent's two copies, left in the hopes that Athaya would eventually open herself to its truth. She clearly had not done so; the only pages that had been torn out were those detailing the sacrament of absolution.

Abbess Helene held up the broken book before the princess' eyes. "Can't you see, Athaya? You recognize the means of your deliverance, though you struggle against it with all your might. I pray each day that you will succumb to God's will and realize that absolution is your only route to—"

The moment the cursed word passed the abbess' lips, Athaya stopped her private recitation. Her eyes threatened a greater destruction than did the storm clouds gathering on the horizon.

"You speak of *that* again," she growled, curling her fingers like a cat baring its claws. "Just like the one who was here before you. Bloodthirsty—"

"Surely you realize that it is the only release from your pain. If you submit to Him, then He will forgive your brief dalliance with magic and grant you a place in His kingdom."

Athaya lurched at the abbess, waving both fists and coming within inches of striking her. "Liar!" she cried. "They are coming. They are coming for me, and then I will be *free*! Free of you, free of this place, and—" She broke off suddenly, clutching her head as if trying to keep it from splitting apart. "Free of it *all*!"

"Who is coming?" Edwina asked nervously, eyes darting to every corner of the room as if fearing imminent invasion.

Her headache abruptly forgotten, Athaya smiled a cat's grin at the old nun, slow and well thought out. "Just 'they.' Maybe the Devil's Children. Maybe demons." Then her eyes narrowed mischievously, and she taunted her two visitors with low and knowing laughter. "Or maybe the Devil himself."

Edwina gulped loudly and retreated to the doorway, muttering a string of prayers for divine protection. The abbess, however, stood her ground and funneled her growing horror into the most devastating glare she could produce. "No one is coming for you, Athaya. You must put aside that foolish notion and submit to what God wishes of you."

But if the abbess had intended to discourage her, she found that her words had quite the opposite effect. "God!" Athaya declared, eyes aglow with triumph. "Yes, of course! God's own angels came for me once . . . they shall come again!"

At first the abbess merely scowled, puzzled by such a peculiar declaration. Angels? What idiocy was this? The fact that it smacked of heresy was, considering Athaya's reputation, far from surprising and not at all relevant. Then she thought back to what the king had told her about Athaya's thwarted escape from the square at Kaiburn and grasped the reason behind the princess' claims.

The abbess chewed on her lip as if it were a piece of tough mutton. The tales of *that* incident were disturbing indeed. It was said that a priest-turned-wizard, the same man who had imprisoned Athaya's magic with the sealing spell, had later attempted to rescue her by summoning a host of angels to distract her captors. The abbess had been quite shaken when she had first

heard that tale—God's messengers lending aid to the Enemy?—
but the king himself had sworn that these "angels" had been
nothing but a magician's trick. They were a mere illusion—
sorcery, pure and simple, and sorcery of the worst kind since it
dared to craft things of God's kingdom.

Abbess Helene shuddered at the implications of such an appalling display of magic. What might the commonfolk think
when confronted with such a magnificent, yet false, vision?
Might it not lure unsuspecting souls to Athaya's grasp, deluded
into believing that magicians actually consorted with the angels,
and were thus divine beings themselves?

"No," the abbess said firmly, banishing that last, faith-
shaking thought. "That was only a trick—an illusion. The king
told me so himself."

But Athaya was undaunted. Although a crinkle in her brow
revealed that she suspected the truth of the abbess' words, she
did not grow discouraged. Instead, a blanket of peace settled
over her, and a slow smile spread across her face like sunrise.
She took up a pillow from her narrow bed and clutched it to her
breast, reaching out for one last hope so steadfast that nothing
could destroy it.

"Then *he* will come, if the angels don't."

Abbess Helene began to chew on her lip again. The faraway
look in Athaya's eyes was ample evidence of who she was referring to. Yes, the king had mentioned something about him,
too. Although his Majesty was so swollen with hatred for the
man that he had refused to speak his name, he did mention that
Athaya had a lover—one that should have died in Kaiburn's
square that day, but who escaped while the illusory angels har-
ried the king and his men. That the princess would take a lover
did not shock the abbess in the least; it was generally known
that Athaya had been living in the forest as an outlaw, almost
entirely in the company of men, while she began her diabolical
crusade. An utter disgrace to the house of Trelane!

But in retrospect, the abbess considered grimly, Princess
Athaya had never been anything else.

Athaya closed her eyes, contentedly hugging the feather-
stuffed pillow as if it were her lover himself. "He will come,
and I will tell him I should have said yes. Should have said yes.
He will come, and I will tell him that I should have said yes."
As she repeated the words again and again, her voice lapsed into
a dull monotone. It was as if she were reciting a lesson from

memory, convinced that it was vitally important, but no longer quite certain as to why.

Seeing Athaya distracted with her litany, Edwina crept up behind the abbess and tugged on her sleeve with blue-veined fingers. "My Lady Abbess, please—let us go from this place at once, before she grows violent."

The abbess waved her back reassuringly. "Not yet," she said, the glimmer in her eyes revealing that she was brewing some sort of plan. "We may yet be able to make her see reason."

Edwina let out an indelicate snort of disbelief. "Reason? I daresay she's far beyond that now."

"Perhaps," the abbess said, still not taking her eyes from the princess. "But it occurs to me that we may have been taking the wrong approach with her."

Gathering her strength, the abbess carefully took Athaya's arm and guided her to the narrow bed. They sat down together on the thin straw mattress, Athaya still holding her pillow protectively against her chest. The clouds had thickened rapidly in the last quarter hour, and Athaya's eyes glowed white as pearls in the darkness. After a moment of silence, the abbess reached out and gently smoothed back her hair—a futile gesture, since the wind merely sent it fluttering again.

"I am sorry, Athaya, but the man you speak of cannot come for you. Don't you remember?" She clasped the princess' hand in a show of sympathy. "He is dead these three months past. He died in the square at Kaiburn."

A horrible silence fell over the room, and but for a single blink, Athaya did not move. The wind grew ever fiercer, and a flash of lightning split the sky, its yellow glare reflecting in her still and staring eyes. In the distance came a menacing roll of thunder.

When Athaya finally spoke, her voice was hushed and grating, and her words nearly lost in the winds howling about her. "What did you say?"

The abbess licked her lips, sensing progress. She sensed danger also, but was committed to finishing what she had begun. "I said that the man you love is dead. You thought he escaped, but in truth he did not. He was burned at the stake . . . as befits a heretic." She paused to swallow, still stroking Athaya's cold and clammy hands. "Don't you remember?"

Again, silence. Another flash of yellow, and another roll of thunder, this one closer than the last, promising destruction.

Athaya rose to her feet and staggered slowly to the window, asking silent counsel of the storm. As the abbess stared at her, silhouetted against a backdrop of green clouds and lightning, muscles slowly growing taut, breath quickening, she realized her mistake. But it was too late, and the storm broke forth in a hellish rage.

Athaya whipped around with a howl of impassioned fury, her nails ripping the pillow casing in two and sending clouds of white feathers and shreds of torn linen to the wind. With an earsplitting shriek, she hurled herself at the abbess, tearing at her veil and robe as if her aim was to rip away cloth and hair and flesh itself until she reached the bones beneath. Emitting a strangled cry, Sister Edwina rushed forward and tried to pull the princess back, but her feeble strength was no match for an outraged madwoman.

"Lies, all of it! Lies!" Athaya shrieked, tears of confused rage streaming down her cheeks. "He will come for me and then I will be *gone*. Gone from here, and gone from you, and gone from all the lies you tell me!"

The abbess grappled with her as best she could, but already she bore the wounds of battle. Four bright red streaks marred each cheek where Athaya had raked her nails across them, and the abbess' wimple was torn and stained with blood. Then her eyes went round with new terror as Athaya took the ends of her stole and wrapped them once around her throat like a noose, pulling tightly until the room began to go black . . .

"Saint Gillian defend me!" she choked out, trying desperately to break Athaya's inhuman grip on the stole. Then Edwina was there grasping a broom in her hands, and with every ounce of strength in her old bones, she cracked Athaya over the skull with the handle. Though the blow as not enough to quell Athaya's wrath, it set her off balance and gave the abbess the opening she so desperately needed. Abbess Helene roughly shoved her attacker aside and bolted from the pallet, sending Athaya sprawling to the floor atop broken pieces of crockery.

Athaya gasped in pain as earthenware fragments dug deep into her flesh, but it did not slow her onslaught for long. Snatching up one of the knifelike shards of pottery from the floor, Athaya scrambled to her feet and rushed forward, seeking a pair of throats to slit. But as she came within inches of the abbess and Edwina, an uncovered foot went down on another of the piercing shards and drew blood, causing her to stumble and cry out in pain.

It was all the time the two nuns needed. Thrusting all dignity aside, the abbess and Edwina bolted out of the room in full retreat. With shaking fingers, the abbess pulled the door closed behind them and shot the dead bolt home.

"Come back!" Athaya howled at them, throwing herself against the door only seconds after the abbess had locked it. "Let me have *your* blood! Come back and let me absolve *you*!"

Safely out of the cell, the abbess and Edwina let out the breath trapped inside their lungs and whispered numerous prayers of gratitude for their deliverance. They could still hear Athaya wailing and hammering her fists against the door, but for the moment they had found shelter from her lunacy.

"She obviously doesn't require her magic to kill us," the abbess remarked dryly, once her heartbeat had slowed and her breathing had returned to a normal level. She touched her fingers to her cheeks, and as her veil was already ruined, used it to blot off the blood from her wounds.

"With respect, my Lady Abbess," Edwina began hesitantly, still clenching the broom in front of her like a quarterstaff, "perhaps you ought not to have told her the man was dead."

The abbess shot her a blazing glare usually reserved for unruly novices. "*That* appears to be obvious," she snapped back, furious with herself for triggering the debacle.

A bone-rattling crack of thunder directly overhead made the two nuns jump simultaneously, and they made a hasty departure, having had quite enough of the guest cloister for one morning. Edwina propped the broom against Athaya's door and trailed after the abbess, cracking her finger joints, deeply troubled by what Athaya had said. "Is it true that this man might come for her?" she asked. "The king warned us that someone might try to rescue her . . . her lover, or another of her friends."

"If any of them were going to come, they'd have done it long before now," the abbess replied shortly, still smarting from the wounds to both flesh and dignity. "And how can they come at all, since they have no idea where she is? No one does except the king and his council. And even if her friends did manage to find her, it would do precious little good at this point. I doubt Athaya would recognize any of them given the way her mind has been deteriorating these past few weeks. Now do stop worrying on so," she added gruffly, her nerves scraped as raw as her cheeks from Athaya's attack. "You grow tiresome."

Edwina nodded in silent apology, clutching one hand over her chest as if afraid her heart would burst from the rapid pace they were taking. "If only she would consent to absolution," she wheezed, shaking her head.

"You saw her face when I so much as mentioned the word." The abbess cursed under her breath, refusing to harbor any guilt for such a transgression under the circumstances. "But if this goes on much longer, I won't wait for her consent. Oh, Edwina, please don't gape at me so," she went on, seeing the older woman's jaw drop sharply. "I wouldn't think of taking such liberties with God's law. Well, I might think of it," she conceded, "but with diligent prayer, I trust I'll be able to resist acting on the temptation.

"Besides," she continued more amiably, her temper improving as the distance from Athaya's chamber increased, "I suspect that the princess is already near her breaking point. Each day she tries to hide her growing pain from us, but each day it becomes more difficult for her to do so. And despite today's outburst, if she eventually comes to believe her lover is dead, then that should finally convince her to stop struggling. I know it seems a cruel thing to do," the abbess admitted regretfully, "but if a brief period of earthly sorrow means she will consent to absolution and save her immortal soul, then I think it a fair price. Soon, Edwina, she will beg us to absolve her." The abbess took in a deep and cleansing breath, letting it out slowly to expel all the stresses of the morning. "And then *all* of us will be at peace."

CHAPTER 2

※❊※

"**W**ELL, *I* CERTAINLY DON'T WANT THE POST," the young earl of Tusel remarked, shaking his head so vigorously that it dislodged a feather from his plumed cap. "Why, I'd rather be sent to the salt mines of Feckham and set to digging with my bare hands." The other Caithan lords seated around the long, walnut table nodded and chuckled softly among themselves, echoing their comrade's sentiment.

The king, on his feet at the head of the council table, merely smiled his understanding. "I didn't plan to appoint you to it, Thomas," Durek assured him, absently adjusting the collar of gold links draped across his shoulders. "You've served me too well this past year for me to reduce you to such a fate."

The earl sighed in exaggerated relief. "Thank the good Lord for that. I am far too accustomed to the activity of the capital to be banished to such a backwater and barbaric place as Sare." He glanced at the tips of his fingernails and then began to buff them on the front of his creamy yellow doublet. "Why, even the most highborn islanders garb themselves in leather and sheepskin like common crofters instead of donning a decent silk or velvet. I've even heard that some still wear dagged sleeves, and those went out of fashion nearly a century ago."

"Then perhaps you would make the best lord marshall after all," the man at his left suggested, nudging him with an elbow, "so that you can not only rule the Sarians but instruct them on the latest fashions as well."

The earl shot a horrified glance at his king, afraid that his Majesty might find merit in such a suggestion, and then promptly launched into an extensive discourse about youth and inexperience—qualities he possessed in abundance, and which, he asserted, rendered him completely unsuitable for the post.

Trying not to grin too broadly, the king returned to the crimson-cushioned throne set on the low dais at the head of the council chamber. He tossed back the folds of his summer-weight mantle and settled himself into the chair with, if not ease, then the indication that he was gradually growing more familiar with its contours. Although not yet thirty, Durek was older than his years, in bearing as well as appearance, but it was a fate he did not disparage as it lent him an air of authority most young men sorely lacked, and all young kings sorely required. Today, like most days, he garbed himself in sober colors with few jewels— much like his father in that, the council sometimes said among themselves, if not in other ways—and wore a gold band inlaid with rubies on his brow.

Durek squinted against the bright sunlight streaming through the latticed windows to make diamond-shaped patterns on the wainscoted wall. "I realize that this is not the choicest position in the realm and that nearly everyone I could think to appoint to it would doubtless prefer to remain here in Delfarham. But the fact remains, my Lords, that Sare is a protectorate of the Crown and must be respected as such. Its people may be less 'refined,' " he added, tossing an amused glance at the fashionable earl of Tusel, "but they *are* my subjects."

The king shifted to a more comfortable position in his throne. "But with DeBracy dead—God rest his soul," he appended with a polite if somewhat obligatory air, "someone will need to take his place as lord marshall by the end of the year. We needn't make the appointment today—DeBracy's chancellor can see to things for a short time—but the task must be accomplished in the next two or three months. Our new marshall needs time to arrange his affairs and reach Sare before winter sets in. So think on it, my Lords," he concluded, settling back among the crimson cushions, "and bring me your recommendations as to who best deserves this singular honor."

Responding like a well-rehearsed chorus, the king's council chuckled at this touch of royal sarcasm. But in the rear of the chamber, farthest from the king, one man was not laughing. Mosel Gessinger, duke of Nadiera and brother to his Majesty's stepmother, slouched down in his chair and seriously considered volunteering for the unwanted post himself. He was loath to divulge his interest in front of the others—speaking out in council was something he customarily avoided, and were he to do so it would be the talk of the court for days—but the idea nagged at his mind all the same.

And why should he not volunteer? By anyone's account, he was highly dispensable. He had no real influence at court—nor any desire to obtain it—and even though he claimed a dukedom, his sharp-witted cousin ran the estate in everything but name. Nor did he take care to look like a duke, clad as he was in a silk-lined robe that claimed nearly as many decades as he did, and a soft-crowned cap with a frayed brim and a listless, gray plume. In the eyes of king and council—and his own, some days—Mosel was nothing more than a gaunt, old man waiting to die, with nothing left to offer the world. Who better to journey to a distant island that the kings of Caithe had, throughout much of history, virtually ignored, and govern a reclusive and close-mouthed people who would not obey him anyway? Secretly, he was somewhat surprised that no one had nominated him for the post already.

"—something that might interest you, Lord Gessinger."

Mosel caught only the last of what his king was saying and bolted upright in his chair swiftly enough to prove to everyone present that he had not been listening. The man seated across from him chuckled scornfully under his breath, whispering something about doddering old fools.

"I said," Durek repeated, unperturbed, "that our next piece of business might interest you in particular, Mosel."

With a flourish, Durek produced a large sheet of creamy vellum adorned with two forest-green ribbons. "I have here a letter, recently arrived from Ath Luaine." He glanced at his council over the top edge of the paper, one brow arching slightly. "It would appear that King Osfonin of Reyka is upset with me."

Durek scanned the page, searching for a particular passage. "I shall spare you a reading of the entire text, but here is the gist of it . . . Osfonin condemns my guardsmen for what he terms 'their unjustified and brutal attack on, and the abduction of, Jaren McLaud, son of my trusted lord Ian, and the foul murder of his valued servant Brice.' "

He lowered the parchment and paused, silently gauging the reactions of his councillors. Most were unsurprised; the council had predicted weeks before that a letter like this would arrive eventually. Only Lord Gessinger's face changed markedly, cheeks flushing red with the knowledge that the aforementioned ambush had only taken place because of his failure to keep four of Durek's men—his captain included—in check. Instead of returning home from their unsuccessful bid to reclaim Athaya from Osfonin's court, the guardsmen had doubled back to Ath Luaine and abducted McLaud instead—the Reykan wizard who first taught Athaya about her inborn magic, and, as the king vehemently insisted, was ultimately the cause of his late father's death. At the time, Durek had been well pleased with his captain's initiative. Mosel gripped the edge of the council table with bloodless fingers, suddenly fearful that the king had changed his mind and would now choose to blame the entire calamity on him.

Durek, noting his council lord in such grievous suspense, smiled lazily before he spoke again. "Of course, I have already shown this letter to Captain Parr and assured him that he was, in my opinion, quite justified, and that I fully support his past actions."

Mosel let out his breath so loudly that several of the other men turned disdainful glares upon him for such a show of cowardice. "But what of Prince Nicolas?" he blurted out quickly, eager to shift the council's attentions to something other than his own discomfort. Worry lines creased his sallow forehead. "Wasn't his Highness still in Ath Luaine on an extended holiday?"

"That he was," the king replied. "But this letter also informs me that my brother has departed the Reykan court; in light of Osfonin's ire, I imagine he no longer feels welcome. It doesn't say where he has gone, so I can only assume he's coming back here." Durek paused and sighed wanly at the men seated before him. "But since Nicolas rarely does what I assume he will, that presumption could be altogether premature."

Durek allowed the council to exchange a few mumbles of assent before he went on, this time more solemnly. "But Osfonin does not only write to vent his spleen at us," he said, snapping a wrinkle out of the parchment. "He is sorely tempted to launch an attack on Caithe out of vengeance, and I believe he might well do it at the slightest provocation."

A swell of impassioned voices rose in the council hall. There had been no talk of war in Caithe for years—not since Durek's father, Kelwyn, had reunited the shires and put decades upon decades of civil wars to rest. As was often the case, the younger lords chattered excitedly at the prospect of battle, while the older ones grumbled at its folly and expense.

"While such a threat might not otherwise worry me," Durek continued, silencing his council with a gesture, "we must recall that there is already trouble enough *within* our borders. My sister's followers are still lurking about—they're quieter now, but we can't be fooled into thinking they're gone. If we spend time and resources defending our borders from Reyka, that gives Athaya's zealots every opportunity to spread unchecked through Caithe. They may even appeal to Reyka for aid—and get it—if we went formally to war. If there is one thing I do *not* want, my Lords," the king added severely, "it is a host of Reykan wizards infesting our land and teaching magic to good Caithan citizens."

The murmurs began again, growing louder as the disastrous implications of the king's words came clear to them. Durek held up his hand, again calling for silence. "As it is, Osfonin has stopped just short of declaring war on us and has instead declared his borders open to any Caithan seeking to flee from absolution. Granted, this could lend some degree of momentum to Athaya's allies, but we must all remember that people have fled to Reyka before. Osfonin's edict, in effect, changes nothing. And we cannot do anything about it short of declaring war on them, which, as I've told you, is much more to Reyka's advantage than ours at the moment. Thus," he concluded, setting the paper aside, "we do nothing, and try not to provide Osfonin with the provocation he is surely seeking."

Disgruntled frowns appeared on the faces of the council at the need for such caution, but no one denied the truth of the king's words. "What we need," growled one of the older lords, "is to get rid of the Lorngeld once and for all. Then Reyka will have no interest in us, nor us in them." The grizzled man scanned the council, his challenging gaze drawing many nods of assent. Although King Kelwyn had tried to form an alliance with Reyka only the summer before, most of the Caithan council had been adamantly opposed to friendship with what they termed "a nest of heretics and Devil-worshipers." Clearly, their feelings had not changed.

Durek also nodded as the man's gaze came to him, features

settling even further into solemnity. "And that, my Lord, brings us to the main purpose for this meeting. The Bishop's Curia has brought us a proposal and begs us to give it our most serious consideration."

He motioned toward the door, and a uniformed guardsman stepped out of chamber, promptly returning with a clergyman clad in a black cassock and blood-red stole. A silver Saint Adriel's medallion gleamed against his chest like a harvest moon in an October sky. Exuding confidence, he swept into the council chamber like a knight entering the lists, his clipped, militant deportment wildly incongruous on a man who had vowed to spend his days tending souls instead of battlefields. Imposing height and a crown of black hair edged with silver lent him an aura of malevolence, and dark brown eyes flicked over each of the assembled lords in quick appraisal, silently judging which were likely allies, and which likely foes.

"Bishop Lukin," the king said formally, gesturing to an empty chair at the table. "Be welcome to this council."

"Thank you, sire." The bishop sat rigidly on the farthest edge of the chair in silent pronouncement that he would have vastly preferred to stand. He carried with him a thick sheaf of papers bound with red cord, which he placed at the end of the council table nearest the king.

"Archbishop Ventan is not with you?" Durek asked, glancing to the door.

"No, sire. He complains of indigestion . . . again." Lukin's lip curled up just enough to reveal how little he thought of such an excuse. "He has therefore allowed me to serve as spokesman for the Curia."

"Very well, then," the king replied, giving Bishop Lukin the floor with an outstretched hand. "You may proceed."

The bishop sprang from his chair, too accustomed to preaching from a pulpit to address the council sitting down. He did not speak right away, but allowed the pointed silence to grate upon his audience, honing their attention to a sharp and painful edge. Silently, he paced the length of the chamber, changing direction with quick, crisp turns. Were he in uniform with a halberd propped against one shoulder, Mosel mused, he would be the very image of a sentry patrolling the castle battlements.

"My Lords," the bishop began at last, his teeth glowing white against deeply tanned skin, "you are all aware of the recent events surrounding his Majesty's sister, Athaya Trelane.

Most of you were present at her trial last spring where she was
found guilty of heresy and treason." He spun around and gripped
the back of his chair as if to keep it from escaping the chamber.
"But still her people endanger the public, fueling unrest by
teaching fiendish spells and renouncing the sacrament of absolution. And there has already been one shameless instance of
tampering with the sacred wine. Abominable! Sabotaging the
hallowed rites of the Church!"

Mosel rubbed his chin as he recalled what had been said of
that incident during Athaya's trial. The son of a rich Kaiburn
clothier—Jarvis, that was the name—had undergone the rite of
absolution shortly after his magical talents emerged, but instead
of deadly *kahnil*, the chalice had contained nothing more than
a powerful sleeping potion. By the time the bishop discovered
the deception, Athaya's allies had already spirited the boy away
to freedom.

Inwardly, Mosel wondered which vexed the bishop more: that
he had been deceived, or that one of his own priests had doc-
tored the wine right under his nose.

"These fanatics must be stopped before Athaya's 'crusade,'
as I've heard it called, gathers any more footing in Caithe," the
bishop continued, slapping one fist into the opposite palm. "We
must act now, before her allies recover from their leader's loss
and find a way to go on without her."

"There's been little enough noise from the Lorngeld since
Athaya was sent to Saint Gillian's," Thomas of Tusel remarked,
shrugging negligently. "I've heard of no recent disturbances in
my shire."

"Then you are most fortunate," the bishop replied curtly, his
contempt for such complacency barely contained as he strode
purposefully to the edge of the dais. "In Kaiburn we are not so
lucky. Many folk sought out the princess' allies shortly after her
appalling speech in the city square last May, all of them brimming with rebellion."

"And at least one of them brimming with riches," the king
mumbled, scowling darkly at the tips of his boots.

Lukin's self-assuredness cracked for an instant, and he cast
an uncertain glance at his king. Mosel enjoyed a secret grin,
glad that the king had squelched Lukin's arrogance so soundly. Everyone at court knew the tale—his prisoner, Jaren McLaud,
had not been the only thing to slip out of the king's grasp that
day in Kaiburn. During the riot that ensued after the wizard's

bolt to freedom, a priceless crown of corbal crystals, brought for protection against wizardry, had been stolen out from under the noses of his Majesty's guardsmen by a bedraggled stripling of a boy. Perhaps the latter was not directly Lukin's fault, but the king had seen fit to blame him for the theft nonetheless, judging him ultimately responsible for the moral fiber of his flock.

"But without Athaya's presence, this foolish crusade is leveling off," observed the councillor seated to Mosel's left, a balding gentleman with two tufts of gray hair over each of his ears. "Several good citizens in my shire have already seen the truth of their error and returned for a proper absolution."

Lukin's eyes suddenly flashed in warning. "Yes, we can all hope that Athaya's absence puts an end to it entirely, but I prefer not to risk Caithe on such a feeble thing as hope. Athaya's allies still exist. I receive at least one report each week of someone preaching in one village or another, espousing her cause. The people are slower to believe without seeing the princess herself, but some of them *do* go to her. And even one lost soul, my Lords, is too many."

Mosel's brows went up slightly. Care for the souls of others was not a thing known to concern Bishop Lukin overmuch.

Fire burned higher behind the bishop's eyes; he was enjoying this sermon well. "The Lorngeld are a dangerous people. When their magic comes upon them, they succumb to madness and loose their cursed spells on innocent folk. Absolution is the only route to their salvation, but it is absolution that Athaya Trelane and her band of zealots seek to abolish!" The bishop's voice rose to a fevered pitch, filling the vaulted chamber like the swell of a pipe organ. "Her people preach the divinity of magic and instruct others in the use of their hell-sent spells, saving their lives but damning their souls! And if her allies succeed, my lords, we shall have a nation overrun with wizards who will use their wicked powers against those who have them not and they will wrest this land from those who rightly rule it!" He gestured dramatically toward the king, nostrils flaring with exhilaration. "We have peace, my Lords—peace, after countless years of civil war. Will we allow these magicians to conquer us and thus make us servants of *their* Creator and not *ours*?"

Despite the bishop's dire predictions, Durek could not help but smile. Over the past few months there had been persistent rumors that seizing the crown was Athaya's ultimate plan, but never had anyone used them to such marvelous effect. The council was stricken speechless, horrified at the future that Lukin held up before them.

"My Lord Bishop," Durek put in softly, "we applaud your impassioned words, but we are already aware of the danger my sister presents. Well, not Athaya herself—not anymore," he added, the shadow of satisfaction passing over his eyes, "but her ideas and her allies. The proposal, if you please?"

The bishop's eyes flashed briefly, like the spark of flint on steel. He was not a man who liked having his fine sermons curtailed, but considering his past discord with the king, he quietly let it pass.

"As I say, the Lorngeld are a dangerous people. It is the opinion of the Curia that they must be destroyed. King Faltil did it once before, over two hundred years ago. We can do it again."

The councillors murmured among one another, some with guarded skepticism, others with an obvious thirst for blood. "But how can we possibly succeed?" one of the lords asked. "Faltil wielded magic of his own against the Lorngeld. We have no such sorcery to aid us."

"We did once," Lukin grumbled, half to himself. He exchanged a glance with Durek, both of them recalling the wizard-priest, Aldus, who had first aided and then betrayed them. "But we do not want their help, even were they to turn against their own kind and offer it. Athaya trains her pupils well," he warned the council bitterly, "and once in her grasp they find it virtually impossible to escape. The Father of Lies claims them fully.

"Our solution is this," he continued, sloughing off the remnants of old rage. "The Curia proposes the establishment of a Tribunal, to be headed by a man of his Majesty's choosing, whose sole purpose will be to root out these heretics and punish them."

Ignoring the flurry of whispers that his words had spawned, the bishop pointed to the sheaf of papers on the table. "This document was written by me and duly signed by a majority of the Curia. It sets forth a detailed plan: how many men we shall require, where to deploy them, what methods we plan to use to identify these heretics, and what punishments we intend to mete out to them—and to those who aid them. We also propose to grant rewards to those who aid us by revealing which of their neighbors are engaged in such heinous activity."

Despite the warmth of the sun-drenched chamber, Mosel drew

his robe closer around his shoulders, gripped by a sudden chill. It seemed insufferably wrong for this man of God to couch the Lord's work in terms of battle tactics . . . estimating the numbers of soldiers required, plotting their positions on the field, selecting the right time for an attack. But it *was* war he was planning, Mosel realized with gnawing dread—a war against the Lorngeld such as had not been waged in over two hundred years.

"You mean an *inquisition*?"

He did not realize he had spoken his thoughts aloud until he caught Bishop Lukin scowling blackly at him. Mosel's cheeks burned hot as coals. Because he rarely spoke—and voiced few useful opinions when he did—he knew the bishop was doubly irritated by his challenge.

"I speak of a vehicle of justice, Lord Gessinger," the bishop replied, forming each word with meticulous, and vaguely patronizing, care.

"B-but if, as you say, Athaya's movement is beginning to die out, then why bother with this Tribunal at all? Without Athaya to lead them, won't her allies eventually give up and disappear?"

Lukin waved him off impatiently. "Fanatics are an erratic lot, my Lord. They rarely give up so easily. If we strike now and crush this rebellion while still in its infancy, we will spare ourselves a worse situation later."

"But such violence . . . turning neighbor against neighbor . . ."

The bishop abruptly changed his tactics. "You cannot mean to say that you *condone* these heretics? That you grant them a right to speak their seditious views?"

Mosel quickly grew flustered under the bishop's penetrating gaze. "I . . . I didn't say that—"

Conscious of the sweat beading on his brow as he fumbled for a more intelligible response, Mosel fervently wished that another of the councillors would speak up and voice the same concern. But as the silence progressed from oppressive to humiliating, Mosel was grimly reminded that in all his years at court, he had only possessed one true ally, only one friend ever willing to stand by him in extremity. And unfortunately, Queen Cecile had departed for the southern shire of Halsey last autumn to await the birth of her second child, and there was no indication as yet of her return.

Never before had Mosel missed her friendship so acutely.

"I think all that Mosel is saying," Durek said, languidly

rescuing his councillor from Lukin's ire, "is that the Curia is proposing a rather extreme measure."

"Yes, your Majesty. But as you yourself once observed, extreme measures are the only ones Athaya and her people seem to understand."

Durek nodded once, conceding the point, and the bishop cast a self-satisfied glare at Mosel before returning to his seat, his sermon done.

The king took up the imposing document and skimmed it, his fingers tugging absently at sparse tufts of a brown beard dusted with early gray. "This Tribunal . . ." he began tentatively, shifting his gaze to Lukin, "it *is* a drastic solution, but that is not to say that it lacks merit. Yet I must be frank with you, my Lord Bishop. I have held my crown less than a year. My father ruled over twenty years and still rules the hearts of many Caithans. I am new to them, and to do a thing like this so early in my reign . . ." His words trailed off as he sank into several minutes of quiet contemplation.

"We shall consider the Curia's proposal most seriously," he went on at last. "However, I shall not make a decision of this magnitude in haste, nor will I have any member of this council advise me until they have thought the matter through quite thoroughly. A final decision may take time."

Lukin lowered his head in confident acquiescence. "As you wish, of course. But I must remind your Majesty that the sooner we cut this canker out of our midst, the sooner Caithe can heal from its wounds. And cutting it out will ensure it does not grow larger."

A faint smile of amused respect graced the king's face, as if to compliment Lukin on his perseverance. "Duly noted, my Lord Bishop."

Stretching stiff leg muscles, Durek pushed himself out of his throne and tucked the Curia's document under one arm. "My Lords, this is clearly a larger subject than we can deal with today. I shall review this proposal tonight and then grant each of you a time to do the same. After that, we can meet again and discuss what should be done."

Durek adjourned the meeting and strode out of the chamber, the bishop close on his heels. The councillors lingered, casually exchanging opinions on the Curia's idea as they helped themselves to wine from the chamber's sideboard.

"A daring proposal, this 'Tribunal,' " remarked the balding man to Mosel's left.

"Indeed it is," Mosel replied. "I wonder if his Majesty will sanction it."

"Why on earth would he not?" the man exclaimed, brows shooting up in surprise. "Surely you do not countenance letting these . . . these *wizards* do as they please and send all of Caithe to the Devil along with them? No, no, no. King Faltil had the right of it two centuries ago. Wipe *them* out before they wipe *us* out."

"I'm not sure that is their intent—"

"God, man, you're not *defending* them?"

Mosel cringed at the accusation—the same accusation that Bishop Lukin had flung at him only moments before. "No, I—"

"I should hope not, or you shall be one of the first this Tribunal sets afire."

Although his companion did not mean for the blow to strike so deep, Mosel felt his bones go soft at the merest thought of such a death. "I only pass on what was told to me—in Reyka—during my recent journey there," he explained awkwardly, conscious that he was beginning to perspire again. "As the Reykans have it, the Lorngeld have no desire to conquer Caithe at all. They simply wish to return to the way of life they had before King Faltil—before the Time of Madness, when they were taught how to use their magic as soon as the madness came upon them. Perhaps they are misguided," he added hastily, seeing the other's growing look of outrage, "but they may not be as power hungry as we assume."

The balding man bolted to his feet, his chair squealing loudly on the flagstone floor as it was pushed abruptly back. A handful of other councillors idly turned toward the source of the noise, and Mosel's companion, noting he was being observed, lowered his voice and continued in harsh whispers.

"Mosel Gessinger, you are indeed a fool. You voice no opinion on anything through countless council meetings, and the one subject you *do* champion is the one certain to get you into the most amount of trouble!"

"I do not champion them—"

"You come close, my Lord, to spouting the very words that Princess Athaya used to defend herself at her trial. For your sake, I will tell no one what you have said just now—especially

his Majesty.'' Appalled, the man stalked away without looking
back.

Mosel pushed away the cup of wine he had poured for himself
and slunk from the chamber, keenly conscious that in offering
another viewpoint, he had not simply been playing a uniquely
literal game of Devil's advocate, but had placed himself in great
jeopardy—a position he was wholly unused to occupying. But
this idea of an inquisition—or a Tribunal, as the bishop would
have it called—shook him to his very soul. Surely such a thing
would be the ruin of Caithe and not its salvation as the Curia
proposed.

Eager to escape the stifling confines of the castle walls, Mosel
stepped out into the small courtyard adjoining the council hall
and seated himself on a carved stone bench beside a cluster of
rosebushes. Letting out a dispirited sigh, he reached inside his
shabby robe and drew out a pendant on a slender chain, a coin-
sized medallion of triskelion design that, though always kept
hidden, was the only truly elegant part of his attire. He placed
his finger on the clasp that would open the silver disk, then
closed his eyes and let the ornament fall back against his chest.

The old sadness had returned of late, pressing like a physical
weight on his brittle bones—an ache that had nothing to do with
age and infirmity. God, why did he keep the thing? Why, when
it offered him soul-deep sorrow instead of the comfort he had
expected? After so long, such keepsakes should lose some of
their power. And this one had, for a time. But now its potency
was back, and the memories it evoked were more sorrowful than
ever. Sorrowful, because the power to heal was in his hands and
he found his courage lacking.

Wearily, he linked bony fingers together and rested them on
his lap. Throughout the summer months, as June turned to July
turned to August, he felt something from deep within pushing
at him. Pushing him to do a thing that he, and no one else,
could—or would—do. But being unaccustomed to bold moves
of any kind, he found that such knowledge kindled his fear
instead of firing whatever spirit of adventure he might once have
possessed. And he *had* possessed one once; he had not been an
old man all his life. Asking for the Sarian marshalcy would have
been an ideal escape, but deep inside, from that part of him that
pushed, he knew that hiding in an island thicket like a frightened
rabbit would not only fail to lessen his pain, but would inevitably

consign others to the same misery that had tormented him for over forty of his sixty-two years.

Mosel sighed quietly, massaging his eyes. God, how bad would the pain have to get to make him act? And how many others would have to suffer while he debated with himself day after day after day?

More than were suffering now, he realized, if Bishop Lukin persuaded the king to sanction this Tribunal.

After a quarter hour of quiet, if not peaceful, contemplation, he grasped the pendant and tripped open the latch. He touched his finger to the dried petal tucked inside the medallion, its dead and withered form looking even more pitiable next to the living blooms around him.

"Oh, Rose."

Then, with that whispered word, the *pushing* inside of him became too much to bear. His conscience, having wailed and clawed outside the walls of his resistance these forty-odd years, had won the siege at last. The walls were breached, and they crumbled to dust never to be raised again. He could push back no longer.

And thus it was that six hours later, Mosel's hands snapped the reins of a dun-colored gelding as he urged the beast through the winding, moonlit streets of Delfarham. It would have been sensible to take an escort, but this was a thing he had to do alone. It would likewise have been sensible to wait until morning—a lone man riding at night was extending an open invitation to thieves—but his mission had waited long enough.

Swallowing his fears, Mosel turned his horse toward southern shires . . . to the city of Kaiburn and the heart of Athaya Trelane's rebellion.

CHAPTER 3

※◆※

JAREN SHRUGGED THE BURLAP SATCHEL FROM HIS SHOUL-
ders and hurled it to the ground in frustration, sending up
a cloud of dust. More defeated than weary, he slumped
down on the floor of the sheepfold and ran dirty fingers through
even dirtier hair, finding no relief at being home again—or what
served as his home in Caithe—after ten long weeks of travel.

"Another false trail," he said bitterly, closing his eyes as he
leaned back against the rough-hewn blocks of stone forming the
fold's wall. "And it was our last lead."

Across from him, Master Tonia struggled into a cross-legged
position, the cool earthen floor a welcome relief from the oppressive heat of an August afternoon. She tucked a wisp of graying hair back inside her scarf and wiped sweaty hands on the
rumpled apron draped carelessly over her tea-colored kirtle. "I
know you're tired, Jaren. Lord knows I am, too—and my bones
are a good thirty years older than yours," she said, hoping to
inject a measure of cheer into what was proving to be a very
cheerless afternoon. She offered him a heartfelt smile, but Jaren
was thoroughly mired in his own misery and only managed to
flick Tonia a glance of hopeless dejection.

"All we can do is see if there's been any news since we've
been gone and then set out again," she continued, unwilling to
let him sink too deep into despondency for fear he might never

30

extricate himself. "Don't lose faith, Jaren," she admonished him kindly. "If you lose that, you've truly lost everything."

"Faith," he spat, as if such a thing were beneath contempt. "If that was all it took to find Athaya, then we'd have done it months ago. You'll excuse me if I find myself running a bit short on faith these days."

A guilty knot formed in his belly the moment he voiced the bitter sentiment. As a member of the elite Circle of Masters, Tonia deserved his utmost respect, and for the past few days he had treated her little better than a household servant who can do nothing right in the eyes of an exacting lord. And like a well-trained servant, she had silently borne the brunt of his foul moods, which only made him feel worse than he already did.

"She's trusting us to find her, Jaren," Tonia said quietly, without a spark of anger. "Are we going to just throw up our hands and give up because we haven't succeeded as quickly as we'd hoped? Why, if Athaya had thought that way, she would have given up this crusade of hers long ago." Tonia paused, holding Jaren's gaze with the intensity of her own. "Are we going to give her reason to lose faith, too?"

Jaren lowered his head in shamefaced apology, a shock of overlong hair falling over his eyes like a golden veil. "I'm sorry, Tonia—I don't mean to keep snapping at you. I just can't help feeling that time is running out . . . that it might already be too late."

Ever pragmatic, Tonia made no attempt to offer false comforts. "I know. I'm worried sick about her, too."

The two of them lapsed into silence. Idly, Jaren began sketching pictures in the dirt with the sharp end of a broken twig, but no matter what he set out to draw, each sketch invariably became the image of a young woman; a woman with beguiling blue eyes, and whose face was framed by a storm cloud of black hair.

He knew he shouldn't be so disappointed by their lack of progress—from the day he and Tonia had set out in search of Athaya, they had been forced to accept that they were chasing down nothing more substantial than rumors—but somehow he had expected that at least one of the rumors would lead to her. He and Tonia had listened carefully to the myriad speculations flying through Kaiburn and its surrounding villages about where the princess had been taken, but to their dismay, a different tale seemed to spring from every mouth. Athaya was being taken to the king's holding at Taulone—no, it was his country house in Gorah. Some said she was bound for the convent of Saint Brigit's in the west, others were certain it was the Sisters of the Blessed Sacrament in the south. Many swore they had seen the king's coach escorting Athaya to her prison; the coach had gone north, south, east, west. Some claimed they had seen the king himself leading the procession, while others declared that it was not the king at all, but merely the sheriff and a squadron of guardsmen escorting the shire's tax money to the capital.

Purchasing horses with some of the funds Osfonin had granted Athaya the previous spring, Jaren and Tonia scoured the Caithan countryside armed with this confusing jumble of clues, scrying for Athaya with their vision spheres in every city, town, and hovel. But in the end their spheres had shown them nothing, and now they were home again, empty handed, no closer to finding Athaya than they had been nearly three months before.

"Why is this happening?" Jaren asked suddenly, glancing toward the sheepfold's entrance as if hoping someone—preferably someone with Godlike authority—would promptly stride in and provide him with an answer. "We could have been married by now, and I'd be worrying about being a good husband to Athaya instead of worrying whether she'll *live* long enough to marry me at all."

Tonia smiled at him in heartfelt sympathy. "At least you know she wants to marry you. That's more than you could have said last winter."

Jaren nodded, but miserably. That cruel twist of fate had never ceased to torment him. Athaya had refused his proposal at first, hoping to spare him the dangers faced by wizards in her homeland, but shortly after arriving in Caithe with her fledgling band of crusaders, she'd admitted to Tonia that she had made a terrible mistake. Before she could return to Reyka and set things aright, Jaren had been arrested by King Durek's men, and Athaya entrapped by the bishop of Kaiburn. And but for a brief glimpse on the day he almost died, Jaren had not seen her since.

"It's so frustrating," he said quietly, squinting against the bright sunlight in the doorway. "I love her so much . . . I'd do anything for her. But I can't even find out where she is so I can help!"

"Jaren—"

"It's been three months, Tonia. Three *months*. And you know what Master Hedric said. A few days under the sealing spell wouldn't matter, and one or two weeks might not do too much damage either. But Athaya's magic has been bound since May and this is the middle of August!'' In a fit of temper, Jaren snapped his drawing-twig in two and threw the broken pieces into the dirt, fouling his latest sketch.

Tonia gazed at him with anguish, like a mother who sees her child in pain and knows she can do nothing to assuage it. ''We're doing everything we can, Jaren. We just have to keep looking. Come,'' she said, struggling to her feet, ''let's have a cup of ale and then go back to the camp and rest a while. We've had too little of either these past few weeks.''

Tonia poured two cups of amber-colored liquid from the barrel stored in the rear of the sheepfold, while Jaren used the toe of his boot to remove all traces of the now-ruined sketch from the ground. Accepting the cup from Tonia, Jaren shuffled to the doorway and peered out at the activity around him—activity he hadn't spared a glance for earlier, having been too distracted by his journey's lack of success. Scattered in the expanse of warm grass between the sheepfold and the forest were sparse clusters of fledgling wizards practicing their spells. Some were casting vision spheres and witchlights, some sketched intricate path-maps on wax tablets, and others popped in and out of view as they worked their cloaking spells. But even if a generous handful of wizards were hiding under such cloaks, and even if he assumed that another generous handful were back at the forest camp, Jaren still felt a sting of dismay upon realizing how few of them there were. He was certain there had been at least fifty when he and Tonia had departed.

Now he counted less than twenty.

Seeing him poised in the doorway, a woman detached herself from a pair of young men who were practicing setting protective wards around one another. She wiped the sweat from her brow with the edge of her sleeve and started up the slope toward the sheepfold. With her brown hair, tanned skin, and chestnut-colored eyes, the woman resembled a wood nymph out of legend. Of late, however, she had little of a nymph's natural grace. She walked with an unsteady gait, one hand rubbing her lower back while the other rested atop the child she was close—very close—to delivering.

She said nothing as she approached the sheepfold. There was no need to ask how he and Tonia had fared. Returning without

Athaya meant only one of two things: they had not found her, or they had found her too late, and she was dead.

"There are fewer than before," Jaren observed, standing aside to let her enter the fold. "Without Athaya, they're starting to leave us."

Gilda nodded sadly. "Two more left during the night. That makes over thirty since last month that have come and gone without getting proper training. The bishop's raids haven't helped convince them to stay, either. The camp is safe enough, what with all the wards and illusions, but we've had to post sentries around the sheepfold to watch for soldiers. No one's been hurt yet, and the raids are trickling off, but everyone's still jittery. There are only eighteen left now."

Jaren swirled the ale in his cup without drinking any. "Not much . . . eighteen in all of Caithe."

"There was a day we had only one," Tonia reminded him, sagelike eyes silently urging him not to lose hope. Then she turned back to Gilda. "Where are the others?" she asked, holding out a third cup of ale. Instead of drinking it, Gilda merely dipped her fingers in it and rubbed the cool liquid on her brow and throat. The heat, added to the extra weight she carried, was making her sweat profusely.

"Kale and Cameron are repairing the roof of the dormitory back at the main camp. It hasn't rained much, so they've made good progress; we should have a few more usable rooms before winter. Ranulf was helping me with the tutoring this morning, but he went into Kaiburn a few hours ago to post some more leaflets and do a bit of impromptu preaching. Bishop Lukin has been out of the city for the past few weeks, so we're using his absence as a chance to press our cause. Unfortunately, Ranulf hasn't been getting a very warm reception in Kaiburn these days," she added. "The bishop has threatened to excommunicate anyone who gets caught listening to us, and the last time Ranulf so much as mentioned Athaya's name in public he very nearly got himself lynched."

Jaren took a sip of the cool ale. The story had been much the same with him and Tonia. While searching for Athaya, they had also used the opportunity to spread the news of her crusade to other parts of Caithe and encouraged all Lorngeld wishing to escape absolution to seek out the wizards who taught magic in a sheepfold near Kaiburn. They took care never to say such things until just before they planned to move on, however, since these speeches often prompted a mob of outraged citizens to take up an assortment of sharp-looking farm implements and chase them out of the shire.

"Ranulf was also going to check in with Rupert and see if there are any new rumors about Athaya. There's been nothing so far," Gilda added, glancing regretfully at Jaren. By now, his relationship with the princess was well known to them all.

Jaren nodded glumly and swallowed the rest of his ale in a single gulp. If a new rumor were circulating through Kaiburn, it would be certain to reach the popular Blacklions tavern before long, and its owner, Rupert, whose son was among their remaining students, would be certain to pass the information on to them as quickly as possible.

"So you've been teaching eighteen students all by yourself today?" Tonia asked, eyes widening. "Why not ask Foster to help you? His spells were coming along quite nicely."

Gilda shifted her weight from one foot to the other, her face downcast. "He was one of the two who left last night," she said. "He told me it was one thing to have a Trelane leading us, but that without Athaya we don't have any sort of legitimacy at all. I tried to convince him to stay, but it was no use." Gilda splashed another few drops of ale on her forehead. "At least his threat of madness was gone, and he'd learned to control his spells enough to avoid accidents. Maybe that's what finally convinced him to go when he did."

"I'm sure you did the best you could," Tonia assured her. Then she took a long, assessing look at Gilda's face and bunched up her lips in mild displeasure. "Just be careful not to overburden yourself. I know there's been a shortage of tutors since Jaren and I left, but you'll need to keep your strength up for the day that baby finally arrives." She gave Gilda a good-natured grin. "That's when the real work begins."

Tonia finished the rest of her ale and dabbed the foam from her lips with the frayed hem of her apron. "Well, now that we're back, let's see what sort of progress our pupils have made. The ones we have left, anyway," she added under her breath, drawing her brows into a frown.

Taking her usual brisk pace, Tonia led them toward a half-dozen wizards clustered in the shade of an apple tree. Jaren squinted against the sunlight; no, at a second glance it was a maple tree, but one clever wizard had peppered the branches with witchlights, and was now plucking them like ripe apples and banishing them, one by one, back to oblivion. As they approached, the students abandoned their spell-work; witchlights winked out, vision spheres dissolved. A man wearing spectacles looked up from the open book resting in his lap, while another student suddenly materialized beside him, leaving off a deftly cast cloaking spell. Despite a chorus of pleasant greetings, Jaren could tell that each of them was inwardly noting that he and Tonia had returned alone. Some hid their disappointment well, others failed completely.

"I see you're almost done with the *Book of Sages*, Girard," Jaren said to the young man with the book, trying not to reveal his relief at seeing that not everyone had deserted them. "Finished memorizing the Succession of Circles yet?"

"You didn't find her."

The bluntness of the remark effectively pierced the delicate bubble of faith that Jaren was trying so diligently to sustain.

"No," he replied solemnly. "Not yet."

Girard was quiet for a moment, debating something inwardly, and then closed the book decisively and got to his feet. "Then I'm going."/

"Going? Where?"

"Anywhere but here," he replied curtly. He gathered up the lightweight cloak he had been sitting on and shook off the bits of dry grass that clung to it. "I'm the son of a master builder and I know enough not to put up the walls before the foundation is set. Whole damned thing caves in otherwise."

"Girard—"

But he didn't have to explain. Neither did any of the others who had left before him. He had been willing to follow a Trelane, sister to the king, Kelwyn's only daughter. It was quite a different thing to commit himself to another of her crusade's founders, none of whom were Caithan born. It didn't seem to matter that Athaya had cultivated a rather questionable reputation even before she had become a practicing magician and been tried for heresy; her father's name and reputation hung about her like a glamour, lending her an almost legendary air. She was still of royal blood, and the people of Caithe had not forgotten that.

"I made up my mind a fortnight ago that I'd be on my way if you didn't return with the princess." Girard draped his cloak over one shoulder and handed the book over to another of the students. "I owe you thanks for what you've taught me—all of you," he said, encompassing Jaren, Tonia, and Gilda with his gaze, "but I just won't stay any longer. Maybe if Princess Athaya comes back, then I will, too."

Girard set a fast pace toward the forest's edge, no doubt to fetch his belongings from the camp. Tonia hurried after him, but her pace was not as brisk as before, as if knowing that no matter how persuasive a speech she delivered, it would ultimately prove futile.

"Damn," Gilda muttered. Jaren's brow went up—it was the first time he had ever heard her swear. "I was hoping he might become a magic tutor eventually. He already knows his letters and he learns so quickly . . ." Her voice trailed off as she saw Girard and Tonia slip into the woods, the sadness in her eyes betraying an expectation that only one of the two would return to the sheepfold.

If Athaya comes back. Girard's words echoed like funeral bells in Jaren's mind. If. Quickly, he forced his thoughts away from the possibility of failure. Tonia was right—he had to keep faith, even if that faith was growing harder to sustain with each passing day.

Having drunk his fill of disappointment for one day, Jaren resolved to return to the camp for some much-needed sleep. He made his excuses to Gilda and was heading for the forest's edge when he caught sight of a huge, broad-chested man loping across the meadow at a steady clip, his fiery-red beard and hair standing out like a beacon in the green-gold grass. Despite his somber mood, Jaren cracked a smile; he liked Ranulf a good deal and had missed his ribald humor these past few months. A retired mercenary from the Isle of Sare, Ranulf Osgood was a coarse but immensely likable man who belched when the mood suited him and scratched immodestly in any vicinity he happened to itch. And beneath his boorish exterior, Ranulf was as desperate to see Athaya safely home as the rest of them.

"You look like hell," he said in welcome, taking in Jaren's sweat-stained shirt and breeches. He did not ask about Athaya— the answer was there to read in Jaren's eyes.

Jaren's shoulders sagged. "That's fitting, Ranulf. I feel like hell, too."

Ranulf jerked a thumb in the direction from which he'd come. "Someone's in the city looking for us," he said. Sweat ran in tiny rivers down his face and throat, and while his soldier's body was still in good condition, he panted loudly as he tried to catch his breath.

"Is that so unusual?" Jaren replied. "That's what we hope people will do."

"This one claims to be a friend," he said as he wriggled out of his shirt and used it to towel off his face. His gaze grew disturbingly intense. "And he's asking for you by name."

Frowning, Jaren folded his arms across his chest and stared thoughtfully at the ground. Precious few people in Kaiburn knew him by name, and most of those who did wished him dead. "Then either our curious friend is not a friend at all," he observed, "or he's an outright fool. If he doesn't take care who he asks, he'll get himself arrested for consorting with heretics."

"Oh, he knows what he's about, all right," Ranulf countered. "His first stop was Sir Jarvis's house—somebody *not* too likely to turn him in. The man started asking about the sheepfold—not that it's any secret, mind you—but then he mentioned your name specifically and said he'd come all the way from Delfarham to see you. Jarvis got suspicious, figuring him for one of Durek's men, and left a message for me at the Blacklions."

"So who was our mysterious visitor?"

Ranulf shook his head. "Wouldn't give his name. Wouldn't say anything at all except that he had an urgent message for you. Jarvis says he was an old man—maybe sixtyish—dressed like a lord who's seen better days. Sound like anybody you know?"

Jaren picked at a thread from his own battered attire and grinned faintly, recalling the days not long ago when he had dressed as befitted a duke's son. "Sounds exactly like someone I know," he replied. Then the grin faded, replaced by wariness. "And it also sounds like a trap."

"Could be the king trying to collar you again."

"My thoughts exactly." Jaren walked in a small circle, rubbing his chin while he wove his thoughts into a plan. "Do we know where to find this man?"

"Jarvis told him to come back to the house at noon tomorrow, and then sent him off to the Blacklions for the night. Rupert'll keep an eye on him in case he tries anything."

"But he won't get a chance to try anything," Jaren declared. He turned his gaze south toward Kaiburn, eyes alight with subtle mischief. "If this is a trap, Ranulf, then we're going to be the ones to spring it. I think I'll go into the city tonight to pay a call on our 'friend'—and talk to him on our terms, not his.'' He lifted an inviting brow at Ranulf. "Care to join me?''

The mercenary beamed his approval, boldly displaying a gap which had once been home to two large teeth. ''Aye, and why not?'' he said, clapping Jaren soundly on the shoulder. ''It's been too long since I've been out for a pleasant evening's ambush.''

As the bells of Kaiburn Cathedral chimed the eleventh hour of the night, Jaren and Ranulf slipped wraithlike through the winding side streets and into the timeworn but popular Blacklions tavern. Welcoming lamplight and the tempting scent of roast mutton greeted them as they circled the common room and approached the grizzled, potbellied man filling his guests' wine goblets. When he saw them enter, he finished doling out the rest of his flagon and then motioned them to a corner near the kitchen door.

''Thought I'd see you here afore the night was over,'' he said to Ranulf with a crooked smile. He cocked his head toward Jaren. ''This the one he's looking for?''

Ranulf nodded. ''Which room did you give him, Rupert?''

''Last one on the left. Paid for a room all to himself, too— we don't get so many as has that kind o' money. Not and are willin' to spend it here.'' The man dug down into the pocket of his smock and handed over a slender iron key. ''Here. Just try not to get blood on anything, eh? That room was just scrubbed down, and the chambermaid will be out for blood herself if she has to do it again this month.''

Rupert strolled away to tend his customers while Jaren trailed Ranulf up the stairs and headed toward the rear of the tavern's upper floor. Torches lit the dim hallway at either end, and the greasy, black smoke made Jaren's eyes water.

''This is it,'' Ranulf whispered, stopping in front of a weathered oak door. He pressed his ear against it, then fumbled to set the key in the lock, his wizard's fingers unused to such a mundane means of entering a locked room. A turn of the key, and the chamber turned over with a soft click.

They checked the corridor to make certain it was deserted, then shrouded themselves under cloaking spells so that their quarry would suspect nothing until it was too late. Ranulf pushed gently on the door, and it swung open with a low-pitched creak, sending a slant of golden torchlight cutting across the freshly scrubbed floor.

Inside, the sound of wispy, rhythmic breathing stopped abruptly, replaced by a puzzled grunt from underneath the coverlets; their quarry had not been sleeping so soundly after all. "Hmmph? Who's there? Oh, of all the—" With a hand over his eyes to shield them from the torchlight, the man slid out of bed and staggered across the floor, spindly legs tangling themselves in the folds of his nightshirt. Jaren and Ranulf stepped silently past him just before he pushed the door closed and listened to him mutter his irritation over faulty locks as he returned to the warm sanctuary of his bed.

Moonlight lent the room a silvery glow—enough light for Jaren and Ranulf to position themselves on opposite sides of the bed without stumbling into anything. Ranulf slid his dagger from its sheath with a cool hiss of steel. He and Jaren dispersed their cloaking spells in unison, and an eyeblink later, Ranulf's blade was pressed against the drowsy man's throat.

"All right, you—wake up and 'fess up," he growled, using his other hand to tighten his grip on the collar of the man's nightshirt. "You wanted to find us and here we are. Now start talking."

The man jerked fully awake in an instant, and the sight of Ranulf's eyes blazing not a handspan from his own prompted a stream of panic-stricken babbling. "Who . . . what? Oh, dear God—the money's over there . . . in my boots. Take it. Take anything you want—"

"We don't want your money," Jaren replied coolly. "And we don't want to harm you. I just want to know why you were asking for me at Sir Jarvis' house today."

The man rambled on, still woozy with sleep. "Asking for—? Who are you? I told you . . . the money's over there."

Jaren frowned. That voice—it was familiar. He couldn't quite place it, but he had heard it not too long ago. But not here. Not in Caithe.

With a whisper and a subtle twist of his wrist, he conjured a small witchlight, bathing the chamber in ruddy light. He heard the man's sharp intake of breath; few Caithans were used to seeing even the simplest of magics. But when the fiery glow fell across the bed, illuminating every wrinkle and crease in the old man's face, Jaren's jaw dropped in surprise, and the witchlight lay forgotten in his palm.

"Lord *Gessinger*?"

"I knew it!" His dagger in one hand, Ranulf hoisted the old man into a sitting position with the other, as if he were no heavier than a feather pillow. "You're one of the king's cronies, ain't you?" he demanded, shaking his victim violently. "You're setting my friend up, ain't you? Ain't you?"

"No, please . . ."

"Wait, Ranulf—let him go." Although the Caithan lord had personally delivered King Durek's warrant for Athaya's arrest to the Reykan court some seven months ago, Jaren remembered that Gessinger was the only member of the Caithan delegation who had spoken to him with anything remotely resembling civility. In fact, Lord Gessinger had seemed rather sorry to have brought the warrant at all.

"So let's have it, my Lord," Jaren said, careful not to reveal whatever sympathies he harbored. Gessinger was still the king's sworn man, and that was something Jaren dared not forget. "What does a member of Durek's council want with me?"

The old man leaned forward, clutching an armful of bedcovers tight against his chest. "The convent of Saint Gillian's. On the northern coast, about ten miles west of Eriston."

Jaren stared blankly at the man; Gessinger's sudden change of subject had thrown him. "What?"

"That's where Princess Athaya is."

The room fell deathly quiet, the only sound being Lord Gessinger's ragged breathing. Jaren felt his heart swell to bursting with joy, the day's disappointments suddenly forgotten. Still, he forced the disbelief to come; he had heard too many rumors, all of them false. But though he tried to prevent it, Gessinger's words had cast a spell upon him, a spell of hope that set his spirit to soaring as it had not done in months.

"Why should I believe you?" he challenged, channeling his emotions into a facade of harsh skepticism. He let go of the witchlight, leaving it to hover on its own above the bed, and leaned in close to the old man. "The last time we met, you were looking to take Athaya back for trial, not looking to be her friend."

"The fact that I am revealing the princess' whereabouts to anyone outside of the council, much less to you, already condemns me to death if I am discovered." The old man's fingers kneaded the bedcovers anxiously. "That's why I did not seek you out at this . . . this 'sheepfold' I have heard about. Your people have no cause to love me . . . and I feared to be seen among you. But since you and I had met before, I thought you would give me a chance to help.''

"Well, now, that's all very touching," Ranulf remarked, darkly sarcastic, "but if you were that hell-bent on rescuing Athaya, why come to us? Why not just go and fetch her yourself?"

By now, Gessinger's nerves were beginning to fray badly. "I thought of doing so at first, but I knew I'd never be able to get inside the convent myself—not without being recognized. The convent is near the border of my own shire, and the abbess knows me. But you . . . you have magic! You have the power of invisibility; I have heard the king speak of it, and—'' He broke off at that, his gaze flicking from Ranulf to Jaren as he suddenly realized why he had not seen intruders in his room until they were upon him. "Oh, please," he continued, setting that thought aside, "you have only to find out the truth for yourself. Go to Saint Gillian's, I beg you."

"And fall right into a trap you've set up for me?" Jaren countered. "I've already been ambushed once by Durek's men, and it almost got me burned at the stake." It took conscious effort to force the gruffness into his voice, and Jaren did not think he could maintain his attitude of skepticism much longer.

The Caithan lord continued to knead the blankets with bony, agitated fingers. "Please, you must believe me. I was present at Athaya's trial—I *know* that's where she is."

Jaren patently believed him, but he took care not to look the least bit convinced—not yet. "Then why didn't you help her three months ago when she was taken there? Why wait until now?" Jaren glared at him, the ruddy glow of the witchlight glowing like hellfire in his eyes. "I'm sorry, my Lord, but you'll have to give me something better than a simple promise of good faith."

Briefly, Jaren closed his eyes. *Faith. Just once, my Lord, let simple faith be enough . . .*

Ranulf edged closer to the bed. "You heard the man," he prompted menacingly.

Absently, Gessinger brushed his fingers over a pendant hanging from his neck, the silver disk conspicuously brilliant against the drab linen nightshirt. His eyes grew distant and melancholy. "I . . . am not a man of action, sir. It gives me no pleasure to admit that. I was hoping that one of you would be able to locate her with magic and see to her rescue and that I would not have to involve myself. But as time went by with no news of her escape . . . I just couldn't stand idle any longer.''

He paused, as if inwardly debating the wisdom of his next words, and then lifted his head with newfound fortitude. ''If it will help to convince you, then please—look into my thoughts and see the truth of what I say. I know you can do it; Kelwyn often did such things when his councillors swore their oaths to him.''

Jaren blinked his surprise. Lord Gessinger was not afraid of being touched by magic, and that only strengthened Jaren's faith in him. ''As you wish,'' he replied. No need to mention that he would have insisted on a truth-test anyway, whether Gessinger proved willing or not. This way, it would be easier for both of them.

He bade Gessinger to lie back and close his eyes, then brushed against his mind, reaching out to see the thoughts that resided there. There was some small resistance at first, normal for any-one unused to being probed, but it soon fell away like a weak-ened wall crumbling to dust at the first stone cast from a siege engine.

And then it was there for Jaren to read as clearly as guiding runes on a dark night: the startling maelstrom of emotion that had brought the councillor to this point. There was no dissem-bling in this man; Gessinger opened his soul to scrutiny and showed not a wisp of deceit, only ancient scars and the new spark of resolve that had been kindled from them.

It came in a dizzying swirl of images, but common to them all was a girl, young and vital with dark hair and bewitching eyes. First he saw her strolling through a garden rich with roses— her namesake—arm-in-arm with a dashing young nobleman, neither of them able to take their eyes from the other. Then the image shifted, and he saw that same girl suddenly touched by madness as the power within her began to bloom. But the bud was never allowed to flower, and Jaren saw roses again, this time in the bouquet she carried at her absolution. And when it was done, he saw a broken man, not yet twenty, gathering the fallen petals from the chapel floor and weeping over them.

And with the images came a rush of emotion; the aftermath of that horrible day—the crushing weight of futility, the knowl-edge that nothing was worth living or fighting for. If a girl of such spirit and beauty could be cut down in the name of God, then what was the point of anything? All that remained was to live out his days and die—to join his beloved in death as he could not do in life.

Jaren gently severed the mind-link, trembling from the intensity of their contact. When he drew back, he saw the lord's eyes glistening with fresh tears and knew that he was close to them himself. After what he had just seen, he felt vaguely ashamed of himself; his own anguish was suddenly not as overwhelming as it had seemed that afternoon. While he still feared for Athaya's life, at least he could still cling to the hope of finding her alive—of bringing her back to Kaiburn and making her his wife. The man huddled before him had no such hope remaining.

"So you see?" Mosel said softly, his voice breaking. He opened the pendant, touching his finger to the withered petal, gathered up from the chapel floor so many years ago. "I lost everything when I lost Rose. A few years ago, when Kelwyn began questioning the old laws regarding the Lorngeld, I began to hope that things would change—that perhaps others would not have to suffer as I did. My hopes faded again after he died, but suddenly his daughter was there, taking up his cause. And now . . ." He shook his head slowly. "I cannot let my hopes fade again; not while I have the ability to free her and set her back upon the path she's chosen." A shadow of fear passed over his eyes, and he clutched the pendant tightly in his hand as if to gain courage from it. "Dark times are coming to Caithe. The Lorngeld—and those who love them—will need their leader. They will need a Trelane."

It was an ominous prediction, but Jaren had no time to ask for an explanation. Reeling with new insights and fresh hopes, he staggered from the bedside, turned his back to the others, and, standing in a pool of gentle moonlight, commanded his vision sphere more forcefully than he had ever done in his life.

"Tonia," he cried into the sphere, "Tonia, hear me!"

He waited, tapping his foot with profound impatience. A few moments, and then he whispered a brisk word of triumph. "Tonia? Oh, thank God. Quickly, pack up everything we'll need for—how long did you say?" he asked Mosel, firing the question over his shoulder like the bolt of a crossbow.

"It is over a fortnight by coach—"

Jaren groaned under the weight of this news. "God, so *long*." He muttered a quiet curse that he lacked Athaya's unique talent for translocation; then the journey would take mere seconds instead of weeks. "Tonia, pack up everything we'll need for a month," he resumed into the sphere. "I know where she is, Tonia. *I know where she is.* And we've got to leave tonight."

Jaren banished the vision sphere with a rough wave of his hand, shaking off the last tendrils of fog from his fingertips instead of allowing them to clear naturally. Then he spun around and gripped the nearest bedpost as if needing its support to stand.

"I'm grateful to you, Lord Gessinger," he said, so charged with emotion that his mouth had trouble forming the words. "Thank you. All of Caithe is in your debt."

Mosel lowered his eyes, embarrassed by such praise. "I'll be grateful as well when Princess Athaya can thank me herself. But please," he said, throwing back the quilts, "wait for me to dress. I want to come with you. I know the roads—I can take you there."

Jaren's reply was firm, but kind. "No. You've traveled far enough, and the fewer of us there are, the faster we can go. Besides, you said earlier that you're known in that shire—if anyone recognized you it might cause trouble for all of us. I have to go to her . . . I'm going to marry her, my Lord," he blurted out, feeling the need to share something with the old lord in return for his tragic account. "She's *my* Rose. And a friend, Tonia—the one I just called—she has to go as well. She's the only one in Caithe who can release Athaya from the sealing spell that hinders her power."

Mosel nodded his understanding. "Then go, and I bid you godspeed. But please tell me when you've returned," he pleaded, desperate to know whether his effort would bear fruit. "Oh, and one more thing—"

He reached down and pulled a fat purse of coins from his boot, and pushed it into Jaren's hands. "Take this for your journey. It should be enough for horses, food . . . anything you need for the princess."

Jaren's eyes widened at the weight of the pouch. "It's very generous, but we can't possibly—"

"No, take it. From here I go to Halsey to see the queen—to let her know what I have done. If I'm in need of coin, her Majesty will assist me until I return to the capital." For the first time that night, he smiled, and the simple gesture made him look years younger, brimming with vitality like the nobleman Jaren glimpsed in his memories. "When you return, you can send word to me—to us—there. Queen Cecile has long been Athaya's friend and will be anxious for news of her safe return.''

Jaren nodded once, then tied the purse to his belt and bolted toward the door. ''Come on, Ranulf. There's no time to lose.'' At the last moment, he stopped and glanced back, fumbling for words. ''My Lord, please forgive the way we woke you—''

''Apologize later,'' Mosel said, shooing them out the door with a wave of his hand. ''You've got a long journey ahead of you and you'd best get started. Oh! But if you would, sir—please take this with you?'' Wistfully, he glanced up at the witchlight still burning above his bed. ''It is lovely, but . . . I'm not sure I could explain it to the chambermaid.''

He watched with rapt attention as Jaren snuffed out the little globe, then sighed, but this time without sadness. ''How I should have liked to see Rose make one of those . . .''

CHAPTER 4

❋

JAREN AND TONIA TOOK SHELTER FROM THE MISTING RAIN beneath the cascading branches of a willow tree just outside the gates of Saint Gillian's. It was unseasonably cool for the first night of September, even in this northernmost tip of Caithe, and while Jaren was nevertheless accustomed to the early autumns of his native Reyka, he drew his cloak tight around his throat so droplets of rain would not wriggle their way inside his collar. Thick clouds shrouded the moon; the only light of any kind was the subtle, whitish glow of Master Tonia's vision sphere as she scried for Athaya Trelane.

A breath of wind swept a battery of icy raindrops off the willow branches and onto his head, and Jaren stifled a mild curse, observing strict silence so as not to disturb Master Tonia's concentration. Then the glow of the sphere faded, and Tonia's hands were empty once again. Her gaze shifted toward the north, and her lips moved in a troubled prayer that Jaren could not hear.

"Tonia?" Jaren prompted, deeply disturbed by the grave expression on her face. "Did you see her? How is she?" Another question—are we too late?—was poised on the edge of his tongue, but he couldn't bring himself to utter it.

"Come," Tonia said, setting off toward the gate at a rapid pace. "We must hurry."

The evasive answer kindled white-hot fear in Jaren's heart,

47

but he dared not ask for further explanations. Master Tonia was rarely secretive, and if she chose to keep something from him, he was fairly certain that it was something he did not want to know just yet. Wordlessly, he followed her to the convent's single entrance: an ancient iron gate with a postern door in the boundary wall to its right.

"I saw the sea through an open window beside her, so her cell must be on the north side," Tonia said. "And with this place being well nigh off the map, I doubt the good nuns worry too much about intruders. It should be simple enough to get most anywhere we need to go."

True to her word, Tonia set her palm over the tired lock on the postern door and loosed it with a whispered word. One push, and the pockmarked door swung open with a groan of protest. "Now cast a cloaking spell for both of us," she instructed, just before stepping through the doorway. "I'll want to conserve the rest of my strength for Athaya."

Jaren complied without delay, and they crossed the windswept convent grounds, passing unseen through silent courts and gardens like a cool draft, never encountering a single living soul. If the nuns of Saint Gillian's observed the traditional services, they would have retired hours ago. But for Tonia, the only sign of life Jaren could detect was the cry of a sleepless gull that haunted the nearby shore.

"That must be the guesthouse," Tonia whispered, pointing to the narrow, L-shaped building that formed the northwest corner of the wall. "And I'll wager she's being kept on the top floor."

When they were safely through the guesthouse door, another lock falling prey to a wizard's touch, Jaren let the cloaking spell disperse. The spiral stair leading to the cloister's upper level was windowless and dark, and Jaren lit the way with a small witchlight cupped in his palm. Reaching the top, they crept down the hallway, one on each side, cautiously testing the latch of every door they passed. When Jaren reached the iron-banded door at the end of the corridor, he gasped in exultation and, without regard to her rank, grabbed Tonia by the arm and hauled her unceremoniously across the hall.

"She's in here!" Jaren tried to keep his voice to a whisper, but he was wild with excitement and it came out as a barely muffled shout. "It's the only one that's bolted."

He put his ear to the door, listening expectantly. But the silence that greeted him was oppressive, and somehow he knew it did not mean that Athaya slept in peace, but indicated something far more ominous.

We've come for you, Athaya, he sent out, hoping that she would hear him. But still the silence remained.

Jaren drew back the bolt and stepped inside.

The cell was blanketed in darkness and inhumanly cold; both windows were open to the chilling winds that swept in from the sea. His witchlight lent the cell a hellish and dungeonlike air, its reddish glow dancing in each of the puddles speckling the floor. Wooden dishes were heaped in disarray upon a table, and his eye caught something tiny and black scurrying across the half-eaten bits of cheese. The bed was empty—*empty,* Jaren realized, feeling his heart skip a beat—and its coverings lay in a rumpled heap in one corner.

Oh, please God, he begged inwardly, knowing that his faith would be shattered forever if this journey to Saint Gillian's, so fraught with hope, was yet another false trail. But then he recalled that Tonia had spied Athaya with her vision sphere only a few minutes before. She had to be here somewhere. Unless . . .

Unless something had happened since then.

Then he glanced to the open windows, and hot bile began to rise in his throat. He and Tonia had shunned the open road and approached Saint Gillian's from the shore, and as they had picked their way up the steep incline, he'd noticed that the north wall of the convent was flush with the rocky outcrop on which it had been built. Now it was easy to see why this wing was an ideal spot for a prison cell; other than the inside door, the only exit was the window—a window that opened onto a hundred-yard drop to the rocks below.

No, he told himself, futilely trying to banish the vision. *Damn it all, I've come too far . . . she's suffered too long for it to end like this!*

"Jaren."

He turned around quickly at Tonia's hushed call, grateful for any excuse that would keep him from those dreaded windows. "There," she whispered urgently and pointed to the pile of bedcovers in the farthest corner of the room.

Jaren sent the witchlight to the corner, illuminating the darkness with its ruddy glow. At first glance, he saw nothing more than threadbare cloth piled carelessly at the foot of the pallet. But then he saw what Tonia had seen . . . slender, ivory fingers—most with chipped and broken nails—clutched around a handful of coarse wool, and the tip of an unslippered foot protruding from the motionless heap.

His heart began to race. "Athaya—"

He lurched forward, but Tonia's hand was quick upon his shoulder. "Be careful, Jaren," she warned him. "Don't frighten her."

Jaren knelt beside the huddled form. Slowly, he drew back the blankets one by one as if peeling back the petals of a rose. One blanket, and he saw her arms, pale flesh peeking through the rents in her sleeves; a second blanket, and he saw her legs, shrouded in folds of coarse gray wool—the ragged remains of what had once been a novice's robe. And a final blanket, drawn back, revealed a waterfall of ebony hair, now an unruly mass of knots and tangles, but heartbreakingly beautiful all the same.

With trembling fingers, Jaren brushed her hair aside to look upon the face he had not seen in months.

He was not prepared for what he saw.

"Oh God, Athaya—"

She was so thin, so terribly thin, cheekbones jutting out like knives pressed against her flesh from within. Her lips, once achingly tender, were cracked and bleeding. But worse, when he parted the curtain of tangled hair, it revealed a forehead wrapped in bandages crusted with dried blood. He gestured the witchlight closer, despairing as its reddish glow worsened the sharpness of her bones and robbed her flesh of every hint of life.

Tonia pointed to a bloody stain on the wall, just above the level of her eyes. "Trying to make the pain stop, no doubt," she said quietly, shaking her head in unconcealed pity. "Distracting herself from the seal's pain with something more bearable . . . or at least more familiar."

Jaren placed one hand on Athaya's shoulder and shook her gently. "Athaya? Can you hear me?"

She did not move. Jaren could not even hear her breathe.

He gathered her up into his arms like an injured child, holding her close against his chest and rocking her gently in hopes that the rhythm would rouse her. "Wake up," he whispered in a lyrical voice, like a bard speaking the words to a song instead of singing them. "We're here, Athaya. We've come for you. It's Jaren . . . and Tonia's here, too. Please wake up."

She moaned softly at that, waking slowly as if floating up

from the bottom of the sea. Her nose twitched once, and her breathing became audible again. Jaren lifted a tendril of her hair and wound it gently around his fingers. "Come back to me, Athaya."

She cracked open her eyes like the break of dawn, and Jaren's heart took flight.

Silently, she stared up at him, and he smiled giddily, drowning in the blue depths of her eyes. Then, after struggling to comprehend that she was no longer alone, Athaya's gaze grew wise. She drew in a sharp breath and, just as Jaren opened his mouth to speak again, released a shriek of terror that threatened to crack the very rock on which Saint Gillian's was built.

"Get out!" she cried, writhing out of Jaren's gentle grasp as if his arms were crescents of fire. "Leave me alone—alone, alone, *alone*!" She curled her fingers into fists and pummeled his chest and shoulders with a flurry of savage punches. "Go away or I'll kill you, I swear I will! I've killed people before . . . I know I can do it—"

Dodging the worst of Athaya's blows, Jaren managed to grab hold of her wrists and tried to temper the flow of rage. He gave a sharp, mental command for the witchlight to drift closer, hovering only inches above his head. "Look, Athaya! Look at me . . . it's Jaren. Everything's all right now. You're safe."

Howling in fury, Athaya pulled out of his grip with unexpected strength and scrambled to her feet. She struck the witchlight with her fist and dashed it into a hundred pieces, the tiny scraps of light bobbing in the air like drunken fireflies. Jaren flinched from the slender lance of pain caused by the shattered spell. An even worse pain lanced his heart, but it had nothing to do with his magic.

He got to his feet and tried to approach her again, but he had taken only a single step before she lashed at him again, kicking out with a bare foot. "Get back!"

Jaren obeyed, and retreated a few steps in hopes that it would calm her. "Athaya, please listen to me—you're safe now. I've come to take you away from here."

"Take me—" She broke off, pausing to consider the idea. Jaren thought he saw a flash of elation in her eyes, as if some deeply buried part of her knew what he offered, but her distrust soon resurfaced, more potent than before. "No, I'll not," she said in a voice pitched menacingly low. "I'll *not* go with you. No. You'll never absolve me. Never! That's what I told *them*, and that's what I'm telling *you*. I won't let any of you trick me . . ."

Then she dropped to her knees, fumbling underneath the sorry little bed, and before Jaren had time to blink, she sprang up with a broken broomstick in her hand and struck him full in the jaw with the hard rod of oak. He reeled back from the jarring blow, and would have fallen had Tonia not been there to steady him. His hand went up to rub the tender jaw and it came away slick with fresh blood.

"Now get out," Athaya warned again, waving the broken broomstick before her as if brandishing a sword. "Get out, or I'll crack your skull open next time."

Then her eyes went suddenly blank, glazing over as some other thought ascended to power in her mind. She stepped back to the corner and brushed her fingertips over the patch of drying blood on the wall. She stared at it hypnotically, as if she'd never seen it before, suddenly unconcerned that Jaren and Tonia were still in the room. "I've seen what's inside a man's skull when it bursts . . . all red and gray and blackness. And it's going to happen to me this time. Soon," she added, shuddering visibly. "I can feel it. So very soon . . ."

Jaren's soul cried out in horror, his stomach threatening to erupt not only from the thought of such a grisly fate, but from Athaya's raw display of madness. Tonia put a hand on his shoulder and gently drew him back.

"She doesn't know us, Jaren—she thinks we've come to absolve her. It's probably what the abbess has been pressuring her to do ever since she was brought here. And refusing to give in is the only thing left in her entire world now . . . the only thing she understands. That, and the pain of the seal."

"Be silent!" Athaya wheeled on them in a fury, her gruesome reverie abruptly broken. "Stop plotting against me! I know what you're doing . . . talking about me . . . about what to do with me. I'm not going anywhere with you—either of you! Everything you're telling me is a *lie*!"

Her voice rose to a piercing shriek, and Jaren cringed at the earsplitting volume of it. "Athaya, please be quiet—they'll hear you." But his voice lacked conviction, as if he knew she would not obey or understand.

"If there's anyone within earshot, they'd have been here long before now," Tonia assured him softly. "And in her condition, she probably cries out so often that the nuns don't even bother to come anymore.'' Tonia lapsed into thought, and the lines in her weathered face became even more pronounced. "But one thing is certain—we can't help her if she's going to insist on beating the daylights out of us. If I distract her, can you get close enough to put her to sleep?''

Jaren touched the angry red welt on his jaw, but nodded his agreement. "Just be careful. She's pretty good with that thing.''

Moving cautiously, Tonia skirted around to Athaya's left, giving a wide berth to the broomstick still clutched in her right hand. "It's very cold, Athaya,'' she said, her voice smooth as a new mother's cooing to her child. "Do you mind if I close these shutters? The floor is wet, and—''

"No. I want them open. The wind . . . it reminds me . . .'' She turned vacant eyes to the night sky, forsaking the thought.

"But you're shivering, Athaya. Wouldn't you like to go someplace warm and dry?'' Tonia gestured toward the east. "There's a cove a little ways down the beach, and I have blankets there, and wood for a fire, and some soft, green cheese. Wouldn't you like that? Look, I can point out the entrance to the cove from here.''

Soothed by Tonia's lilting voice, Athaya warily lowered her weapon and drew closer to the window, keeping a safe distance but clearly tempted by the promise of warmth and comfort. Again, some part of her seemed to yearn for what Tonia offered, but was hindered by forces too powerful to overcome.

"Can you see those lights?'' Tonia went on, pointing to an arc of reddish guiding runes roughly a quarter mile up the eastern shore. "Don't worry if you can't . . . you might not be able to until your power is restored. We left them there as markers. The cove is not so far, and we can be there very soon. And you can rest . . . you must be tired, Athaya. Yes, so tired . . .''

Noiselessly, Jaren stepped around behind Athaya, likewise keeping a safe distance. Tonia's voice continued in its rhythm. "And as I told you, there will be a warm fire and thick blankets, and perhaps I can even mull some wine—''

What that word, the fragile link she had forged with Athaya was shattered. "Wine!'' Athaya shrieked, wheeling around on Tonia with wild eyes. "*Poisoned* wine . . . you're one of them, I knew it!'' Athaya swung her weapon back and cried out, ready to deal a deathblow to her enemy. In the same instant, Jaren leaped forward and grabbed hold of the stick, jerking it roughly out of her grasp. The motion pulled Athaya off balance and she tumbled back into his arms, but, like a cat who despises to be held, she turned on him and raked his cheeks with her nails, kicking and wailing in fury at the loss of her weapon.

"Sleep, Athaya," Jaren commanded, pressing his palm against her forehead. It was hard to concentrate on the spell with Athaya clawing and kicking at him—God, his shins would be purple with bruises by morning!—so Tonia added a touch of her power to his own. Athaya struggled far longer than he expected her capable of, but in a matter of minutes, she went limp in his arms, surrendering to their combined spell. Breathing a sigh of relief, for Athaya as well as his shins, Jaren lowered her onto the pallet and drew one of the coarse blankets over her.

"I shouldn't have mentioned the wine," Tonia remarked with chagrin as she knelt at Athaya's side. She touched her fingers to Athaya's temple and nodded approval. "She'll not wake for a while. Let's get her out of here while we can."

Jaren blinked his disbelief. "Get her—Tonia, we can't wait another minute! You've got to release her. Do it *now*!" he cried imperiously, as if he were Overlord Basil himself, issuing a command to the Circle.

"I can't do it here," Tonia began, taking no offense at his urgency since she knew the depth of feeling that aroused it. "I didn't tell you before—you'd only have worried over something neither of us could change. Releasing her . . ." She paused, reluctant to lay the burden of knowledge on him. "It won't be painless, Jaren. And I don't have any idea how long it will take; no one has ever been under a seal this long—not and lived to tell about it. Once I begin to free her power, we can't risk being interrupted. Lord only knows what it might do to her if all that power was released at once."

"But—"

"It's not like lancing a boil, where all the poison comes out in a rush and that's all there is to it. It takes constant monitoring, and the pressure has to be eased a little bit at a time. And even if everything goes well, she won't recover overnight, not after so long. There's even a chance . . ." Tonia trailed off, unsure how to phrase her thoughts. She turned back to Athaya, now sleeping soundly. "Well, best not to dwell on that."

"A chance she won't recover at all?" Somehow Jaren had always known it was a possibility, but he'd taken great care to deny the truth of it. Now that Tonia had voiced that fear, he felt its cold reality strike him harder than the blow Athaya had dealt him with her broomstick.

"That's why I wanted to travel up from the coast; why we staked out that cove in the first place. I had to make sure there was a safe place we could take her—somewhere isolated where we could work without interruption."

"But how much time will we need? The moment they realize she's gone, the abbess will send to the nearest village for men to search the countryside. The cove isn't that far—"

"They won't order a search if they don't think she's missing." Shrugging off some of the gloom gripping them both, Tonia flashed him a confident smile. "I got the idea when we were coming up from the shore, and the look on your face when you first saw those open windows convinced me that it's the perfect ruse."

Jaren was puzzled at first, disliking any idea that didn't immediately relate to Athaya's freedom from the seal, but he quickly realized the implications of Tonia's plan as he watched her collect an armful of dishes, a cup, one of Athaya's cast-off shoes, and the broken piece of broomstick, and hurl the lot of them brusquely out the window. Then she tore a scrap of fabric from the hem of Athaya's tattered gown and snagged it to the edge of one shutter, as if it had caught when she'd jumped . . .

"And they'll assume the tide carried her body out to sea. Simple." Tonia nodded, pleased with her work, and clapped the dirt from her hands with satisfaction.

Jaren, however, was not so easily appeased. He went to the window and looked down at the objects scattered with deadly abandon on the rocks below. The scene was so convincing that it sickened him. "But they'll tell the king she's dead! And he'll tell the entire country." He wheeled around in disbelief. "Tonia, we're having a hard enough time keeping students at the camp without—"

"If she gets through this," Tonia interjected, "then everyone will find out soon enough that she's alive. And if not—" She glanced down at Athaya, watching her sleep in deceptive peace. "If not, then we won't be able to keep it a secret forever. Now snuff out these witchlights and let's go," she said curtly, waving her hand at the tiny red globes as if brushing aside a cloud of gnats. "We have much to do before this night is over."

* * *

Leaving Saint Gillian's was far more arduous than entering had been, what with Athaya's dead weight to carry down the rocky incline to the shore, but Jaren shouldered the burden gladly—the chance to hold her close again rendered her weightless in his arms. The rain was not misting now, but fell in fat, icy drops that slid into his eyes and blinded him like tears. He spotted the cove only by way of the fiery guiding runes Tonia placed there earlier, welcoming beacons for anyone with a wizard's sight.

When Athaya was comfortably settled on a makeshift bed of dry blankets, Tonia built a small fire while Jaren illuminated the cove with a ring of small witchlights. Neither of them expected anyone to be strolling along the shore at such a late hour— especially in such dismal weather—but to make certain that their vital work would not be interrupted, Jaren bounded the cove mouth with wards. A milky-white sheen hung elegantly over the entrance like a curtain of fine samite as the wards sent out subtle signals to discourage passersby from seeking shelter there.

Finally, Tonia said that she was ready to begin, although the solemn manner in which she delivered that announcement made Jaren's flesh creep with apprehension. He could only imagine how frantic he would be had Tonia not prepared him for this moment. Although it was strictly against Circle rules, Tonia had taught him how to use the sealing spell in case something happened to her before Athaya was found. Knowing what to expect—however unpleasant—helped take the edge off his fear.

Tonia knelt on the ground and cradled Athaya's head in her lap and bade Jaren sit beside her. She took in three deep breaths, letting out each one with calculated slowness. Then she turned to Jaren and held his gaze intently. "I'll warn you again, Jaren— prepare yourself. Athaya will be in a great deal of pain." A look of pity crossed her face, regretting in advance what she had to do. "If I were a battle surgeon, I'd have her down a few bottles of strong wine before I start," she murmured, then shrugged off the grim thought and turned back to Jaren. "Just try not to get rattled . . . no matter what happens. I'll need a steady hand to support me."

"What should I do?"

But he answered the question himself long before Tonia did. *Anything, Athaya. Anything for you . . .*

"Just be there with me—in her mind," Tonia explained. "Be ready to do anything I ask. I probably won't need you, but it's best to take precautions. Oh, and slip this into her mouth." She handed him a short strip of leather, which he gently lodged between Athaya's teeth. ''Having something to bite down on might help her get through this.''

With that, all preparations had been made. *Now follow me,* Tonia sent to him, placing her hands on each side of Athaya's head. *Follow . . . and pray for the best.*

Jaren slipped inside after her, drifting behind Tonia's ghostly presence until they came to the place they sought—the entrance to Athaya's paths, where all her spells resided. The entry chamber resembled a dimly lit cave, its walls smooth and shiny like polished ebony. On one side was a slab of gray stone one shade lighter than the walls. Faint symbols were carved in the wall above the slab, but instead of shedding their usual benign glow, the runes pulsed and throbbed like an infected wound, randomly flashing their anger and illuminating the dark chamber like red lightning.

But worse than the blazing runes was the powerful aura of chaos lurking behind that door, bubbling and churning like a vat of boiling lead. The turmoil intensified as Jaren and Tonia drew closer, the imprisoned magic a living thing that suddenly sensed that someone had come to set it free.

You'd better hold her down, Jaren, Tonia advised him, brushing her fingertips against the bloodied bandages still wrapped around Athaya's forehead. *Her power won't be easy to contain and if it causes her too much pain she might try to harm herself again.*

Jaren obeyed promptly, but he did not like the worried edge to Tonia's voice. He swung one leg over Athaya's body, pinning her to the ground with his own weight, and pressed her shoulders down with his hands.

He felt Tonia's readiness resonate throughout the chamber of Athaya's mind. Her presence moved toward the gray slab of stone, preparing to turn it aside and, little by little, release the pressure of the magic trapped within the paths beyond. As she approached, the chaos behind that door howled and grew more fierce, like a storm entrapped in a porcelain jar, eager to shatter its vessel and wreak its fury upon the world.

''*Aperi potentiam,*'' Tonia whispered.

At her command, the door to Athaya's paths shuddered and began to roll aside, its movement slow and laboring, like a drawbridge straining against rusted chains. Tonia braced her presence against it, holding the stone such that only a crack would appear to let the power trickle slowly out from behind. Athaya whimpered in pain the moment the crack appeared, as if her flesh had just been sliced open with a blade. Magic seeped from its prison like blood from a wound, but the pressure of it forced the crack to widen, despite Tonia's efforts to hold the stone in place. The seepage of power turned to a steady stream, and the faster it flowed, the more Athaya's pain increased. Her whimpers soon turned to choking sobs, and every breath seemed a torture to her.

Jaren, help me! Tonia commanded suddenly. A minute had not yet gone by, but already she sounded tired and winded. *The pressure . . . her magic is too strong, I can't hold it—*

He joined her, bracing himself against the onslaught of power rushing against the door—angry power too long confined. But before a pair of heartbeats passed, he knew that even their combined strength would never be enough; they could not hold the stone in place. He felt their combined force of will being overwhelmed like tender saplings in a raging flood, and within seconds, the stone exploded from their grasp, borne away by the strength of that flood, and Athaya's magic was set free in one great blast of adept-level power.

The eruption engulfed them, but still they struggled to replace the stone and contain it, all the while knowing their efforts would be useless. Athaya opened her eyes and screamed with unholy pain, as if one of her limbs had just been severed, and she writhed wildly under Jaren's weight. She clawed at his face and arms with sharp-edged nails, as if he were the cause of her torment, but still he held her firm.

Athaya's screams shook him to the center of his soul, so helpless was he to stem the tide that caused them, and it was several moments before Jaren could calm himself enough to speak. But he had to reach her somehow; to find the mind within that tempest, trapped in the raging vortex of its own power.

"Fight it!" he cried, using all of his strength to keep her pinned to the ground. "Don't let it win. You can get through this, I know you can. I love you, Athaya!" He shouted the tender words so that she might hear them over her screams. "I'm waiting for you. Fight your way back to me so I can tell you that I love you!"

Then a blast of heat seared his right side as the campfire flared up into an unnatural column of flame. In perfect unison, he and

Tonia dove from the fire and rolled in the dirt, dampening the sparks that showered over their clothing.

Jaren's eyes met Tonia's at the same time, each reflecting the same dreadful thought. *Her spells are free now . . . but she can't control them at all.*

Then the rocks encircling the fire suddenly began to explode one by one, the force of Athaya's magic reducing them to piles of fine sand. Jaren scrambled away from the shattered stones and backed himself against the cove wall, all the while sensing something else far more deadly. Something building in the air around him, making it electric . . .

The next thing he knew, Tonia was at his side, pulling him to his feet. "Get outside the wards—now!"

Jaren had never heard such urgency in Tonia's voice before, and an icy shiver snaked through his limbs, freezing his blood. "We can't just leave her—"

"NOW!"

It was not the advice of a friend; this time it was a direct order from a member of the Circle. But Jaren still resisted, loath to leave Athaya to the mercy of her own power. Then the air began to crackle and hiss, touched with the scent of sulfur, and Jaren suddenly decided to obey, all too certain of what was coming next.

It started as a scream from deep in Athaya's throat, then recast into a string of deadly words. *"Ignis confestim sit!"*

Tonia and Jaren were only inches beyond the cove mouth when a streak of green fire lashed out from behind them with killing force. Only the seemingly fragile wards saved them from a savage death, deflecting the coil and sending it hurling back inside the cove. They raced across the sand, pausing to catch their breaths only when they were safely ensconced behind a boulder near the waterline. The wards should, if they held, keep Athaya's wild spells contained within the cove, but Jaren suddenly doubted the strength of his own spells against those of an adept wizard—and a raving one at that.

He peered around the boulder, watching in fearful silence as more fire-spells ricocheted off the inside walls and the wards, lighting up the interior of the cove like fireworks. The coils were frighteningly strong—more so than any she had conjured in the past—and never before had he known them to give off such a smoky, potent smell.

"God help her, Tonia, she's going to kill herself."

Without thinking, he started to rush back to the cove, but Tonia gripped his arm forcefully and hauled him back behind the boulder. "We can't do anything to help her . . . not now. All we could accomplish in there is to get ourselves killed, too."

But the power inside the boundary had grown too great to contain, and it was with strange relief that Jaren saw his wards torn apart as if they were nothing more substantial than cobwebs. No longer confined to the cove, the fiery coils of lightning snaked across the beach, hissing in fury as they touched the cool waters of the sea. At that same moment, a storm broke out above them, the rain coming in blinding sheets—a hot, steaming rain, like water dumped from a washbasin. Wind drove the waves with angry force, impaling them on the rocks lining the shore.

A brilliant flash of lightning lit the sky, and at the same time, another streak of green fire shot out from within the cove. The two forces met in midair, touching off an unearthly roar of thunder more menacing than anything that had ever come from the skies alone, as if war between heaven and hell had finally come to pass.

"My God, what's happening?" Jaren said aloud, covering his ears as lightning and arcane fire met again with a deafening crash. But he didn't need Tonia to answer his question—he had been a magic tutor long enough to know exactly what was taking place around him. He knew all about a wizard's *mekahn*—that time of trial when magic first appears and presses for release, when madness and unmastered spells become an outward sign of the mind's inner turmoil. And this . . . this was a *mekahn* gone wild, each wayward spell a sign of the chaos boiling inside Athaya's mind; a chaos more dangerous than any *mekahn* could ever be, for Athaya was fully trained, and knew far more spells— many of them deadly—than a fledgling wizard could hope to know.

Then, as quickly as it had come, the storm abated. The rain passed on, the wind died away, and an unnatural silence fell over the shore. But instead of relief, Jaren turned to Tonia with a potent sense of dread.

"My God, you don't think—"

He couldn't bear to finish the question. There were few explanations for such a sudden cessation of power, and one of them was too horrible to contemplate.

With dire impatience, Tonia and Jaren waited a few moments

to make sure the spells had truly stopped, then crept cautiously back to the cove.

Blankets, food, and clothing were scattered recklessly across the sand, strewn about by the wild winds of magic. The fire crackled with benign intent, but the walls of the cove were scarred from the onslaught of fiery green coils, patterned burns looking like black runes carved into the stone. And in the center of it all, Athaya sprawled facedown in the earth as if she had collapsed after trying to stand, dust from the shattered stones coating her hair and clothes like ash.

Tonia knelt at her side and touched two fingers to the side of Athaya's throat, flinching briefly as she sensed aftershocks of pain. "I feel a pulse. And she's breathing. She must have simply passed out." Tonia let out a heavy sigh of gratitude and rubbed her eyes wearily. "It was the best thing she could have done, under the circumstances."

Jaren dropped to his knees beside her. Both of them were exhausted and battered and slick with hot rain and sweat. He reached out and combed Athaya's hair with trembling fingers, whispering her name even though he doubted she could hear him.

"You're free, Athaya," he said, pushing her hair back so that he could see her face. "You're free. Please come back to me, Athaya. Please come back—"

"She's through the worst of it," Tonia told him as she tucked a dry blanket around Athaya's motionless form. "She has strength I never dreamed possible. It may take a while, but with proper rest and food . . . I think she'll recover."

Jaren glanced up, still wary. "Physically, you mean. What about—"

"Her mind?" Tonia sighed again, unable to give him the assurance he sought. "I don't know, Jaren. I'd promise you the world if I thought it would help, but I can't. I just don't know."

Although he was tired unto death, Jaren got up and staggered out of the cove, craving a moment of solitude. He walked to the waterline and stared up at the sky. It was clear now—some small benefit from Athaya's rage—and the clouds and rain that had lingered for most of the day had moved to the southeast, perhaps to plague the king in Delfarham. The sea was calm, licking the shore like a cat gracefully touching its tongue to cream, and a brilliant array of stars formed their age-old patterns in the late summer sky, offering countless promises that they would burn there forever.

But the beauteous night could not comfort him.

She would probably recover physically; he knew he should throw himself prostrate on the ground and thank God for that. But what about her mind—her soul? What about that part of her that made Athaya *Athaya*?

And that would be the cruelest joke of all, he thought bitterly, sinking to his knees in the cool sand. That Athaya should be mad forever, destined to grapple with this mutant breed of *mekahn* and all its inherent torments. And with Athaya's magic freed, carrying with it all the dangerous potential of an adept wizard . . .

Jaren shivered. That was a grave threat indeed. She would likely deal herself a hideous death and take others with her in such great and awful madness.

He scooped up a handful of wet sand, absently molding it between his fingers. All that he had wished for had come to pass: Athaya was free of the convent, free of the seal, and here, warm and alive at his side. But despite all of that, Jaren's heart was heavy with the knowledge that she was still as far away from him as she was before.

And this time, only fate—the ineffable magics of God—could say whether she would ever return to him again.

CHAPTER 5

✠

FAR TO THE SOUTH, IN THE SOLAR OF THE QUEEN'S AN-cestral home of Halsey Manor, Prince Nicolas Trelane steadied himself against the window casement, one arm braced on either side of the narrow embrasure as if struggling to keep the wall from tumbling down around his ears. Before him, the pink and orange ribbons of a late-September sunset crowned rolling green hills still untouched by autumn, but the scene held no beauty for him. The news he had just received cast a pall over his soul, and his typically ebullient manner was eerily subdued.

"It can't be true . . . it just *can't* be."

Queen Cecile and Lord Gessinger, both seated near the hearth, stared at one another in silent disbelief. Between them, Cecile's tiny new daughter slept soundly in her rosewood cradle, oblivious to the catastrophe around her.

The letter, bedecked with royal red ribbons, trembled in Cecile's hands as she read the passage again. " '. . . and it is my duty to inform you that our unfortunate sister has taken her own life and that her final judgment now rests in the hands of God.' " Cecile paused, choking back a sob. "There's more," she went on, her voice unsteady, "but it's just a spate of nonsense about suicide being one of the wiser things Athaya's ever done, and that God may see fit to grant her mercy for removing her cursed magics from His earth, even though it wasn't done by means of a proper absolution.''

The king's callous assessment of Athaya's death cut through Nicolas' state of shock like a whetted blade. He wheeled around with a hiss of rage. "It's a lie!" he cried, pounding his fist against the casement so hard that the glass rattled in its fittings. "It's nothing but a damned, hideous lie!''

Nicolas did not realize he'd been shouting until a pitiful wail arose from the snugly wrapped bundle in the cradle; Caithe's newest princess had been rudely awakened from her nap. Cecile summoned a handmaid to take the baby somewhere more peaceful to sleep, then abandoned Durek's letter on her chair and went to Nicolas' side. She leaned against him, blond curls falling limply over his shoulder, craving solace as much as he.

"It's impossible," Nicolas insisted, shaking his head in staunch denial. "Athaya wouldn't *do* such a thing. She'd never give up like that—not after everything she's been through. Not after everything she's risked . . .''

Cecile dabbed at her tears with the delicate lace cuff of her honey-colored gown. "I know, but—oh, God help us both . . . what reason would Durek have to lie about a thing like this?''

"He's wished Athaya dead for over a year now," Nicolas retorted, spewing out bitterness in every word. "Perhaps he thinks that if he tells everyone she's dead, they'll forget all about her and what she was trying to do for the Lorngeld. And damned if it might not work, too," he added sullenly.

The prince ran troubled fingers through a crop of sun-bleached brown hair as he turned to Lord Gessinger. He gazed upon the Caithan lord with growing desperation, groping for reasons why Athaya could not possibly be dead, but slowly coming to the awful realization that it might not be a lie after all.

"Does it say how she killed herself?'' Nicolas asked, longing to know exactly what had happened despite the horror of it. "Does it say if her body has been returned to Delfarham? Not that Durek would be decent enough to give her a proper funeral," he added spitefully, glaring at the offending piece of parchment as if trying to set it afire by the heat of his gaze alone.

Mosel picked up the letter and scanned it, then sighed dejectedly. "No. He urges her Majesty to come home again, that's all.''

"I suppose if . . . if this is true, he sees no need to punish me anymore," Cecile said, trying to suppress an undignified sniffle. Then her eyes grew hard, and she brusquely flicked a tear away. "Or perhaps he's suddenly realized he has a daughter now and feels obligated to take a look at her."

Nicolas let out a laugh completely devoid of mirth. "And you wanted to know why I came straight here from Reyka instead of going back to Delfarham." Suddenly exhausted, he sank down into the chair Cecile had abandoned, taking little comfort in the sumptuous cushions. "Why should I have ruined what was left of the summer by going back home and listening to more of Durek's verbal excrescence about the Lorngeld when I could spend time with you and my new little niece?" One edge of Nicolas' lip curled up slightly. "Even at the tender age of two months, little Lillian is a far better company than my brother will ever be."

Cecile smiled, but it was a smile marred by sadness. The month since Nicolas' arrival had flown quickly, their happiness together too rudely shattered by Durek's awful news.

"This is all my fault," Mosel said quietly, rubbing his bloodshot eyes. His face was more sallow than Nicolas had ever seen it, and his shabby gray robe only served to emphasize his misery. "I waited too long. I should have gone to Kaiburn right away instead of spending the summer hoping Athaya's friends would find her on their own. Oh God, I'll never forgive myself for this. Never!"

Cecile sat down on the footstool before him, golden skirts pooling around her feet like spilt honey. She clasped his aging hands firmly in hers. "Please don't say such things, Mosel. You did more than anyone could have asked; you were very brave to risk going to Kaiburn."

"I was so happy," he went on, too awash in his own grief to find solace in her words. "When Jaren left for Saint Gillian's, I thought everything would be set right again. If only I hadn't wasted the summer debating whether or not to get involved! And if Bishop Lukin hadn't brought up the issue of this Tribunal, I wouldn't have gone to Kaiburn at all. That's how brave *I* am, your Majesty," he finished, his lips trembling with shame.

Too restless to sit still for any length of time, Nicolas left his chair and returned to the window to stare gloomily at the smoldering embers of sunset. "Stop blaming yourself, Mosel. Consider that a command from both the queen and myself." He tried to force a smile to punctuate his jest, but it would not come. Instead, he bowed his head. "I can't begin to imagine what

Jaren is going through right now." He glanced over his shoulder at Cecile. "He asked her to marry him, you know."

The queen gave a listless nod. "Yes, you told me."

The three of them lapsed into strained silence for a time, and Nicolas began to pace the room in frustration, still grasping for answers. "I wonder if this Tribunal is more than just a proposal," he speculated, recalling what Mosel had told him of the bishop's plans when he had first arrived at Halsey. "Is it possible that it has already been formed? That it might be at work even now?" A harsh edge of anger crept back into his voice. "If that is true, then perhaps Bishop Lukin arranged to have Athaya secretly murdered." His eyes flashed, eager to find a target for his rage and a more plausible explanation than suicide for his sister's supposed death.

"I don't think so, my Prince," Mosel replied. "He had only just presented the idea to the king. I don't doubt his Grace capable of murder, but even if the king and council approved the Curia's proposal the next day, I doubt that even the industrious bishop of Kaiburn would have had time to plan and carry out a murder in the name of this Tribunal so quickly. Besides, if he had planned her death, I think it likely that he would have spread the word that she had finally consented to absolution. Such an act—proof that Athaya had finally surrendered to the demands of the Church—would have helped the king's cause far more than news of her suicide."

Nicolas scowled his disappointment, mentally tossing aside the theory. He paced in silence, inwardly finding and rejecting countless other explanations. When he finally spoke again, his voice was so strange, so thick with suppressed wrath, that Cecile turned to stare, if only to assure herself that the words were indeed coming from Nicolas' mouth.

"I swear to you, Cecile, if this is true . . . if Athaya really *is* dead, then it's the same as if Durek killed her by his own hand." He curled one hand into a fist, clutching an invisible weapon. "It's damned fortunate that I'm not in Delfarham right now, or I might be tempted to take a knife to that brother of mine." He glanced briefly at Cecile, aware that he had just spouted opinions as treasonous as any Athaya had been accused of, but the queen responded with an eloquent shrug, unwilling to chastise him, but equally unwilling to speak in defense of her husband.

"And I'll wager he hasn't wasted any time spreading this news all over Caithe," Nicolas continued, his eyes narrowing to tiny slits. "It's just the weapon he needs to destroy what Athaya's accomplished once and for all. That, and this damned Tribunal."

Cecile gazed up at him, blue eyes barren of hope. "What are we going to do, Nicolas? What can we possibly *do*?"

"You, Cecile, are going to stay here and not get involved with any of this," he replied hastily, going on before she could voice a word of protest. "You've got the baby to look after, never mind the fact that Durek has already punished you once for speaking out in Athaya's favor. Defy him again and Durek might do worse than send you back home to cool off—he might just pack you off to Saint Gillian's in Athaya's place. Then who would see to it that the next generation of Trelanes is raised with any sense? As for me . . ."

Nicolas fell into a brooding silence again, this time for several minutes, weaving plans behind his eyes. Soon, taut muscles relaxed as he settled into a decision, and though he did not smile, Cecile detected the shift in his expression.

"You're plotting something," she accused gently. "And I have every reason to believe that I'm not going to like it."

Nicolas strode to her side and took her hand, his eyes reflecting the bonfire of conviction now burning inside of him. "A Trelane has to lead this crusade, Cecile. Only that name can lend it the credibility it needs to succeed. It's starting to die already, what with Athaya gone—I heard as much on my way back from Reyka." He gave her hand a determined squeeze. "And if Athaya can't lead it—for whatever reason—then damn it all, I *will*!"

Cecile gasped, fingers flying to her mouth, but she quickly assembled her scattered emotions into proper order again. "Nicolas, you can't!"

"My Lord!" Mosel exclaimed, jumping to his feet as quickly as feeble legs would permit.

"And why not?" Nicolas went on, blazing with desire. "What better things do I have to do? Go back to Delfarham? No, I can't be satisfied with that life anymore. I've spent twenty-two years as little more than a convenient appendage to this family—an extra prince, handy to have around in case the king finds himself in need of an heir. And once Mailen was born," he added with a shrug, "I wasn't even needed for that. I'll admit it's been an easy life, but . . . oh, maybe I'm just getting older and I'm finding out there's more to life than a bottle of good wine and a pretty girl to share it with. I want more, Cecile . . . I *need* more. And I don't think I ever realized that until I saw the risks Athaya was taking. I'm a Trelane too, and Caithe's future is my responsibility. I can't sit back any longer and let Athaya do all the work.''

Cecile stared at him unblinkingly, as if seriously questioning whether this was truly Nicolas, or some clever illusion crafted by magic. But Mosel was roused by the prince's impassioned speech and went down on one knee before him, his head bowed.

"I know I'd be of little use to you, your Highness, but there's nothing for me in Delfarham. There never was. Well, nothing but my shrewish sister," he added, glancing up wryly, "but I'd be glad never to see Dagara again. If you go to Kaiburn, then take me with you."

Nicolas laid a hand on the lord's frail shoulder and bade him rise. "I appreciate the offer, Mosel. But if you truly want to help, I think the best place for you is in Delfarham. You can keep an open ear at the capital. But for you, Cecile and I never would have heard about this Tribunal, nor where Athaya was being kept. You can inform me of what Durek and the Curia are up to; no one should suspect you."

"I'll admit to that, my Prince. My king and his court think little enough of me—"

Nicolas flushed scarlet, ashamed of the way his remark had been construed. "That isn't what I meant—"

"I know. But it's true . . . few at court bother to mind their words in my presence." He smiled wanly. "My reputation will serve me well."

At long last, Cecile decided that this was not an illusory Nicolas and managed to recover her tongue. "Nicolas, you may mean well, but you're no Lorngeld . . . you don't know the first thing about magic. Although I'll grant that you do know quite a bit about rebellion," she added dryly. "As much as Athaya, it seems."

He inclined his head at the compliment. "I learned from the best," he conceded. "And while I may not be able to work magic, I know a lot more about it than I used to. I left Ath Luaine in the company of one of the most talented wizards in Reyka; we parted ways near Kaiburn, and he went off to find Athaya's camp. He taught me a great deal during our journey."

Then, no longer able to contain his energy, Nicolas turned on his heel and headed for the door.

"Where are you going?" Cecile asked, spying the slightest curl of a smile on Nicolas' lips. It was not his usual grin of mischief, however, but something more mature, drawn from depths that, in the past, he'd found little reason to fathom.

"Why, to Kaiburn, of course," he said, "where there are plenty of people who know about both magic *and* rebellion. And I want to leave now, before I wake up and realize what a foolishly risky thing I'm doing."

Then the smile vanished, replaced by fierce determination. "I'll wait for Jaren to get back from Saint Gillian's . . . with or without Athaya. And if it turns out that we really have lost her," he added, his voice breaking only slightly, "then I'm going to do everything in my power to take her place. And then Durek will have to answer to *me*."

The first thing she sensed was the smell of bacon cooking and the familiar crackle and hiss of hot grease. Tendrils of smoke tickled her nostrils, threatening to make her sneeze. Her clothes were stale and damp with sweat, but the coarse woolen blankets draped over her kept off the worst of the chill. Somewhere not too distant, waves washed gently against an unknown shore, determined to lull her back to sleep. Her eyes were closed, and it seemed too much trouble at the moment to open them.

"I'll be gone for the better part of the day," a woman's voice came from somewhere very close; a voice pitched low, as if not wishing to draw undue attention to itself. "Once I fetch our horses from the village, I'll buy a wagon and load it with more supplies. I'd best get some more sage and rosemary while I'm there—hmm, maybe a bit of balm, too." The woman paused, and sighed gently. "Her fever may have broken, but she's still weak as a lamb and might not stand up well to a relapse. But it's been three weeks, and we simply can't stay here any longer; we've got to get Athaya back home before the few students we have left decide to desert us, too." Then came another pause, the clink of coins being poured into a pouch and the snap of a buckle being hitched. "You going to be all right here alone?"

"I'll be fine, Tonia. And I'll take good care of her, I promise."

That voice! Athaya stirred deep within, some part of her demanding to awaken and rise up despite the oppressive lethargy that pressed her to the earth as if she were buried under a mound of heavy snow. It was a voice last heard in her dreams, and one she never thought to hear again.

"Don't look for me before dark," the woman said. Another murmured word of farewell, then the muted sound of footsteps retreating in the sand.

The crackle of hot grease ceased shortly after that, followed by the quiet gurgle of liquid being poured into a cup. Athaya felt the brush of rough cloth against her arm as he sat down beside her to eat his breakfast. Bacon . . . the sumptuous smell of it pulled her farther out of her torpor, and her stomach growled in envy. She tried to remember when last she had eaten and found that she could not. In fact, she could not remember much of anything. Cold wind, a locked room, rage. So much rage . . .

Every fiber of her brain was alive and tingling now, like flesh warming from frostbite, and her raw muscles ached, each and every one of them, as if she had been carrying a too-heavy burden for too long a time. But her awareness of the pain helped rouse her even more, and she could sense in some indefinable way that it was not a dangerous pain, but a healing one that would gradually subside.

She tried to crack her eyes open, wanting—needing—to see; to prove that this was not another of her mind's heinous tricks. The lids were hard to open, sealed closed by dry tears, but she squeezed them shut to form fresh tears and then they yielded easily. Her sight was slightly blurred, as if she looked at the world through a badly formed pane of glass, but even the first, foggy glimpse of her surroundings revealed that this was no prison cell and that the figure at her side was no bride of God determined to see her absolved.

It was no trick this time. It couldn't be. He was too real, there beside her, staring at the fire as he absently sipped ale from a dented tin cup, unruly blond bangs cascading over his eyes like a waterfall. He was just as she remembered, if more haunted and timeworn, fine lines wrinkling the once-smooth places around his eyes and making his face look pitifully bleak.

She knew the words she wished to say. They were framed perfectly in her mind, but her mouth was slow to obey. It held a pasty taste, and her tongue felt like the skin of a peach. So, forgoing speech, she lifted her hand—so difficult, as if her flesh had turned to lead—and touched his sleeve.

The gentle motion startled him, and ale sloshed from his cup and into his lap as he turned to her, eyes wide with shock as if she were a corpse that had suddenly come back to life.

"Jaren—" Her voice was little more than a dry, scraping sound. "Is it you? Is it really you this time?" She was reluctant to believe, after all this time; so many dreams had been shattered before . . .

"Oh my God, Athaya—" He thrust his breakfast dishes aside, ale and bacon grease soaking the sand, and scooped her up into his arms, holding her tight against him. "You're back. Oh, thank the Lord, you've come back—"

Unbidden, the tears began, and she forced out each word through long and ragged breaths. "They told me you were dead. I was so frightened. I wasn't sure . . . I couldn't *remember*. But I didn't believe them. I knew you'd come . . ."

The warmth and strength of his embrace pulled her farther from the realm of sleep, but she was too exhausted to leave that realm for long. Already her muscles cried out for more rest, and her mind grew woolly, drifting slowly back to unconsciousness. But she had to say it—now, while she had a chance. She had let too many other chances slip away.

"I should have said yes," she said, clinging to him with every scrap of strength she had and savoring the mingled scent of smoke and seawater on his skin. "I meant to. I wanted to. Oh God, I should have told you yes."

"It's all right, Athaya," he murmured, rocking her in rhythm with the waves. "You don't have to explain anything now."

"There wasn't time to tell you—"

"You're well, Athaya. You're alive and well and that's all that matters."

"I wouldn't blame you if you didn't ask again . . . if I hurt you too much. But I have to tell you . . . I tried before, but Aldus called to me and the bishop took me away—" Vaguely, Athaya knew that she was beginning to ramble; it was taking more effort than she expected to remain lucid for even a few moments. Her eyelids fluttered closed against her will as gentle oblivion beckoned her back, not yet ready to free her fully.

"Athaya, don't worry about it anymore. There's no need. I understand."

"Do you? Oh, do you?"

She felt fingers in her hair, gently brushing it from her face. His skin was rougher than she remembered; the skin of a common man and not a noble's son, and she loved it all the more for its imperfection. "Of course I do."

One last time, she forced her eyes open, not yet ready to let him slip from her sight. Then, for the first time, she noticed the fading bruise on his jaw—a large, purple blotch gradually turning to yellow. Gently, she touched her fingers to it. "What happened?" she asked, her voice badly slurred from exhaustion.

He smiled, and almost laughed, as if recalling a private joke. He brushed her palm with a kiss. "Nothing, Athaya. Nothing at all."

And his voice was so reassuring, like the whispered promise of an angel, that she let herself drift to the very brink of sleep, knowing that she would rest more peacefully than she had in months . . . or perhaps years. Oblivion was no longer a prison to be feared; now it was a place of healing.

From a distance, she heard his quiet murmurs of comfort, and once, a whispered prayer. And content with the knowledge that the words were said at last, she slipped away into dreams, knowing that only sleep—blissful sleep—would make all things well again.

CHAPTER 6

❊❊❊

"**A**THAYA TRELANE, GET BACK INSIDE THIS WAGON this instant!" Tonia scolded, reining two sorry-looking mares to a halt. She glared down from her perch on the driver's bench, waiting in thinly veiled vexation as Athaya strolled leisurely alongside the rickety contrivance instead of riding in it as she had been ordered to do at least a dozen times.

Athaya glanced up like a child caught eating sweets before supper—not sorry for the sin, only sorry to have been discovered. But how could she be blamed? A gentle breeze caressed her face, the clover was cool beneath her feet, and the air was touched by the crisp scent of autumn—nothing like the cold, dead place where she had spent the whole of the summer, all musty darkness and clammy stone walls. Was it so surprising that she would prefer the outdoors to yet another prison cell, this one with wheels?

"Can't I walk for just an hour or so?" She pouted a little, but Tonia had already turned away, voiding any persuasive power the gesture might have held.

"Absolutely not. I let you walk for an hour this morning and I won't have you overexerting yourself. Besides, you should be thankful you've got the means to ride at all," Tonia added. "You'd never believe what I had to pay for this decrepit old thing—convincing those villagers to part with one of their wagons during harvest was harder than getting ol' Basil to crack a smile.''

Athaya's eyes widened a bit; Tonia must have had a difficult time indeed. Overlord Basil, head of the distinguished Circle of Masters, was among the most ill-natured persons Athaya had ever met and the day she saw him smile would be the day the sun rose in the west.

"Then if I have to ride, can't I at least sit up there with you?'' she persisted. She knew she was being a perfectly awful patient, but since she didn't feel in the least bit sick or tired, it was hard to take Tonia's well-intentioned advice to heart. It was impossible to lie back and rest when she wanted nothing more than to run through the sun-warmed grass and feel her heart pumping hot blood through her limbs, each new surge telling her that she was alive . . . gloriously alive.

Tonia rolled her eyes. "Not until after sundown. Too much sun wouldn't be good for you—might bring your fever back.''

"But—''

"You may as well give up,'' Jaren advised, his head poking out from beneath the wagon's canvas covering like a turtle's out of its shell. He had been silently observing Athaya's attempts to wheedle what she wanted out of Tonia, all the while grinning in detached amusement as if everything she did was cause for delight. Although she was warmed to know that his amusement was born of love, Athaya suspected that in his current state of bliss, she could throw a tantrum worthy of the most spoiled of princesses, and Jaren would simply smile in adoration and murmur praises to her irrepressible spirit.

"It's for your own good, Athaya,'' he said, offering his hand so that she could climb back inside the wagon. "You've been sick—in case you've forgotten.'' For a moment, his eyes clouded over with memory, the amusement gone. "We almost lost you.''

Athaya fell silent at the reminder, realizing how foolish her complaints must sound to them. Days ago, Jaren had described everything that had happened in the cove—her delirium and spate of deadly spells—and since she remembered nothing of it, the tale held a morbid sort of fascination for her. Still, she was horrified by the knowledge that she easily could have killed all three of them unknowingly, like doing murder while sleepwalking.

"Well, I'm better now,'' she persisted, brushing that unpleasant thought aside. "In case *you've* forgotten. Last night when you thought I was asleep, I heard Tonia say that I was making a remarkable recovery.''

Jaren scowled his reluctance to concede that point, aware that it would only fuel her determination to walk instead of ride. "If you value her opinion that much," he said, turning the argument against her, "then do what she tells you to. She was a midwife back in Ulard, you know and can work quite a few healing spells. She knows what's best for you."

Athaya voiced a few more obligatory grumbles, but knew they would be as fruitless as those she'd voiced the day before . . . and the day before that. Oh, she had been content to ride at first, sleeping away the lingering effects of the sealing spell. Now, after seven days of dull travel, she felt alert and strong and hungry for activity. But as she had no desire to fall ill again so soon after regaining her health—and her sanity—she grudgingly accepted her fate, scowled her displeasure, and settled back amid the straw in temporary defeat.

"Now, Athaya, let's pick up where we left off before your attempted escape," Jaren said with a wry tilt of his brow, and Athaya was tempted to pinch him for being so smug. Unlike herself, Jaren did not chafe at the confines of the wagon; his years as a magic tutor had accustomed him to long hours spent in libraries and thus he was content to sit beside her day after day, exercising mind instead of body. In doing so, however, he had lapsed into his old tutor's role—much to Athaya's dismay. He filled his hours by questioning her almost constantly, determined to awaken those corners of her memory that still slumbered. And while Athaya welcomed every moment of his presence—a presence she had prayed for until she fell incapable of praying for anything at all—his well-meant interrogations rekindled unpleasant childhood memories of the schoolroom at Delfar Castle, where she was drilled by a neverending string of royal tutors, all of whom had thrown up their arms in despair at her indifference to her lessons. She wanted to give Jaren the answers—if only so that he would stop asking questions—and was angry when she could not. Whatever book contained them was closed to her for now, like one of Master Hedric's secret tomes held shut by binding spells.

"Now, what's the last thing you remember?" Jaren asked her, resuming his oral examination.

The last thing I remember, Jaren, is your asking me that same question not twenty minutes ago. Athaya bit back the caustic reply. "Nothing specific—just scattered images. Wind. Lots of wind. And storms . . . several of them."

"And when was the last storm that you recall?"

"June, perhaps," she replied, shrugging carelessly. "I seem to remember getting plums with my supper around that time."

"Do you remember what month it is now?"

Athaya glowered at him. "September. You told me so just yesterday. Honestly, Jaren, my memory may be spotty but I'm not stupid. Even *I* can see the leaves beginning to turn."

"There's no need to get irritable—"

"I am *not* being irritable!"

Tonia let out a merry chuckle, shaking her head from side to side. "God bless us, the two of you are bickering like married folk already."

"I wouldn't need to argue with him if he didn't keep treating me like a half-witted invalid," Athaya retorted with good-natured scorn. She picked up a piece of straw and began to shred it restlessly between her fingers. Gradually, a grin of mischief spread across her face. "Maybe I should try a spell of translocation," she said with seeming idleness. "Then I could avoid this whole, boring journey and simply wait for the both of you in Kaiburn."

"Don't you dare," Tonia warned her, shooting a fiery glare over her shoulder. "You've barely used your spells since the fever broke and you have no way of knowing how reliable they are. Granted, you don't seem to be having any trouble with them," she added with a thoughtful frown, unable to explain why that should be so, "but I won't have you testing yourself with the most taxing spell you know."

Athaya sniffed her opinion of this decree, then resumed shredding bits of straw with vigor, convinced that her physician was being too overprotective. Granted, she had used her magic sparingly in the past week—and always under Tonia's scrutiny—but even Tonia was forced to concede that she had met with extraordinary success. Admittedly, she hadn't conjured anything more taxing than a simple vision sphere and she'd gotten a slight headache the first time, as if she had flexed an injured muscle an inch too far. But after that, her spheres and witchlights came as strong as they ever had—even stronger sometimes, when she was fed and well rested—all to Tonia's profound mystification.

Inwardly, Athaya was wildly relieved. One of her worst fears had been that she would never regain her former level of power; at the very least, she expected her spells to be extremely frail. However, if her physical health had returned so rapidly, why should it seem odd that her spells would rejuvenate at the same pace?

"I just can't explain it," Tonia reflected, chewing on her lip in puzzlement. "You were delirious for three weeks and *poof!* Not seven days later you're up and about and ready to dance around Maypoles."

"Hardly Maypoles," Athaya replied dryly. "It's September, as Jaren so desperately wishes me to remember."

Jaren let out a puff of exasperation, but again, the very sight of her—safe and sound and full of life—seemed to appease him, and his annoyance soon dissolved into a smile.

"And you haven't developed any side effects," Tonia went on. "Well, except for a bit of memory loss. But when you think what might have happened . . ." She shuddered as her words trailed off, and even Jaren shifted his weight uncomfortably.

"I have one side effect," Athaya observed, raining destruction upon yet another stalk of straw. "I'm bored to death from riding in this cart."

Jaren reached out and plucked the hapless piece of straw from her fingers. "Get used to it," he advised, "because we're not stopping unless we have to. We want to get back to Kaiburn as soon as possible. There are people there that need you, Athaya." His gaze turned somber. "Or at least there were when we left."

This time, Athaya offered no further complaints. When Jaren first told her that there were eighteen students at the sheepfold, she could barely contain her excitement. She was surprised to find that he and Tonia regarded this as bad news, because there had once been nearly fifty. Fifty! It was only when they reminded her that students had been steadily leaving the camp, unwilling to remain without Athaya's presence there, that she understood their urge for haste and bowed to it.

They stopped for the night near a copse of clean-smelling pines, and Tonia prepared a simple but hearty pottage of barley, bacon, onion, and garlic. After driving the horses all day, she was the first to grow tired and soon crept into the back of the wagon with her blanket, welcoming the bed of straw that Athaya had disdained all afternoon. Athaya spread her own blanket over a bed of pine boughs, content to be sheltered only by stars.

Over the past week, Athaya's appetite had recovered just as

quickly as her health and her magic, and Tonia had not been asleep for an hour when Athaya claimed that she was hungry again. Mumbling something about oubliettes, Jaren promptly set about making griddle cakes to supplement the pottage. Athaya soon heard a series of hissing sounds that shouldn't have been quite so loud, then wrinkled her nose at the tendrils of black smoke that spiraled up from the shallow iron pan. Jaren scraped the flat cakes onto two plates and set one before her, a fallen log acting as a makeshift trestle table.

"One thing I *do* remember, Jaren McLaud, is that you once told me you couldn't cook. Then, as I recall, I was hungry enough not to care." She gazed suspiciously at the ovals of blackened batter on her plate. "Now, however, I'm beginning to see your point."

Jaren offered her the spatula with a flourish and, inclining his head, gestured graciously toward the campfire. "Then, my Lady, I humbly bow to your superior skills."

"My—? Oh no," she said, shaking her head as she gently pushed the spatula away. "If you ate anything I cooked, you'd probably come to regret ever having rescued me." She pulled the stopper from a small pot and tipped it upside down to let the amber-colored liquid dribble out. "Besides, they won't be so bad drowned in syrup."

As Jaren smirked at her and began to eat, Athaya gazed at the last vestiges of the ugly but fading bruise on his jaw—the only flaw on that tanned and smooth-boned face. It had taken several days before she had wrested the truth of the incident from him, and even though he refused to hold her accountable for striking him, the angry, purple welt made her cringe with guilt each time she looked upon it.

"I'm sorry I've been so difficult lately . . . and that I snapped at you earlier. You don't deserve it—not after everything you've been through on my account."

"Bickering like married folk already," Jaren recalled with a wistful smile.

It was the first time either of them had mentioned the subject directly; in unison, both of them realized it and fell suddenly silent. Athaya hadn't mentioned Jaren's proposal since the day her fever broke, hoping that he would broach it first, but Jaren hadn't said a word either, perhaps fearing that she had forgotten what she'd said to him in the cove. But now it was time to set all such foolishness aside. That, Athaya knew, was precisely what had driven them apart in the first place.

"I owe you so many explanations, Jaren," she said at last. "I acted like a fool in Ath Luaine last winter. But I was so afraid . . . afraid that you'd end up just like Tyler. Nicolas told me that it was ridiculous to think I could keep you away from me if that's where you really wanted to be. He said that it was boneheaded of me to refuse you." Athaya glanced sidelong at him, noting the slightest hint of a grin. He wasn't going to argue the point.

"I think Nicolas is very perceptive," Jaren said simply. He set their plates down in the grass, and then folded her hands inside of his. "You can't go through life assuming that everyone who cares about you is going to wind up hurt—or dead. After all, you and Nicolas have been close all your life and nothing terrible has happened to him yet. And what about Lord Gessinger? He took risks for you, too, and as far as I know, he's safe enough."

Athaya nodded, still slow to believe that Lord Gessinger—old Mosel, of all people—was the ultimate cause of her freedom. That tale surprised her far more than her unexpected success with her spell work. Even if Athaya had known that the council lord once lost a loved one to absolution, he still would have been the last man at court she would have suspected of such intrigues.

Apparently he knew that, too.

"Nicolas told me that I wanted other people to risk things I wasn't willing to," she went on, continuing her confession. "It was true . . . but it wasn't enough to make me change my mind. Not then."

"It's a risky thing you're doing. Correction—*we're* doing. But I'll take my chances." He reached out and dabbed a drop of syrup from the edge of her mouth. "It's not as if I'd be marrying you under false pretenses."

Her expression changed, subtly but markedly. It was a small thing, but his words had finally given her the precious proof she needed that—for once—the dream wasn't going to be snatched away. "I didn't know if you'd still want to," she began, trying to swallow a world of relief in one gulp. "Not after the way I treated you. I hoped so . . . I prayed for it. But I wasn't sure."

Jaren wagged a finger in her face. "Athaya Trelane, after what I've been through these last few months, you'd better agree to marry me or I'm going to take you right back to Saint Gillian's and leave you there."

Athaya tipped her head to one side, pretending to consider the matter. "Then I suppose I'll have to agree," she said. She leaned forward, sending a river of black hair flowing over her shoulders. "Just as I should have done the first time."

Gently, she pulled him close and sealed her promise with a sweet, burned kiss tasting of syrup. All afternoon she had yearned to run—to feel blood pumping through her veins—but now, without so much as a single step, she felt her heart race and her blood surge through every limb, her flesh coming to life as it had not done in months. Then, her supper momentarily forgotten, she fell against him, and for the first time that day she felt no restlessness or hunger for activity, but was content to remain exactly where she was, unmoving, nestled like a child in the crook of his arm.

Then she sighed wistfully, looking off into the trees. "Of course, now comes the hard part."

"The *hard* part?" Jaren exclaimed. He let out a hearty laugh that rang like chapel bells through the tiny clearing. "God help me, Athaya, between the time I first asked you to marry me, and today, when you finally accepted me, I've been abducted, thrown into prison, very nearly executed, and most recently, cudgeled by a madwoman with a broomstick. And that doesn't count what I went through *before* I proposed to you. If all that was the easy part," he concluded, laughing again, "then I'm certain I don't want to know what the hard part is."

Athaya gave him a good-natured scowl. "All I meant," she began crisply, "was who will we get to marry us? Certainly nobody in Caithe. I doubt we could saunter right up to Bishop Lukin and ask *him* to do it. Aldus would have, but . . ." She trailed off, sadly recalling the priest's undeserved fate.

"Not so big a problem—we'll simply have it done in Reyka. If your translocation spell is as strong as your other spells seem to be, we could go there any time we wanted to."

Athaya rolled her eyes, chagrined that she had overlooked such a simple solution herself, but her face quickly clouded over with frowns. "Trouble is, I'm a little nervous about showing my face anywhere in Reyka these days. Overlord Basil has probably heard about all of this by now and would relish a chance to tell me that I got exactly what I deserved for teaching Father Aldus that damned sealing spell in the first place."

"Oh, I wouldn't worry about that," Jaren assured her. "Master Hedric will defend your reasons—especially if doing so will

annoy Lord Basil.'' He smiled wanly at the ongoing friction
between his former teacher and the Overlord. "So it's settled.
After we get back to Kaiburn and let everyone know we're fine,
we'll go to Ath Luaine and find someone to marry us. Now that
I've got you, Athaya Trelane,'' he warned, "I'm not about to
let you slip away from me again."

Athaya smiled her approval at such a fate, then picked up her
plate and finished the rest of her supper in silence, giddy with
joy; joy at the balmy night with its scent of pine and necklaces
of stars; joy at the warmth and security of Jaren's arm around
her; and yes, even the joy of blackened griddle cakes swimming
in syrup; for, she thought, it was perhaps the sweetest thing that
she had ever tasted since—burned or no—they had been lovingly
made by his own hand.

Nine days after they left the cove near Saint Gillian's, September gave way to October and the weather turned noticeably
cooler. Although she was loath to admit it in light of all her
recent complaints, Athaya was grateful that she had the straw to
keep her warm and the wagon's canvas roof to shelter her.

She peered at the world through an opening in the canvas,
gazing at a sloping field dotted with sheaves of wheat, freshly
tied. Although the sun had not yet broken the horizon, dozens
of country folk were already working the fields, bringing in the
precious harvest. It had been a hot, dry summer throughout
much of Caithe—or so Jaren had told her—and on those infre-
quent occasions when they had stopped in a village to buy bread
and ale for Athaya's ever-clamoring stomach, they had heard the
country folk grumbling about the poor harvest, muttering among
themselves that there might not be enough grain to see their
families safely through the winter.

They decided to make another such stop toward midday, but
they had been gone from their encampment less than an hour
before the wagon suddenly rolled to a stop.

"Why are we—oh!" Poking her head out from under the
canvas, Athaya saw billows of black smoke spiraling up from
somewhere over the next hill. She heard the frightened squeals
of animals, and once, the echo of a human scream.

"We'd better go around," Jaren said. He was seated beside
Tonia on the driver's bench this morning, having finally relented
in trying to refresh Athaya's memory.

Tonia fretted with a wisp of gray-streaked hair that peeked

out from beneath her scarf. "We could . . . but it'll take the rest of the morning to circle back to the road again."

"Better to get home a few hours late than get caught up in some sort of local trouble."

"No," Athaya said firmly, her voice noticeably flat. Her eyes narrowed, then widened again, as if in recognition. "Someone there needs our help. I feel . . . traces."

Her distracted manner revealed her meaning more than her words, and Jaren and Tonia also cast out, searching for signs of a wizard struggling with burgeoning spells. Unlike their native Reyka, there were few enough wizards in Caithe that it was easy to sense power being used, and easier still when such power was fueled by the madness of the *mekahn*. But after a few moments of silence, they exchanged doubtful glances with one another and, in unison, turned and gazed at Athaya curiously.

"I can't sense anything," Tonia said, a hint of surprise in her tone. While Jaren's ordinary abilities might preclude him from picking up signals that an adept like Athaya was sensitive to, Tonia clearly expected that with years of experience behind her, she would not be so constrained. "Are you sure?"

Athaya was puzzled by the question. "Of course I am. It's faint, but . . . can't you feel it?"

Tonia grunted noncommittally. "Come on," she said, snapping the reins. "Let's get to the bottom of this."

They crested the hill and came upon a scene of ruin. It was a tiny village, but the damage to it was vast. Several thatched rooftops were burning, animals and children scattering fearfully in all directions, and in the village green, dozens of bloody-faced folk were raining blows on one another with flails and hoes and fists.

Then Athaya saw a young girl running toward them on the road, apron strings flying as she fled the destruction clutching a basket of eggs in her arms. Athaya jumped out of the wagon and stood in the girl's path. "Please, stop! Can you tell us what's going on up ahead? What village is that?"

The girl appraised her warily for a moment, but as Athaya did not look much like a robber—the gray nun's robe, while tattered, still had its uses—she offered them a curt nod of greeting. "That there's Pipewell, ma'am." She was still breathing heavily, but now that she'd put some distance between herself and the village, her fear had subsided. "I only just went in for me day's eggs and I nearly got myself killed! An' look," she added, scowling into the basket, "now three of 'em's broke."

"But what's all the trouble about?"

The girl clicked her tongue, as if scolding a child. "A nasty business. Wizards, don't you know. There's one of 'em been found here—cracked the millstone this morning just by lookin' at it, I hear—and folks is fightin' over whether to take him to the priest or sneak 'im off to one o' those magic schools folk here have heard tell about."

"I see," Athaya said solemnly. She heard Tonia and Jaren exchange a flurry of whispers, wondering why they had not sensed the wizard's presence yet. "Do you know who this wizard is?"

The girl shrugged noncommittally. "Not right well, no. But Alec is the reeve's son, and the reeve ain't told the priest about him yet. Says he won't, neither. Some folk think he should, is all, but others don't want to cause trouble. Me, I'm keeping my nose out of it. Might get it broke, otherwise," she added, glancing back over her shoulder at the village, "just like me eggs."

"I won't keep you any longer. Thank you." When the girl continued on her way, Athaya headed toward the village on foot, motioning Tonia and Jaren to follow.

It was a small riot in a small village, nothing more. But as she drew closer, the smoke and blood and angry words weighed heavy on her. In a sudden—and unpleasant—flash of insight, Athaya envisioned riots like this breaking out in every village and every city. Until she had begun spouting words of salvation, Caithan wizards had gone quietly off to die. No riots . . . but no options. Now that had changed, and while it would never be enough to silence her, the burning rooftops and bloody faces showed her the price her crusade would exact. It was civil war, just as Durek said. But no matter how many deaths this civil war might command, Athaya knew that they would be nothing compared to those multitudes who had already been led away quietly to absolution. The price, however high, had to be paid.

The wagon rolled into the village green just as the fighting was beginning to abate—some folk had retreated to lick their wounds, others were busily dousing fires or scurrying after frightened pigs and chickens. But while the blows had ceased, at least for the moment, spirited words were still being exchanged across the green.

"But Father Bartholomew has to be told!" one aging man

with a full head of snowy-white hair shouted. "Damned fools, have ye all sold your souls to the Devil to think the boy can be let to live? He's got to be carted off and absolved."

"That may be," a younger man replied, wiping away the trickle of blood that seeped from his nose, "but I ain't for doin' it and getting myself in trouble with the reeve. One bad word to the bailiff and next thing you know we're all given extra work."

A third man nodded soberly. "Aye, he can hold a grudge, that one, and with my crop ruined by the drought, I'll need every penny I have. Even a small fine could mean my family starves this winter."

"But we don't have to tell Father Bartholomew anything!" one young boy, several handspans shorter than any of the men, cried. "Haven't you heard the news? No one with magic has to die anymore. Princess Athaya will save them!"

"Then it's you who hasn't heard the news, boy," the white-haired man snapped, tossing him a condescending glare. "Good news, if you ask me. Princess Athaya is dead. Killed herself. One o' the king's messengers brought word of it to the manor not a fortnight ago."

Athaya's hand flew to her mouth as she sucked in a gasp of shock. She spun around to face Tonia and Jaren. "Killed my . . . what are they talking about?"

Tonia flashed a query at Jaren, who promptly bit his lip. "I was supposed to tell you about that," he said sheepishly, pitching his voice low enough so the villagers would not hear. "Right before we left Saint Gillian's, Tonia threw some of your things out of the window so the nuns would think you jumped and wouldn't bother to send out a search party. Once we had you back, I was so happy that . . . I guess I forgot."

"And you accused *my* memory of being faulty!" But she had little time to dwell on that now. The first, terrible thought that crossed her mind was that if these remote villagers had heard such a preposterous tale, then so had everyone else in Caithe. If students were leaving before, she realized, then this could drive the rest away entirely.

She strode purposefully toward the villagers, only to be greeted with a stony glare from the white-haired man. "Off with ye; this is none of yer affair."

"Isn't it?" Athaya replied, stepping forward. "You've got a wizard among you and that makes it my affair."

"What are ye, a priest now? No, a nun by the look of it," he added, glancing with distaste at the torn remains of her gray novice's gown. "And a shabby lookin' one at that. Who sent you struttin' in here actin' as if ye own the—"

"Tell me where I can find this man," she said simply, leveling him with a look so full of confidence and purpose that he was left speechless with surprise. "I can help him."

The young boy hurried to her side, his eyes sparkling with curiosity. "Are you a wizard?"

"I am. As are my two companions."

A chorus of murmurs rippled through the villagers, and many of them drew back in fear, hands going to their weapons. Others looked at her hopefully, as if she was an angel sent to them in answer to their prayers.

"Alec's at the reeve's house," the boy told her excitedly. "It's that big stone one next to the mill."

Athaya thanked him and set off toward the house, Tonia and Jaren trailing along behind her. No one made a move to stop them—three wizards in a village as small as Pipewell was a vast army indeed—nor did anyone dare to inspect the contents of their wagon, fearful of what horrors it might contain.

"Jaren and I still aren't picking up anything," Tonia murmured. "Whatever disruptions you sensed must be gone now."

"Almost. From what I can tell, he's not in bad shape . . . not yet. His *mekahn* has barely begun."

They hadn't gone twenty yards when a fair-haired man and woman staggered into the green from behind one of the cottages. The woman was moaning in pain, clutching a twisted arm across her chest, and the man, his face spotted with blood, was struggling to keep her on her feet.

"I need help!" he cried. "Where's Miriam? Somebody fetch her, quickly! Emma's arm is broken."

"Miriam's gone," one of the village women said. "She left last night to deliver a child over in Oxbridge. And she took her apprentice with her."

"Let me help," Tonia interjected smoothly, stepping up to the injured woman. "I know how to set a broken bone." She smiled at the woman to comfort her, then glanced up at the man. "Are you her husband?"

"No. Her brother. Emma don't have a proper husband yet." His dry tone revealed that it was an old argument between them. "She's twenty years old. Should have married years ago and set about having children."

"You don't want their help, Ethan!" one of the village men called out. "They're wizards . . . they'll drink her blood!"

"Oh, shut up, you old fool," he snapped back, barely sparing the man a glance. "I don't believe that horseshit and neither should you." He studied the three strangers again, curious, but not fearful.

Tonia gently examined his sister's grotesquely bent arm. "How did this happen?"

"She got in the way of the fighting—got hit by a flail. Meant for me," Ethan added, lowering his eyes in chagrin.

Tonia turned to Jaren. "Go on ahead to the reeve's house," she said softly. "You can handle Alec alone—Athaya says he's not very far along. He'll probably just need someone to explain what's going on and what his options are. I'd like Athaya to stay with me."

Jaren nodded and departed, while Tonia and Athaya followed Ethan and his injured sister into one of the few cottages undamaged by fire. He prodded a goose out of his way with his foot and laid Emma down on a narrow pallet of straw.

"I'll need wood for a splint and cloth—about this much," Tonia said, extending her palms, and Ethan left to fetch the items. She patted Emma gently on the shoulder, and brushed back a lock of her wheat-colored hair. "Just close your eyes," she whispered soothingly, "and this will all be over before you know it."

Now, Athaya, Tonia sent, *I want you to put her to sleep and keep her that way so she won't feel any pain while I reset the bone.*

Athaya closed her eyes and did as she was told, touching Emma's mind and whispering comforting phrases until she drifted off into a deep sleep. Athaya was not highly trained in the use of healing spells, but sensed Tonia's concentration as she aligned the splintered bone and knitted it back into a seamless whole. The arm would be tender for a while, and while Athaya suspected it would heal perfectly well without the aid of a splint and sling, she knew why Tonia had requested them. Given the volatile temper of the village, there was no need for anyone to know that the woman had been healed by wizardry.

Once the bone was set, Tonia went on to soothe her patient's lesser injuries—a bruise here, a cut there, a burn. Athaya relaxed into her task, joining with Emma's mind and sending messages of sleep to her patient, until . . .

Athaya's eyes snapped open. What on earth? There . . . something was *there*, inside the woman's mind. It was small but unmistakable, like a single diamond set upon an expanse of black velvet. Athaya had touched the minds of those with magic and those without, but she had never seen its like before. It was tiny as a mustard seed, but held the radiance of a thousand candles.

Tentatively, she reached out, probing the little speck of light . . . and flinched back in shock as she realized what she beheld. It was small, but oh, what it contained!

Tonia, look at this! she sent excitedly. *Touch her mind and tell me what you see!*

Startled by the force of the message, Tonia grumbled a rebuke for breaking her concentration, then paused to look. *Nothing unusual,* she replied. *Am I supposed to see something?*

It's a . . . how can I describe it? A seed. Right in the center of her brain. Look! There it was, glowing brilliantly in the darkness like a single star. How could Tonia miss it? Tonia was a Master . . . how could she not sense its presence—its potential? An entire universe, in which dwelt all the powers of God, nestled in a space no larger than a pinprick.

A seed of what? came Tonia's baffled reply.

Athaya was close to trembling as she responded, more certain than ever of what she beheld. *Power. Magic. This woman . . . she's a wizard, Tonia. Or will be one day, when her* mekahn *comes.*

Tonia looked up sharply, her eyes as wide as Athaya had ever seen them. "That's impossible!" she said aloud. "Do you know what you're saying? The *mekahn* is the only sign there is . . . the only sign there ever *has* been. No one has ever been able to tell who is a Lorngeld and who isn't before the *mekahn*." Then she paused and drew in her breath with a soft hiss, holding it as if afraid to let it go. "And no one has ever been under a sealing spell as long as you have, either—not and lived to tell about it." She peered into Athaya's eyes as if seeking something hidden behind them. "First you sensed that wizard's presence and now you sense this. I wonder just what that sealing spell did to you."

Athaya laughed nervously and averted her eyes. "Tonia, you're scaring me."

Tonia's reply was barely audible. "You're scaring me, too." Then she shivered violently, as if someone had just dribbled cold water down her back. "Let's keep this quiet for now . . .

we don't have any idea what we're dealing with. We can't very well stay here for who knows how many months—or years—to see if Emma develops magic, and if you've made a mistake, any hint that she might be a wizard could cause another riot like the one out there.''

"But what if it isn't a mistake, Tonia? What if it really *is* a seed . . . what dormant magic looks like before the *mekahn*?'' The possibilities were staggering. If it was possible to identify who was a Lorngeld and who was not *before* the madness came, then so much destruction could be averted! People could plan for magic to enter their lives, not be rudely jolted by its arrival. God, was there even a chance one could be trained in advance as well, so as to avert the madness entirely?

While Athaya's head was spinning with ideas, Tonia's face was unexpectedly grave. "If you're right, then we may have a worse problem than we realize. Can you only imagine the hordes of folk who'd be throwing themselves at your feet begging to be tested? Wanting to find out whether absolution was in their future or not? The whole of Caithe would be in a panic. And it may not even be right to know such a thing in advance!'' she added, her face lined with strain. "How can we know that God would approve of this?''

"But maybe He already has. Maybe He granted me the gift for a reason, and all I have to do is find out what it is.''

"Maybe,'' Tonia said, shaking her head in a rare show of confusion. "Maybe. I just don't know.''

Jaren slipped into the cottage just then, whistling cheerfully. "Our wizard is just fine. A little confused, but—'' He broke off abruptly when he saw the impassioned looks on their faces. "Hey, what's going on?''

"I can't go into it now, Jaren,'' Tonia said tersely, aware that Emma's brother would return any moment with the splint and cloth. "But Athaya has discovered an extraordinary side effect of the sealing spell.'' She glanced at Athaya once more, as if studying a curious artifact. "I may be wrong, but if I'm not, we can't risk letting anyone hear about this—not until we understand the implications.''

"Implications? Of what?''

"Later, Jaren,'' she said with finality. "You said Alec is fine?''

Jaren frowned at her evasiveness, but knew better than to press for details. "For now. I asked if he wanted to come to

Kaiburn with us, but the offer made him nervous. He said he'd never be able to get away until after the harvest anyway, but that he'd think about it. But Athaya was right—his *mekahn* is still in the early stages. He won't be in too much danger if he waits until November to come."

When Ethan returned with wood and cloth, Tonia made a crude splint and sling for his sister's arm, a kindness for which, despite her protests, she was persuaded to accept a dozen fresh eggs in payment. The village green was still crowded with people when they returned to the wagon, and Athaya didn't have to guess what—or who—they were discussing so animatedly. The sudden presence of three wizards in Pipewell seemed to have quelled the villagers' dispute, perhaps convincing many of them that they now had worse problems than one unpredictable reeve's son.

Undaunted, Athaya strode regally to the center of the green; one task remained before she departed this place. She climbed onto the rim of the village well. It wasn't a very dignified platform from which to make a royal proclamation, but considering that the only other nearby structure was the stocks, it would have to do.

"Your friend Alec is indeed one of us," she called out, paying no mind to the rumbles of discontent from some of the villagers. "And he may yet choose absolution. I pray he does not, but I will force no one to believe as I do in the sanctity of magic. All I wish you to know is that he and those like him do not have to die. Send them to Kaiburn, where I can teach them. Or Kilfarnan," she added, remembering the scholarly Dom DePere and his plans to further her cause in the west. "Another of my friends has started a new school of magic there."

Then one woman near the front of the crowd gasped loudly and pointed at her in sudden recognition. Athaya offered her a subtle nod. "The king's messenger that came to your manor? He was wrong, my friends. Tell everyone in the village—in every village." Her gaze swept over the crowd, charging everyone present with a sacred duty. "Tell them that Athaya Trelane has returned."

CHAPTER 7

❈❈

THEY BEGAN RUNNING TOWARD THE WAGON THE MOMENT it crested the hill and came within sight of the sheepfold. Tonia had contacted Ranulf with her vision sphere two days before to alert him to their return, but even though Athaya's friends and followers were expecting her, their reception was warm and enthusiastic.

The moment the wagon rolled to a stop, Jaren scrambled out of the back and lifted Athaya down, setting her gently in the grass amid Ranulf, Gilda, Kale, Cameron, and over a dozen others. The next few minutes were a dizzying collage of embraces and faces—some new and unknown, others familiar and dear—and to Athaya's surprise, she even received scattered bows and curtsies from those who felt it proper to acknowledge her royal heritage, however much the outlaw she might be at present. Jaren and Tonia withdrew to the outskirts of the crowd, allowing Athaya to have the adoration all to herself.

"Decided against taking holy orders, I see," Ranulf remarked dryly, freeing her from a suffocating, bearlike hug and touching stubby fingers to the sleeve of her ragged nun's robe. "Good thing. Somebody so hell-bent on setting Caithe on its ear never would have survived the rule of obedience."

Before Athaya could think of a suitable rejoinder, Kale stepped forward and went down on one knee before her, bowing his head in obeisance. A former member of the King's Guard, Kale

had stayed at her side since she had been forced to flee Delfarham over a year ago. His formal homage not only surprised her,
but touched her deeply. "Dom DePere sent a messenger from
Kilfarnan a few days ago asking whether the news was true,"
he said, "but none of us had any idea what to tell him."

"Aye, the ol' bookworm has been frantic, all right," Ranulf
added, chuckling softly. "His messenger is still here—been
bunking in one of the empty rooms at the dormitory. I'll send
him back to Kilfarnan with the good word."

Athaya lifted one eyebrow. "Then I gather you've all heard
the announcement of my supposed demise?"

"Weeks ago," Cameron said, pushing to the forefront. Al
though not yet fourteen, the erstwhile pickpocket had sprouted
almost to Ranulf's height over the summer, and Athaya had to
force herself not to gape. "The king made sure the news came
here first—to discourage us. Folks talked of nothing else in the
city for days," he went on, gazing up at her with devotion. He
offered her an awkward smile. "Must be nice, being so popular."

Athaya couldn't contain a hearty burst of laughter. "Notorious is more like it, Cam. There's a big difference."

Then she turned her attention to Gilda, now in her ninth month
of pregnancy and impossible to overlook in any crowd. "Tonia
tells me you've been doing most of the tutoring while I've been
gone. I can't tell you how grateful I am—and proud."

"It was harder when there were more of them to teach,"
Gilda replied as she wiped a trickle of sweat from her brow.
"There are fifteen at the sheepfold now," she added, anticipating Athaya's next question. "Only thirteen are actual students,
though." Her eyes flickered briefly toward a pair of newcomers
set apart at the rear of the group—a striking, auburn-haired
woman and a similarly colored man almost as burly as Ranulf.
For a moment, Gilda looked as if she were about to say more,
but the impulse passed. "Frankly, after we heard the news of
your death, I'm surprised we didn't lose them all. But that will
change now." She smiled, and her face glowed like a rosy dawn
breaking over the eastern horizon. Considering that Gilda had
once been hostile toward magic—as was her husband, who drove
her from their home the day he discovered she possessed it—
her blatant enthusiasm for their cause warmed Athaya's heart.

Then a dark-haired woman that Athaya had never seen before
wormed her way through the cluster of people. She touched the

sleeve of Athaya's robe as if it was of gossamer, fragile as a
butterfly's wing. "Miraculous," she murmured, searching
Athaya's face for confirmation that she was truly flesh and blood,
and not a wraith come back to walk the earth after death. "God
surely has His hand in bringing you back to us, your Highness."

"I have no doubt that He did," Athaya replied. "But it wasn't
a miracle exactly. Just the work of devoted friends. Or more
accurately," she amended, "one devoted friend . . . and one
husband-to-be." With that pronouncement, the embraces began
anew, as those she knew and those she had yet to know both
offered their congratulations with equal fervor. Even in her reduced state, she realized, a royal wedding was still something
to be celebrated.

"Let's be going back to the camp now," Tonia said in her ear
a moment later, drawing her away.

"But we've only just arrived. I want to meet the new students
and catch up on what's been happening in the city and . . . and
just *be* here." Fondly, she looked across to the squat, stone
sheepfold. Decrepit and weatherbeaten, the thatch-roofed magic
school was still the most beautiful thing she'd seen in weeks.

"I know you'd rather stay," Tonia told her, "but there's
someone waiting for you at the camp—been here a few weeks,
I gather. Ranulf told me about it when I contacted him yesterday.
He wouldn't tell me who it was, though. Apparently your mysterious visitor wants to surprise you."

Tonia instructed Kale and Cameron to take the wagon and
horses into the city and sell them—much to Athaya's gratification—and then set off at a brisk pace toward the forest, Athaya
and Jaren following arm-in-arm. The path back to the camp was
unchanged, but several times Athaya was misled by unfamiliar
illusions—to counter the bishop's raiding parties, Ranulf altered
their form and placement every few weeks—and so she had to
rely on the runes alone to guide her around the false brambles,
bogs, and gullies obscuring the camp. The insubstantial runes
glowed like streaks of fire on the tree trunks, marking a path
through the dense forest for any with a wizard's sight to see
them.

Athaya had guessed the identity of her visitor long before she
reached the clearing—who else was always popping up at unexpected times, always to her delight? And who else would insist
his presence be kept secret? She found him playing a game of
solitaire in the grass beneath the bell tower, whistling content-

edly each time he placed another card in position. His shirt and breeches were stained at the elbows and knees, his light brown hair was frosted with bits of leaves, and he looked as much a king's child as Athaya did herself. And that, Athaya thought, was how she loved him best.

Stifling laughter, she crept up behind him and made a wriggling gesture with one finger. *"Figuram visionibus praesta,"* she whispered, conjuring the illusion of a black snake slithering menacingly toward the prince. It took him a moment to notice it, so intent was he upon his game, but when the motion caught his eye, he let out a shriek wholly unworthy of his royal upbringing. He scrambled to his feet and stumbled backward, spraying cards everywhere with abandon, and fell into the outstretched arms of his waiting sister.

"Nicolas, it's so good to see you!" she cried. "I thought you were still in Ath Luaine."

His eyes darted back to the grass, upon which there was now no snake, and wrenched his face into a good-natured scowl as he proceeded to hug every wisp of breath out of her lungs. "I'm glad I knew you were coming ahead of time, Athaya, or I think I'd be embarrassing myself with tears right now." He released her from his loving grip and looked down at the scattered cards at his feet, sighing in mock-despair. "And I was winning that game, too."

Jaren and Tonia had joined them by then, and Nicolas offered a brotherly embrace to Jaren, and a gracious kiss on the cheek to Tonia. "My, my," Tonia exclaimed, chuckling softly, "I've never been kissed by a prince before—not even by Felgin." She glanced sidelong at Athaya and cocked her head knowingly in Nicolas' direction. "I like this one."

"I'm in debt to both of you," Nicolas told them. He shook his head from side to side, as if not quite believing that Athaya stood before him in the flesh. "If I were king, I'd grant you all the land from here to the Sea of Wedane and give you coins enough to drown in as reward for what you've done."

Athaya regarded him wryly. "If *you* were king, Nicolas, they never would have had to rescue me from that prison in the first place."

"Ah. Good point."

Tonia excused herself to go find something cool to drink in the kitchens, while the others gathered up the scattered playing cards and sat down on a log near the campfire. But suddenly,

Athaya's joy at seeing her brother again was sharply curtailed, and she sprang back to her feet.

"Nicolas, do you realize what you've done by coming here? If Durek ever finds out about this, he'll pack you off to prison, too!"

"Oh, I rather doubt it," he replied carelessly, shuffling the cards. "Even assuming he did find out—and I don't see how he could, since anyone who claimed to have seen me here would have to explain just what *they* were doing here, too—I don't think he'd do anything drastic. Remember what I told you a long time ago about needing to put a few more heirs between you and the Crown? I figure his Majesty will need at least two more sons before he can safely get rid of me. He's only got the one, you know. Then again, maybe you don't . . . Cecile just had a baby girl, bless her!"

"Oh, I'm so glad!" Athaya exclaimed, appeased—at least for the moment—by Nicolas' explanation. "How is she?"

"She's fine. It was tough going for a while, but—oh, Athaya, this is ridiculous! I can tell you all my news later. Right now I have to hear about you." He set the cards aside and put a protective arm around her shoulder. "From what I've heard, you've been going through something far worse than just having a baby. But you look so well! I was expecting you to be ill or tired or—"

He cut himself off abruptly, but the troubled look in his eyes told Athaya what he had been about to say. "Not quite sane?" she finished for him. "No, Nicolas. I'm fine."

If not exactly back to normal, she added inwardly. She exchanged a knowing glance with Jaren, who had been just as stunned as Tonia when she had finally told him of the strange new talent she had uncovered in Pipewell. But until she learned more about it, she thought it prudent not to mention it to Nicolas. If such a thing was a puzzle to trained wizards, then Nicolas would be baffled indeed.

"I came back from Reyka with a wizard-friend of yours, and he told me more about what a sealing spell could do to you than I ever wanted to know." Nicolas shredded a dry leaf between his fingers, betraying his concern. "He's still here, by the way. In fact, he's waiting to see you right now." Something sly crept into her brother's eyes. "The two of us became rather close during our journey. We talked about you a lot. Both of you," he added, turning to Jaren.

"Prince Felgin?" Jaren asked, eyes brightening at the prospect of seeing his old friend again.

Nicolas chuckled, as if at a private joke. "Hardly. When I left Reyka, Osfonin was pressuring Felgin to stop dillydallying and find himself a wife. He won't be leaving Ath Luaine until he gets one, I'm sure—not if he wants to keep his head. No, this wizard is much older."

"Master Hedric . . . it must be!" Athaya exclaimed. She jumped to her feet and hastened across the clearing, Jaren close on her heels.

"Athaya, wait—"

She heard Nicolas call to her, but did not turn back. The moment her foot touched the chapel's threshold, however, she wished she had. Athaya jerked to a stop as if she'd walked into a shielding spell, and Jaren careened into her, sending them both stumbling clumsily over the threshold. The robed figure standing at the altar with his back to them was too tall to be her old teacher.

Hearing them enter, the man turned in a sibilant swirl of brown wool. Athaya's heart promptly sank into her slippers.

"Overlord Basil."

His smile was vaguely predatorial, teeth glowing white in the chapel's dim light. "You remember me."

Indeed she did. Being brought before the Circle of Masters was one of the more nerve-racking experiences of her life, and Lord Basil had done little to make it easy. But he was not quite the same as she remembered; not the same elegantly clad gentleman who was most at home amid the polished marble floors and gilt trim of the Circle Chamber. In his drab traveling attire, boots crunching on dry leaves that had blown through the chapel's open windows, he appeared more fallible. He still had the cool, stony gaze she remembered, but it was different this time. Somehow, it struck her as more . . . crafted.

"Wise, holding your tongue. Waiting to see what I know before giving anything away. Wise." He nodded approvingly, and his tone was suspiciously free of wrath. "But you need not keep silent. I have been here for several days and Ranulf has told me everything. To his credit, I had to order him to speak. He's a loyal man."

Basil knew everything? Athaya's heart sank even farther. And it had been such a pleasant day so far. Glancing at Jaren, she was secretly gratified to note that he looked no less uneasy than she did. If she weren't convinced that the Overlord would only find them later, Athaya would have cast a spell of translocation that very instant to take herself and Jaren somewhere far from his acerbic eye.

"My Lord—"

"You knew it was a Circle spell," he said as he came down the aisle, slowly advancing on her like a cat toward its prey. "You can be sure I will speak to Master Tonia about this as well; she takes much blame for allowing you to do such a thing."

"Please don't blame her. She only let me teach Father Aldus the spell because there was no other way . . . and there wasn't time to ask the Circle! Without the seal, one of our students would have been poisoned and Aldus would have been discovered by the bishop during the ceremony—" Athaya knew she was babbling, but the Overlord's condemning gaze fouled her tongue and robbed her of eloquence.

"Don't bother making excuses, Athaya," he said evenly. "They won't do you any good at this point."

Athaya leaned against one of the stone pews for support. "I gather that news of this has reached Reyka, then."

Basil nodded. "Around midsummer. Of course, by that time we already knew something had gone wrong. Shortly after the news came to Ath Luaine that Jaren's servant was found murdered—and I am sorry for that, Jaren," he added sincerely, "a craftsman named William came to the palace to see Lord Ian. He said that a man—a Caithan man—had been asking about the two of you a week or so before, claiming he was trying to protect the princess from an assassin. Obviously that wasn't his intention at all."

Jaren's eyes narrowed at the memory of his captor. "Captain Parr."

"That's when Hedric realized what was happening. Since he knew that the Circle was to be kept informed of your activities in Caithe, Athaya, he contacted me right away. And when Prince Nicolas made plans to return to Caithe after the news arrived of your trial and imprisonment, I decided to join him. By the way," he added, "his Majesty wishes you to know that he did not ask your brother to leave his court. Osfonin invited him to stay as long as he wished, but he was too worried about you to remain. As for me," he went on, molding his face back into an expression of indignation, "I think you know why I have come."

Athaya heard herself swallow.

"As Overlord of the Circle of Masters," he said, his voice crisp and formal, "I formally condemn your actions in teaching a secret spell to one not sanctioned its knowledge, in blatant violation of the strictures of the Circle."

Jaren fidgeted beside her, drawing Basil's glare. "And yes, Jaren. I know that Tonia has taught you the spell as well."

"My Lord, I can explain—"

"—but under the circumstances, I suppose that couldn't be helped. If something had happened to Tonia, then Athaya would have truly had no hope remaining. It was wise of her."

Such unexpected benevolence stripped Jaren of any ability to reply beyond a series of silent blinks.

Basil came a step closer to them, and suddenly the stone facade crumbled. Instead of the imperious Overlord, Athaya saw before her a mere man, capable of faulty judgment—and forgiveness. "However," he began, lips poised on the brink of a smile, "speaking simply as Basil Avalon and not as the Overlord, I think you could not, in good conscience, have done other than you did."

Athaya knew her mouth was hanging open in a most undignified manner, but she was too astonished to close it. Sympathy? From Basil? The same man who once accused her of masterminding her father's murder and plotting to use her magic to gain the Caithan throne? The Overlord's change of heart surprised her far more than Lord Gessinger's hand in her escape had ever done.

"Hedric was worried about both of you—as was I," Basil added awkwardly, as if confessing something he was vaguely ashamed of. "But Hedric's position keeps him in Ath Luaine—his new assistant is inexperienced and can't be left unsupervised quite yet—and so I came here to find out what had become of you. Despite what you may think, I am deeply grateful to find you both well. And now that I have," he concluded, pressing his palms together as if preparing for prayer, "I suppose my mission is complete and I shall be returning to Tenosce."

Athaya knew that this was the proper moment in which to invite him to stay as long as she wished, but something kept her from speaking. Overlord Basil had been the stuff of nightmares until his very hour; did she really want him to remain? Luckily, however, Basil filled the silence himself, and to Athaya's surprise, he didn't seem to be expecting any such invitation. No, he expected something quite different.

"It is a long journey, especially to make alone." Athaya detected a vaguely martyred lilt in the Overlord's voice. "Unless I leave now, I shall never make it back before the weather turns cold. Snow comes in October quite a number of times." He was hinting at something—not very subtly, Athaya noted—and she had to make a conscious effort not to smile.

"If you'd rather, my Lord, I could take you there."

Basil utterly failed to hide his delight. "Now, that would be logical, wouldn't it? This translocation spell of yours . . . the experience would be remarkable, I'm sure. But it is a selfish request; you've only just returned, and—"

"It will be no inconvenience," she assured him, knowing he desired nothing so much. Apparently he had gotten over his initial resentment of her rare talent. Inwardly, she decided not to risk ruining his sanguine mood by telling him about the seeds just yet; resentment might flare up again, worse than before. "In fact," she continued, "Jaren and I were planning to return to Reyka anyway." She paused, taking Jaren's hand. "To be married."

Basil nodded his approval. "I expected as much," he said, chuckling softly as he shifted his gaze to Jaren. "Your father has been rather vocal in his fears that you would do just that. But you have my congratulations, nonetheless." He turned back to Athaya. "Will you have the ceremony at Glendol Palace, then, or in Ulard?"

"Actually, I'd love to have it here," Athaya said wistfully, gazing about the sorry little chapel. "Many wizards died here during Faltil's scourge, and holding a wedding here would sanctify the place again, I think. But there's not a priest in all of Caithe who could marry us—not legally, anyway. I was excommunicated last winter," she added offhandedly. While excommunication would have had most Caithans trembling in peril of their souls, Athaya had grown used to regarding her spiritual status with pride, like a wounded soldier who shows off hardearned scars.

Just then, a vagrant smile lifted the edges of Basil's lips. "You could have the ceremony here, if that's what you wish." Suddenly, the smile bloomed wider. "Being the Overlord of the Circle does have its privileges, you know—rather like being captain of a ship."

"You mean *you* can do it?" she blurted out.

Basil's eyes reflected amusement at her reaction. "I can. Wizards are as much priests in Reyka as are the priests themselves, Athaya. Perhaps even more so, since they carry God's mark. As Overlord, I have the authority to perform marriages providing that one of the two people involved is a Lorngeld.''

Athaya almost laughed aloud. A few months ago, Lord Basil seemed as eager to see her on the receiving end of a headman's ax as did Durek and his Curia, and his offer to act as priest for them was only slightly less unexpected than having Bishop Lukin volunteer to do it himself.

She and Jaren gratefully accepted his offer. ''Then afterward, if Tonia thinks it's safe for me to go ahead and try my spell of translocation, Jaren and I will take you back to Reyka.''

''And I'll let my father know he's acquired a new daughter-in-law,'' Jaren said with happy resignation. ''I can see his face turning purple already.''

Athaya had no doubt that it would; Lord Ian had long seen fit to blame her for all the calamities that had befallen Jaren since the day he first set foot on Caithan soil. Not that they weren't indirectly her fault, she admitted, but she certainly hadn't ensorcelled Jaren into following her, as Ian seemed to think. But perhaps it was easier for Ian to blame Athaya than to accept the notion that Jaren had a rebellious streak in him, and wasn't proving to be quite as dutiful a son as the Reykan duke might have liked.

''Your father will be glad enough to see you all in one piece,'' the Overlord assured him. ''In light of that, I think he'll approve your choice of bride quickly enough. After all, I was rather suspect of her myself until recently. But my eyes have been opened . . . as will Lord Ian's, I imagine.''

Then he turned to Athaya, his expression abruptly earnest. ''I was harsh with you during our first meeting, your Highness,'' he admitted, and although he didn't voice the actual words, Athaya belatedly realized he was apologizing. ''However, being in the company of Prince Nicolas for several weeks has convinced me that perhaps I was too hasty in my judgment. He defends your honor quite convincingly, and anyone who can inspire that sort of devotion—in a brother, and in others,'' he added, motioning to Jaren, ''deserves more respect than I initially chose to grant.''

Athaya was honored by the compliment—surely it was one of few Lord Basil gave to anyone. But something he said bothered her, like the faint beginnings of an itch. "So you and Nicolas became friends, did you?"

"We had nothing but time on our hands during the journey, and your brother is a charming sort of individual—it would have been difficult for us not to become friends. He told me all that had happened to you since your magic came—and a little about your father, and Rhodri, and your brother Durek." Then Basil's eyes twinkled unexpectedly, and in a most unsettling manner. "And a few other stories I found rather entertaining."

"Such as?" Athaya asked warily, sensing a small knot forming in her stomach.

Evasively, Basil began adjusting the folds of his traveling robes. "Actually, he asked me not to tell you."

As if on cue, Nicolas chose that moment to saunter into the chapel, whistling gaily. "Everyone on good terms again?"

"Everyone except the two of us," Athaya said, peering at him suspiciously. She set her hands on her hips. "Just what kind of stories have you been telling him about me?"

Nicolas offered his most innocent and winning smile. "The truth, Athaya . . . nothing but the truth."

Athaya bit her tongue to keep from swearing in front of the Overlord. She had spent most of her childhood years—and a good number of the adult ones—getting herself into the most awful kinds of trouble; the truth would be bad enough.

"Don't pick a fight with him just yet, Athaya," Jaren cautioned lightly, folding her neatly inside his arms. "You'll want him in your good graces for the wedding."

Nicolas' brows shot up. "The—?" Then his surprise melted away and he laughed with unbridled jubilation. "Well, it's about time you two got yourselves straightened out."

Athaya accepted his kiss of congratulation, but as he turned away to offer Jaren a brotherly embrace, she took hold of his arm and whispered into his ear. "I'll drop it for now, Nicolas, but after the ceremony I want to know exactly what you've been saying to Overlord Basil."

That same night, on a cool October evening blessed by a full moon and adorned by a jewel box of stars scattered across the black velvet sky, Athaya Trelane and Jaren McLaud were married in the forest chapel.

It was not the kind of wedding she had dreamed about as a girl, Athaya thought as Nicolas escorted her down the aisle.

Back then, she had envisioned Saint Adriel's Cathedral bedecked with roses, a satin gown stiff with gems, and all of the Caithan nobility in attendance. And it was not Jaren who had awaited her in those dreams, but another man, long since lost to her. But she no longer grieved at Tyler's death, thinking of him with fond remembrance and sure in the knowledge that he would bestow his blessing upon this marriage, having always placed her happiness above all things in his heart.

Now, looking upon the makeshift altar cloth of autumn leaves, the candles glowing serenely from within hollowed pumpkins, and her simple peasant's gown of deep green wool, Athaya thought that nothing—not all the pomp and ceremony that Caithe could muster—could surpass the beauty of the dream turned to reality, since the man she most loved in all the world was waiting to take her hand, preparing to be hers from now until the end of their days.

Basil greeted the small congregation, bestowing blessings upon them all; then, after Nicolas kissed his sister's cheek and formally released her into another's lifelong care, Athaya accepted Jaren's jeweled wizard's brooch as a token and offered her own to him, until such time as the tokens could be replaced with rings. And when every vow was said and every prayer offered up to the heavens, Overlord Basil looked down on the bride and groom with paternal pride.

"May you one day unite this land as steadfastly as you yourselves are united today," he said, drawing the ceremony to a close. "Do so, Athaya, Jaren, and Caithe shall flourish forever."

When the formal ritual was over, the assembly spilled out of the chapel and into the clearing so that the informal festivities could begin. One of the newest students at the camp was also a harper, and he, along with Kale and his hand-carved flute, played dancing tunes far into the night. Ale and cider flowed freely, a haunch of venison roasted on the spit, and gaiety echoed from every tree in the forest.

"So, how does it feel to be his Majesty's brother-in-law?" Ranulf asked the groom loudly, slapping him on the shoulder so hard that the ale sloshed from Jaren's cup.

"I'd be honored if his Majesty wasn't so hell-bent on trying to kill me."

"Durek's going to hear about your escape before long, you

know," Nicolas pointed out to Athaya. "God only knows what he'll do. Try to get rid of you again, most likely."

"Hell of a wedding present," Ranulf drawled. He planted a kiss of congratulations on Athaya's cheek. "Ask him for a rope o' pearls instead." He belched with great volume, then teetered away in search of more ale.

"Of course, hearing you're not dead will be bad enough," Nicolas went on, "but one of these days he's going to find out about this wedding and really hit the rafters. Oh, I wish I could be there to see his face when the news reaches Delfarham that you're alive and well." He sighed with the vaguely peeved air of having missed an exceptionally good party. "I'm sure his expression will be priceless. Absolutely priceless."

In those rare moments when she wasn't either dancing or being congratulated, Athaya made an effort to speak briefly with each of the new students. They came from every walk of life: a tinker, a baker, a handful of farmers, a wine merchant, and even the wife of a neighboring baron. Some were overtly enthusiastic about their magic, others quietly confused, and one or two were still terrified for their souls, but Athaya spoke to them all with gentle gratitude, thanking them for their courage and promising to protect them as well as she was able.

By far the most animated newcomer she encountered was the auburn-haired woman that she had seen at the sheepfold that afternoon—one of the two that Gilda had said were not students. Shortly after the ceremony was ended, the woman scurried up to her, brimming with good wishes and compliments. Her hair was windswept and unkempt, her kirtle deeply wrinkled, but that did not detract from her creamy skin and brilliant green eyes. Were she to tidy herself up a bit, Athaya thought, she would be quite striking indeed; a rival to any noblewoman.

"It's such an honor to meet you, your Highness!" she cried, dropping a low if somewhat clumsy curtsy. "I've heard so much about you, and to be here for your wedding . . . why, never in my life did I dream of such a thing!" In an instant, her smile was replaced by a look of grave concern. "Oh, and what you've been through o'er the summer—I heard the others talkin' about it and it sounds right awful. Awful! But I didn't understand some of what they said—I don't have the power myself, you know. Sealing spells and all . . . quite an odd thing, to my mind. Would you mind so much if I asked a thing or two?"

"Certainly," Athaya said, trying not to laugh at the woman's good-natured but bountiful flow of words, "if you'll tell me your name first."

The woman slapped her cheeks with both palms. "Oh, silly goose! Where's me head," she said, blushing. "Connor's always sayin' I'd walk off without it if it wasn't latched on. I'm Drianna, my Lady. Drianna of Crewe. Connor's me husband—o'er there, by the ale, as usual." She gestured to a husky, red-haired man standing next to Jaren and Nicolas at the ale barrel. Nicolas, Athaya noted, was watching Drianna with detached interest—the prince was never one to let a lovely woman slip past his gaze.

"So what did you want to know?"

"Oh, ever'thing," she replied, making an all-encompassing gesture with her hands. "Like did it hurt much? Did it ruin your magic?"

Athaya gave her a brief summary, but pointedly omitted everything relating to Emma and her seed of magic. For the moment, that volatile knowledge was going to stay between herself, Jaren, and Master Tonia. "And my power wasn't ruined at all," she said at the end of her tale. "In fact, I'm stronger now than I was before."

Drianna's eyes were round, enchanted by the tale. "Stronger! 'Tis a blessing, truly."

"One I paid for, believe me," Athaya told her solemnly. "I don't remember much from that time, Drianna. And yes," she added more quietly, "it did hurt."

Drianna suddenly looked repentant. "Oh, I'm sorry, my Lady, to be bringin' up unpleasant things on such a happy night for ye. 'Twas only my curiosity. Connor says I have too much for me own good, and that I'm forever prying too much."

"That's all right," Athaya assured her. "If you've come to help me, then you've every right to know. But you've said that you don't have magic—is your husband a Lorngeld, then?"

"No, neither of us. But my brother's one," she added quickly, as if afraid Athaya would send them away if they could not produce proper credentials. "That's why Connor and I want to help you. We can't teach spells or any such thing, but—oh, there must be something we could do!" If it was possible for her eyes to light up any further, they did so. "I know! You need someone to look after you proper. I was a lady's maid afore I got married—'twas years ago, of course, but I haven't forgot the knack of it. And you a newly married lady—you'll not be wanting to bother yourself with chores that I could do.''

Athaya was grateful for any offer of help; there was always work to be done even after the lessons of magic were done for the day, but it was not exactly the genteel sort of assistance that Drianna was offering. There was a constant need for someone to help with the cooking and washing, with repairing the crumbling monastery, and with the wholly unglamorous task of digging latrines. And as more people came to the camp—as Athaya fervently prayed they would—the workload would only increase. In light of that, having her own personal lady's maid seemed a frivolous thing.

''Why don't we talk about that later,'' Athaya suggested, putting her off in hopes that Drianna might find a different niche for herself on her own. Then, in an effort to change the subject, she scanned the assembly around her; aside from Connor, she saw no one sharing Drianna's ruddy coloring. ''Which one is your brother?''

Drianna shook her head, and her red hair burned in the firelight. ''Not here. He went to the other school in Kilfarnan. We were closer to it when his power came. We'd just come over from the island a few weeks before.''

''Ah, yes—you said you were from Crewe. That's in Sare, isn't it?''

''Aye. But there wasn't much work for glassmakers there now that the repairs to the Lord Marshall's manor are done—glass is me husband's trade, you see—so we came to the mainland. When we was near Kilfarnan, Connor heard there were repairs being done on the cathedral here, so he came hoping to find work.''

Athaya was about to ask if he had been lucky enough to find any, but was distracted by the sight of Ranulf standing at a distance, though just within earshot, and glowering at Drianna with blatant distrust. He did not approach them, but merely belched and gulped down some more ale as he continued to stare. Athaya made a mental note to talk to the mercenary when his head wasn't clouded by ale; he was from Sare . . . was there a reason he would take such an instant dislike to a fellow islander?

Then Jaren appeared at her elbow, and Drianna scurried away to rejoin her own husband, offering profuse apologies for taking up so much of her time. Athaya turned to him, realizing that it

was the first time they'd been able to speak to one another since
the festivities began.

"Can I see you alone for a minute?" he asked.

He guided her to the shadows behind the bell tower, and
before she could ask what he wanted, he gathered her close and
pressed his lips to hers, warming her blood. "I think everyone's
kissed the bride tonight except for me," he observed, showing
no eagerness to rejoin the celebration. Then he touched his fingers to the cross-shaped brooch pinned to his doublet—her
brooch, that she had given him in token—and his expression
shifted, as if in recognition.

"I was so proud when Hedric gave that to me," Athaya told
him. "It made me feel as if all those lessons meant something
. . . as if I'd finally accomplished something important."

"Did he tell you?" Jaren asked, looking up.

"Tell me what?"

"This brooch. It was his. His teacher gave it to him . . . oh,
fifty years ago. He must truly care about you, Athaya. Enough
to give this to you, and not to any of the hundreds of other
wizards he's trained. Of course, I can see why he loves you so,"
Jaren went on, "I fell into the same trap myself." He pulled her
close again, winding silky curls of hair between his fingers. "I
can't even begin to tell you how happy you've made me."

"You don't have to tell me," she whispered, pressing up
against him and brushing her lips across the fading bruise on
his jaw. "You can show me later."

"Later?" he asked, as his breath began to quicken.

Athaya peered around the edge of the tower. Ranulf was telling a bawdy tale to an attentive audience—a tale she'd heard
several times before—and those who weren't laughing were already dozing from an overabundance of ale and food. No one
would miss them if they slipped away now . . .

You're right, she sent. *We've both waited far too long for this.*
In a matter of moments, they were climbing the steps to the
dormitory's second level, and then quietly slipped into Athaya's
little room.

Someone had been there before them. Rose petals were scattered on the pillow and coverlet, and a flagon of wine and two
goblets were set on the overturned barrel that served as a table.
A thin piece of linen had been folded into makeshift drapes,
falling open just enough to let a moonlit breeze filter in and
scent the air with pine.

Athaya smiled, deep from the heart. They had no finery, no money, and no servants, but she counted herself among the luckiest of women because of what they did have. They shared a soul . . . and would share more before the night was done.

Athaya closed the door and fell against it, gazing around her with serene joy. "There were times I never thought I'd see this room again . . . much less have you here with me."

And there were times, so many times over the last year, that she never thought to find happiness again. It was exactly one year ago that she had fled Caithe for her very life, blinded by sorrow and despair. But Jaren had been with her then, and he was still here with her now, even after these last tempestuous months. Perhaps her side was not the safest place for him, but, she knew now, the best places aren't always the safest ones.

She glanced up, realizing how close he was to her, feeling the warmth, though there was no fire. As if she were light as a pillow, he gathered her up and set her gently on the bed amid the scented petals scattered there. He handed her a cup of wine, offered a toast to the rest of their lives, and then bent over her, running a fingertip from her chin to the hollow of her breasts.

She averted her eyes, smiling secretly.

What is it? he sent, lapsing into the easy intimacy of thought. Spoken words were too distant now . . . too jarring.

Right now, she began, daring again to scry the depths of those brown eyes as she placed a palm on his cheek, *I don't know how I ever refused you.*

Deftly, he kissed the wine from her lips. *I'll let you make up for it*, he offered.

Athaya was happy to oblige.

CHAPTER 8

✖✖✖

L ATER THAT SAME NIGHT, FAR FROM THE PALLET WHERE Athaya and Jaren lay entwined in each other's arms, the king of Caithe was rudely awakened from a sound and pleasant sleep to receive the most appalling news he'd heard in months.

"What in the name of all the saints do you mean she's *alive*?" Durek sat bolt upright in the great feather bed, then after a moment's silent gaping, leaped out, his legs ensnaring themselves in the folds of a white linen nightshirt. The royal hair was matted and sticking out wildly in all directions, and the light from a single oil lamp on the bedstand turned his Majesty's face haggard and sallow.

He repeated his question, shouting at his guard captain from a distance of mere inches. Captain Parr, however, did not shrink under the king's wrath, not because he possessed unusual courage, but because he was no less irate than Durek himself.

"She was seen in a village called Pipewell, sire," the captain said through clenched teeth. His vigilant brown eyes were hard as polished agate. "There were two others with her; judging from their descriptions, one of them was undoubtedly Jaren McLaud."

With a shriek of outrage, Durek spun around and clutched at his hair, threatening to pull out the fine, thinning strands by the fistful. "Damn her. Damn them all! God, what have I done to deserve such torment? That girl was spawned by a demon—if I ever doubted it before, I'm sure of it now. Alive . . . it's impossible. Impossible!''

It was the closest thing to a tantrum that he'd had since his childhood years, and even the unflappable Captain Parr raised his slender brows in surprise. Bishop Lukin, who had accompanied the captain on his unpleasant errand, stood quietly in the shadowy corner, his black cassock rendering him almost invisible, and frowned at the king's unseemly display.

Then Durek spun around and gave his captain a brutal shove toward the bedchamber door. ''Get out!'' he shrieked, his cheeks flushing purple as an overripe plum. ''Out! And bring me no more damnable messages!''

As if it were a routine dismissal, Captain Parr merely bowed and departed, making no effort to quicken his stride. When he was gone, the bishop crept from his dark corner like an insect venturing from its lair to trap its dinner. He helped himself to a chair near the foot of the king's bed and folded his meaty hands in his lap.

''He was only the bearer of bad tidings, sire. He did not cause your sister's escape.''

''Preach to me some other time, Bishop,'' Durek snapped, slumping down despairingly onto his bed. He closed his eyes and pressed his forehead against the carved oak bedpost. ''Well?'' he asked gruffly, not bothering to look up. ''You're obviously here for a reason, so spit it out.''

''I think you know what I have come to say,'' Lukin began, with the arrogant condescension of knowing one's cause is just and others are simply too blind or dull-witted to see it. ''Your sister's allies have now dared to violate the sanctity of convent grounds, freeing the princess and deceiving all of Caithe into believing her dead. By now, they are no doubt traversing the countryside proclaiming Athaya's 'miraculous' return to her people. Your Majesty,'' he went on, holding his palms up in entreaty, ''what further proof do you need that something must be done?''

Durek groaned. ''I knew it. This business of a Tribunal again. Tell me,'' he added, opening one eye to peer at Lukin sardonically, ''how is it that Archbishop Ventan never speaks on this subject to me, when from you it is all I hear?''

''With respect,'' he replied, in a tone that suggested he was about to make a less-than-respectful observation, ''I believe the

esteemed archbishop is beginning to bow under the weight of
his years and is therefore less willing to do battle with the forces
of evil that have been turned loose upon the world. His living is
comfortable; he sees no need to risk that, preferring, perhaps,
to wait and hope the Devil—and his children—leave Caithe on
their own.''

Despite his ill humor, Durek let out a bemused chuckle. "Odd
how he gets indigestion every time the subject arises.''

"Like all good sons of the Church, the archbishop fervently
believes that the Lorngeld are a damned race. We both know,
however, that he has long been a man more given to words than
to action. He is reluctant to declare open warfare on Athaya and
her people. Thus, the idea of a Tribunal distresses him.''

"In other words, he'll support a war as long as he doesn't
have to fight it personally.''

The bishop tilted his head to one side. "One could say that,
sire.''

Durck sat up straight and began rubbing away the deep, leaf-
shaped impression that the bedpost had made on his forehead.
His gaze was suddenly shrewd. "This was all your doing, wasn't
it? Oh, you let the Curia have some credit, that was benevolent
of you. But you thought up this whole Tribunal idea yourself,
didn't you?''

The bishop shrugged modestly. "Someone had to take the
initiative. Princess Athaya—''

"Is the bane of my very existence!'' the king shot back, pushing himself back to his feet. His wrath returned, potent as before, but this time more controlled. Athaya. It was always
Athaya, making misery for him at every turn.

Durek's feet were soundless on the carpet as he paced the
room, still reluctant to concede to the bishop's request. He had
read the Curia's proposal so often that he had committed most
of it to memory, debating with every word whether, righteous
as a Tribunal would surely be, such a measure would be prudent.
He shivered as he recalled the more gruesome parts of the proposal; the Tribunal would grant no mercy, and their methods of
gaining confessions of guilt were not for the faint of heart. The
penalty for those fleeing absolution was death—but not so easy
a death as absolution. No, once that chance was spurned, all
that remained was fire or dismemberment. And the penalty for
those who aided such rebellious Lorngeld was only slightly less

dire; an easier death—perhaps merely the noose—but death all the same.

If there was a bright spot to this bloody prospect, Durek mused, it was that all lands and possessions of those found guilty would immediately revert to Church and Crown. A unique sort of war, wherein the enemy finances its own destruction.

But while this plan might work—and swell the coffers of Caithe in the bargain—Durek still balked. Did he wish his name linked to such a thing throughout all of history? A fine thing if it succeeded—King Faltil earned the love of the people two centuries ago with just such boldness—but what if it failed? When the false news had come of Athaya's death, Durek secretly hoped that her crusade would die away on its own and a Tribunal would not be necessary. But now everything was changed, and he grew increasingly certain that, whatever reservations he might have, the bishop's proposal—drastic though it was—held the only solution for a lasting peace in Caithe.

"The people shall think me bloodthirsty if I agree to this Tribunal," he observed, his voice challenging the bishop to put such fears to rest.

Lukin returned his gaze steadily. "They shall think you a tool of the Devil if you do not," he replied smoothly. "And what matters blood when spilled for a righteous cause, my Lord? The greatest crusades of the world's history run deep with blood, my Lord, but God rewards all of his soldiers with glory and riches in heaven.

"If you do nothing, sire," he continued, "the people will mock you. They will think you afraid to stand up to your own sister. They will think you fearful of the Lorngeld. Athaya's crusade must be destroyed before such things come to pass. Better the people think you bloodthirsty, my Lord," he added ominously, striking the final blow, "than incapable."

Durek's nostrils flared, but he quickly turned his back to that remark and strode seethingly to the window, steadying himself with a lungful of sea-salted air. Yes, he was aware of the rumors . . . of the whispers exchanged behind his back. Hushed doubts of his skill at kingship, and speculations about whether he could ever be the king his father was. Kelwyn reunited a land torn by civil war. Would his son now have it rent again by a handful of treasonous wizards?

There would be no going back once he agreed . . .

But damn it all, he wasn't going to let Athaya defeat him! He, not his sister, was the rightful ruler of Caithe, and if he could not stop one foolish girl, could not enforce his will upon his people, then he did not deserve his crown.

And if this Tribunal succeeded—God, a tempting thought—and every trained wizard in the land was vanquished, and the sacrament of absolution again reigned supreme as the one, true way of mastering the Lorngeld's madness, then his name would be praised in Caithe for generations. Durek Trelane, the man who delivered his people from the threat of the Devil's Children.

And then, perhaps, they would forget Kelwyn.

"Then so be it," he said, speaking the words as if reading a death sentence. "You have your Tribunal."

He did not need to turn around to know that Bishop Lukin was smiling like a sated lover. "You are wise, Majesty," Lukin replied. "Better to wage a quick and bloody war than to delay acting until the infection becomes incurable."

Turning his back on the city of Delfarham sprawled out beneath his tower, Durek returned to the bedside and wrapped one hand around the bedpost as if clutching a scepter. "As Archbishop of Delfarham, the job should rightly go to Ventan," he said, thinking aloud. "Unfortunately, Daniel may have an ample stomach, but not the kind needed for this sort of work." He gave the bishop an appraising look. "You're a ruthless sort of bastard," he growled in grudging respect. "I therefore appoint you, Jon Lukin, as Chief Justice of this Tribunal, and charge you with the task of stopping my sister's crusade once and for all. Use whatever means you require; recruit all the men you need." His gaze frosted over with hatred. "I want Athaya stopped at all costs."

In a rare show of gratitude, the bishop went down on one knee before him, and to Durek's surprise, waited to rise until bidden to do so. Suspecting it would be a great while before the normally haughty clergyman humbled himself again, Durek savored the sight for a full minute before motioning him to stand.

"So, Chief Justice . . . what will be your first move?"

"As with any army, to mobilize my men," Lukin replied, flexing his stiff knee with subtle irritation. "Several monastic orders have already offered their services to the Tribunal, but the most effective, I think, will be the Order of Saint Adriel. Throughout history, they have proven themselves to be the most militant and well disciplined brotherhood in Caithe."

Durek lifted his brows. "And you, I recall, were educated at one of their priories."

The bishop inclined his head in modest gratitude. "I am, perhaps, biased in my opinions," he admitted freely, "but the Curia supports my view that the brothers of Saint Adriel are best fitted to serve as Justices for the Tribunal—they are the least tolerant of such evils as her Highness represents and the most aggressive in eliminating them. All I need do is contact Preceptor Mobarec, and he will alert the priories."

"How long will you need? How long before these Justices of yours are out hunting wizards?" Durek fired the questions impatiently; now that his decision was made, he was eager to see it put into action.

"Provided I find enough messengers, only a matter of weeks. Tentative arrangements were already made before the proposal was brought to the council; we required only your consent to begin. If all goes well, there will be commissioned Justices operating in every shire by the end of October."

Durek knitted his brows; he was pleased with the bishop's initiative, but piqued that he had acted so predictably and played right into Lukin's hands. Efficiency was all well and good, but the bishop's obvious assumption that his king would eventually acquiesce bordered on effrontery.

Yes, such men were a trial . . . but they always got the job done.

"You have your messengers. As many as you need."

The bishop nodded serenely; he had not expected any other reply. "I will dispatch them first thing tomorrow." He paused, and when his Majesty did not pose another question, he took a step back, as anxious as the king to put the plan into action. "If there is nothing else . . ."

"Yes, go," Durek said, suddenly exhausted. "We will speak of this again tomorrow." He began to yawn, but swallowed the impulse; there was one thing he had forgotten to say—something he suspected Lukin had long been waiting to hear. He pitched his voice low, as if whispering conspiracies. "If you succeed in this," he added, just as the bishop reached the doorway, "then be sure I will remember it when the time comes to appoint a new Archbishop of Delfarham."

Lukin's mouth twitched only slightly, but the look in his eyes was unmistakably triumphant as he bowed his thanks and slipped out of the chamber, silent as a wraith.

Alone at last, Durek crept wearily back into his bed. He was vaguely unsettled by what he had just done—he was not fully accustomed to the risks a king must bear—but Lukin obviously shared none of his reservations. *And why should he?* Durek mused bitterly. It was not *his* name that would be reviled should the Tribunal fail in its commission; it was not *his* crown that would be lost should Athaya usurp him. And Durek had already been warned of that possibility by Ventan and many others— that what Athaya truly desired was not merely to free her people from oppression, as she termed it, but to free them of their oppressive king as well and take her brother's place on the throne of Caithe.

The bishop, however, feared nothing; he was afire with zeal for his task. Despite his holy profession, he had earned a com- mission that any soldier would kill to obtain. He had an army that was his to command, a dangerous enemy to be extin- guished, and the indisputable knowledge that the power of Al- mighty God was on his side.

And if he can bring down this self-appointed savior that I must suffer to call sister, Durek thought as he pulled the satin coverlet over his shoulders, *then may God grant him a special place in heaven.*

Late—very late—on Athaya's first morning as a married woman, she and Jaren met Lord Basil outside the chapel, all of them ready to leave for Reyka. Master Tonia hovered nearby as well, not to join the party in their return to her homeland, but to seize one last chance at trying to talk them out of making the journey at all.

"I just don't like the idea of you taking the both of them," she muttered to Athaya, tapping her foot restlessly on a shady patch of grass still laced with dew. "Ath Luaine is a long way off. How do you know you've got the strength to get there alone, much less with two passengers?"

Athaya smiled indulgently at Tonia's protests; after the pre- vious night, she was far too content with the world to let any- thing, or anyone, irritate her. She leaned against the chapel's ivy-covered wall, shoulder-to-shoulder with Jaren and decided that at this moment, if Durek himself were to appear at the camp, she would be quite incapable of wrath and would merely invite him to the campfire to partake of ale and sausages.

"It's not the distance that matters, Tonia; it's how many others I take with me. But I've carried someone before—Cordry, remember?''

''Only a few miles,'' Tonia reminded her.

''As I said, the distance doesn't matter—well, at least that's not what Master Credony thought.'' Granted, Athaya hadn't actually tested the theory herself, but if one of the wisest wizards in history had come to such a conclusion, who was she to question it?

''Oh, stop clucking about like a mother hen, Tonia,'' Basil chided gently. ''I'm perfectly willing to take the risk if she and Jaren are. The experience will be worth it.'' But despite his cool comportment, Athaya knew that Basil was wildly eager to depart on their arcane journey. He did not deign to show it, however; long years of service in wizardry's highest office had trained him to hide his emotions well, and only his restless fingers, constantly rearranging the folds of his traveling cloak, betrayed his childlike enthusiasm.

Tonia's brows remained deeply furrowed. She studied Basil and Jaren as if estimating their combined weight, then turned her attention back to Athaya. ''But to work such a powerful spell so soon after your illness . . .''

Just then, Athaya felt Jaren's subtle laughter ripple through her mind. *I could assure her that you've got all your strength back*, he sent, *but it might not be tactful to explain exactly how I found that out*.

''Tonia, I'm fine,'' she replied hastily, feeling her cheeks tingle with warmth. ''Or have you forgotten about my miraculous recovery?'' Athaya purposely avoided Jaren's gaze for fear she would break into a foolish grin; it had been a rather lively night.

Realizing that Athaya, Jaren, and Basil were going to leave no matter what she had to say about it, Tonia simply murmured a few words of defeat, wished them a safe journey, and trudged off toward the campfire to cook her breakfast. Her path crossed Nicolas', who sauntered up to the departing trio chewing contentedly on a sausage as thick as his wrist.

''Off on your honeymoon, then?'' he asked, wiping a trickle of grease from his chin. His eyes were slightly bloodshot from the previous night's ale, but other than that he was as spirited and cheerful as ever.

''Not exactly,'' Athaya said with a trace of regret. ''We're only going to Ath Luaine to deliver Lord Basil and let everyone at the palace know that Jaren and I are safe. We'll be back tomorrow night.''

''Now that the word is beginning to spread that Athaya's alive and at large again, she can't be away from Caithe too long,'' Jaren explained. ''People have to see her and know that we haven't given up.'' He laid a hand on the small of her back. ''Maybe after things settle down a bit, we'll be able to slip away somewhere for a few weeks.''

Athaya smiled, but wistfully; such a time of relative peace was a long way off. ''And what are your plans, Nicky?''

Nicolas took another juicy bite of sausage. ''As soon as I finish my breakfast,'' he said, full-mouthed, ''I'm off to Halsey to let Cecile and Mosel know you're alive and well—if the news hasn't reached them already. I'm sure they'll want to see both of you as soon as possible.''

''Tell them we'll be there,'' Athaya assured him. She kissed his cheek in farewell, grimacing when her lips came away slick with sausage grease. ''And tell Cecile I'm anxious to meet my new niece.'' She dabbed at her lips with the back of her hand. ''I'll wager even our little princess isn't as messy with her meals as her uncle Nicolas.''

Nicolas touched an oily finger to her nose and then wandered off toward the creek to wash his hands.

Once he was gone, Athaya motioned Jaren and Basil into the chapel so that she would be free of distractions for her spell-work. ''One last thing before we go,'' she cautioned them. ''Translocation drains my power and tends to make me dizzy. You two might need to hold me up when we get there.''

Jaren nodded once, his anticipation making it difficult for him to stand in one place. He was excited yet nervous at the prospect before him, like a young soldier's first time at sparring with metal blades instead of wooden ones—a thrilling experience, but one with a new and unpredictable element of danger. ''Anything else we should know?'' he asked.

''I don't know if you'll experience the same things I do—the only other passenger I've had was out cold at the time. Oh, and whatever you do, don't let go of my hands. If you break physical contact with me during the spell, there's no telling where you'd end up . . . assuming you'd end up anywhere at all.''

The looks of alarm that Basil and Jaren exchanged made Athaya realize the implications of what she'd said. Until that moment, she had never considered the dangers of translocation—not in casting the spell itself, but in being transported by someone else. My God, what *would* happen if one of them were to let go of her? Would they drop out of the sky over unfamiliar lands? Would they end up in this world at all? Or would they be abandoned in that between-place of passage—not dead, but no longer quite alive?

Athaya quickly abandoned that train of thought; if she dwelled any further on it, she might change her mind and refuse to take either of them anywhere. "Just don't let go," she said again, and on that ominous note, the three of them joined hands—firmly.

Athaya closed her eyes and drew air deep into her lungs. She felt the power surging through her, strong and vital, as she drifted down into her paths, gliding through those darkened passageways of her mind for the spell she sought. Then, when she stood at last before the rune-marked alcove—the place that spoke of flight and freedom—she called a picture of her destination into her mind's eye; saw Master Hedric's study in all its infinite detail, from the flagstone floor blemished with blots of spilled ink, to the tops of the cherrywood bookshelves, coated liberally with dust.

"Hinc libera me," she whispered, hurtling into that vortex of swirling white light and colorful images too numerous and fleeting to identify, and where all the sounds of the universe clamored in her ears at once. Her body vanished for that instant, leaving only consciousness behind; but, though she could not feel her flesh, she sensed the presence of her companions—two solid and unchanging forms clinging to her in the turmoil.

Slowed by her burden, she did not pass through the chaos quite as quickly as in the past, but soon she was expelled from that place-that-was-not-a-place and thrust back into her body with a psychic jolt. She felt warm hands in each of hers, and heard two sharp intakes of breath, like a pair of drowning men gulping precious lungfuls of air. When she opened her eyes, Jaren and Lord Basil were staring at one another in wordless rapport, their foreheads glistening with sweat. Athaya had never seen the cool and illustrious Lord Basil so thoroughly shaken, and she found such added evidence of his humanness quite refreshing.

Then Basil pressed his fingers to each temple, steadying himself. "Where in the name of God *were* we?"

"Nowhere," Jaren answered softly, his grip still tight on

Athaya's hand as if afraid of being sucked back into that unearthly realm. "Or everywhere. I don't know which." He
blinked a few times to chase off the daze, then slipped his arms
supportively around Athaya's waist. "Do you need to sit down?
Are you dizzy?"

She frowned as she shook her head; she was as shaken as he,
but for an entirely different reason. "No. But I *should* be. I don't
understand—"

Then, from somewhere very close, a loud *thump* severed their
dialogue, and all three travelers jumped in unison. Athaya turned
sharply toward the source of the noise, and there, in the doorway
leading to the adjoining library, stood a dark-haired young man
gaping at them in mute astonishment. At his feet were no fewer
than a dozen books that had just slipped out of nerveless fingers.

"Colm?" came a voice from the library. "What was that
noise?" Then came the sound of a chair being pushed back,
scraping harshly across the flagstones. "Lord, what have you
broken this time?"

Master Hedric emerged from the inner library in a swirl of
dark blue robes, scowling at the pile of books on the floor. But
just as he was about to comment on the young man's clumsiness,
he caught sight of his three visitors and the admonishment died
on his lips. Letting out a wholly uncharacteristic whoop of glee,
he hurdled the heap of books as nimbly as his aged legs would
allow, and scooped Athaya into his arms in a forceful embrace.

"God be praised, you're safe! Both of you," he choked out,
throwing a slender arm around Jaren as well. "There were times
. . . oh, but never mind that now. Thank God. Thank God!"
Then, when he lost the strength to squeeze them any harder, he
glanced toward Overlord Basil and offered him a vaguely peni-
tent nod. "I'm sorry, my Lord—you're most welcome, too, of
course."

Basil brushed off the unneeded apology with an obliging wave
of his hand.

"I see you've met my new assistant," Hedric said, gesturing
back to the young man now scrambling to pick up the books
from the floor. "And frightened him half to death, I see," he
added with a chuckle. "Colm, go find Prince Felgin and send
him to me. But don't tell him why. Hurry!"

Colm pushed his armful of books into the nearest shelf and
hurried out of the study, tossing one last furtive glance at the
three newcomers as if still uncertain whether they were real or

not. Once he was gone, Hedric laughed quietly. "Colm's a fine boy, but he's still awfully nervous. I suppose he's young enough to be impressed by my position—High Wizard to the King and all that. He stammers and drops things a lot, but he'll get over it. Jaren did. Eventually."

Hedric led the others into the library and passed out generously filled goblets of wine, toasting their safe return. "I see Athaya's introduced the two of you to the miracle of translocation," he observed, unabashedly proud of his former student's talent. Aged yet youthful eyes twinkled as he glanced sidelong at the Overlord, visibly tempted to remind him just how adversely he had reacted when Athaya first discovered the spell in her paths. Instead, he merely asked: "Tell me . . . what was it like?"

"Unsettling, to say the least," Basil said, adjusting the folds of his traveling cloak as if it would help set his rattled world back to rights. "But it was thrilling, too. It was like being in a carriage when the horses bolt; I had no control—all I could do was endure the ride and hope I didn't end up dead at the end of it."

Jaren nodded vigorously. "I felt exactly the same way. All that light and color and noise—it was dizzying. Is that what you see, Athaya?"

"What?" Athaya pulled herself up with a jerk; she had only been half-listening. "Oh, yes," she began, looking distractedly into her goblet, "the same. Only . . . it's different this time. Not the light and color—that's exactly as I remember it—but me . . ." She shook her head as if listening for a rattle that wasn't there. "I shouldn't be feeling this way."

"Perhaps I shouldn't have given you that wine so soon after the translocation," Hedric said worriedly.

Athaya set the goblet down on the nearest bookshelf. "No, it isn't that. It's just that I've always felt light-headed after a translocation—and I was carrying two others with me this time. I should be feeling worse, not better."

Then, remembering yet another side effect of the spell, she twisted her wrist and conjured a witchlight with ease; the fiery globe burned as brightly as it ever had. Athaya's eyes widened noticeably. "And I've never been able to work spells right afterward either. My magic was always too weak."

"Perhaps you're just getting better at it," Hedric suggested.

"It might be the sort of spell that you can develop a tolerance to. There's still a great deal we don't know about translocation."

"Or perhaps it's yet another side effect of the sealing spell," Jaren said quietly, gazing into her eyes as if scrying for an image in a vision sphere.

Hedric was instantly alarmed. "What side effects? Athaya, what haven't you told me? Has the seal harmed you?"

Athaya didn't have a chance to do anything but shake her head in denial, for at that moment Prince Felgin swept boldly into the chamber without knocking; he knew what Hedric's summons had meant. He crossed the room in three swift strides, looking every inch a prince in his crimson tunic and fur-lined mantle, black hair trimmed precisely at his bearded chin. Laughing brown eyes glittered as brightly as the ruby-studded band encircling his forehead.

"Damn, but it's good to see you two again!" he burst out, almost shouting. Athaya grinned—the prince, like most Reykans, was not known for his reserve. He greeted Jaren with a fierce hug, pounding him heartily on the back, then bent down and kissed Athaya firmly on the lips.

"Careful, Felgin," Jaren warned good-naturedly. "I'm not sure I like other men kissing my wife like that."

"Your—?" The prince threw his head back and whooped with delight, while Master Hedric offered more subdued congratulations. His smile was broad, but betrayed no surprise; he had long expected such happy news.

Then Felgin drew Jaren aside, pitching his voice low, but loud enough so that all could hear. "I thought you came back to tell us you were *safe*. You'll never get any peace and quiet with a wife like that."

"That," Jaren replied, "is exactly what I'm counting on."

Wine goblets were filled again, and Athaya spent the next quarter hour describing the previous evening's wedding, offering enough detail so that Hedric and Felgin could feel as if they had attended the ceremony, drunk the ale, eaten the venison, and danced to the flute and harp until they'd fallen exhaustedly into their beds. And Athaya took special delight at the startled looks on their faces when they learned who had performed the ceremony.

"Perhaps you can do the same service for me one of these days, my Lord," Felgin said. "Not quite yet, of course," he added quickly, seeing a silent chorus of raised brows around him. "But Father's been after me like a hellhound to find a wife and settle down. If I have to endure one more day of having eligible young ladies paraded in front of me like horseflesh at a fair, I may just go find a pleasant cliff somewhere and jump."

Basil sputtered indignantly. "Prince Felgin!"

"Although if I don't pick a wife soon," Felgin muttered, "my father will probably throw me off himself."

"That reminds me," Jaren began, his ebullient mood suddenly dampened. "Is my father at court? I'd better get it over with and tell him I've gotten married." He offered Felgin a crooked grin. "Maybe we'll be meeting at the bottom of that cliff before long."

Felgin drained off the last of his wine. "I'll take you to him," he offered. "I think he's out in the mews. And then I'm going to find *my* father and have him order one hell of a feast for tonight. A wedding feast!" The two of them departed at that, Felgin bidding Athaya good-bye with another kiss—this one safely on the cheek.

Left alone with Hedric and Basil, the conversation quickly turned to a more serious topic than that of weddings. "Jaren said something earlier about side effects," Hedric began, studying Athaya's pupils with a physician's scrutiny. "The sealing spell . . . has it injured you?"

"No. Quite the opposite, in fact."

Athaya brushed over the worst of the story, admitting that she remembered little of her ordeal after the first few weeks, and went on to explain about her unusual strength—not only her rapid physical recovery, but her increased ability with the translocation spell as well. And lastly, she told them about the seeds of power . . . about what she had seen in the village woman's mind.

"I can't be positive, of course—not unless I go back to Pipewell someday to find out whether Emma ever developed magic. But I *know* that's what I saw."

She saw Lord Basil's lips poised to say "nonsense," but he cut himself short, perhaps realizing that this was precisely what he had said of the translocation spell—a spell which he now had ample evidence was anything but nonsense. Instead of dismissing her description of the seed as the boast of a young upstart, he seemed awed—and more than a little unnerved. Hedric, however, had learned long ago never to doubt Athaya's tales and chewed on his lip intently, his mind reeling with the significance of her newest skill.

"What's happened?" Athaya asked, hoping that one of the Masters could shed their wisdom on the subject. "What did the seal do to me?"

An immediate answer was not forthcoming. Both of them fell silent, exchanging puzzled glances as they pondered the problem. Athaya impatiently waited for a response, growing vaguely disturbed by the amount of time it took for two such venerable wizards to come up with one.

"It is often said that in these forms," Hedric said at last, gently pinching the pale, wrinkled flesh of his forearm, "to look full upon the face of God would lead to madness. So we can only look at reflections of that face; the sun and stars, the sea— His creations. I think this is what really happens during the *mekahn*. It is our first taste of the divine—an unsettling one, to be sure. The voices . . . the chaos. Much like the between-place you pass through during translocation." He paused as if that connection was somehow important, noting that Basil chose that moment to shift uncomfortably in his chair, and then went on. "Perhaps during your time under the seal, you were too closely confined with your own power; communed too intimately with your own manifestation of the divine. You came too near, perhaps, to learning secrets that God did not wish you to know— at least, not yet. That could explain why you have no memory of those final days."

"Our gift is indeed a double-edged sword," Basil mused, his eyes focusing on a ball of dust on the carpet. "Our power is fatal to us if seen in all its glory, but just as fatal if we do not learn to use it at all. It is up to us, then, to find the proper balance."

Athaya felt oddly unsettled; all this talk of the divine being fatal was making her nervous. She hadn't meant to encroach on God's realm and pry into His secrets—if that's indeed what she had come dangerously close to doing.

"And now that I think on it," Hedric continued, "there may be a logical explanation for what's happened to you. The first time you held a vision sphere, you had more luck with futures than most wizards have in a lifetime. Perhaps that talent was somehow enhanced by the sealing spell. Seeing these 'seeds' is like seeing the future, but in a different sort of way.

"And the increased strength you have—that also makes a certain kind of sense. Unusual bursts of strength are quite common during the *mekahn*. If, as I suspect, the *mekahn* is a taste of the divine and if that's indeed what happened to you under the seal, though far more intensely, then it's no wonder you have great strength . . . at least for the time being."

"You mean this might not last?" That would certainly put an end to her concerns about the ethics of this talent. If it was going to fade away, such concerns would be rendered academic.

"Bursts of strength almost always fade after the *mekahn*. This talent of yours? It might last; it might not. I'm afraid you're on your own this time, Athaya," he said. His eyes shone, envious but not jealous, like those of a proud father who knows that his child will achieve what he never would.

"Does that also mean I'm the only one who can figure out the scruples involved in all of this? Whether I'm ever supposed to *use* this talent or not?" Briefly, she explained why it would spell disaster for Caithe if the populace discovered—or heard even the most insubstantial rumor—that there was a way to determine if they were host to the dormant, and widely cursed, powers of magic. But did that mean the talent should never be used at all, or should never be used in Caithe? The two were very different things, and spells were traditionally guarded or forbidden because of their own inherent dangers, independent of the ever-changing politics of the world.

"I think your instincts have provided the answer already," Hedric replied pensively. "It does not seem fair to use the talent for some if you cannot use it for all. It's simply too volatile, given the situation in your homeland."

"I tend to agree," Basil said, "but as Hedric said, you are on your own this time." He frowned out of habit—a faint echo of his former distrust that he quickly dispelled. "But I think we can trust you to make the right decisions. I might not have said that six months ago, but I'm fairly certain of it now."

Hedric raised his bushy white brows, unaccustomed as he was to Basil's reformed opinions of his protégée. Indeed, Athaya was not quite used to them herself, but was grateful to have finally earned the Overlord's confidence.

"Well, now that I'm satisfied that you're all right," Hedric said, refilling Athaya's goblet, "what about your work? Have you succeeded in converting the masses yet?"

Athaya laughed wryly. "Hardly that. A few dozen, maybe."
She spent the next few minutes bringing Master Hedric up to
date with all the news from Caithe and on the faltering state of
her crusade. And since he'd been instrumental in gathering the
first few members of her fledgling army of wizards, she also
told him of Dom DePere's ambition to further her cause in the
west, of Tonia's wise and steadying influence, and of Ranulf's
infectious good humor. "And Ranulf is loyal to a fault," she
added, turning to Hedric. "I can't believe I ever distrusted him—
now I know better than to question your judgment."

Hedric shrugged modestly. "Old age has to be good for
something."

Across from him, Basil's gaze grew dark. "Not all wizards
from Sare follow the Sage, Athaya. Ranulf Osgood is a pleasant
exception."

"The Sage?" Athaya didn't like the solemnity that had settled
over the Overlord of a sudden, and it made her shiver. "I was
talking about Ranulf's having been a mercenary; he fought
against my father in the civil wars. But I've heard you mention
Sare before . . . something about a cult. Is there something I
should know about it?"

Basil threw a silent query at Hedric.

"I saw no reason to burden her with that at the time," Hedric
replied. "She had enough to worry about getting started with
her crusade."

"True . . . but now she should be aware." Basil sipped
thoughtfully at his wine. "There's not much I can tell you,
Athaya, but the little I've heard about them isn't good. Basically,
these cultists claim that their gift of magic gives them the right
to dominate others—that they were chosen by God to rule the
earth. They even have the audacity to call their leader the Sage—
an insult to our most revered and learned Masters."

Athaya reflected on the *Book of Sages*—the central part of any
wizard's library. The wizards whose writings were collected in
that book were among the greatest in history. That the leader of
a small cult of magicians would dub himself Sage was audacity
indeed.

"How long have they existed?"

"I understand the cult was formed shortly after your country's
Time of Madness—what, two hundred years ago? An indirect
result of the scourge, I believe, but I doubt anyone knows the
actual history of it except maybe the cultists themselves. To my

knowledge there have never been more than a handful of them, and they keep to themselves for the most part. Thanks be to God,'' he added under his breath.

Hedric plucked a book from a nearby shelf and flipped through its pages until he found the passage he wanted. ''They call themselves the *Magisteri*,'' he informed them. ''If I recall my Old Sarian correctly, that means 'Gods on earth.' ''

Basil snorted his opinion of that claim. ''Of all the pretentious drivel.''

''I can't translate much of this,'' Hedric went on, squinting at the pages, ''but it seems that the wizard who founded the cult prophesied that one day they would receive a sign from God that it was time for their ascent to power.''

''What sign?'' Athaya asked.

Hedric slid the book back on the shelf. ''No one knows—no one outside of the cult, that is. It's a secret they've never revealed.''

''I wonder . . .'' Athaya began, rising to her feet and pacing in a wide circle around the room. ''There's a Sarian woman at our camp. Ranulf certainly seems to distrust her—he was glaring daggers at her last night, though I haven't asked him why yet. Maybe he knows her. Or maybe she's a member of this cult.''

''Is she a trained wizard, then?''

''No. Neither is her husband. She says her brother is, though— apparently he went to Dom DePere's school in Kilfarnan when his magic came.''

Hedric shook his head. ''Then I doubt either one of them is of the *Magisteri*. Why bother to associate with a people who fervently believe they're superior? And if her brother has just come into his power,'' Hedric went on, ''then why send him to Kilfarnan for training and not back to the cult, if that's where their sympathies lie?''

Athaya accepted the argument with a nod. ''True. I don't have any reason to distrust her. Although I'm not exactly sure why she's come to us. The only thing she's offered to do so far is be my handmaid, and that's something I've learned to live well enough without.''

''You're bound to attract curiosity seekers,'' Hedric said with a wave of dismissal. ''Just welcome them as you do everyone else. Who knows? One of them might turn out to be a valuable ally one day.''

Athaya grinned, glancing sidelong at Lord Basil. ''Yes. We

can become friends with the most unexpected people, can't we?''

"Just don't publicize it too widely, if you please," the Overlord replied, squaring his shoulders as if to reclaim a perceived loss of dignity. "I have a reputation to maintain."

CHAPTER 9

❈

A THAYA AND JAREN RETURNED FROM ATH LUAINE THE
next evening, after a whirlwind thirty-six hours of feast-
ing, dancing, and reunion with her friends at the Reykan
court. She departed not only with Lord Ian's good wishes—as
surprising a reformation as Basil's—but with a purse filled with
Reykan gold that Ian had given his son when Athaya wasn't
looking. "He said it's to help the Lorngeld," Jaren had told her,
"but you know as well as I do that it's really a wedding present.
He won't admit it, but I think he's warming up to you."

Athaya smiled her gratitude, wondering if she would ever be
able to work such magic on Durek, Bishop Lukin, and the myriad others whose opinions of her were still quite icy.

The first thing Athaya did on her return from Reyka was dispatch Kale to Halsey Manor to tell the queen that she intended
to visit in three days' time. "You should find Lord Gessinger at
Halsey—and Nicolas, too. Just remember to tell them when
Jaren and I are coming—three days from now, precisely at noon.
And make sure they're alone in the solar. I don't want to frighten
any of Cecile's women the way I did Hedric's assistant," she
said, envisioning a cluster of aghast handmaids fainting in unison upon her arrival, "and he's *used* to magic."

Over the next two days, it became clear that news of Athaya's
escape from Saint Gillian's had reached far beyond the small
and isolated village of Pipewell. Two new arrivals came the first

day; on the second day, five; and the third day, seven, all of them claiming to know at least one more family contemplating whether to send one of their own into the princess' care. And the words these newest Lorngeld spoke upon arrival were variations on a common theme: "Athaya's return was the sign I was waiting for," one said; "It was an omen that God wants us to live and not to be absolved," said another.

Athaya spent every spare minute getting to know her new students, learning about the places they came from and listening to them talk about their families, not all of which knew about or condoned their burgeoning powers. She met Terrence the thatcher, Darien the bard, Coby the chandler, Nathan, whose father owned the Blacklions tavern, Lyssa, an unmarried woman who feigned pregnancy so her family would send her away in disgrace for the months it would take to birth her power, and dozens of others belonging to every trade and rank.

And though she was elated at their ever-increasing numbers, Athaya soon realized the need to step cautiously when surrounded by such a concentration of wayward magic; fledgling wizards practiced their spells everywhere and at all times of the day and night, and Athaya was forever being startled by unexpected illusions—her heart still raced at the memory of the wild boar that Coby conjured—and jumping back from cook fires that had a tendency to flare up when someone grew tired or angry.

For the most part, Athaya left the details of her students' training and spell-work to Tonia, Gilda, and Jaren, all of whom were infinitely more patient than Athaya knew herself to be. And because she planned to be gone from Kaiburn fairly often, spreading her message of salvation to as many villages as she could, she thought it best for no one to rely on her exclusively for their training.

At her elbow almost constantly was the zealous Drianna, eager to help in any way she could. Athaya had only to take one step toward the ale barrel before Drianna placed a full goblet in her hand; she had only to mention the growing October chill before Drianna ran to fetch a cloak. The Sarian woman had clearly not forgotten her determination to be a lady's maid, and although Athaya had gently explained that such services were not necessary, Drianna merely took the refusal as a sign that she had to prove herself and tried all the harder to gain Athaya's acceptance.

Drianna's attentions were flattering, but made Athaya feel

vaguely uneasy. True, she had grown up surrounded by ladies-in-waiting, but now, after living outside of the law for a full cycle of seasons, she had come to enjoy doing many routine chores herself. But on the day Athaya first revealed that she found pleasure in sweeping out her chamber, or helping Ranulf brew the camp's ale, or even donning her own clothes, Drianna had reacted as if she had uttered blasphemy.

"But you . . . you're a Trelane, my Lady!" she exclaimed. "Such things are far beneath you."

"Not much is beneath me these days," Athaya remarked dryly—she had been digging a new latrine at the time. "Or haven't you noticed that we're all outlaws here?"

This anomaly puzzled Drianna, but she refused to concede the point and proceeded to snatch the shovel out of Athaya's hands. "But the people must respect you! They must see that you are their princess and were born to rule over them. And they'll never see that if they find you digging holes for others to . . . to . . ." She stamped a delicate foot in protest. "It simply isn't done!"

"Drianna, one of the things I'm trying to accomplish is to stop people from doing certain things simply because it's always been done that way—absolution, to be specific."

"It's not the same," Drianna puffed, as if she hadn't understood Athaya's argument in the slightest, and proceeded to dig the trench herself. "Just because you want the peasants to follow you doesn't mean you have to lower yourself to their level."

Athaya thought this an odd statement coming from one who had, only the day before, freely admitted being the daughter of a poor and landless serf, and who had only reached the station of lady's maid because she once caught the eye of a wealthy nobleman. But because it was easier to give in than to argue such a minor point, Athaya let Drianna have her way and submitted to being served—and having latrines dug for her—whether she liked it or not.

"Is there anything else I can get for ye?" Drianna asked on the morning that Athaya planned to leave for Halsey. They stood in the small room that Athaya and Jaren shared, and Drianna had just finished lacing up the back of Athaya's forest-green kirtle—the one she had been married in only five days before. Jaren waited patiently in the doorway, gazing longingly at Athaya as if he was imagining undoing those laces even as Drianna was tying them.

How about a little peace and quiet? he sent to Athaya, shading an errant grin with one hand.

Athaya flashed him a glance of helpless understanding as she turned around to face Drianna. "No, I'm fine. You've already helped me change my dress and braid my hair, besides fetching my breakfast—that's quite enough for one morning. Perhaps you can look after Gilda today; her child is due any day now, and she needs help getting about more than I do."

Drianna's face fell slightly; for all her professed enthusiasm, she was not near so attentive to Tonia, Gilda, or any of the other women, but the sympathetic glances they tossed at Athaya from time to time revealed that they were rather glad of it.

"Will you be using your magic to get there, then?" she asked Athaya, eyes glittering like a pair of well-cut emeralds. When Athaya nodded, Drianna beamed, "Then that means you've been there before, right? Or you couldn't go by magic?"

Athaya let out a thin sigh. For not having magic herself, Drianna was endlessly curious about how it worked and was especially fascinated by the more exotic spells that Athaya alone could cast. Perhaps she was only curious on her brother's behalf—for all Athaya knew, he could be an adept like herself, heir to the same level of ability—but at times, Drianna's constant flow of questions became as irritating as Jaren's persistent attempts to rekindle her memory during the journey back from Saint Gillian's.

"I went to Halsey a few years ago, just before Cecile and Durek were married. I should be able to picture the solar clearly enough to get us there. Not that I have much choice," she added. "I can't just appear on her doorstep and announce myself—Cecile's in enough trouble because of me, and I won't heap any more on her head by being seen there. Now, Drianna, please go and tell Tonia we've gone and remind her that we'll be back in a few days."

"But could I stay and watch you go? I'd love to see you disappear. Tonia says it's a sight, and—"

Jaren took her elbow and, with gentle firmness, guided her to the door. "Please—just tell her we've gone."

Resentment flared briefly in her eyes, but it was quickly dampened. Grudgingly, she curtsied and left the room.

"We'd best be off," Athaya said to Jaren, glancing out the window at the sun overhead, "it's almost noon. If Kale has done his job—and he always does—then Cecile will be expecting us."

She tossed a cloak over her shoulders and took Jaren's hand, then closed her eyes and slipped into her paths, following the now-familiar route to the spell of translocation. A whisper, a jolt, and a pair of heartbeats later, the stone floor of their room was replaced by a costly carpet, and she and Jaren found themselves in the queen's solar at Halsey Manor. Kale was posted at the door, while Cecile and Lord Gessinger were seated together in a wide bay window overlooking a private courtyard. Sunbeams flowed over them through the latticed glass, making Mosel's threadbare robe look an even paler shade of gray and, in contrast, setting the gold at the queen's ears, throat, and fingers to glittering each time she made the slightest move.

Both of them were gaping, staring at the patch of air above the carpet that, filled with nothing but dust motes only a moment before, had suddenly given birth to Athaya and Jaren.

Cecile's delicate blond brows formed two perfect arches. "Incredible. Kale told me what to expect, but . . ."

She shook her head, at a loss for words. But when the initial shock was past, Cecile rose to embrace Athaya, soundly failing in her attempt to hold back tears at their reunion. Wiping her eyes, she offered her embrace to Jaren as well. "Welcome to our family," she said, kissing him once on the cheek. "Durek won't like my saying that, but you're welcome nonetheless." Then she lowered her eyes remorsefully, as if confessing sins to a priest. "I must apologize for my husband's treatment of you in the past. What he's done to Athaya is bad enough, but you . . . you're not even one of his subjects."

"No. But now it's worse," Jaren replied in a tone that assured her no apologies were necessary. "Now I'm one of his relatives."

Cecile's eyes spoke her gratitude at Jaren's lack of bitterness. "Speaking of new additions to our family, Nicolas has taken the baby outside—they'll be up in a few minutes. I've left orders for no one else to be admitted; we won't be disturbed for the rest of the day."

Athaya went to the window and gazed out upon the lush, well-kept grounds of Cecile's ancestral home. Graveled walks wound gracefully around a garden rich with rosebushes, and the apple trees were heavy with fruit. In the courtyard below, Nicolas made a game of tickling his niece's nose with a fiery orange leaf plucked from a sugar maple, supremely content to spend his time in the unprincely pastime of doting over infants.

Jaren turned to greet Lord Gessinger, thanking him again for his part in Athaya's escape. Athaya offered her indebtedness as well and kissed the man lightly on each cheek. His skin was dry as parchment on her lips.

"You saved my life," she said simply, looking anew at the man whom she—and many others—had long ago dismissed as a dull and useless member of the Caithan court. "If I can do anything for you—"

Mosel's fingers instinctively closed around the pendant at his throat. "Just save them, Athaya. Save them all."

Athaya embraced him again. *I'll try, my Lord. That I can promise you.* "But it's been two months since you left Delfarham," she said with concern. "Won't Durek question your absence?"

"It would be the first time he ever has, my Lady," Mosel replied self-effacingly. Then he loosened his collar, as if the room had suddenly grown too warm. "There is much else to occupy his interest these days."

The last was added with particular grimness, and Athaya tossed an inquiring look at Cecile. "Athaya, there's something you must know." She bade them all be seated, and, as if on cue, the sun dipped behind a cloud and dimmed the light in the solar.

For the next quarter hour, Mosel summarized the council meeting he had attended in August, making only the briefest mention of Osfonin's scathing letter and the death of the Sarian lord marshal, whom Athaya knew only slightly from her childhood and therefore could not mourn. Most of his speech was devoted to the Curia's proposal for eliminating the spread of wizardry in the land. With every word, Athaya felt her blood grow cooler; she felt Jaren's hand tighten on hers.

"And it's even worse than that," Cecile added when he was done. "I just received word two days ago that Durek has approved this Tribunal. He's appointed Bishop Lukin as Chief Justice, and the ranks of his inquisitors are to be filled by the brothers of Saint Adriel. The arrangements have already been made."

"Adrielites," Athaya said, expelling the air from her lungs. "Not men to be trifled with."

Mosel nodded his accord. "Yes, they're a humorless sort. They seem to think that if one is enjoying life, then one is obviously living it wrong. And since you've made a habit of telling

the Lorngeld that they should savor their gift of magic,'' he
added, ''you're an ideal target.''

''My God,'' Athaya whispered, ''it's Faltil's scourge all over
again.'' She stared at the wainscoted walls, picturing lurid horrors in the paneling's benign patterns: blood, betrayal, torture,
death, and families forever torn asunder. And all because of
magic. Wondrous magic, bestowed by God. ''So he's declaring
war on me at last.''

''We knew it would come, Athaya,'' Jaren said quietly. ''This,
or something like it.''

''I know. But that doesn't make it any easier to accept.'' She
got up and returned to the window, shivering despite the sun.
The courtyard was empty and quiet now—Nicolas had gone and
taken his laughter with him. ''One of two things will happen
now. The people of Caithe will either join me in greater numbers, or they will hunt me down and flay me alive for bringing
this horror down upon their heads.''

Jaren came to join her at the window. ''If it's any comfort to
you, that's probably exactly what Durek's thinking right now.
He's got to be wondering if his subjects will consider this Tribunal a blessing or a curse; wondering whether they'll come to
love or hate him for it.'' He rested a hand on the nape of her
neck. ''That's the price of leadership . . . and you're both paying it.''

The somber mood was abruptly broken by Nicolas' entrance
and the sound of contented gurgles emanating from the bundle
of ivory blankets cradled in his arm. Out of that bundle, Athaya
saw five tiny fingers reaching up to tug on the prince's chin.

''Cecile, at your earliest convenience, would you kindly tell
your ladies that just because I am a man does not therefore mean
I am going to drop this baby on her head the first chance I get.
I used to carry Mailen around when he was smaller than this.
They were eyeing me like vultures the entire time, ready to
swoop down the moment I did something wrong.''

His smile faded at the solemn tableau before him.

''They just told me about the Tribunal,'' Athaya said by way
of explanation. ''Nicolas, you knew about this weeks ago. Why
didn't you tell me?''

''But you'd only just come back! What was I to do—bring up
such a delightful subject at your marriage feast? Besides,'' he
added darkly, ''at the time, I didn't know that Durek had actually approved the damned thing.'' He bit his tongue on the curse,

then shrugged it off, realizing that the infant was far too young to be corrupted by it.

"Well, you could have warned me," Athaya began again, but Nicolas silenced any further admonishments by pushing the baby into her arms. She protested at first, fearful of dropping the wriggling bundle, but the child's bewitching blue eyes and seraphic smile soon persuaded her to accept.

"What is her name?" Athaya asked suddenly, realizing that no one had yet told her.

"Lillian," Cecile replied. She smiled warmly at Mosel and touched her fingers to the back of his hand. "Lillian Rose."

Athaya gazed down at the child cradled against her breast and gently brushed her fingertips against the downy tufts of honey-colored hair. What would the future bring for this little one? She was a princess of Caithe—no doubt she would marry a prince, as Athaya was to have done . . .

Was to have done, before her magic came. Would that be Lillian's destiny as well?

She could find out . . . and yet, she could not. Hedric was right and so were her instincts; she felt it more strongly now. It would be unfair to use her gift for selfish knowledge, giving her friends and family advantage over thousands of others doomed to ignorance. And at this point, she realized, there was no proof that her prophetic talent was reliable; she would not know that until the day when—or if—Emma of Pipewell became a wizard.

Athaya handed the child back to Cecile, who let out a shallow sigh and placed her daughter in a rosewood cradle near the window. She rocked the cradle gently with one hand, while the other curled into a tight fist at her side. She gazed intently at her daughter as if trying to peer into her future, unaware that Athaya had the ability—if not the sanction—to do so.

"This isn't the kind of world I want for my children!" Cecile burst out. Her voice was hushed, so as not to frighten the child, but carried an undercurrent of frustrated rage. "Fighting and bloodshed . . . God in heaven, I know it sounds naive, but why can't we just leave each other to go about our lives in peace?" She spun around in a swirl of cream-colored satin. "I'll never forgive Durek for agreeing to this Tribunal. Never!"

Athaya wanted to comfort her, but found she could think of nothing to say. Peace seemed such a simple thing to ask; why, then, was it so difficult to achieve?

"He didn't used to be this way," Cecile went on, looking

absently to one side as if addressing an invisible presence. "Or maybe he was, and I didn't choose to see it. My father told me I was to marry Kelwyn's heir, and I was happy to obey; I had never met Durek, but simply assumed that he would be as noble a man as his father." A shadow passed over her eyes. "I have never been more wrong."

Cecile stepped away from the cradle and into a pool of dappled sunlight. She was the picture of fragile beauty in her blond curls and lace-trimmed silk, but inside dwelt a core of unyielding strength, and now, an indelible mark of sadness. "I tried to love him. I wanted to. But he is so . . . *remote*. So distant." Cecile reached up and clutched the rope of pearls around her neck as if it were a shackle. "At first I thought it was my fault for not being able to reach the deepest part of him. Only later did I begin to suspect that there was no depth to reach; that there was nothing I would know after four years that I had not known in the first four hours of our acquaintance. Oh, I think he cares for me in his way," she admitted, tilting her head to one side. "If nothing else, he loves me for the son I gave him. But it wasn't what I was expecting." The queen sighed, emitting a sad, breathy laugh. "Perhaps I listened to the minstrels overmuch as a girl, never realizing that they weren't singing about the real world."

Then, realizing she had perhaps said more than a queen should, even to friends and family, Cecile waved off her despondency as if dismissing a bothersome servant from the room. "But enough of this brooding," she said, forcing a smile as she returned to her guests. "I make myself melancholy over things I cannot change."

"But you still haven't gone back to Delfarham," Athaya observed quietly.

"No. Durek gave me leave to return the moment he heard the tale of your death, but I replied that I was still wearied after the birth. Since the child is a girl, he is in no particular hurry to see it," she added, vaguely spiteful, "and so I think I will extend my weariness well into the winter. And if Mailen were here . . . oh, but for my son I might never go back at all."

"Have you sent for him?" Athaya would have liked to see the boy herself—he was little more than two when she had left the capital a year ago and would be much changed by now.

"Of course I have—several times. And I miss him terribly. But Durek refuses to send him." Cecile laughed with a bitterness seldom revealed. "The boy's not yet four, and still Durek fears that I will corrupt him with talk of justice and mercy if I have him all to myself in Halsey. Worst of all," she added with exaggerated scorn, "I might dare to teach him not to regard wizards as the Devil's Children. *That* Durek would never forgive."

Kale smiled at her sadly, and spoke for the first time. "He misjudges you, my Lady."

"He misjudges all of us," Cecile replied, her gaze shifting in turn to Athaya, Nicolas, Jaren, and Mosel. For a moment, her face reflected deep-seated frustration that she could do little to change her husband's opinions, but as soon as it had come, she let her disappointment fall from her shoulders as if throwing off a too-warm cloak. Turning to a more pleasant subject, she asked Athaya about her wedding, and though Nicolas protested that he'd already told her everything there was to tell, Cecile silenced him and claimed she wished to hear it again.

Athaya remained another hour at Halsey, but as the afternoon wore on, she knew that they would not be able to have privacy of the solar much longer—Cecile's ladies would grow curious. But she was reluctant to depart; Kale would return to the camp, of course, but who could say when she would see Cecile, Mosel, or Nicolas again?

"Jaren and I should go," she said at last, gathering up her cloak. "We'd like to get as far as Dubin by nightfall."

Nicolas made a swirling gesture with his hands. "What, no magic?"

"Not this time. We're planning to visit a few villages on the way back to Kaiburn and show people that I'm definitely not dead and that I'm still determined to teach magic to anyone who wants to learn. But I haven't been to any of the villages in this shire before, so we can't travel the easy way."

"Before you go," Mosel said, rising to his feet, "you should know that there are those at court who dislike the idea of a Tribunal. They won't say so publicly, but . . . well, people have never been overly careful of what they say in my presence. Most were friends of your father's who supported the Reykan alliance last year. None of them are on Durek's council, of course—he culled out anyone even remotely tolerant of the Lorngeld the moment he was crowned. I cannot promise that these men will help you, but you may wish to approach them and find out if they are willing to join your cause."

He passed on a half-dozen names. Athaya had considered contacting her father's allies some months ago, but had decided to wait until her fledgling crusade showed some promise of success. Now that she had risked trial and imprisonment, the lords of Caithe would be more likely to believe that she was serious and not simply playing at rebellion. And now that she was gaining more of a following, she felt more confident asking them to shelter the Lorngeld from the Church and to allow new schools of magic to be established in their shires. Most of the names Mosel gave her were men she had already planned on seeking out, but one or two others were welcome surprises—or would be, if she could persuade them to help her, or at the very least not to betray her to the Tribunal.

"Then perhaps that is the answer to this riddle," Cecile said, turning to Athaya. "I have a private message for you from the earl of Belmarre, my neighbor to the south."

Athaya frowned. Belmarre . . . the name of the shire was vaguely familiar, but she could not remember ever meeting its earl. Perhaps he was someone she had encountered only briefly at court years ago—in her other lifetime.

"The earl knows of my friendship with you—who does not, by now?" Cecile added dryly. "He asked me that if I ever had a way to contact you, I should tell you that he wishes to speak to you. He said nothing more than that," she said, shrugging helplessly. "He was not one of Kelwyn's closer friends, but perhaps he is willing to offer you his aid."

Athaya felt a flutter in her stomach, though she couldn't tell if its source was excitement or apprehension. Aid from an earl—that would be a godsend indeed! But was it that simple? Durek's men had set traps for her before . . .

"It could be a ruse," Jaren cautioned, echoing her own thoughts back to her.

Athaya nodded, but the possibility of gaining an earl's support was too tempting to resist. *If this is the bait Durek is using*, she thought with an air of recklessness, *then he's chosen the right kind*.

"How far is it to Belmarre?"

Late that afternoon, Athaya and Jaren arrived at the gatehouse of the earl's castle, their ears and fingers numbed from a brisk October wind—a rude harbinger of the coming winter. They had walked the five miles from Halsey; having never been to Belmarre before, Athaya could not use translocation, and they dared not be seen riding on horses known to be the queen's. The autumn sun was sinking low in the sky when they told the gate-keeper their business. He seemed little inclined to admit them so late in the day, but when Jaren told him that they bore a message from the queen, he acceded readily enough.

A sentry led them across the inner bailey and into a rustic, timber-beamed hall and bade them wait until the earl returned from his afternoon ride. He ordered a kitchen maid to bring each of them a goblet of mulled wine, and within the half hour, the earl of Belmarre strode into the hall to greet his guests. He was a slim but robust man in his early forties, whose cropped, brown hair curled neatly inward just beneath his chin. Athaya liked him at once; clearly an unpretentious man, he was dressed little better than his guests and smelled strongly of horses and he smiled at them as if they were visiting dignitaries and not simple couriers.

"You have a message from the queen?"

Athaya glanced at the kitchen maid, now busily sweeping out one of the hall's six fireplaces. "Of a sort," she said, framing her reply carefully. "I've come to tell you that I have received your message. You asked to speak to me, my Lord. Her Majesty was to tell me so when we next met."

Recognition dawned on the earl's face. "Ah, yes . . . I remember. Beth," he said to the kitchen maid, "would you leave us, please?"

The maid curtsied and slipped away, and the earl offered a bow to his royal guest. "Your Highness, I thank you for coming." Then his eyes twinkled, and he indulged in quiet laughter. "It's gratifying to learn that you haven't killed yourself—I've been hearing rumors of your return for days now."

He shifted his gaze to Jaren, "And I can guess who you are. The Reykan wizard, yes? The one his Majesty keeps trying to get rid of?"

"The same," Jaren acknowledged proudly. "Jaren McLaud of Ulard, my Lord."

"And my husband," Athaya added, equally proud.

The earl's brows shot up. "Your—? Well, *that* news certainly hasn't traveled this far south."

"It hasn't had time," Athaya explained. "It only happened a few days ago. But the hour is late, my Lord, and I don't wish to keep you—is there something you wished to discuss with me?''

The earl shifted his weight, looking sheepish, though with the cool control of a man long accustomed to authority. ''Actually,'' he admitted, ''my message was something of a ruse. It wasn't I who wished to see you, but my steward. He didn't know how to reach you, and I told him I would use my friendship with the queen to lure you here.''

''I see.'' The word *lure* set Athaya's nerves on edge, but her instincts did not sound any warnings; the earl struck her as a sincere and trustworthy man.

''I regret the falsehood, but I think you'll understand Adam's reasons after you speak to him. But he asked to see you alone,'' the earl added, turning apologetically to Jaren. ''I'd be glad to show you about the place in the meantime . . . perhaps offer you something to eat?''

Jaren glanced sidelong to Athaya. *I'll stay with you if you want me to.*

No, I'll be all right, she sent back. *If this was a trap, he would have sprung it by now.*

''I'd be honored to wait with you, sir,'' Jaren replied.

The earl summoned the sentry posted at the hall's entrance. ''Inform Adam that he has a visitor: the woman he wished to speak to about his son.''

Ah, so that was it. Athaya exhaled, slightly disappointed. She had let her thoughts run free during the walk from Halsey, convinced that the earl had requested this audience to offer his support. But no, this was a more ordinary tale—a man whose son struggled with the fury of the *mekahn* and who wished to place him in Athaya's care. She would be glad to accept, of course—that was her entire purpose in Caithe—but felt irritated with herself for building her hopes so high.

After giving his steward a few moments to prepare, the earl asked Jaren to wait in the hall while he showed Athaya to the steward's apartment. The man occupied all three levels of the castle's south tower, the earl explained, and lived there alone, attended only sporadically by the castle servants. Their meeting would be suitably private.

Ascending to the tower's second level by way of a steep and narrow staircase, the earl knocked on a weathered door edged with blocks of sandstone. A gravelly voice gave permission for his guests to enter, and the earl led Athaya into a brightly lit

chamber of elegant simplicity, adorned by few but well-chosen
pieces—a walnut table, a silver pitcher, a set of porcelain dishes.
It was not the home of an extravagant man, but of a modest man
with modest needs.

The steward stood near an arched window with his back to
them, as if bracing himself for this meeting by grasping one last
moment of meditation and then slowly turned to greet his guest.
He was a stooped man of perhaps sixty years, clad in a plain
crimson gown lined with black silk. Fair-skinned, he had likely
been blond in his youth, but his thinning locks and cropped
beard were now fully gray. But it was the vibrant, green eyes
that struck Athaya motionless: eyes that she knew so well—
though on the face of another, younger man—that the earl did
not have to speak his name. Athaya knew who he was . . . dear
God, she knew too well.

"Your Highness, this is my steward, Adam Graylen."

The man bowed to her, and Athaya's tongue went dry as
sawdust. No wonder the name Belmarre had sounded so familiar! This was the place of Tyler's youth—Tyler Graylen, the first
man she had ever loved and the first to die in her defense. He'd
often spoken of his father, the steward to an earl with lands in
southern Caithe; it was Cecile's friendship with the earl that had
led to Tyler's employment in the King's Guard over four years
ago.

Athaya gazed upon the man that had fathered him and was
suddenly afraid. Not of physical harm, but of harsh and cutting
words . . . of painful memories and blame. Why else could he
wish to see her, if not to berate her for leading Tyler to his death?

It was not the sort of trap she had envisioned, but under
Adam's serene scrutiny, she felt just as tightly snared. Only the
knowledge that she had the power to vanish by magic at any
moment gave her the strength she needed to remain.

"Thank you, m'Lord," Adam said, and before Athaya could
plead with him to remain, the earl departed to rejoin Jaren in
the hall.

Athaya tried desperately to read the steward's face, but it was
carefully controlled, revealing nothing. He gestured to a high-
backed chair near the fireplace. "It was good of you to see me,
your Highness. Would you care to sit?"

Suspecting her knees might buckle if she did not, Athaya took
the chair gladly. When Adam pressed a cup of cool ale into her
hand, she gulped it down. Daring an upward glance, she saw

him quietly studying her, as if trying to see her as Tyler had and discern those qualities that had so enchanted his son.

"I don't know what to say to you, sir," she told him after a moment of strained silent. "Frankly, I'm surprised you wanted to see me, considering . . ."

"Please, call me Adam," he told her in a gentle voice. "And be assured that I did not ask you here to shower you with curses. I do not despise you. I did, just after it happened," he admitted, "and for a long time after that. But not now."

The room fell silent, but for the subtle crackling of the fire, and Athaya could feel her heartbeat slow its feverish pace as her initial fears were put to rest. Adam swallowed a mouthful of ale, and his achingly familiar eyes grew dreamy as he looked into the past. "Tyler wrote to me every so often from Delfarham. After the first few months, I knew he was in love. All those flowery phrases . . . I began to think I'd raised a bard instead of a soldier." Adam chuckled, and a wistful smile lifted the corners of his mouth. "But he never told me the lady's name. I never knew it was you, until—" He sipped at his ale again. "Until he was gone."

Athaya closed her eyes, allowing the pain of his loss to wash over her, dulled by time but not forgotten. He was gone, but his memory would be with her always—memories of the time he had urged her to learn all she could of her magic, knowing that if it was of her, then it could not be evil; of the time he had defied his king's command to arrest her for Kelwyn's murder, and in doing so, planted the seed of his own destruction. And most vivid of all, she carried the remembrance of that death, forever seeing the silhouette of his severed head against the clouds: Durek's grisly warning to all those who would dare defend a Devil's Child. All the sealing spells in the world would never erase that image from her mind. But perhaps it was best that she always retain it, for it was that final blow that gave her the will to go on and the determination to lead the Lorngeld to a better future than what Caithe and its Church chose to grant them.

"You must blame me for his death—"

"No," Adam replied. "Or better to say no longer."

Athaya set aside her empty goblet and laid one hand gently atop of his. "I loved your son, Adam. Had I been born into any other family, we would have spoken of marriage long before we did." She smiled inwardly at that, thinking what Drianna would surely say about princesses marrying castle guardsmen: It simply isn't *done*.

Athaya paused, weighing her next words carefully. "I'm married now," she told him, hoping he would not take it as a slight against his son. "My husband is with the earl. Jaren knew your son, though only briefly. Tyler hated him at first," she confessed, laughing through her tears as she recalled Tyler's deep distrust, convinced that Jaren was trying to corrupt Athaya with magic and turn her power to evil purposes. "But they became friends—eventually."

"Then I'm sure he's a good man," Adam said with conviction. Silently, he refilled Athaya's goblet. "My son was a fine judge of character, my Lady. If Tyler liked Jaren, then Jaren is a man worth liking. And if Tyler put his trust in you instead of in the king, then he had a damned good reason for it. Your cause must truly be just, my Lady," he said, fixing his green eyes upon her. "My son never would have died for a poor one."

Athaya smiled; she believed that as fervently as Adam did. "If it helps, sir, then know that but for your son, I would not be defying the law and offering the Lorngeld an alternative to absolution. Tyler's death gave me the will to do so, so that others might be saved from such senseless deaths and the grief that comes of them."

She suspected that Adam knew this already, but the glow of tranquillity in his eyes revealed that he was glad to hear it nonetheless. "I honor your mission, your Highness. In fact, that is why I asked to see you. I have something for you."

Adam stepped into an inner room and emerged with a small, ironbound chest. He set it on the table before her, unlocked it with a slender key, and bade her open it.

Athaya lifted the lid, and her eyes went wide at the sight before her. The chest was filled with silver coins! And not just coins, but a collar of gold links, a ruby ring, and several ornately jeweled brooches.

"It was meant for Tyler," Adam explained softly. "A part of his inheritance. But now I want you to have it." Again, his lips turned up in a wistful smile. "He would have wanted that."

Athaya gazed at the chest as if she had never seen such riches before, and her mind reeled with possibilities. She would be able to feed and clothe those who came to her and had no means of their own; she would be able to buy paper and ink to print more leaflets espousing her cause; she could even use some of the money to build a *real* school of magic, to take the place of the sheepfold . . .

But *this* . . . surely it was all he had.

"I can't possibly take this. It's . . . it's just too much."

"Please—you must. The earl is a good man, and has promised to see to my needs until I die. I have no family—my wife's been gone these thirty years and Tyler was our only child. I'd rather see my money go to the people you're trying to help than sit in a strong room gathering dust." He touched his fingers to her shoulder. "If there had been somewhere for you to go when your magic came, your Highness, then my son would not have been forced to defy his king and sacrifice his life for what he believed in. It hurts all of us, this rite of absolution . . . and I want to help stop it."

Athaya gazed into his aging eyes, realizing how many of his father's traits Tyler had inherited—loyalty, generosity, and an inborn need to see justice done in the world. Not the Tribunal's idea of justice, rife with blood and swords and threats of damnation, but divine justice. God's justice. What an irony, Athaya mused, that the two were not even remotely alike.

Athaya arranged for the treasure to be sent to her in care of Sir Jarvis in Kaiburn, knowing that a fine carriage escorted by guardsmen would not be an unusual sight at the door of the wealthy clothier. The room had now grown dim with twilight, and Athaya knew that she and Jaren would need to leave the earl's castle and seek shelter for the night. Odd, she thought, but when she had entered Adam's chamber, she wished only to escape; now, however, she only wished to stay and listen to Adam's tales of Tyler's childhood while she recounted her own memories of his last few years.

"If there is anything else I can do for you, you have only to ask," Adam told her, as he guided her to the door. "To honor my son's memory, I will help in any way that I can."

"You've done a great deal already," she told him, barely able to speak the words. She embraced him with affection and offered a kiss of gratitude. "I will use your gift wisely. And I thank you. All the Lorngeld thank you."

And as Adam escorted her back to the hall, Athaya realized that she had gained a far greater treasure than a chest of silver and gemstones; she had gained a father's forgiveness and support. And for that, Athaya resolved, she would be a faithful steward of his generous gift.

CHAPTER 10

✳✳

SIX DAYS LATER, ATHAYA AND JAREN RETURNED TO THE
sheepfold with both good and bad tidings to pass along to
their followers.

The news of Adam's gift would be welcome indeed; Athaya
would keep the actual amount in the confidence of her closest
friends, but it would comfort everyone to know that her crusade
had the means to continue unhindered for a while and that its
leaders would not be diverted from the vital tasks of preaching
and training by having to spend an inordinate amount of time
struggling to survive. Adam's silver, combined with the gold
from Jaren's father, would keep the core of her following fed
and clothed for many months.

In addition to their newfound wealth, Athaya and Jaren had
met with a respectable level of success on the way home from
Belmarre. The villages they had visited were much like Pipewell
in that the folk were both curious and wary of the notorious pair
of wizards in their midst, and only once were Athaya and Jaren
forced to make a precipitous exit after someone had threatened
to fetch a corbal crystal from a nearby church. Nonetheless, a
woman in the first village had promised to send her daughter to
Kaiburn within the week, and a newly married couple in another
village were following only two days behind them so that the
husband, whose budding magic was nearing the dangerous stage,
could be properly trained.

Unfortunately, Athaya feared that these good tidings would inevitably be overshadowed by news of the Tribunal. "All this talk is making me nervous," she said, as they crossed the fallow fields west of the sheepfold. "Sometimes I wish these so-called Justices of the Tribunal would hurry up and start rampaging through the countryside so I can stop jumping at shadows."

Jaren nodded his sympathy. "An enemy you haven't seen yet is worse than one you have. And I'm certain the rumors about the Tribunal are the main reason that the earl wasn't more willing to help us."

Athaya sighed in disappointment. While she had been with Adam, Jaren did his best to persuade the earl of Belmarre to join their crusade, but to no avail. "It doesn't make sense," she said, shaking her head. "He welcomed us into his home knowing who we were; he trusts his steward completely—"

"And he sympathizes with what we're trying to do, if that's any help," Jaren continued. "But he's not willing to risk his neck—or the necks of his tenants—by being one of the first Caithan lords to back us publicly. I hinted that one of Durek's councillors had already allied himself with us—I didn't mention Gessinger by name, of course—but even that wouldn't sway him." Jaren paused for a moment to work a stalk of dry straw from his boot. "At least he promised not to stand in our way; that he'd overlook it if one of us started teaching magic in his shire, or if a few of his nineteen- or twenty-year-old tenants suddenly vanished for a few months."

Athaya pulled the folds of her cloak closer about her as they proceeded up the slope; the wind had picked up, scattering colored leaves like scraps of cloth, and the sky bore the grayish-green tint of a coming storm. "That's something to be thankful for, I suppose. And in the end, that kind of passive support will be just as effective as people actively working for us."

"Or giving us vast sums of money," Jaren added.

Athaya turned to him, watching the wind tousle locks of overlong blond hair that arched over his forehead like thatch. "I'm glad you don't mind my accepting Adam's gift," she said, this time more quietly. "I wouldn't blame you if it bothered you."

"Bothered me?" he said, puzzled at first. "We can put it to good use. Oh, now I see . . . you think I might be a bit jealous of Tyler's ghost." He stood before her, resting both hands on her shoulders. "Athaya, I told you long ago not to worry about that. I'd never ask you to forget him; I'd never want you to. If you hadn't known him, you wouldn't have become the person you are today. And besides,'' he added lightly, grinning as he resumed his stride, ''you've never asked me to forget all the women *I* knew before I met *you*.''

It took a moment for his remark to register, and then Athaya hastened to catch up with him. ''What women?'' she said, taken so completely by surprise that she didn't think to conceal it. ''You never told me about any women—''

Jaren's laughter made her suspect that he was exaggerating, but Athaya didn't bother to question him further. Such things hardly mattered now. Nevertheless, Athaya decided to keep her magnanimous thoughts to herself, and simply scowled at Jaren good-naturedly as she linked her arm in his.

They reached the sheepfold to find that Ranulf, Cam, and several of the neophyte wizards had knocked a hole in one side of the squat structure, as if planning to build a second entrance. On second glance, however, Athaya realized that the stones had not been dismantled methodically, but had been blown out from the inside. She saw another handful of men rethatching the roof with a mixture of rye straw and bracken—or, more precisely, putting a new roof on a structure which no longer had one.

''What happened here?'' Athaya asked Tonia, as she emerged from the damaged sheepfold with a jug of fresh cider.

''Oh, we had a slight accident yesterday. Marya—she's a new girl from Feckham—well, she was practicing her weather-spells and called up a bit too much wind. The poor girl was terribly embarrassed, but once I told her about the time you called down a thunderstorm without thinking to come in out of the rain first, she felt better.''

Athaya smiled wanly as she surveyed the sparse number of students at the sheepfold today; with the little school under repairs, most of the others had remained at the forest camp for their lessons. And that, Athaya thought, was probably how it should stay. Even though Gilda said that the bishop's raids had trickled off over the summer, the sheepfold was still well known as a haven for wizards; with their growing numbers, it was best that only a few people be at the fold to greet new students, leaving the others safely back at the camp under the protection of wards and illusion. With the onset of the Tribunal, Athaya suspected that the raids might well return.

"Gilda must be back with the others, then?"

"She's back at the camp, all right, but she's not teaching spells today." Tonia smiled broadly. "She's nursing her new son. Nathan is looking after her students for the time being—he's barely done with his own training, but he's got a knack for teaching. Drianna's caring for Gilda and the baby, though with only a fraction of the devotion she shows to you. She'll be thrilled to know you're back."

"Who?" Athaya asked dryly. "Drianna or Gilda?"

As Tonia departed to pass out cups of cider to the others, Cameron emerged from the sheepfold with an armload of straw, dropping it at his feet the instant he caught sight of Athaya. He hurried toward her, his gangly gait as awkward as a colt's, the result of arms and legs that stubbornly refused to grow at the same rate.

"Is it true?" he asked. His voice broke in midsentence—a tentative and unsuccessful venture into manhood—and his cheeks colored slightly. "It's all they're talking about in the city. Has the king really sent an army of priests out to kill us?"

Athaya sighed heavily; so the news had reached Kaiburn at last. "I'm afraid so, Cam," she told him. "I heard it directly from the queen. But don't worry the others by speaking of this just yet—I'll call a meeting for tonight and tell everyone what I know." *Not that I can put their fears to rest*, she thought glumly. *But at least I can warn them what we're up against.*

Cam nodded gravely, but was unable to suppress a glint of excitement at the prospect of battle. He went back to his work, passing by one of the men climbing down from atop the sheepfold's roof. Although the man's back was to her, Athaya realized there was something all too familiar about his build. Her suspicions were confirmed when he jumped down from the ladder and sauntered to her side, grinning like a jester as he picked bits of straw from his hair.

"Nicolas? What are you doing here? I thought you went back to Delfarham."

"At the moment, I'm apprentice to Terrence, the master thatcher." Nicolas pointed to the stocky young man lashing the straw bundles to one another with spars of hazel; Athaya had met him briefly on the night of her wedding. "He is teaching me to fix a roof—did you know those bundles of straw are called yealms?" he added, his eyes shining with the thrill of new knowledge. "Fascinating. And I, in turn, have promised to teach him something princely—perhaps the fine art of carrying on a pleasant conversation with someone you despise." Nicolas glanced back to Terrence and laughed quietly. "He's too polite to say so, but I suspect he finds me the most inept apprentice he's ever had."

Athaya plucked another random piece of straw from her brother's hair. "You still haven't told me why you're here thatching rooftops. If you don't get back to Delfarham soon, Durek will think something's happened to you."

"As if he'd care," Nicolas replied sullenly, kicking at a stone like a disgruntled child. Athaya waited for his smile to return—Nicky never sulked for more than a few seconds at a time—but it remained conspicuously absent. "I meant to tell you days ago . . . I'd made up my mind the day I first set foot in your camp, but I knew you'd make a fuss." He gazed up at the fresh-tied thatch atop the sheepfold, admiring his handiwork with sublime approval at having built something with his own hands instead of simply paying others for their labor. "You see, Athaya, much like my extended holiday in Reyka, I've decided that I rather like it here."

"Nicolas, what are you saying?" Athaya asked, but the churning feeling in her stomach told her that she already knew the answer.

"I just didn't come for a visit. I came to join you. To put it bluntly, I'm not going back to Delfarham," he concluded, leveling her with a look of resolve as steadfast as the forest oaks. "I want to help, Athaya. I'm staying. For good."

Jaren extended a hand of official welcome, but Athaya was quick to restrain him. "Not so fast, Jaren. I know Nicky better than you do—I'm sure he's only teasing. He does, about most things."

"Not about this," Nicolas replied, and still the smile did not return. "Maybe I'm finally starting to grow up. Of course, I never expected it would be my little sister who would inspire me to do such a thing," he added, almost wistfully. Then he gazed at her with a bone-chilling degree of solemnity—something Nicolas did only rarely—and spoke from the very bottom of his soul. "I've got to do something with my life, Athaya, and I've chosen this."

Athaya shook her head in stunned disbelief. "But Durek—"

"Has told me to get out of his sight a hundred times," Nicolas finished hastily. "This time I'll obey him."

Athaya knew she was gaping, but couldn't help it. Had Nicolas lost his reason?

Or had he, like she had done only a year ago, finally found it?

"And don't you dare tell me it's too dangerous," Nicolas went on, plucking the fears from her mind before she had a chance to voice them. "Might I remind you what happened when you tried to say that very thing to him?" He jerked a thumb at Jaren, who clearly agreed with Nicolas but was being tactful enough not to say so. "He would have been better off coming to Caithe with you in the first place, but you made him stay behind in Reyka so he would be safe, whereupon he was promptly abducted by Durek's weasel of a captain and dragged here anyway. Besides, I know you're planning to contact all of Father's old friends—how can you ask them to join your crusade but turn me away?"

"That's different!" she protested, although she could hear her voice growing weaker, her words less forbidding. "Nicolas, you're a prince of Caithe; you're second in line to the Crown—"

Nicolas threw up his arms in triumph. "Exactly! I'm a Trelane, Athaya. Caithe is my responsibility, too."

Athaya sighed heavily; how could she possibly counter that argument? It was precisely the same reasoning she used herself. "God knows our family doesn't need any more outlaws in it," she murmured, although there was no longer any force behind her words. "Durek will disinherit you, just the way he did to me."

"It hasn't seemed to harm you any," Nicolas replied, his elusive smile at last returning. "In fact, I'd say it's done you good."

Just then, Terrence called down for more hazel switches, and Nicolas trotted off to resume his work. He whistled contentedly as he ascended the ladder with an armful of split branches, looking every inch the contented peasant without a princely thought in his head.

"We'll talk about this later, Nicolas," Athaya warned, but as she turned back to Jaren and caught his playful smile, she knew that this was one battle she had already lost.

At the forest camp that evening, Athaya called her following together to warn them of the king's Tribunal. She sounded the camp's bronze bell at dusk to summon everyone to the chapel, and her stomach fluttered as she approached the little church, thinking that this must be how soldiers felt on the eve of battle: willing to fight, but wondering whether they would live to see another sunset.

A light snow was falling—unusual for southern Caithe in mid-October—and blanketed the clearing with a thin layer of stardust that crunched beneath her boots. Inside, Jaren was placing a ring of witchlights over the altar to light the chapel, and the palm-sized orbs cast a ruddy glow over the expectant—and openly apprehensive—faces of the congregation.

When everyone was assembled, Athaya walked up the aisle to the front of the chapel feeling oddly like a priest about to conduct holy service. And although she wore no vestments, her cloak felt to her like a chasuble and her marriage brooch a bishop's ring of office. She had never spoken to all of her following at one time before, but her nerves were eased by the knowledge that they were a receptive audience and nothing like the angry mob she had addressed in Kaiburn's square five months ago.

"First of all, I want all of you to know how glad I am that you are here—although my welcome comes a bit late to those of you who have been here all summer." Athaya let her gaze fall on each of the newcomers in turn, offering her silent gratitude. "You've risked quite a bit in deciding to accept your magic and not give in to absolution, and I'll do everything I can to help and protect you while you're here."

Athaya ran her fingers along the edge of the altar. "As you've probably noticed by now, our efforts fall into three main areas. We need to keep on making ourselves known—recruiting new members, as it were. We have to make certain that everyone in Caithe knows what we're offering. For that reason, you may not see me in the camp very often during the next few weeks; I want to spread the word of what we're doing here in as many places as I can before the winter sets in." *If it hasn't already*, she thought, glancing out of one window; the snow was falling faster now.

"Secondly, we have to teach the wizards who come to us and save them from the worst of the *mekahn*. If there are a lot of them, it could seem for a while as if we're trying to push back the tide with our bare hands. Even now, there are roughly five tutors to nearly thirty students, and we're somewhat strained for help. In other words," she said with a smile of entreaty, "once you've mastered your own magic, those of you who would like to teach others are strongly encouraged to volunteer. Nathan, I've already heard that you're doing a fine job.'' She nodded her thanks to Rupert's brawny, fair-haired son.

"Lastly," she went on, her smile fading, ''we need to watch our backs. I don't have to tell you that what we're doing isn't exactly popular—at least not with the king and the Church. We're safe enough here at the camp—the failure of the bishop's men to find it over the summer is proof of that—but we can't hide the sheepfold the same way; others must be able to find us as you did. It's common knowledge that we're there; the fact that you've had to post sentries around it attests to that. Our enemies know where to find us, too."

Several people shifted uncomfortably at the spoken need for defense; they knew exactly which enemies she was referring to, but none of them said a word.

Athaya felt their tension and her palms grew moist in response; she had come to the part of the speech she'd been dreading. "But there's another reason I've called you here tonight," she began, astonished at how silent the chapel had suddenly become; were she only to pause and listen, she might have heard the snowflakes touch the ground. "Some of you have heard rumors about a Tribunal, charged to destroy anyone with the powers of magic—and anyone who offers him or her aid." Athaya drew in a steadying breath, and the air filling her lungs was thick with the musty scent of dead and dying leaves. "I've recently learned that these are not rumors at all. The king and his Church have formally declared war upon us."

A chorus of voices rose in fearful crescendo, but Athaya pressed on; she had a duty to tell them the worst of it. "And since the Bishop of Kaiburn has been appointed Chief Justice, I don't think I need to tell you the kind of methods his Tribunal will employ to obtain confessions of guilt. You have only to think back to the darkest time in our people's history—back to the Time of Madness and the scourge which caused it."

The looks of stark terror that crossed their faces told Athaya that they knew their history well. During King Faltil's massacre of the Lorngeld two centuries before, showing mercy to the Lorngeld was itself a crime punishable by death. Once stripped of their power by corbal crystals, the wizards' bodies had been abused in the most heinous of ways; by blades, by fire, or by the sheer simplicity of tearing limb from torso. Although trained to deal with violence, even experienced soldiers like Ranulf and Kale exchanged queasy glances at the possible fate before them.

"What about my wife?" one man called out, moving to stand in the aisle. "I would have died anyway, but not Martha. If they find out she's married to me . . . that she knew I came here . . . my God, they'll kill her!"

"I can't promise you they won't," Athaya told him, unable to hide the brutal truth from him. "Knowing that the ones you love might be hurt because of you isn't easy to live with—believe me, I know that as well as any of you. But we can't fight for our *own* lives without taking that risk. In the end, when absolution is a distant memory and the Lorngeld are no longer called the Devil's Children, then no one will have to live in fear for themselves or their families."

The man mumbled something under his breath as he returned to his seat. Athaya wasn't sure if she had reached him, but at least he had not stalked out of the chapel. That, in itself, was something; a tiny victory amid a massive war.

"Talking about how wonderful the future will be doesn't help us now!" a fair-haired woman cried, whose bloodless fingers clutched at the folds of a threadbare cloak. It was Marya, the one who had inadvertently demolished the sheepfold's roof. "We'll be captured by the Tribunal the day we leave this camp to go back home!"

Jaren addressed the woman pointedly, but without criticism. "You'd be dead already but for Athaya. Why not stay and help us teach others? If we trained every Lorngeld in Caithe, then the Tribunal would never be able to kill us all— we'd win by virtue of sheer numbers. At this point, we've nothing to lose."

"A fine thing for you to say," a man grumbled from the rear of the chapel. "One who can run home to Reyka with his tail between his legs as soon as things get bad."

Jaren bristled at the remark, and Athaya craned her neck to see who had spoken—a lanky but taut-muscled man with features as sharp as his tongue. Ah, yes . . . Sutter Dubaye, one of the newest arrivals. Gilda had warned her about him. A baron's son, he had defied his father and refused absolution. Faced with the prospect of losing his lands to the newly formed Tribunal were it to be discovered that his son was a wizard, Lord Dubaye had chosen to protect the lands by publicly disowning the son. Thus, Sutter had come to the camp an embittered young man, resenting his magic for what it had lost him, and refusing to acknowledge what he had gained. And according to Gilda, who had supervised most of his early training, he was reckless with his power to the point of stupidity; knowing he should be dead by absolution anyway, he had no concern for what remained of his life.

Before Sutter could say another word, Ranulf was behind him clutching a fistful of his fine linen collar. "Jaren almost burned for Caithe, you spoiled little pup," he growled into the younger man's ear. "I'll wager *you* haven't risked so much for anything in your short life."

Sutter twisted out of Ranulf's grasp with a hiss of wounded pride. "Everyone talks of fighting for our right to use our magic, and yet we do nothing but cower in these woods like common criminals. I say if it's a war the king wants, then we should give it to him!"

A murmur of agreement rumbled through the chapel, and Athaya knew that this was one notion she had to quash immediately. "And what would that prove? Only that we're as violent and corrupt as everyone thinks. No, our main goal is to teach magic to those who want to learn. We'll defend ourselves if we're attacked, of course, but I don't plan to go out and look for trouble."

"But—"

"This is the kind of battle best fought one person at a time, Sutter." She shifted her gaze to the others. "Every one of you who came to this camp has already struck a blow to those who would absolve you, and that will only continue as our numbers increase. If we eat away at the Tribunal's foundation long enough, it'll collapse on its own. We won't have to fight. We will have already won."

Sutter stared at her, dumbfounded. "But how can you expect to seize the throne *that* way?"

Athaya gaped at him. Was she never to be free of this suspicion? "Let me make one thing clear, Sutter," she said firmly, keeping a tight rein on her outrage. "I have no designs on the throne nor any wish to see Durek toppled from it. Much as I might wish otherwise, our laws declare him the rightful king of Caithe. I only want to change his perspective on a few things in as peaceful a way as possible."

"You're sure about that?" Nathan challenged from the first pew, visibly skeptical that anyone so close to the throne could not possibly covet it. At first, Athaya was surprised that such a suspicion would be voiced by a man who, judging from everything she'd been told of him, was dedicated to her cause and who was proving himself a successful tutor as well. Then she saw beyond the challenge itself and knew that had he asked the question precisely because of his loyalty. Like Athaya herself, he was willing to defy his king for what he believed in, but was not willing to challenge Durek's right to *be* king. That was taking rebellion one step too far.

"I'm sure of it, Nathan," she replied calmly. "I swear it on my father's name."

He nodded slowly, seemingly appeased by her choice of oath, but Sutter was not so amenable. "But why waste time doing this the hard way?" he went on, increasingly agitated. "If we were to depose him, then that makes Mailen king—and Prince Nicolas would be regent until the boy's of age." Sutter pointed to the prince. "*He'd* give us what we want."

Nicolas bolted to his feet and shot a murderous glare across the aisle. "How *dare* you think that I would be party to a plot like that?" he snapped, as furious as Athaya had seen him in a very long time. "Opposing the king is one thing . . . killing him is something else. That's something Athaya would never do."

"She's done it once before," Sutter grumbled under his breath, and Athaya heard a chorus of indrawn breaths at the insolence of his words. Nicolas moved to strike him, but Athaya silently waved him back.

"Leave him be," she said, imbuing her words with a composure she did not feel. "I'm used to such ignorant remarks."

Her cool tone, combined with the prince's show of ire, convinced Sutter that perhaps he had gone too far. "Then can't you just bewitch him, for God's sake?" he said, turning back to Athaya with a sheepish look on his face. "Change the king's mind by magic, if you won't do it by force?"

"I wish it were that simple," she replied, "but we have a responsibility to use our gifts ethically. We must change the king's mind without abusing our power and without resorting to violence."

Marya, however, was unmoved by such talk of lofty ethical concepts; her thoughts were utterly absorbed with the looming specter of the Tribunal. "But fire and torture—oh, isn't there anywhere safe we can go? Caithe is no place for us now . . ."

Much as she wished her people would choose to stay and help instead of flee, Athaya nodded. "Reyka has opened her borders to anyone who fears to remain here," she announced, glad for the chance at turning the subject away from such dangerous topics as ousting the king. "Unfortunately, Durek knows this as well as we do, and I suspect that the Tribunal will post spies at the border and in the port cities to catch people trying to leave. Getting there won't be easy."

This news spawned another chorus of muttering. Only Drianna looked unconcerned—but then, Athaya reflected, she had looked that way all night. Vaguely bored, she swung one foot to and fro, impatient for the others to stop talking so that the meeting could come to an end. Apparently she did not feel her brother's life was in any danger at Dom DePere's school in Kilfarnan.

"You won't abandon us, will you?" Marya asked, still wringing her cloak with anxious fingers. "You won't go to Reyka and leave all of us behind?"

Athaya shook her head resolutely. "No, I started this and I'm going to finish it. I'll not leave Caithe until it's over, win or lose. That I promise you." She paused and leaned back against the altar. "What I can't promise you is that any of this is going to be easy. The Tribunal is the greatest challenge we're going to face. But if we can defend ourselves against this unjust persecution, and if we can prove that we're not going to give up no matter what they do to us, then someday the king will have no choice but to let us be.

"We know the storm is coming," Athaya said in conclusion. "Now all we can do is wait . . . and pray we're stronger than it is." She let those words hang in the crisp night air for a moment, and then, her benediction spoken, Athaya walked slowly down the aisle and out into the clearing, where the snow around the chapel grew ever deeper.

The next morning dawned cold and frosty, and snow crunched under Athaya's boots as she emerged from the dormitory and went to the kitchens for breakfast. The mood of the camp was subdued after the previous night's meeting, and those students who were already awake and attending to their lessons went about their work with a sobriety that had been absent only a day before. Their eyes offered wary greetings as she passed, hoping she had no more bad news to bring them.

Drianna was already in the kitchens when Athaya arrived, busily chopping up leeks and cheese for her mistress' eggs, and for once, Athaya was glad to be waited on; she had not slept well the night before—neither had Jaren, who was still abed—and her eyes remained fuzzy and tired. She poured herself a cup of watered ale as she waited for her eggs to cook, and as she sipped at it, Ranulf strode in with a large burlap sack balanced on his shoulder. Athaya had asked him to collect Adam Graylen's treasure from the Jarvis house that morning, but he had clearly returned with more than a chest of silver. A sleepy-eyed Nicolas strolled in after him, curious at the sack's contents.

"Look what just arrived for us," Ranulf said. He flung the bundle down on the kitchen table so hard that Athaya's cup of ale nearly overturned. "It's from Kilfarnan."

He untied the burlap sack and pulled it back to reveal a bolt of cloth. Reverently, as if it were the costliest silk, he laid it out on the table.

Drianna looked up from her skillet and glared at the black fabric. "But it's just an ordinary bolt of wool," she said, unable to see any wonder in such a mundane thing. "And you can't even dye it a decent color. What's so special about that?"

Athaya barely heard her, so astonished was she by the sight; it was the most remarkable fabric she had ever seen. The wool itself was not unusual, but clinging to it, edging both sides like a border of fine embroidery, were bright red runes—stitches of light instead of thread.

"What is it?" Athaya asked, not tearing her eyes away from the cloth.

Ranulf touched his fingers to the bright red marks as if to prove that they would not rub off. "It's called runecloth. Cordry Jarvis sent it. There's a letter, too—from Mason." He handed her a folded sheet of parchment.

Athaya smiled warmly. Cordry had been her first student of magic, but one whose first love would always be the manufacture of cloth. Apparently, he had found a way to—quite literally—weave his two talents into one.

"But what's so odd about it?" Drianna asked impatiently. She held one edge of the cloth close to her eyes and scowled at it. Nicolas squinted at the fabric as well, equally puzzled, but electing to wait for an explanation instead of demanding one.

"The runes—oh, I don't suppose either of you can see 'em," Ranulf said. "Cordry's bought himself a mill and set up shop. He says he's found a way to set guiding runes into the cloth like dye so they won't fade and have to be reset. Damned clever," he observed, surprised that Cordry, whom he'd once dismissed as a lovestruck fool, could have accomplished anything so useful.

"Apparently, Mason has been getting the cloth from Cordry and giving swatches of it to all of his students," Athaya said, scanning the Dom's letter. "That way, they can recognize one another, but nobody else is the wiser. Not a bad idea."

"But there's nothing there!" Drianna protested, still working a corner of the cloth between her fingers.

"Runes are something that only wizards can see," Athaya told her. "That's why you need to have one of us with you every time you go out to the sheepfold; otherwise, you'd never find your way back. The rest of us just follow the rune trail." Athaya picked up the bolt of cloth, judging its weight. "How much did Cordry send?"

"Just the one bolt for now," Ranulf replied, "but it's enough for us to give a piece to everyone in camp."

Athaya nodded her agreement. "I think it's time I went to Kilfarnan. I'm anxious to see how Mason is faring, and he writes that he'd like me to come and meet his students when I get a chance—one of them in particular." She smiled up at Drianna. "Maybe your brother is making a name for himself."

"What? Oh, aye," Drianna said absently. But without being able to see the runes, the cloth held no fascination for her and neither did the rest of their conversation. She set Athaya's breakfast before her, then departed for the dormitory to deliver a plate to Jaren as well.

"She has a brother who's a wizard?" Nicolas asked, once she was gone. "Funny, she never talks about him."

Ranulf frowned at the door, as if suspecting that Drianna was still listening behind it. "Aye, and that husband of hers never talks about anything at all unless you wrestle the words out of him—he's almost as bad as Kale. And speaking o' that," he added, "Kale's outside keeping an eye on Adam's treasure chest for the moment, but I was thinking of hiding it under one o' the flagstones in the chapel, just like we did with that corbal crown.''

''Very well—but let's not put all of the money in one place. I'd like to think we can trust everyone in the camp, but . . .'' She thought of Sutter instantly. ''I'd rather not take any chances. But before you go,'' she added, seeing Ranulf edging toward the door, ''I'd like to ask you something.'' She speared a sausage with her knife and took a bite. ''Drianna seems harmless enough, but you seem to distrust her. Why? Do you know her?''

''No. But you can't trust Sarians—I should know, bein' one myself.'' Seeing that Athaya was silently requesting more of an explanation than that, he went on. ''I don't trust her because she's nosy, and Sarians ain't the nosy type. Why d'ye think Caithan folks know next to nothing about that island, anyway? Because Sarian folks like it that way. They keep to themselves and expect others to do the same. And besides,'' he added, idly surveying Athaya's plate in hopes there would be leftovers, ''she came here practically beggin' to be our slave and then glares daggers at anybody who asks her to do something, as if she was the queen o' Caithe herself. Anybody but you, that is . . . I guess she's impressed by royalty.''

''She doesn't offer to wait on *me* hand and foot,'' Nicolas observed. ''Maybe she's only impressed by royalty *and* magic.''

''Do you think she knows something about the cult?''

Ranulf met her gaze. ''You know about them?''

''Yes. And so do you, obviously. Why haven't you mentioned them before? Maybe you can tell me something more than what either Hedric or Basil could.''

''Oh, I doubt as I'd know much that those two don't,'' he said, ''but I didn't say anything to you so's you wouldn't think I was involved with them. You weren't too sure of me at the start, you know,'' he reminded her with a half grin. ''But as to the *Magisteri*, they think that magicians are destined to rule the world. And their leader—the Sage—is simply the lucky bastard powerful enough to kill off anybody who tries to overthrow him.''

''The one with the most potent magic wins?'' Nicolas asked.

''That's what they figure. And God sanctions it all,'' he added sourly. ''Trial by combat and all that. They're a scary bunch, and there's more of them than folk think.''

''How many?'' Athaya said, suddenly worried. The existence of a large group of trained wizards just off the Caithan shore should have delighted her—a pool of potential magic tutors just waiting to be tapped—but instead she was unsettled, knowing that they obviously held a very different view of their power than she or any Reykan-trained wizard did.

Ranulf scratched at his beard. "Well, nobody knows for sure. But it's more than just a handful of wild-eyed fanatics, that I can tell you. There's easily a few hundred of them, and some of the spells they use—spells of sickness and mind control—were banned by the Circle years ago. What they do all day I don't know. Wait for some prophet to tell them it's the right time to start their world takeover, I expect." Ranulf turned aside and spat on the floor with contempt. "But they can wait until there's icicles on the Devil's rooftop for all I care."

"This cult," Nicolas began, his face intent. "It could be a problem if they start making trouble for us."

"Maybe," Ranulf said with a shrug. "But why would a bunch of wizards who've been in hiding for years suddenly decide to come to Caithe at a time like this? And even if they did, the minute they heard about this Tribunal, they'd go back to their bolt holes and wait until the trouble blew over."

"Sare . . . I've got it!" Nicolas lurched against the table, knocking over Athaya's cup and drenching her eggs in watered beer. Before she could complain about her ruined breakfast, he reached out and grasped her shoulders. "You didn't want me to stay at the camp, did you?"

Athaya frowned. Why did she get the idea that even if she said no, she wasn't going to like Nicolas' next proposal.

"Well, no—"

"Fine. But I'm going to help you anyway." His feet moved side to side in a little dance, and his eyes were alight with mischief. "Congratulate me, Athaya," he said, holding his hands out as if awaiting applause, "you're looking at the new lord marshall of Sare."

Athaya bolted to her feet, sending the toppled ale cup spiraling onto the floor. "The *what*?"

"The post has been open for months. Nobody's crazy enough to volunteer for it—Mosel told me so. Nobody but me, that is. And Cecile told me that Durek is getting desperate—he's got to pick a victim soon."

"You? Lord marshall of Sare?" The idea of Nicolas being lord marshall of anything struck her as vaguely ludicrous—his buoyant and sometimes reckless nature didn't seem suited to the routine tasks of administering the island's government. But her long-held image of Mosel Gessinger had changed drastically in the last few months; perhaps it was time to take a new look at her brother as well.

"Of course! Don't you see? I can check up on this cult of yours and see if they're up to something. And all as part of my job! No one will be suspicious in the least."

"But why on earth would Durek give you the post?"

"To get rid of me; oh, Athaya, do you honestly think he wants me underfoot at court? Look—not everyone's heard you're back yet. I'll just ride into Delfarham, heartbroken over your death, and ask Durek to send me away so I won't be tormented by the memories. He'll send me away so fast—"

Athaya waved off that idea. "Nicolas, the news of my return is spreading too quickly—he'll never believe you haven't heard it. Especially once he finds out you've been to see Cecile."

"I suppose you're right. Well then," he said lapsing into exaggerated despair, "I shall tell him that I cannot reconcile my feelings of conflict any longer; that I'm torn between my duty to Caithe and my devotion to you; that the best thing would be for him to send me away so that I can serve Caithe without being tempted to seek you out." In an eyeblink, the mask was gone. "Think he'll take the bait?"

Athaya didn't have to consider it. She knew how Durek's mind worked. Of *course* he'd take it . . .

"Mosel was planning to leave Halsey yesterday," Nicolas went on, caught up in the excitement of his new future. "If I leave today, I can catch up with him on the road to Delfarham. He still needs to come up with a reasonably plausible explanation for his disappearance from court—oh, Durek might believe that Cecile sent for him, but it wouldn't hurt to embellish the tale a bit. Maybe we can cover for each other somehow. So," he said, flashing his smile to Ranulf. "Where might I find this Sage?"

"You're awfully confident of getting the marshalcy," Athaya observed.

Nicolas winked at her. "I'd wager that treasure chest of yours on it."

"The Sage's fortress is in the highlands, on the eastern side of the island," Ranulf told him. He rubbed his beard and thought for a while, debating. "But why don't I take you there myself? Assuming Athaya can spare me for a while, that is. I know the way, and folks might be more likely to talk if they see you with a Sarian—unlike Drianna, most islanders tend to be damned tight-lipped with strangers. And if there's any trouble, you might need a wizard's protection—and not a wizard who thinks he was born to rule the world." He turned to Athaya. "But if you'd rather I stayed . . ."

"Of course I could use you, but I hate to send Nicolas off alone—"

"Then it's settled," Nicolas said, before she had a chance to change her mind. "We'll go to Delfarham together. I'll hide you away somewhere in the city until I'm ready to leave, and then you can meet up with me . . . oh, maybe at the port in Eriston. You can claim to be going home to Sare, and take the same ferry. We'll make a show of becoming fast friends, and then I can appoint you to some post or other in my new household."

Ranulf nodded his approval of the scheme, while Athaya stood temporarily mute; their plans had been spun so quickly that she didn't know exactly what to think of them yet. "But the Sage," she began, after a moment's pause. "We don't know anything about him, other than he thinks himself superior to anyone who doesn't have magic. Being lord marshall might not impress him."

Nicolas looked down his nose at her. "If I can ingratiate myself with Overlord Basil—whom you once said didn't like a soul on this earth—then I can ingratiate myself with the Sage. Master Tonia even told me that I was more of a wizard than you are, since, as she put it, I 'got that old mule to smile.' "

Athaya laughed softly and threw up her hands in surrender; if anyone could handle such a daunting task as befriending the Sage, Nicolas could.

Then, taking up a sharp carving knife, Athaya cut three strips of runecloth from the bolt. "Take these with you, then," she said, folding two of the strips into Nicolas's hands. "One for you and one for Mosel."

"Ah, a lady's favor!" Nicolas said, draping the black cloth over one shoulder. "I shall wear it into battle with honor."

"Take care of him, Ranulf," she told him, offering him the third strip of runecloth. "And don't dice with him, even if he begs you to. He's terrible at it and will resent you for taking all his money."

Ranulf laughed heartily, accepting the charge with a casual salute. "I'll keep him out of trouble. And I'll be back as soon as I can. Can't have you running this rebellion of yours for long without my valuable advice, now can I?"

"Excuse me then, Athaya, Ranulf." Nicolas offered them a graceful bow and headed for the door. "I'd best go practice being sullen and tormented. I'll be performing for his Majesty the king within the week!"

CHAPTER 11

※※

"A ND THIS," DOM MASON DePere PROUDLY SAID, making a sweeping gesture toward the burned-out shell of a tithe barn, "is my college."

Athaya smiled at his choice of word. It didn't look like much of a college yet, but the scholar's brown eyes gleamed as he gazed upon the sorry little structure as if it were no less majestic than the spires of the prestigious Wizard's College in Reyka. But it was his own creation, and calling it his "college" reflected his hopes of what it would become rather than the ruin it currently was.

For all its faults, he had chosen a good location for his school. The barn lay on the outskirts of a thinly populated village roughly two miles west of Kilfarnan. Thus isolated, Mason could insure that outbursts of untrained magic, inevitable when training new wizards, would attract a minimal amount of attention. The wards around the barn were strong, and more than once during their approach, Athaya was convinced that the guiding runes were misplaced and veered off instinctively before Mason pulled her back into the trail. And being a master of illusion himself, having taught the art for several years at Wizard's College, Mason's little school was well-disguised. The phantom bog surrounding the barn even smelled of moss and still water, but once past it, the tumbledown barn shimmered into view, cone-shaped dwell-

162

ings and canvas tents surrounding it like a village springing up around a new castle.

"It isn't much," Mason admitted, seeing the barn through Athaya's eyes, "but at least we know we won't be driven off the land." Mason's perpetually composed features relaxed into a broad smile. "It's part of Cordry's mill property, and he's given it to us . . . his donation to our cause."

Mason guided them around the east side of the barn—or what was left of it. Something had ripped a giant hole in its side like a gaping wound, and burned wood was piled on the ground beside it. "We rebuilt that wall once, but one of my students had an accident with his witchlights not long ago and burned it down again." He placed his hand on the large leather bag tied to his belt. "The money you brought should help us repair it before the worst of the cold weather arrives—thank you."

"You owe your thanks to a man named Adam Graylen," she told him, "but you're welcome just the same." She had delivered nearly half of Adam's gift to Mason so that her crusade could flourish in other shires and was glad to know it could be put to use right away.

Then Mason's hand was on her elbow. "Come, let me take you inside—my students are eager to meet you. It isn't much warmer, what with the wall half-gone, but at least there will be a fire and something hot to eat."

Athaya and Jaren followed him willingly; after ten days on horseback with nothing more palatable than dried fish and apples to sustain them, a hot meal would be a blessing. The air was unseasonably cold for the third week in October, and she was shivering despite her hooded cloak, fur-lined boots, and heavy wool mittens. Jaren and Mason, however—both native to the northern reaches of Reyka, where snow was commonplace from September through May—found the weather refreshing and wore nothing on either head or hands.

Inside, the barn was a hive of activity. No fewer than forty students were divided into groups and diligently pursuing their lessons, some holding the delicate orb of a vision sphere between their fingers, while others practiced warding spells and perfected the fine art of illusion. All of them, no matter what their task, worked under the watchful eye of a more experienced wizard. Closest to the entrance, one man cast a shielding spell before him, while a woman—presumably his wife by the delight she took in her task—tossed stones at him in rapid succession, laughing as each one struck the invisible shield and bounced harmlessly aside in a shower of blue sparks.

The activity came to a halt the moment Athaya appeared in the doorway, and the barn fell conspicuously silent, all eyes turning to her. Laughing quietly, Jaren leaned close and whispered in her ear. "Your reputation precedes you."

Athaya glanced at him sidelong. "Is that good or bad?"

As she soon discovered, it was good. Mason escorted her to each group and introduced the students by name, and most offered sincere thanks for, as one said, "showing them a better future than absolution." Except for one surly fellow who still grumbled his doubts about whether she was spreading heresy or not—she didn't bother to point out that his very presence here made him, in the Church's eyes, as great a heretic as she was—Athaya was given a surprisingly warm reception. Since the start of her crusade—and truthfully, for the better part of her life— warm receptions were not things she was used to, and it was a refreshing change. As princess of Caithe, Athaya garnered far more attention from Mason's students than Jaren did, even after he was introduced as her husband, but Jaren merely smiled graciously, thinking nothing of it. In fact, as with Drianna's lack of attention, he seemed rather grateful for it.

After they had taken a full turn around the barn, Mason led his guests to the west corner, farthest from the open wall. This part of the barn served as the group's living quarters, and individual sleeping areas were marked off by makeshift tents and blankets suspended by strings, like bedsheets hung outside to dry. In the center was a common area with a large fire ringed by dozens of straw mats.

Before she sat down, Athaya scanned the people in the barn one more time, looking for someone specific. "Have you had any students from Sare?" she asked Mason offhandedly. "Someone at our camp had a brother who came here." Odd, but Athaya could not recall that Drianna had ever mentioned his name. "Probably fair-skinned with red hair . . . maybe an accent?"

Mason put a finger to his chin, thinking. "We did have someone who fit that description, but it was a woman. She's been gone since September."

Athaya shrugged, but simply because Mason did not recall the man didn't mean he had not been here. With so many students to attend to, there was a chance that Mason might forget one. Athaya tried not to dwell on the other possibility—that Drianna's brother had never arrived at all.

"I've only lost two so far," Mason told her, with the attitude of one who expects failure to be an occasional part of success. "One simply couldn't accept the fact that her power wasn't some kind of curse and ended up hanging herself from the rafters." Remorsefully, he glanced up to one of the ceiling's timber beams. "The other went into the city and never returned—rumor has it that he was arrested by the Tribunal, but no one knows for sure."

"The Tribunal . . . you've seen them, then?"

"They're already making routine patrols in the city. The main abbey of Saint Adriel isn't far from here, and the Preceptor was one of the first to receive the king's orders. Aren't we the lucky ones?" he added wanly.

"It looks as if you've set up shop in a rather hazardous location."

"True," he admitted. "But the sheepfold falls within Bishop Lukin's jurisdiction, and he's the Chief Justice. Just whose location is worse?"

Athaya glared at the Dom good-naturedly. "Thank you so much for reminding me of that."

"But on a brighter note," he went on, "you'll be glad to know that two of my students have gone south to start another school near the coast. I haven't heard from them yet, but I made them a ward key so we could keep in touch with panels. Traveling can be risky these days—I've heard the Tribunal has started watching the main roads, looking for people who might be on their way to one of our camps."

Athaya nodded her approval of his plan; she had used a panel to attend her first meeting with the Circle of Masters, and recalled the rune-etched stone that had allowed that window of magic glass to pierce the wards surrounding the Circle Chamber. She made a mental note to create a ward key for Mason before she departed. With such a device, the two of them could speak to one another—or any of their other offshoot schools—without ever leaving their own camp.

That evening, when the work of the day was done, Mason's followers provided Athaya and Jaren with a simple meal of rabbit stew, bread, and fresh-baked apple tarts. "I'm sorry I can't offer you better ale," Mason said as he offered her a goblet of watery liquid, "but the harvest was poor this year and grain is expensive. Maybe we'll be able to buy a bit more now that you've enriched us.''

Athaya surveyed the people gathered around them and smiled warmly. ''I'm not sure I should admit this, Mason, but you've got a healthier following than I do at the moment.''

''Healthy, perhaps—but nervous.'' Mason sipped at his own ale and grimaced slightly at the taste.

Although she suspected she could say little to ease their distress, Athaya stood up after the meal was over and made a brief address to Mason's students, drawing her words from what she had told her own people in the forest chapel. Like her own following, this group grew silent and anxious when she spoke of the Tribunal. Unlike her own, however, they had already lost a fellow wizard to it.

''How will we fight them?'' A wiry young man rose to his feet, and Athaya recognized him as one of Mason's assistant tutors. ''When do we march against the Tribunal?''

Athaya groaned inwardly—another Sutter Dubaye, ready to draw his sword and start slaughtering the enemy. ''We're not marching anywhere,'' she said, and then offered him the same explanation that she had given to her own people ten days before, detailing how the battle could be won by training one wizard at a time, without resorting to warfare. ''I may be creating an army of sorts,'' she concluded, ''but an army of teachers, not soldiers.''

The man tightened his jaw, displeased with her response. ''Aurel says that for every one of us they take, we should kill one of them,'' he said, oblivious to the suggestion that murdering priests was no way to convince anyone that the Lorngeld were not the Devil's spawn. ''He says it's bound to work—there are more Lorngeld than monks of Saint Adriel!''

Athaya found this piece of news far more dangerous than Sutter's sullen grumbling. It was bad enough that others shared his opinions, but here, at least one man had apparently started acting on them.

She glanced down to Mason, seated on a straw mat beside her. ''Who's Aurel?''

''He's the one I mentioned in my letter,'' the Dom replied quietly, and motioned her to kneel. ''While you're here, I'd like you to speak to him—he's posing a bit of a problem.''

''Has he turned against you?''

''Quite the opposite. He believes in our cause . . . perhaps too much. He's taken to preaching on street corners these past few weeks. I don't mind that part of it—I've done it myself, and it's one way of letting people know why we're here—but some of the things he says are disturbing, things like killing a Justice for every Lorngeld that dies at the Tribunal's hands. I've talked to him about it, but he claims I'm being too cautious and that if we want to win the war, we have to expect to kill the enemy. But Aurel . . .'' Mason paused and shook his head. "He's reckless! It's as if he's daring the Tribunal to come and arrest him, so certain that he can fight them off with his newfound power and be a hero.''

"He's never been close to a corbal crystal, has he?'' Athaya asked, aware that the crystal's pain was highly effective at dousing a wizard's sense of omnipotence.

Mason scowled. "No. I wish he had; the experience might cool his fires a bit. But if he gets himself arrested by the Tribunal, then corbal crystals will be the least of his problems.''

"I'll talk to him,'' she assured Mason. "If I can't persuade him to tone it down a bit, then I'll see if a direct order works.'' She offered the Dom a confident grin and made a small gesture to the others gathered around them. "After all, I outrank him in this army.''

Mason took Athaya and Jaren into Kilfarnan the next day, amid gusting winds that tore away the last, stubborn leaves still clinging to the trees. Aurel was prone to preaching in the city's poorer districts at the noon hour—perhaps hoping that the Tribunal's Justices would be attending midday services and not roaming the streets in search of wizards—and so Mason led them along the city wall to a noisy and pungent square crowded with vendors, craftsmen, and an abundance of pickpockets, where they waited for Aurel's arrival.

Mason bought them fresh corn bread for lunch; shortly after they finished it, their quarry appeared in one corner of the square, just outside a stale-smelling brewhouse. "That's him over there,'' Mason whispered, pointing to a freckled young man with brown hair and compelling blue eyes. He was an average-looking sort who might not earn a second glance from passersby, but his butter-colored tunic and deep blue cloak drew the notice of the poorer and more drably clad people around him.

"He needs a few lessons on how to blend into a crowd," Jaren observed under his breath.

"Believe me," Mason replied, "that's the last thing our hero wants to do."

Aurel climbed atop an empty ale barrel and began speaking to anyone who would listen. Athaya noticed that many cityfolk hastened away when they heard the subject of his sermon; others threw apple cores and bits of moldy cheese, shouting at him to be gone and take his heresy elsewhere, but some lingered at the far edge of earshot, listening to him without seeming to.

Athaya moved forward so that she could hear Aurel's words. Unfortunately, they were as disturbing as Mason had forewarned. Even more disturbing was the fact that no one was bothering to question his line of reasoning.

"We must not hide like cowards from those who seek to kill us!" Aurel was shouting, raising his arms high above his head. "And those of you without the power—surely you have known many of the Lorngeld who were killed before they'd even begun to live. Don't you want vengeance? Weren't their lives worth it?"

He earned a murmur of support with that, and Athaya saw many faces grow sad and angry as they remembered those they had lost. Aurel saw this shift in emotion, too, and took advantage of it.

"We must take up arms and fight our oppressors! If you have the power, then don't give in to absolution. Disobey the Church, as Princess Athaya herself has been urging you to do. If you have the power, then learn to wield it and use it as a weapon—use it to insure victory!"

"Victory!" someone shouted in support.

"Quiet, you fool!" another cried, throwing a handful of pebbles at Aurel, which glanced harmlessly off his shoulder. "Go and preach somewhere else. Do you want to bring the Tribunal down on our heads again?" At the mere mention of the word, several more citizens detached themselves from the crowd and hurried away, fearful of being seen in Aurel's company.

"The Tribunal can never defeat us if we band together and insure that for every wizard that dies, a Justice shall die!" Aurel retorted.

Athaya worked her way to the forefront, flanked by Jaren and Mason. "Is this your own version of absolution, then?" she called out, challenging him. "Killing off the Justices for the sin of threatening you?"

Aurel scowled at his audience. "Who said that?"

"I did," Athaya said, raising her hand. "And I also think you have misinterpreted your leader's beliefs. She would have you refuse absolution if you wish, that much is true, but she would not countenance the murder of those who oppose you—not unless it were in your own defense."

Aurel was visibly angered by this rebuke. "And what gives you the right to question me?" He looked down his nose at her like a master annoyed by a recalcitrant servant.

"Oh, she has a right," Jaren remarked, suppressing a smile. "Especially since she's the one you claim to be following."

Aurel had difficulty using his tongue for a moment, and Athaya used the chance to pick up the thread of his speech. "Aurel, I believe you mean well. But I don't think we should go out and attack anyone. Not even the Tribunal."

"Your Highness?" he asked with a blink of surprise, as if he'd heard nothing that she'd said.

Athaya inclined her head slightly, aware that several folk behind her were backing away, loath to stand too close to the dishonored princess of Caithe. "We should do everything we can to avoid killing our enemies. The moment we cross that line, we're no better than they are."

Then Athaya felt a gentle tug on her sleeve, and she turned to see a thick-jowled man in a costly, fur-lined cloak standing just behind her. "My Lady, aren't you being a bit naive?" he asked, pale eyes intensely curious. "You seem to be urging your people to do nothing but sit back and wait to be arrested."

"I'm urging them to concentrate on teaching magic to those who want to learn," she said. She rubbed at her eyes, suddenly conscious of a dull ache behind them. "I don't want to wage a bloody war with the Church. Caithe's priests can claim whatever beliefs they wish; they can preach that the Lorngeld are the Devil's Children if that's what they believe. But we can elect *not* to believe them and persuade others not to believe them either."

"But that accomplishes nothing!" Aurel retorted from his lofty perch.

Athaya shook her head. "It accomplishes everything, Aurel. Maybe not as quickly as you'd like, but it will work in the end."

"It's cowardly," he protested, though the conviction in his voice was waning.

"It's fair," Athaya responded. "Magic makes us different from others, my friend, but it does not make us better or more righteous."

Athaya debated with Aurel for a few more minutes, gaining silent approval from the increasing numbers of people who drifted closer to hear them. Then she paused and became conscious of a low rumbling, somewhere in the distance. Her heart started to race when she identified the sound as hoofbeats, drawing closer. Next to her, a woman recognized the ominous sound as well and let out a piercing shriek as she bolted into a nearby alley.

"News of our presence here has reached the Tribunal, I fear," Mason said, his eyes growing dark. "Come, this has happened before. I know a place we'll be safe."

Athaya turned to the cloaked man beside her, still hanging on to her sleeve. "I'm sorry, sir, but I must go."

"Please, only a moment longer," he pleaded, transferring his grip from her sleeve to her wrist. "One more question—"

The hoofbeats were louder now, rising in menacing crescendo as a half-dozen men galloped into the square, whipping their black destriers. The monks' hair was shorn in severe tonsures, and each wore a black surcoat emblazoned with a blood-red chalice—the chalice of absolution, and the symbol of Saint Adriel. Athaya had never seen terror grip people's hearts so quickly; as if the riders had been born of hell itself, the cityfolk broke and ran, screaming like souls condemned, knowing that merely to be seen in a wizards' presence was a damning offense.

"Let them come!" Aurel shouted over the din of hoofbeats. "I shall defend you!"

Athaya heard a distant snap, then the whistle of an arrow flying inches above her head. It was aimed at Aurel, who smiled in triumph as he extended his hands before him, as if to welcome an embrace. *"Salvum fac sub aspide!"* he cried, conjuring a shielding spell. The arrow struck the shimmering patch of air and instantly crumbled to ashes.

"Stop it, you fool!" Mason shouted at him. He grabbed a handful of blue cloak and jerked Aurel to the ground. "Don't bait them—we need tutors, not martyrs!"

The force of the crowd swept Mason farther away from Athaya and Jaren than he intended, but Athaya's feet were rooted to the ground, unable to follow him. She had never witnessed such random bloodshed as that which the Justices now inflicted. They refused to let mere peasants slow them; the black-clad Justices drove through the crowd, armed with crossbows and swords, brutally riding down anyone unfortunate enough to step into their path, be they young or old, woman or child. Athaya heard the crunch and pop of bones as limbs fell beneath the horses, ironed hooves grinding them into the cobbles. She saw bright fountains of blood as the priests—men of *God*, she thought, aghast—cut a path through living flesh as if it were dead brush, cursing at those who did not move out of their way fast enough.

For a brief moment, Athaya wondered if Aurel had been right . . . if perhaps violence and bloodshed was the only thing that men such as these could understand.

"Athaya, hurry!" Jaren tried to pull her to safety, but the cloaked man beside her only tightened his stubborn grip on her arm. Then Athaya watched his eyes transform before her; before, they had reflected mere curiosity, but now they burned at her as if she were a pestilence to be destroyed, a canker to be cut out of the city's flesh.

Sensing disaster, Jaren raised his hand to strike, but at the same time, the man reached into his fur-lined cloak, opening the garment far enough for Athaya to glimpse the black surcoat and blood-red chalice beneath it. He thrust his hand into the leather pouch at his belt and drew out a jeweled censer, baring it to the sun. Daylight glittered on rubies and emeralds . . . and brought to life the single corbal at its base.

"You won't be leaving Kilfarnan," he said, dangling the censer by its chain before the wizards' eyes, taunting them. "Let your magic save you now."

It was not too large a gem, but its blow was crippling. The dull ache behind Athaya's eyes—only now did she realize the warning sign for what it had been—turned to needles of white-hot fire. As Athaya felt her knees go weak with pain, some remnant part of her brain told her it was all quite logical—the more powerful the wizard, the more a corbal hurts; her power was recently augmented by the seal. No wonder she had sensed the corbal while it was still in the man's purse! But the discovery did nothing to help the situation; Jaren was affected as well, but not to the same paralyzing degree. He was still on his feet, though unsteadily, and managed to throw himself on the Justice's back, trying to dig his fingers into the man's eyes and force him to loosen his grip on Athaya, but the corbal was doing its work well, robbing him of strength.

"We've been watching that one for a while now," the Justice said, oblivious to Jaren's feeble blows. He cocked his head toward the barrel from which Aurel had been speaking. "He's good at gathering up the ripe fruit, leaving us to take it away. But finding you here, Princess, is an added pleasure indeed."

He turned his face away. "Over here, my Lords!" he bellowed to his comrades, still hacking their way through the crowded square, but coming ever closer.

Realizing that he had little strength remaining—and little time—Jaren tried another tactic. Retreating a few steps from the Justice, he then threw his full weight against the back of the man's legs, forcing his knees to buckle and sending the three of them collapsing into an unruly heap. The censer flew out of the man's grasp, and one sharp-eyed thief, seeing the prize, quickly snatched it up.

A thief . . . but also an ally. "Bless you, Princess!" a woman's husky voice came as she darted away, stuffing the censer into her tattered cloak.

The Justice lacked his weapon, but even from his knees, his hold on Athaya held firm. He waved his free arm, guiding his comrades to their quarry; it would be only seconds before they arrived—most likely with more corbals.

There was only one choice left. Reaching out wildly with her right hand, Athaya grabbed Jaren's arm and held fast. "Hang on, Jaren. We're getting the hell out of here." *Assuming the corbal hasn't scrambled my spells*, she added inwardly. But there was no time to worry about that now; either the spell would work or it wouldn't. She would find out soon enough.

"Mason—"

She twisted around, looking frantically for the Dom, only to see that he had been swept nearly twenty yards from her side by the force of the fleeing crowd. He and Aurel were struggling to reach her, but Athaya harshly waved them back. Mason blinked his surprise, and then, realizing what she was planning to do, turned back and vanished under a cloaking spell, taking Aurel to safety with him.

Athaya closed her eyes, conjuring a mental picture of the forest camp and feeling its peace and safety envelop her. She brushed aside the cobwebs in her brain—the last vestiges of the corbal's disruptive power—and then whispered the words. *"Hinc libera me."*

She plummeted into the chaos more desperately than ever

before; if the Justice refused to release her, then he would simply have to come along. The man's added weight slowed their journey, but suddenly, between heartbeats, she sensed a gasp of horror and . . . the weight was gone. Then, mixed into the images and sounds around her, came an unearthly shriek, and the ragged sounds of suffocation, a man gasping for air. Then she saw him drifting away into the turmoil, his flesh dissolving into nothingness, as if his body had been plunged into a tub of acid, burned away by an unseen fire, and torn apart by unseen demons. After the span of another heartbeat, only the bones were left; after another, even they had gone, leaving behind only the memory of the man and the invisible essence of his being. Athaya's stomach turned over at the sight—real or a dream she did not know, but she had just witnessed a vision of a death far more gruesome than any torment the Tribunal could hope to devise.

When her feet once more found solid ground, she twisted around, shaken and fearful. She was home, back in her room at the dormitory, safe in the Forest of Else.

There was no sign of the Justice; not even a shard of bone had passed through the chaos to the camp.

"Where is he?" Jaren asked, likewise searching for their unwelcome companion. "I thought he came with us."

Athaya could not stop her trembling. "He let go of me, Jaren. He panicked and let *go*."

Jaren's eyes widened at the implications. "Then where did he end up? Somewhere between here and Kilfarnan? Or—"

"Dead. I saw it. I saw his body shrivel to ashes right after he let go of my hand. He screamed at first, but then his voice . . . his whole body disappeared. Something was left . . . his soul, maybe. I didn't have time to wonder."

She glanced down, noticing that she was gripping Jaren's hand so hard that it was bloodless. Despite what had just happened, she knew that she would use the spell again, and knew that she would take Jaren with her when she did. But at that moment, as she tried to stop her knees from shaking, Athaya realized that never before had that between-place proved so deadly. This time, as Hedric had once speculated, Athaya felt as if she truly had encroached too far into God's mysterious realm of secrets and discovered dangers heretofore unknown.

CHAPTER 12

※※

"**M**Y LORD MARSHALL—ER, I MEAN, YOUR HIGH-ness?"

"Either one is fine, Josef," Nicolas replied offhandedly. "I answer to both." He pushed himself away from his writing desk and smiled up at the gaunt wheatstalk of a man who had just stepped into the study—Josef, the island's chancellor. "What is it?"

"Someone is here to see you," he said, anxiously cracking his knuckles as if this was not at all good news. "A messenger."

Nicolas blinked his surprise. He'd met only a handful of people since his arrival in Sare three days ago and received the impression that none of the uniformly taciturn folk was much interested in pursuing the acquaintance. "Who sent him?"

"He . . . did not say, m'lord," Josef replied, despite a knowing cast to his eyes. "Shall I send him in?"

Nicolas sank back in his chair and put his feet up on the edge of a timeworn desk. "Certainly. I haven't anything else to do— you've handled everything so well since DeBracy died that I have precious few problems to attend to."

Nicolas sighed as his chancellor withdrew, wishing that Ranulf was at hand to ease the loneliness of his first uneasy days as lord marshall. But before the two of them began centering their efforts on learning what they could about the mysterious Sage, Ranulf had departed for a brief visit to his old village—he'd mumbled something about a woman he once knew, but refused to offer any further detail—and would not be back until the end of the week. And without the mercenary's ribald good humor, it was proving difficult for Nicolas to keep his spirits up in the crumbling and dismal manor that was now his home; even Athaya's derelict monastery was more welcoming! His bed-chambers were shockingly small, less than half the size of his apartments at Delfar Castle, and the manor itself—Nicolas hesitated to call it a castle—was miserable and drafty and hopelessly dour, as if it still mourned the death of the last lord marshall.

Whenever he needed to cheer himself, however, he simply called to mind the look of astonishment that had graced Durek's face when he had humbly requested the Sarian marshalcy. The king's astonishment was quickly supplanted by suspicion, of course, but a few well-timed teardrops and sobs of agony had convinced him that Nicolas wanted nothing more than to leave Caithe behind him forever, wishing to be a good prince, but no longer able to cope with being caught between his older brother and his outlawed sister. Durek wrote the commission and sent him packing almost overnight, unable to disguise his relief at having one less problem to deal with.

As planned, Ranulf joined his entourage at the port of Eriston, much to the consternation of the prince's honor guard, who felt that such a rough-spoken barbarian was a most unsuitable traveling companion. They crossed the narrow channel in late November, docking on the bleak expanse of Sare's eastern shore—bare cliffs of black slate dotted by a few scraggly pines and bounded in the north by mist-shrouded highlands. It was not a large island—the size of a Caithan shire, perhaps—and if the tiny port was any indication, lightly inhabited. To a man, the Sarians were wholly unimpressed by his arrival, and judging from the few he had spoken to, Nicolas found his new subjects a reclusive people, forgotten by history and seemingly glad of it.

The creak of a door hinge broke Nicolas out of his reverie, and he turned to see Josef usher in a swarthy young man of average height and above-average self-assurance. Like most of the Sarians Nicolas had encountered thus far, the messenger was dressed for warmth instead of style. He wore a heavy sheepskin coat over a tunic of plain brown wool, its only adornment being a chain of pounded bronze links. But his manner lent him an air of authority that his garb did not, and he strode into Nicolas' presence as an equal—if not a superior.

"Thank you, Josef," Nicolas said, and caught the chancellor scowling uncertainly at the messenger as he departed. Almost, Nicolas thought, as if he knew and feared him.

"I am surprised to see you, sir," Nicolas began cheerfully, as he offered his guest a chair near the fire. "I've only been on Sare a few days—too early for messages from the mainland and not long enough for the islanders to start extending dinner invitations." He picked up a flagon from a nearby sideboard. "Will you have some mulled wine? Or perhaps some whiskey?" he added, pointing to another, smaller flagon. "I'm told that's what most folk prefer here."

The man shook his head, his eyes reflecting a patronizing touch of amusement at Nicolas' breeziness. "Nothing, thank you."

"Please don't mind if I do—the calendar may claim that the winter solstice is a month off, but my bones tell me that winter is most decidedly here." Nicolas poured himself a small cup of the locally brewed whiskey and settled down on a cushioned bench across from the stranger. "You've brought me a message?"

"Aye, my Lord. From his Grace, the Sage of Sare."

Nicolas coughed up a mouthful of the whiskey. The Sage! God, did the man already know why he was here?

Across from him, the messenger's amusement deepened. "You have heard of him?"

"Only tales," Nicolas said quickly, not wishing to reveal how he came by that knowledge. "From the servants."

"His Grace, Brandegarth of Crewe, the honorable Sage of Sare, has sent you a greeting." The man rose, as if etiquette demanded that he deliver his message standing up. "His Grace welcomes you to his island—"

"*His* island?" Nicolas exclaimed, with all the indignation that a lord marshall would have been expected to produce. "Has no one informed your master that Sare is a protectorate of the Caithan Crown?"

"Sare does not require Caithe's protection," he said, chuckling his indulgence at what he clearly regarded an absurd observation. "But to continue, the Sage extends his welcome and says that he will not interfere in your duties here as long as you accept his terms. One," he went on quickly, before Nicolas could ob-

ject, "that the Lorngeld of Sare are his domain and that just as
priests answer to God above their king, so do the wizards of this
island answer to the Sage above you." He paused, nodding his
pleasure when Nicolas offered no retort. "Second, no Lorngeld
on this island shall be forced to adhere to your custom of absolution. The priests may preach whatever doctrine they like, but
all of them know that to enforce their will means . . ." The
messenger shrugged negligently. "Well, it would be foolish for
them to try."

Nicolas gulped down the last of his whiskey. "Is there anything else?" he said, feigning defiance.

"Only that to disobey the Sage's wishes would produce a
result that would not be at all pleasant for you."

"Cutting through all the diplomatic claptrap, if I don't play
by his rules, he kills me. Is that it?"

Smoothly, the messenger reclaimed his chair. "That is the
essence of it, my Lord. The Sage does not take disobedience
lightly and has an army of wizards who would willingly vent his
displeasure upon you."

"I see." And just then, Nicolas realized that every lord marshall who had ever come to this island had been greeted with
this very message. Those who obeyed lived out their lives in
quiet obscurity, but those who defied the Sage's authority and
attempted to enforce the absolution laws suddenly vanished,
never to be seen again.

"And I suppose I'm to order all of my men to dispose of any
corbal crystals they've brought to the island," Nicolas went on,
sustaining his mock outrage. Although he had forbidden the
members of his household to display the gem—ostensibly because they were a painful reminder of Athaya, but actually to
protect Ranulf—he knew many of his entourage carried them.
And on Sare, waving corbals about would be like swatting at a
hornet's nest, openly risking the vengeful sting of the Sage and
his followers.

At the mention of the crystals, the messenger's amusement
faded to something darker. "Bits of colored rock hold no interest for the Sage," he said, cool but menacing. "But it would be
respectful of you not to carry them in his presence, or the presence of his people."

"His people . . . like yourself?"

The man nodded imperceptibly. "Be assured, mere gemstones will not deter him in the unlikely event that he wishes to

come see you. He does not involve himself overmuch in the dealings of mainlanders.''

"Crewe, you said," Nicolas said softly. "Brandegarth of Crewe."

"Yes, my Lord."

"I shall remember the name."

The messenger smiled grimly. "See that you do." And with that, he rose and strode out of the chamber without asking for leave.

And why should he? Nicolas mused, as he poured another cup of whiskey. The man knew who his master was, and it certainly was *not* the prince of Caithe.

Josef returned in a matter of moments, rushing frantically into the chamber as if expecting to find Nicolas lying in a pool of his own blood. "Is everything all right, my Lord?"

Nicolas turned away from the window, where he had been pondering the messenger's words as he gazed at the icy rain crusting the countryside. Josef had clearly suspected the messenger's purpose—he had been chancellor to the last two lord marshalls and no doubt knew of the Sage's "terms."

"I'm fine, Josef. And I've been thinking . . . as soon as I'm settled here, I'd like to take a tour around my new home. See as much of the island as I can before snow becomes a nuisance. Plan a route for me . . . and make sure it starts with a stop in Crewe." He saw the chancellor's face go white. He added, "I know a woman from there," he explained, using his acquaintance with Drianna as an excuse. "I'd like to find her family and tell them how she's faring on the mainland."

Josef paused, waiting for Nicolas to say more—or at least admit to the blatant falsehood. When he did not, the chancellor grudgingly murmured his agreement and departed.

Once again alone, Nicolas walked to the fireplace and stared at the dancing flames. Since leaving Caithe, he and Ranulf had been trying to devise a logical way to approach the Sage; never did he expect that the Sage would come looking for him first.

"All right, Brandegarth of Crewe," he said aloud to the flames. "You've made the first move. Now I think it's time to deliver a message of my own."

Athaya picked up another ball of dried meat and berry paste, worked in some melted suet, then cupped it in her hands like a witchlight. *"Esca haec pervivax sit,"* she whispered, laying on a spell of preservation. The pemmican would stay fresh for months without magical aid, but Tonia, seated beside her at the kitchen's pockmarked worktable, insisted that it cost them nothing to add a bit of extra protection. Now that Gilda had fully recovered from her son's birth and could spend more time tutoring new wizards, Tonia had taken it upon herself to supervise the storage of the camp's precious food supplies and insure that they would not be caught short in midwinter. The storehouse might be full now, she often told those who were growing complacent, but the balmy breezes of April were a long way off.

And today, Athaya reflected, spring seemed further away than ever. Although the kitchen was cozy, warmed by magically heated stones and fragrant with simmering pottage, it was wickedly cold outside and had been so for a fortnight. And instead of the graceful blankets of snow which make winter bearable, the forest camp was steadily pelted by hail and varnished daily with fresh sheets of ice. The aching bruise on Athaya's hip was a constant reminder that even crossing the short distance between the dormitory and the kitchen had become treacherous.

Athaya set her pasty creation with the others heaped on the kitchen table, where they would later be wrapped and stored in dry pits behind the kitchens. "I hope we never get desperate enough to actually need these," she remarked, gazing at the unappetizing collection of spheres. "They look horrible."

She expected at least a chuckle of agreement, but Tonia frowned and said nothing, working another mass of paste and suet into an apple-sized ball.

"We will have enough food to get through the winter, won't we?" Athaya asked, unsettled by her companion's silence.

Tonia didn't answer at first, instead staring bleakly at the single ball of pemmican in her hand as if trying to multiply it into hundreds by sheer force of will. "Not if folk keep arriving at this rate," she replied.

Silently, Athaya wiped the suet from her hands with a rag. It should have been good news; her first few months in Caithe had been a constant struggle to persuade a handful of Lorngeld to come to the camp and be trained, and it seemed inconceivable that having too *many* people would ever pose a problem. The abandoned monastery now sheltered nearly a hundred wizards and more were arriving every day, often with their families in tow. And most of them, fleeing the Tribunal's wrath, arrived with nothing more than the clothes on their backs—no food, no money, and no way of obtaining either. Driven from their homes without any way of surviving the winter, many came to Athaya angry and desperate, demanding that she care for them since she was the ultimate cause of their misery. She did so willingly— as a Trelane, it was her duty to defend and succor her people as best she could—but as their numbers grew, she watched her once-impressive treasure dwindle dangerously, the precious coins going to buy grain and blankets and medicines. What would happen once it was gone?

She didn't like to brood on that and was grateful that she had found little enough time to do so over the past month. She and Jaren had only just returned from the southeast shires of Caithe, seeking out three of the six men that Lord Gessinger had hinted might be willing to support her cause. Thus far, her impassioned pleas had accomplished nothing; to a man, every lord she spoke to was fearful of attracting the Tribunal's attention and had asked her, with varying degrees of rudeness, to leave his home with all due expediency. But there were three more lords remaining on Mosel's list, and she planned to speak to them all before the year's end. Perhaps one of them would grant her money, or better yet, allow a school to operate in his shire and offer to provide food and shelter to the Lorngeld who sought sanctuary there.

"We put aside as much as we could," Tonia went on, gazing at the now-completed heap of pemmican balls. "Onions, seeds, nuts, apples, berries . . . and there may be enough fish and dry beans to sustain us, but it's near impossible to buy grain in the city for ale—folks are hoarding what they can get ahold of after such a bad harvest—and the deer in this forest aren't going to have much meat on them come the new year."

"But we still have some of Adam's money left; I only gave Mason half of it. We may yet come across another wealthy benefactor." Athaya rested her elbows on the table. "People won't like it if we have to start rationing."

Tonia dismissed the observation with a snort. "They'll like it even less if we run out of food in January and they end up starving to death."

Athaya nodded grimly. Having spent most of her life at court, she had never known what it was like to go hungry in the winter. The prospect did not appeal to her.

Then, from beyond the doorway, Athaya heard a pair of strident voices, increasing in pitch as they drew closer. Her muscles tensed instinctively; one of them belonged to Sutter. He burst into the kitchen a moment later, red faced and stomping his feet against the cold. Gilda was close on his heels, shaking her finger like a nagging wife.

"I don't care if you *do* find it demeaning, my Lord," she was scolding, laying a heavy dose of derision on the last two words, "you're going to help dig the storage pits whether you like it or not. Now get back out there—"

Sutter spun around in a swirl of fur-lined wool, every inch the wrathful lord. "And freeze to death? God's blood, it's bad enough in my room, much less out in the open!"

"At least you *have* a room in the dormitory," Tonia remarked softly, without looking up. "You're not living outdoors in a canvas tent or a hovel of pine boughs and straw like some of the others."

Sutter's nostrils flared. "At least they have some privacy! I haven't had to share a room since I left the nursery! And that churl Davis insists on having his foul pig stay in our room at night, so the place is even more crowded than it has to be." He sniffed imperiously. "I'm no peasant used to bedding down with animals at night."

Calling on her own reserves of imperiousness, Athaya rose slowly to her feet. Sutter's attitude had never been good, but it had worsened as rapidly as the weather, and she was just as tired of it. "Rant and rave all you like," she said through gritted teeth, "it won't do you a whit of good. The dormitory is already housing three times as many people as it was built to, and that means everyone has to share."

Sutter glared at her, one lip protruding.

"And don't tell me that you deserve better simply because you're a baron's son," she went on, knowing that it would be his next argument. "If you expect *me* to be impressed by that, you're sadly mistaken." This wasn't the first time Sutter had tried to pull rank on the others to gain better food and accommodations, and although she hated to do so, Athaya had often been forced to use the same tactic in order to put him in his place.

"And if you aren't going to do your share of the kitchen work," she said in conclusion, "then you aren't going to do your share of the eating. Is that clear? Now go and dig that pit the way Gilda told you to."

Sutter was stubborn, but not stupid; he knew a royal command when he heard one. His mouth pinched itself into a tight mass of muscle, but the defiance had been effectively wrung out of him. "We should be fighting the Tribunal, not digging pits in the woods," he muttered, then made an impertinent huffing noise and stalked away.

Athaya curled her fingers into fists and resisted the impulse to cudgel some sense into him, not only because of his refusal to abandon the notion of forming an army of wizards to battle their enemies—he had for a while, but news of Aurel's sermon in Kilfarnan had ignited the fire again—but because of his utter lack of willingness to share in the camp chores. Was it so unreasonable to be expected to prepare one's own food? Was it so unreasonable to be asked to share precious living space? The camp's rapidly increasing numbers, combined with the bad weather, meant that every unused corner of the monastery compound had been converted into someone's living quarters. Sutter was not alone in his perceived misery, but no one at the camp had to endure it for more than a few months. Once trained, the wizards would move on.

And in Sutter's case, Athaya would be glad to see him gone.

"He's the worst of the lot," Gilda observed, echoing Athaya's own thoughts. Her cheeks were flushed, but Athaya didn't know if it was from anger or the cold. "He's hard to teach and harder still to like."

"How's his spell-work?" Tonia asked.

"Not very good. He's lazy and only practices his spells when he thinks one of us 'commoners' is showing him up. Ask him to put a preservation spell on something and you can be sure it will rot within the week. No, he only cares about battle-magic. I told him we'd get to that once he mastered the basics, but he just won't listen. And he's got to work harder on his wards," she said worriedly. "The last time it was his turn to ward the camp for the night, he reversed everything and set a spell of attraction by mistake. Thank God the bishop didn't get it into his head to search the forest that night, though after all his failures over the summer, I'd guess he's given up on trying to flush us out of here."

Athaya was just about to warn against growing complacent toward Bishop Lukin's persistence when she heard the brittle crunch of footsteps on ice-crusted snow. Jaren appeared a moment later, snugly wrapped in a cowled cloak and scarf. "Athaya, could you come to the chapel?" he said, tossing back his hood. His face bore a peculiar expression—curiosity mixed with a hint of awe. "Tonia, you might want to come along, too. A new student has just arrived . . ."

With new wizards arriving every day, Jaren had obviously found something unusual about this one to bring it to their notice. Athaya slid her hands into a pair of deerskin gloves and followed him, with Tonia close behind.

Athaya was surprised to find two newcomers inside the chapel, not just one. Nearest the door was a fair-haired woman sipping at a mug of hot cider, and beside her, a man ill-dressed for the weather, shivering underneath a heavy blanket. Athaya noticed that he held his cup of cider with only his right hand; his left was thickly wrapped in linens.

She did not recognize the man, but the woman she knew instantly. "Emma!" Athaya exclaimed. "From Pipewell—"

"Your Highness," the woman murmured, scrambling to her feet to offer a brief curtsy.

Athaya turned excitedly to Tonia and Jaren, each of them well aware what Emma's presence meant, but after exchanging knowing glances, they muffled their reactions so neither of the newcomers would think something was amiss, or that Athaya's surprise was due to anything other than the coincidence of seeing Emma again.

"The moment I knew what I was, I decided to come and find you," Emma explained, her voice soothing as a bard's. "Ethan told me that you helped to mend my arm . . . I'm afraid I don't remember much about it."

Glad as Athaya was to see her, however, one question still nagged at the back of her mind. "How did you find us?" she asked, knowing that the guiding runes leading to the camp were all but invisible to wizards still early in their *mekahn*.

"I brought her through," the shivering man replied, also rising to his feet. He looked at Athaya with respect, and she felt as if she should know him. Jaren and Tonia clearly did, and Tonia was quick to greet him with an embrace. "Girard, I'm so glad you're back."

Athaya tossed a silent inquiry to Jaren.

"Girard was with us over the summer," he explained. "He left in August, just before Tonia and I left for Saint Gillian's."

"I stopped at the sheepfold first," Girard said, "but I can see you've had to abandon it."

Tonia nodded her regret. "Aye, it's too risky there now. Too bad, after all that work we did on the new roof."

With the advent of the Tribunal a month ago, Bishop Lukin had assigned a small band of men to patrol the sheepfold regularly, knowing it to be a haven for the Lorngeld. And losing the sheepfold made it far more difficult for those who needed help to find those who were offering it. Now, folk had little choice but to wander into the forest and hope to be found by one of Athaya's wizards before they died of the cold. Thus, Athaya and the others made a habit of regularly scrying the forest's edge and going out to fetch anyone who seemed to be looking for them. It wasn't an ideal solution to the problem, but they could think of no way to let people know where they could be found without letting the Tribunal know as well.

"What changed your mind, Girard?" Jaren asked. "Frankly, I didn't think we'd see you again."

"This changed my mind." Carefully, he peeled off the soiled linens swaddling his left hand.

Bile surged into Athaya's throat, but she did not turn her eyes away. Girard's hand was little more than a bloody stump of flesh. Every finger had been severed—and recently. The five stumps still flared an angry red, and two were white with infection.

Athaya exhaled slowly. "I don't think we need to ask who did that to you."

"Someone from my village suspected where I'd gone over the summer and told the shire's new Justice—they've been told to question people who vanish for a few months and then return. Damn that Roderick!" he burst out. "We've never been friends, but I never dreamed he hated me enough to turn me in!"

Biting his lip, Girard began to rewrap his hand. "A man came to my workshop one afternoon about two weeks ago, and before I knew what was happening, he pulled out a dagger with a corbal crystal in its hilt. Then two others came in, and they all took me to a room beneath the village church."

Athaya shivered, but knew that this time its source was something far more heartless than the winter cold.

"The Justices already knew I was a wizard—the corbal had already found me guilty of that. But instead of simply absolving me, they kept asking me how to get to your camp; kept wanting to know why the bishop's men failed to find it all summer. And each day I wouldn't answer, they'd cut a finger from my hand. God, I never thought it would hurt so much! The day they were going to start on my right hand, I finally told them that only wizards could find the camp, and then they tried to make me promise to lead them here."

"Themselves and an army of others, I'll wager," Tonia remarked.

Girard nodded. "They also wanted me to name everyone I'd met here. But I just couldn't betray any of you." He looked at Athaya imploringly. "Your people saved my life, and all the Tribunal wanted to do was take it from me. As if they'd really have let me live even if I led them here," he said with unbridled scorn. "I'm not that stupid."

"But how did you get away?" Athaya asked.

"I found out that I have friends as well as enemies in the village," he replied with a grateful smile, "and one of them managed to free me from my cell. I met Emma on the road a few days later—picked up the vibrations from a spell she'd set off by accident. She almost ran off—thought I was a spy for the Tribunal—but I conjured a witchlight for her, and we traveled together after that. Damn, but I wish I'd never deserted you in the first place," he added with a touch of shame. "Then I never would have been arrested."

"You would have left the camp one day," Athaya pointed out, "and your village wouldn't have been any safer then."

Girard nodded sadly. "I suppose not. And now I can never go back again. So I'm here, if you'll have me. To do whatever I can." He glanced down at his ruined hand. "I'll not be going back to carpentry."

"We're always short on tutors," Tonia said. "Gilda had hoped you'd be willing to do that one day."

Girard shook his head and laughed dryly. "I barely knew my own spells when I left . . . I don't know how good of a tutor I'd be."

"You'd be surprised how low our standards are these days, Girard," Tonia replied, arching her brows. "We're desperate for help—there's over a hundred wizards here now."

He let out a low whistle, impressed by their reversal of fortune.

"That reminds me," Jaren said, turning to Emma, "whatever happened to Alec, the reeve's son? I talked to him on the same day you broke your arm."

Emma lowered her eyes. "He's dead. He was afraid to be absolved, but even more afraid to defy the village priest and spend eternity in hell. I don't believe that, though," she added hastily. "How can I burn in hell for something that I was born with?"

"I wish more people saw it that way," Athaya said with a smile. "But if we all do our jobs well, they will." As she spoke, a gust of icy wind swept into the chapel; Girard and Emma, already chilled from travel, began to shudder uncontrollably.

"All right, you two," Tonia said, motioning them toward the door, "into the kitchen with you. I've got some pottage simmering, and you both look in dire need of it."

Their eyes glowed with gratitude for the offer, and Tonia led Girard and Emma, leaving Athaya and Jaren alone in the chapel.

"So," Jaren began, reclining against one of the stone pews, "it looks as if this 'seed' of magic is no longer just a theory. Emma is proof."

"Ironic, isn't it?" Athaya observed. "I get proof of my talent only after I've decided not to use it. But we don't have all the answers yet—I saw her seed only a few months before she arrived—we have no idea how long it's been there. Maybe a seed is only visible right before the *mekahn*. Or maybe I would have been able to detect her power years ago . . . or even from her birth. At this point, I could look at someone and not see a seed, but that wouldn't necessarily mean they don't have one, only that it hasn't developed yet."

"True," he conceded, "but Emma's arrival still confirms one thing: You can tell who's a wizard and who's not before the *mekahn*. And that's certainly never been done before."

Just then, they heard a scuffle and a strangled gasp, and Drianna lurched forward into the chapel, clinging to the doorjamb to keep from falling. "I'm not often so clumsy," she explained, looking up sheepishly, "but there's a big patch o' ice just outside the door." She gestured in the general direction of the kitchen. "I see we've got ourselves a new wizard. Do ye want me to scout about the camp for a place she can sleep until she builds a lodge of her own?"

"That's a fine idea," Athaya said. "And find out if anyone can spare an extra cloak or blanket. It didn't look as if Emma brought much with her."

Drianna bobbed a curtsy and left them, moving much more slowly over the ice coating the chapel entrance.

Once she was gone, Athaya chuckled softly to herself. "I should have thought to arrange a bed for Emma before," she said, tossing Jaren a crooked grin. "After all, we had a fairly good idea she was coming."

Late that night, Athaya sat on the edge of her bed etching runes into a flat piece of stone with the tip of a knife. It was tricky work; her room was chilly despite a pair of braziers, and her hand trembled at times, turning the runes into a series of childlike squiggles. Drianna sat behind her, gently working a comb through masses of her windblown hair.

"So you call it a ward key, do ye?"

"Yes. This one's not tuned to the camp yet, but I've a few that are. Once someone leaves us, they can use this to contact us without being turned aside by the wards. Dom DePere uses them to keep in touch with some of his former students, and I thought it would be a good idea to make some myself."

"Aye, and a fine idea it is. But speaking o' that," Drianna began, her idle chatter turning purposeful, "I've been thinking, your Highness . . . about Girard. I saw what they did to his hand—awful, of course—and knew it could have just as well been my brother. I think Connor and I should go off and try to find him and make sure he's safe. 'Sides, Connor hasn't found any work in Kaiburn and our money's running low. But we can make our own way, don't you worry—you need the food and money you have for the others."

Athaya found Drianna's sudden concern for her brother rather odd—the Tribunal had been at their bloody work over a month now—but perhaps the reality of Girard's injury had changed her mind as nothing else could. "I asked about your brother in Kilfarnan, but Mason couldn't place him. But I'm sure he got there safely," she added, so as not to alarm Drianna unnecessarily. "I didn't have his name and I only guessed what he looked like; it wasn't much for Mason to go on."

"Oh, we don't look at all alike. Different fathers, you know," she said, and Athaya didn't have to turn around to see the arch in Drianna's brow. "And his name's Devyn. Silly of me never to have mentioned it."

The gentle pull of Drianna's comb sent Athaya's thoughts to shifting, and instead of brooding over Girard's harrowing encounter with the Tribunal or the fate of Drianna's brother, she began to wonder whether her own brother had arrived safely in Sare. Cecile had sent word through Sir Jarvis that Nicolas had gotten the post, and Athaya estimated that he would have arrived

there sometime this past week. Of everyone at the camp, however, only Athaya, Jaren, and Tonia knew where Nicolas had
gone, or that Ranulf was with him. It would put both of them at
risk if the news trickled back to Delfarham that Nicolas had gone
to Sare on Athaya's behalf, and so Athaya merely told the others
that Ranulf had gone off to do some recruiting for them and that
Nicolas had returned to Delfarham and that they had traveled
together part of the way.

"Drianna, you're from Sare . . ." she began with seeming
idleness. "What can you tell me about the Sage?"

The comb stopped abruptly in midstroke, then cautiously resumed. "You've heard of him, then?"

"A bit, when I was in Reyka. No one knows very much about
him, though. He's quite a mystery."

"Aye, though not being a wizard myself it's doubtful I'll ever
know much about him. Keeps to himself, he does, he and his
people. But he's said to be a fearsome powerful magician. What
they call an adept—like yourself. Folk frighten their children
with tales of the Sage to make them behave; they say he'll turn
them into pigs."

Athaya smiled. If such a spell existed, she could think of any
number of people on whom she'd gladly cast it other than an ill-
behaved child. Durek perhaps . . . or Bishop Lukin, or better
yet, the whole order of Saint Adriel. She'd create an army of
pigs, able to do nothing worse than root for acorns at the forest's
edge.

"I've heard that his people believe their magic sets them above
everyone else . . . is that true?"

"They probably wouldn't live apart from everyone else in the
island if it weren't so. But I can't right say. I don't have much
to do with wizards—except yours, that is."

Now that Athaya's hair was properly combed, Drianna went
about braiding it for the night. "If I thought I could trust him,"
Athaya began, "I'd be tempted to ask if he'd send me some
wizards to help train the Lorngeld here. People come to us almost every day now, but the number of tutors is growing too
slowly to handle them all. But I won't have them being taught
that having magic means they're better than everybody else or
that it gives them the right to run other people's lives—that goes
against everything I learned from Master Hedric."

"Oh, all that might be just tales, you know. Can't say what
he might not help a princess in need. And a pretty one at that,"

she added, threading a purple ribbon into Athaya's braid. "But I've a question—don't I always, though!—if you have a power that others don't, and you're not supposed to use it to rise up in the world, then what's the magic for?"

Athaya exhaled a roll of laughter. "Sometimes I wonder about that myself. But Master Hedric once told me that it's for each wizard to discover the meaning magic has in his own life." She set aside her ward key and rubbed the itch from bloodshot eyes, exhausted by the events of the day. "Sometimes I think *my* magic's only purpose is to make me utterly wretched."

"Don't talk like that," Jaren chided her as he stepped into the room. "You're our fearless leader."

"I'm not fearless. I'm scared to death most of the time." Athaya turned and gave him a kindly glare. "Have you been eavesdropping long?"

"Not really. I heard you saying something about Sare as I came up the steps."

Athaya let out a sigh. "A fine source of trained magicians, if only I could use them."

"She doesn't want them telling people that their magic makes them better than everybody else," Drianna supplied, as she tied Athaya's hair ribbons into a bow.

Jaren leaned against the doorjamb. "You couldn't really stop them, though, could you?" he reflected, lapsing into thought like a scholar musing upon a new theory. "You told Aurel that the Church is free to espouse absolution, and we're just trying to persuade people not to believe them. Logically, then, why couldn't the Sage try to persuade people that their magic means more than what we tell them it does?"

Athaya didn't care for that line of reasoning; it had an unsettling amount of truth to it. "Just whose side are you on?"

"I'm only making a point."

"That'll be all for tonight, Drianna," Athaya said archly as she rose to her feet. "Jaren and I are going to have an argument now."

Jaren quickly raised his hands in surrender. "No, we're not," he replied. "I'm too tired, and by the look of those circles under your eyes, you are, too."

Drianna smiled knowingly. "If she wants to argue, then you'll argue . . . I know what it is to be married. Oh, but afore I go," she said, turning back to Athaya, "could I take one o' those keys you were making? I might forget to ask later and if I do find Devyn, won't it be fun if he can call you with that little piece of rock instead of coming all the way here to meet ye?''

"I don't see why not." Athaya plucked a tuned key from the windowsill and handed it to Drianna, then bade her good night.

"I think our next trip will have to be our last for a while," Jaren told her, as he began to strip off his layers of winter wool. "No one's said so directly, but some of the students are starting to resent all our absences—they think we're sneaking off to get better meals from our noble friends than they get here.''

Athaya's face tightened into a scowl; it wasn't hard to guess which one of her followers had started *that* rumor. "Sutter is a spoiled child," she retorted.

"And not a very observant one, either. Anyone can see that you're not eating well—you're almost as thin as you were when I found you at Saint Gillian's. You're pushing yourself too hard," Jaren said, growing serious. "You're not getting enough food or sleep and you're working too much magic. All these translocations—''

"Now you're starting to sound like Tonia," she teased, slipping out of her gown and under the coverlets quickly enough to avoid being chilled by the crisp air. "I still have more strength than I had before the seal—it's some compensation for all the hell I went through. Besides, we need to visit the last three men on Mosel's list, plus say our piece in their shires' villages, and I'm certainly not traveling by foot in this weather unless I have to. Once that's done, we can stay here and rest for a while. Now hurry and come to bed," she said, with a glint in her eye that proved she was not so tired as she looked, "I need something other than blankets to keep me warm.''

But as Jaren lay down beside her and wrapped her in the warmth of his embrace, Athaya knew there would be no real rest for a great long time—not while the Tribunal scoured the land for wizards and all who aided them.

CHAPTER 13

✳✳

NICOLAS GAZED UP AT THE IMPOSING LIMESTONE FOR-
tress, its crenellated towers rising majestically into a
leaden sky that threatened yet more snow. His face bore
an expression akin to awe. "God's breath, it makes the lord
marshall's manor look like a dovecote."

Beside him, Ranulf made an indelicate snorting noise. "And
why not?" he grumbled, glaring at the whitewashed citadel.
"The Sage thinks he's the next best thing to God Himself. He's
probably got the damned front gates studded with pearls."

A bitter December wind bit through their cloaks as they urged
their horses toward the castle's twin-towered gatehouse. Although Nicolas had chosen to begin his island tour with the town
of Crewe, only a half day's journey north of his manor, he fully
intended for his first stop to be his last. Though Sare was by no
means large, Nicolas had little love for winter travel; it would
be a simple thing to complain to Josef of his princely discomforts
and plan to complete his island tour when the weather improved.
Once he left Crewe, the tour's true purpose would be fulfilled.

As they drew within fifty yards of the gatehouse, Ranulf reined
his horse to a halt. "Be careful from here on out," he advised,
his words muffled by a heavy woolen scarf dusted with snow.
"These wizards aren't as scrupulous as the ones you're used to,
and I'll wager the Sage is the worst of the lot."

Nicolas nodded from somewhere underneath a heavy cowl.

"Even the name sounds imposing. Brandegarth," he said, testing the name on his tongue like an unfamiliar wine. "Brandegarth of Crewe."

He might have thought it a Sarian oath judging from his companion's reaction. *"What?"* Ranulf said sharply, jerking down the scarf covering his face. He forced his voice low so as not to draw unwanted attention from the gatehouse guards. "Confound it, Nicolas, why didn't you tell me that before?"

A tremor of foreboding rippled through Nicolas' limbs. "You've been gone all week, remember? And I don't have the luxury of a vision sphere for sending private messages. I must have simply forgotten to mention it. Why?" he asked, unsettled by Ranulf's expression. "Is it important?"

Ranulf's eyes were leaden as the sky. "I knew a man by that name once," he began, in a voice as hushed as faraway thunder. "We trained for the army together." He shifted in his saddle, bushy red brows deeply furrowed. "If this is the same man, my friend, then not only is he a damned powerful wizard, but a ruthless, power-hungry son of a bitch on top of it."

Suddenly, Nicolas felt overly warm beneath his fur-lined cloak. "All of Athaya's spells and none of her scruples, is that it?"

"Pretty much sums it up, though it's hard to compare their actual spells; no two adepts are going to have an identical set. But I'd watch your back if you don't want a knife to end up in it," Ranulf cautioned him. "The man I knew wouldn't think twice about murdering a prince."

With that revelation, Nicolas realized that he had been far more content knowing nothing at all about the Sage than knowing this fragment of unpleasant information and he looked forward to his visit a great deal less than he had only moments before. Unfortunately, the guards at the gatehouse had taken notice of the pause in their approach and were eyeing them curiously.

"I'll be safe enough," Nicolas said, trying to lift his spirits as he urged his mottled gray gelding ahead. "After all, I'm only here as the lord marshall's messenger, remember?"

Ranulf glowered at him, openly displeased with Nicolas' choice of ruse. "You'd better be a damned good actor, then. If the Sage gets it into his head to truth-test you, he'll find out who you really are soon enough. And then you'll have to explain why you lied to him." The curl of Ranulf's lip indicated that the Sage was not likely to forgive such a deception. "If he gives you the chance to explain at all."

Nicolas shook off his warnings with a shrug; this was no time to be pessimistic. "Ranulf, my friend, you're addressing the man who made Durek believe that I yearned to come to this island to escape Athaya's dangerous influence. When it comes to deceiving ruthless sons of bitches," he concluded with a grin, "I've had plenty of practice."

Ranulf longed to temper his confidence with more words of doom, but there was no time for anything but a scowl; the gatehouse was before them, and a somber-faced man with an ice-crusted beard stepped out to block their path. He was clad in the colors of night, the silver-edged black livery a perfect complement to the barren winter landscape. He said nothing at first, but merely held out a flat, blue stone engraved with strange symbols. Ranulf stripped off one glove and touched his fingertip to it, and within moments, the symbols on the stone began to glow bright red. Nodding, the guardsman offered the stone to Nicolas, but when he put his own finger to the slice of agate, it remained blue. The guardsman made a haughty sniffing sound and tucked the stone back into his glove.

"You have business with his Grace?" he said to Ranulf, ignoring Nicolas as if he were nothing more than a clod of dirt in the road.

"We come from the lord marshall with a message for the Sage," Nicolas said pointedly, drawing the man's eyes lazily back to him. "And a gift."

The guardsmen considered that for a moment, but when he spoke, he again addressed his question to Ranulf. "Is his Grace expecting you?"

Nicolas balked. The Sage was a wizard of repute and might very well have foreseen his arrival. "I don't think so," he said truthfully. "But would you kindly address your questions to me? I am the lord marshall's envoy, and this is my escort."

The guardsman's lips curled back into a grimace. "A wizard? Escorting one of the lord marshall's *couriers*?" His eyes swept across the mercenary with markedly less respect, as if Ranulf were a wealthy lord who had just announced his intention to take up tanning. Then, Nicolas realized the significance of the blue stone; he had been tested for magic and found lacking and therefore unworthy. Ranulf, because of his gift, was assumed to be the higher-ranking of the pair.

And on Sare, Nicolas reminded himself, that was a very safe assumption.

A second guardsman led them across the snowy courtyard and into a spacious and well-heated antechamber. He asked Ranulf to wait by the fire while Nicolas attended to his errand, and as he called for a servant to see to Ranulf's comfort, Ranulf whispered rapidly into Nicolas' ear. "I'll stay alert for trouble, but don't expect me to come to your rescue unless I have to. If the Sage is the same Brandegarth I knew, then I'll be damned if I want him recognizing me. He might not—it's been a good twenty-five years. But it might lead to questions about just what I'm doing here with you."

So, while Ranulf put his feet up near the fire and had his wizardly needs attended to as if he, and not Nicolas, were the visiting dignitary, Nicolas was conducted to the Sage's private receiving chamber. With every step he took through the winding corridors, he marveled at the richness of the place. Dozens of intricate tapestries decorated the walls, and the windows were luxuriously large, many of them fitted with costly stained glass. Moreover, Nicolas suspected that Sare boasted a silver mine, for evidence if it was everywhere; cups, plates, and candlesticks gleamed from linen-covered tables lining the spacious halls— even the sconces were of silver and not common iron.

If he suspected it before, he was certain of it now; the Sage, not the lord marshall or the king, was the undisputed ruler of this bleak island.

His escort stopped before a vast double door of carved oak, and above it, Nicolas spied an elaborately enameled crest—a cross, flared at each point, and set upon a circle. He squinted at it, knowing he'd seen something like it in the past, then realized that the device was the same as that on the brooches that he'd seen Athaya and Jaren wear—or rather, almost the same. This device was overlaid by a golden crown, the cross and circle serving merely as its background.

While Nicolas studied the crest, troubled by its inherent meaning, his escort stepped inside to inform his master of Nicolas' arrival. Nicolas used these last precious seconds of solitude to take a much-needed and very deep breath. When he was finally led inside, he prayed that he did not look as nervous as he felt.

Somehow, as he had pondered the title of "Sage" over the past few weeks, Nicolas had mentally conjured an image of an older man—a man with rheumy eyes and graying hair, and bony, drooping shoulders—someone a bit like Overlord Basil, perhaps, who would be at home in a quiet chamber filled with books and ink pots and his own ideas. And considering the aura of mystery surrounding him and his little-known cult of wizards, Nicolas also imagined a wily and secretive man—one who lurked in dark corners and slipped poisons into the cups of kings, shunning more blatant forms of attack.

Brandegarth of Crewe was none of these. As the Sage took his measure, silently judging what matter of creature the lord marshall had sent, Nicolas sensed that this was a man with no need for stealth; if he wanted to kill a man, he would simply reach out and snap his enemy's neck with his bare hands—as easy a task as swatting a gnat. He was a tall man in his early forties—piratelike, if Nicolas was any judge, from his swarthy skin and shoulder-length black hair. A heavy torque embraced his neck, each end bearing a small, open-mouthed gargoyle, and thick biceps were adorned with pounded silver arm-rings and striped by a series of fading, ropelike scars. He wore nothing but a sheepskin vest and a pair of woolen breeches tucked into deerskin boots; practical clothing that defied the weather with its scantness. But more than anything else, Nicolas noticed the eyes—piercing green eyes that revealed thoughts constantly in motion, like ocean waters restless with a coming storm, churning impatiently as they wait for the proper time to unleash their full fury.

"So the lord marshall has sent you, has he?" The Sage's voice filled every corner of the chamber, a chamber more sumptuous than anything Delfar Castle could offer and which boasted as many silver adornments as the outside corridors. The silver gleamed red from the pair of witchlights hovering just beneath the ceiling, brightening the chamber with the light of a dozen lamps. The room was surprisingly warm, too—a marked change from the chill of the outside corridor. From somewhere close by, Nicolas heard the strains of a harp and for one unsettling moment he thought it was coming from the large, earthenware jar set near the fireplace.

"Yes, your Grace," Nicolas said, composing himself enough to bow gracefully. "He has received your message and sends this gift in reply."

Nicolas reached into his cloak and drew out a small strip of cloth. He unfurled it and laid it across his arms like a merchant proudly displaying his wares at a fair. He caught the Sage's flash of surprise and tried not to smile his relief. Though to him it was nothing but a swatch of black wool, to the Sage it was embroidered with runelight. Nicolas hoped that Athaya would not mind his giving away her favor, but she was sure to forgive him under the circumstances.

"The lord marshall wishes you to know that your warning was not necessary," he went on, with all the dutiful humility of one bred to serve rather than be served. "He has never harbored any ill will toward your people and has no intention of harming them. He sends this wondrous scarf as a token of his friendship."

Brandegarth picked up the cloth in his hands, nodding his pleasure as he ran fingers through the insubstantial threads of light clinging to the cloth—lights whose placement Nicolas could only guess, judging from where the Sage touched his fingers. "A fascinating article, indeed," he said, sincerely impressed. He glanced back to Nicolas with one brow slightly raised. "And an unusual gift from a Caithan."

Nicolas made no reply to that, but merely conceded the point with a nod.

The Sage admired the cloth for a few moments more, then set it reverently aside and motioned Nicolas to a chair by the fire. No, not a fire, he realized at second glance, but a collection of heatstones like those he had seen in Athaya's camp. But the stones Athaya made had never given off so much warmth, and Nicolas let his heavy cloak slide from his shoulders, quick to see how the Sage could dress so lightly.

But then, he reflected, his eyes drawn back to the fireplace, Athaya's heatstones had not been coated with a sticky-looking substance that looked uncomfortably like blood, either.

"The lord marshall would welcome such marvelous stones as these," he said with a smile, pretending to be as entranced by them as the Sage had been by the runecloth. "His chambers are quite drafty and cold."

"Yes, I'm sure they are," Brandegarth replied, in a tone that indicated he would do nothing to alter that fact. Then he reached for a circle of pottery on the hearth and placed it over the mouth of the earthenware jar like a stopper. Suddenly, the harp music stopped. "Can't let it all out at once," the Sage remarked off-handedly, "or I'd have none left for this evening." Ignoring Nicolas' look of astonishment—this time unfeigned—the Sage lowered himself into a cushioned chair across from Nicolas, wincing as he fought back a twinge of pain. "My messenger, Couric, tells me that the new lord marshall is the king's brother."

"That is true, sir." Nicolas swallowed, hoping that the messenger hadn't also provided the Sage with a description. He deemed himself fortunate that he had not encountered Couric in one of the castle corridors and until reaching the Sage had kept his face carefully shrouded by his cowl.

"An odd place for a prince of Caithe to find himself, wouldn't you agree?" Brandegarth's smile was enigmatic. "Few Caithans are willing to come to Sare for any reason at all, much less to reside. But it is true—had I known who he was, I might not have sent my warning. I have heard of his magical sister and know that she and Prince Nicolas are close."

"Indeed so."

The Sage pondered that for a moment. "Do you know him well?"

Nicolas shrugged indifferently. "As well as one can know a prince, my Lord," he said, with all the aplomb of a courtier.

As he hoped, the Sage laughed softly. "A clever answer. But you are not being truthful with me, sir," he said. He was still smiling, but now there was a sense of advantage behind it. "Or should I say, your Highness?"

Nicolas felt all of his muscles tighten at once, not bothering to wonder whether he should be afraid, but trying to calculate how afraid he should be. Ranulf had been right to warn him. Deluding Durek was one thing, but it was quite another matter to delude a wizard, much less one of the Sage's reputed abilities.

"My father used to test us like that," he said, touching a finger to his temple and searching for the familiar sensation that—curiously—was not there. "I never could hide the truth from him when I was a boy." He studied the Sage's face, but could not tell if the man was merely amused, or was crafting an elaborate method of killing him.

"Until I know whom I can trust," Brandegarth said matter-of-factly, "truth-testing can be a useful habit. There are those who covet my position and would try to obtain it without going through proper channels. But in truth, it was not necessary to test you," he admitted more genially. "Couric conjured your image for me days ago. He stole a drop of you when he went to the manor."

Nicolas was bewildered at first, but then he remembered what

Athaya had told him about a locket that Felgin once made for her; a locket bearing Tyler's image, crafted by a single drop of his essence.

"But I never felt a thing."

"If you had," Brandegarth said dryly, "I would have accused Couric of being clumsy." Then, the subject having lost its interest, the Sage picked up a flagon from a small side table and swirled the contents. "Do you like our whiskey?" he asked, and without awaiting a reply, poured two cups of the amber liquid and handed one to Nicolas.

Nicolas only sipped at it, aware that he had to keep a clear head. "I'm sorry for the deception, but I wasn't certain what sort of a reception I'd get here."

"No need to apologize," Brandegarth assured him, brushing the subject away negligently. "I'm impressed that you were brave enough to come yourself instead of sending an envoy. And I'm flattered that you thought it necessary to be so secretive. Tell me, did you think I would do something vile to you? Turn you into a pig, perhaps?" Brandegarth shook his head, chuckling at the absurdity. "That's what all the young ones are told."

"No, I—"

"She sent you here, didn't she?" he asked, firing the question at Nicolas like a bolt from a crossbow. "Your sister, Athaya?"

"No!" he answered hastily. Until he felt on firmer footing with the Sage, Nicolas wished to keep Athaya's involvement with his presence on Sare as minimal as possible. "It was my idea to come."

Brandegarth swallowed a mouthful of whiskey and peered behind his guest's eyes; this time, Nicolas knew that he was being truth-tested—he felt the featherlike touch of the Sage's mind exploring the insides of his skull.

"So it was," the Sage declared. "Why?"

"There aren't many wizards west of Reyka and hearing about you piqued her interest. She's heard some stories, of course, but had no way of knowing whether they were true or false. I simply came to find out what I could."

Brandegarth looked away, absently running a finger around the lip of his cup. "I have heard stories about her, too." He paused, but was not inclined to elaborate. "What do the Caithans say about me?" he asked, turning back. Green eyes twinkled with delight at the thought of his own notoriety.

Nicolas told him what little he or anyone outside of Sare

knew: that the Sage was the leader of a magicians' cult, that he gained his rank by victory in battle, and that beyond these few facts, nothing else was known.

"Cult," Brandegarth spat with contempt. "Reykans *would* call it that." He pushed the insult to the back of his mind. "Then your sister is no longer in prison?" he asked disjointedly, and although he tried to hide it, Nicolas could tell that the Sage's interest had been roused. "We are isolated here, but news does reach us—albeit several months late. The last I heard, she had been tried and imprisoned for speaking out in favor of wizardry."

"Yes, but she was freed some months ago."

"Ah, I see. And now she wishes to know more about me," he went on, openly pleased. He nodded, as if this was a development he had foreseen long ago. "I think she wants more, my Prince," the Sage said, raising a knowing brow. "I think she wishes my help in this crusade of hers, and that you were sent to request it."

He smiled expectantly at Nicolas, waiting for him to concede the point, but Nicolas merely shifted uneasily in his chair. He didn't wish to anger his host, but lying—as he had already discovered—would be pointless. "Well, no . . . she didn't exactly say that."

The Sage's smile fell away. He was genuinely surprised, but quickly regained his composure. "Ah . . . perhaps she will do so later." He tapped his fingertips in an erratic rhythm, betraying inner unrest. "If she is reluctant to ask for my help, then perhaps she fears that my people will return to Caithe and interfere with her crusade."

That was indeed Athaya's fear, but Nicolas was too distracted to acknowledge it; one of the Sage's words had seized his full attention. "Return?"

Brandegarth smiled indulgently. "Not surprising that your historians would neglect to mention that a handful of wizards did manage to escape Faltil's scourge; it sounds infinitely more flattering to say that Faltil killed them all. No," he went on, "my people have lived on this island for nearly two centuries, your Highness, and we find it quite pleasant."

Although he could think of little basis for his suspicions, Nicolas had a prickly sensation that, while pleasant, the Sage would not find it at all unpleasant to gather more wizards into his fold. Nicolas had lived long enough at court to recognize ambitious men, and the Sage did not strike him as one who would remain satisfied with this small island for long.

"We could have gone to Caithe years ago and offered our aid to your father," the Sage pointed out, sensing Nicolas' doubts and hoping to alleviate them. "It was commonly known that Kelwyn wished to better the Lorngeld's fate. And yet, instead of lending him our support, we remained on Sare."

The explanation was logical, but oddly unsatisfying. "Then you never plan to go back?" Nicolas asked.

"I did not say that, precisely," the Sage replied, his cautious tone revealing that Nicolas was straying into topics he preferred not to discuss. "But the time for our return has not yet come." Then he rose to his feet and handed Nicolas his cloak, putting an abrupt end to their meeting. "However, my Lord Marshall, the time for your return has. I have other business to attend to, and if I keep you here overlong, your household may begin to fear that I have indeed turned you into a pig."

Nicolas accepted the cloak, anxious to leave; the Sage's talk of leading his people back to Caithe one day—however far in the future it might be—had disturbed him. "You're right, of course," he agreed. "My chancellor wasn't happy to learn of my plans to come here today, and I don't want to worry him."

"He was right to feel wary. Your predecessor was wise enough not to defy me, but the lord marshall before him came to this castle and never left it. He was fool enough to bring a corbal crystal into this castle without my consent; apparently, no one had warned him that such disobedience is punishable by death." It was a subtle hint, but one that did not go unnoticed.

When he reached the door, Brandegarth gave his shoulder a friendly pat, as if unwilling for their meeting to end on such an ominous note. "You seem an agreeable sort of fellow," he observed with a nod of approval. "I should like to speak with you again."

"And I you." Nicolas scanned the Sage's chamber again, and his eyes sparkled as he caught sight of a pair of leather-bound cups set upon the mantel. "Tell me," he began, relaxing into his usual charm, "do you play dice?"

The broad smile and crinkle of skin around the Sage's eyes was the only reply he required.

CHAPTER 14

✳

"**B**UT MY LORD, YOU CANNOT TURN YOUR BACK ON them," Athaya said, poised on the delicate edge between persuading the man to offer his aid and outright begging him to do so. "If you have a care for all the people of your shire, then you must reconsider. Both our fathers would have wished it so."

The duke of Castre glowered at Athaya from beneath razor-thin blond brows. He was one of Caithe's most powerful lords and the son of Kelwyn's oldest friend, but at the moment, Duke Arcaius seemed little inclined to concede any bond between himself and Kelwyn's only daughter. He had not even offered her the temporary warmth of a fire, but insisted on seeing her in an isolated corner of the courtyard, away from the curious eyes of his servants.

"You are not welcome here, my Lady." The duke's blue eyes were as cold as the snow-covered earth beneath Athaya's feet. "Neither you, nor your husband. I implore you to leave—and quickly, before anyone discovers you've been here."

"Would you have dismissed Kelwyn from your home had he asked you to support him?" she persisted. "Would your father? I simply carry on what Kelwyn began and I had hoped that you would be among the first to join with me, in honor of our fathers' friendship."

"It's only because of that friendship that I don't report you to the Tribunal,'' he retorted, each word making a crisp puff of whiteness in the air before his face. ''I've a duty to protect my tenants. Just last week, three men from Torrey were burned to death for hiding a wizard in their cow shed. One nameless wizard is bad enough, but the slightest rumor of *your* presence in my shire would bring the Tribunal screaming down upon my head—especially were they to learn you had set foot within these walls.''

''And so we're to let the Tribunal intimidate us into living under bad laws? Into submitting to a 'sacred' ritual that has nothing holy about it?''

Strangely, the duke didn't argue those points. Athaya suspected that he believed much the same as she, but refused to involve himself in what he considered to be someone else's problem. ''Princess, I shall ask you one last time to leave my home before I have no choice but to see you and your husband forcibly removed from it. And tell no one you were here—no one!'' He meant to sound threatening, but his tone only served to reveal how very frightened he was.

The duke turned on his heel and stalked away, and, before another minute had passed, Athaya and Jaren were put outside the gates by the head guardsman, abandoned in the snow like beggars denied a crust of bread.

Athaya huddled inside the folds of her traveling cloak and let out a bleak sigh as she looked back at the castle's iron-studded postern door, now securely closed against her. ''He was our last hope.''

''He was the last man on Mosel's list,'' Jaren clarified. ''Surely there are others willing to help us . . . we just don't know who they are yet.''

Athaya threw him a subtle look of awe, wondering—and not for the first time—how Jaren always managed to sustain a small reserve of optimism in even the worst of times. ''I hope we find out soon, then,'' she said, kicking at a chunk of ice in her path. ''We may be gaining support in the villages, but unless we sway a few lords to our side, it's going to be harder to keep this crusade alive—and harder to finance it.''

Jaren rubbed his hands together, blowing hot breath on them to keep his fingers from going numb. ''Come on, let's go home,'' he said. ''It may not be much, but it's the one place in all of Caithe where no one's going to throw us out into the snow the moment we arrive.''

"Although I'm sure there are a few who'd like to," she replied. She was well aware that not everyone at the camp held charitable feelings toward her, and many openly resented that they could only escape absolution by coming to her for help. "But we need to stop at Blacklions tavern on the way back and see if Cordry's sent us any more runecloth. I asked Drianna to let him know we were running short when she went to Kilfarnan to look for her brother. After that we can go back to the camp and relax for a while. If it's possible to relax," she added dryly, "in the midst of a hundred magic students setting off spells at all hours of the day."

They reached Kaiburn late that afternoon. From a grove of oaks near the duke's castle, Athaya scouted out a deserted alley in the city and translocated them there, sparing them both from walking the nearly one hundred miles between Castre and Kaiburn. The alley was squalid and littered with refuse, the stench barely muffled by the snow, and Jaren was visibly surprised that Athaya had enough familiarity with such a place to be able to work a successful spell of translocation.

"We're near the looca-den where Ranulf and I found Cordry," she explained, smiling at the look of trepidation on Jaren's face as he wondered what other unsavory places she'd frequented before his arrival in Caithe.

Once they reached more familiar streets—no easy task, as the cobbles were slippery and caked with ice and frozen mud—Jaren guided her toward the Blacklions tavern. It wasn't long, however, before Athaya's nose wrinkled at the acrid stench of burned wood. When she and Jaren rounded the corner which should have opened onto a small square fronting the tavern, all that remained was the gutted remains of a building, its roof and walls now nothing but a pile of blackened and ash-covered timber. Half-hidden under the wreckage was the tavern's sign—a pair of black lions on a crimson field, paying homage to the royal house of Trelane. It, too, was nearly burned beyond recognition, and the sight of her family's ravaged crest made Athaya shudder.

Jaren stopped a woman who was trudging past clutching a basket of shriveled-looking onions to her chest. "Excuse me, madam, but can you tell me what happened here? My wife and I have been away from the city for a few weeks, and—"

"Why d'ye want to know?" The woman's voice was both hostile and frightened. "You a friend of Rupert's?"

Jaren nodded eagerly. "Yes, I am."

If he thought the admission would ease the woman's nerves, he was sadly mistaken; her fear only intensified. "Get away from me," she snapped in a hushed voice, then buried her face in a tattered scarf and hurried away.

Athaya shifted her gaze from the retreating woman to the remains of Rupert's tavern. "The Tribunal must have found out about Nathan," she murmured.

"It's a sight, ain't it?" a man remarked from close behind them, and Athaya jumped at the unexpected voice. She hoped he hadn't overheard her, and luckily, his jaunty smile gave no indication of it. "You should have seen the flames—as high as the spires of the cathedral if they were an inch."

"What happened?"

"You haven't heard?" The man chuckled, but it quickly turned into a nasty-sounding cough, full of fluid. Athaya suspected that he would be lucky to survive the winter. "You must be new in town," he went on, after regaining his breath. "The owner—fellow named Rupert—sent his son off to join those wizards living in the forest. And he was mixed up with 'em too—damned foolish business, if you ask me. Anyway, they came to arrest him last week." His smile receded slightly. "You folks know him?"

The look in the man's eye turned greedy, and Athaya's instincts sounded in silent alarm. He was clearly hoping to uncover a few of Rupert's friends so that he could earn a few coins by informing the Tribunal about them. Fine leather boots, out of place among his threadbare cloak and mittens, made her suspect that he had already received similar rewards.

"No," Jaren replied with a shrug of indifference; he'd picked up on the man's change of manner also. "I heard this was a decent place to buy ale, that's all. My wife and I will try elsewhere."

The man looked vaguely disappointed, but brushed it off as if accustomed to occasional failure. "You can try, but there's precious little ale to be had this winter and none that's much good. About the only things there's plenty of in the city these days are rats and bad tempers."

Athaya commiserated with a nod, then took Jaren's arm and moved away at a seemingly casual pace. While Caithe was far from widespread famine, the poor harvest had caused shortages in every shire, and folk were jealously guarding what they had. Most people would survive until spring well enough; the true hardship would fall on the beggars among them—and, as Athaya knew too well, on the Lorngeld who were driven from their homes by the Tribunal. More than once during her travels, Athaya had heard people whispering that the poor harvest and bitter winds of winter were God's punishment for allowing wizardry to run rampant in the land. She could only pray that the weather would improve and that such a sentiment would not cause a backlash against her that she wasn't prepared to handle.

They reached the Forest of Else that evening, and for one dizzying moment, Athaya thought they had stumbled into the wrong camp. She could only gape at the chaos of tents and cone-shaped shelters jammed into the clearing—at least three times the number that had existed when she and Jaren had departed three weeks before. It was as if an invading army had sur-rounded the derelict monastery, pitched a disorderly encamp-ment around it, and placed it under siege.

"My God, there must be hundreds of them," Jaren said, no less astonished than she.

They picked their way through the narrow paths between the shelters, idly counting them as they went. Though they saw few others—no doubt huddled beside the heatstones in their shel-ters—they could sense the increased numbers in the underlying hum of voices, the fitful coughs and sneezes, the cries of dis-gruntled infants, and the thick, pervasive smell of too many people living in close confinement.

When they emerged from the maze on the opposite side of the clearing, Athaya realized why the camp had seemed rela-tively deserted. Dozens of people lingered behind the chapel, many of them dabbing at their eyes with rags while two men shoveled earth into what looked uncomfortably like a grave.

"What's all this?"

They turned in unison at Athaya's voice, and Kale detached himself from the crowd and came to her. "It's Terrence—the thatcher," he replied, bowing his head. "The cold got into his lungs last week, and he just wasn't strong enough to fight it. He . . . died a few hours ago."

Before Athaya could express her sadness, she heard an angry shout of recognition from the rear of the crowd. A cluster of wool-wrapped bodies broke away from the larger knot and ap-proached her—three men, a woman, and a bleary-eyed toddler on the verge of tears.

Unfortunately, one of the men was Sutter.

"It's about time you got back," he said indignantly, as if scolding a wayward child. "While you've been off dining with the great lords of Caithe, we've been here slowly starving to death. If something isn't done damned quick, we're all going to end up just like Terrence!"

"Dining with—" Too shocked to go on, the words evaporated from Athaya's mouth. She had been the recipient of much rudeness these past few weeks, as lords and villagers alike cast her from their homes, but nothing had so soundly insulted her as Sutter's wild accusation.

"Look, Sutter," Jaren began, staving off the argument before Athaya erupted with rage. "We've been gone three weeks and only just set foot back in camp. Give us a few minutes to—"

"Master Tonia says we're each allowed only two cups of ale a day," Sutter railed on, heedless. "Two cups! How are any of us supposed to live on that? And now we only get cheese every other day—and puny quarter round at that. Why, the scullions in my father's kitchens get better rations!"

Athaya leveled him with an icy glare; her people had just buried one of their own, and all Sutter could think about was his stomach. "Then go back and work in your father's kitchens. No one's making you stay here."

Sutter hated to be reminded of that fact more than he hated anything—which, considering the extraordinary number of things he seemed to hate, said a great deal—and fell bitterly silent. But instead of offering relief, his studied silence only served to tighten Athaya's already knotted nerves. Like magic contained by a sealing spell, she suspected that in time, if left unvented, Sutter's simmering resentment would explode.

"Oh, never mind the cheese—we have to do something about the cold," the woman beside him said, hugging her child close against her legs. "My boy's been sick all winter, and I'm always down with a chill no matter how many heatstones I make, and Gilda says there isn't an extra blanket left in the whole camp."

"And something has to be done about all these *people*," another of the men complained. "The tents closest to the trenches reek to high heaven, and all the ashes in the world don't help cut the stench. And unless we clear out some more of these trees, we'll be sleeping on top of one another come the new year!"

"If any of us live that long," the third man added sullenly, sniffling loudly.

Athaya held up her hands to halt the flow of grievances. "Let me talk to Tonia first, all right?" she said, edging away from them. "I'll find out what our situation is and see what I can do."

She ground her teeth together in frustration as she headed for the kitchens. *Lord, I've been back for less than five minutes and already I feel overwhelmed.*

The kitchen was not exactly the haven of solitude she had sought—few places in camp weren't crowded these days—but at lest it was warm, and no one clamored for her attention the moment she walked inside the door. Tonia and Cameron sat at the great oak table kneading bread; Gilda, Girard, and Marya were cleaning a small assortment of fish; and a pair of brawny men were hunched over a large cauldron, concocting a mixture that smelled unpleasantly of turnips.

"Rupert! Nathan!" Jaren cried, hurrying toward the men at the cauldron. "Thank God the two of you are safe. We saw what happened to the tavern and feared the worst."

He quickly presented Rupert to Athaya—after all this time, the two of them had never had the chance to meet—and after a clumsy but well-intentioned bow, Rupert hung his ladle on a peg by the fire and sat down at the table to tell his tale.

"Nathan came back to work at the tavern a week ago—he'd learned his spells, but couldn't decide if he wanted to stay and help train others or not. Some of my neighbors suspected where he's been these past few months, but there wasn't a breath of trouble until a pair of Justices came knocking on my door two days ago. They tried to take me away for questioning, but Nathan distracted them by starting a fire in the kitchen and got me away with something he called a 'cloaking spell.' Nathan said it was better to lose the tavern than let it be given to one of the Tribunal's informers as a reward—and I damn well agree with him," he added forcefully.

Athaya was impressed by the man's fortitude, but the slight twitch of his lip revealed that he would miss his business more than he admitted.

"They may not have intended to," Nathan added over his shoulder, "but since I've no tavern to work in anymore, the Tribunal has seen to it that you've gotten yourselves another magic tutor."

"That reminds me," Tonia said, turning to Athaya as she washed the flour paste from her hands. "I have a message from

Mason; he contacted us with a panel last night.'' The solemn look on her face did not bode well. ''He said to tell you that Aurel is dead.''

Athaya and Jaren exchanged a glance, but neither of them was surprised; Aurel had gambled with his life before and this time he had lost. ''The Tribunal?''

''No. Someone else got to him first. Mason said he was hanged by a mob of city folk. They were so afraid his constant preaching would get them all arrested that they decided to get rid of him once and for all.''

Athaya leaned wearily against the table. ''That's not a good sign. And if it happened in Kilfarnan, it could happen in Kaiburn, too. Or worse, right here at the camp . . . our own people turning against us. All we'd need is a few more hotheads like Sutter.''

''Sutter Dubaye is a puffed-up donkey's ass,'' Nathan said, throwing another turnip into the cauldron. ''All them highborn types are the same, thinking they own the world.'' He spun around quickly. ''Er—not the two of you, of course,'' he added, eyes flitting between Athaya and Jaren.

''Sutter likes to stir up trouble with a lot of words, but I doubt he'd act on them,'' Jaren said. ''He strikes me as the type to back down from a fight.''

Athaya was inclined to agree; she had seen Sutter back down only a moment ago, cowed into silence by her own sharp words. And while he persisted in airing his grievances to anyone who would listen, at least the grievances themselves were becoming more benign. No longer did he preach the need to raise an army of wizards to depose the king; instead, he channeled his hostility into a host of petty and less destructive concerns. He was an irritant, but one that could be endured.

''We can only hope that if folks are mad enough, they'll just up and leave,'' Tonia said, rubbing a spot of flour from her cheek. ''A few have, you know. Kennig and Faye and that woman from Dubin . . . I can't recall her name. Girard was tutoring her.''

''There are a few out there angry enough to leave right now,'' Athaya remarked. ''What's all this about rationing ale?''

Tonia huffed her annoyance at what had obviously become a heated dispute. ''I had no choice, Athaya. I'm sure you saw the extra tents—we're numbering close to five hundred now, and there simply isn't enough grain in the storehouse for everyone.

Even to make the ale we have, I had to dip deeper into our money than I'd planned. And Kale has been forced to assign sentries to watch the storehouse so folk don't up and loot it. I set some guarding spells on it, but a few of the wizards in camp are clever enough to undo them if nobody's paying attention."

Athaya closed her eyes and slowly massaged them—yet one more knot to untangle. "I'll count up all our money, then take a look at the storehouse to see just how tight our belts are going to have to get. Then I can worry about the overcrowding and the cold. And maybe after that, if I'm lucky, I can start worrying about what I'm *really* supposed to be doing: teaching all of these people to use their spells so they can go out and teach others and take some of the burden off the rest of us."

She cast a thankful glance to Nathan, making sure he knew how desperately his help was needed, then moved toward the door. "By the way," she asked Tonia, just before she stepped over the threshold, "did Mason say anything about sending more runecloth?"

Tonia shook her head. "Not a word."

"That's odd," she said, rubbing her chin with concern. "I asked Drianna to arrange it, and she should have reached his camp over a week ago. I hope nothing's happened to her."

"Oh, I wouldn't worry," Tonia assured her. "She's got Connor with her, and there aren't many who'd trouble a man that size. And trying to avoid the Tribunal's road patrols is bound to delay them."

Athaya nodded, her fears assuaged for the moment. "You're probably right. They may not be wizards themselves, but they have just as much to fear from the Tribunal if anyone finds out they were here." She dismissed all thoughts of Drianna and left the kitchens to attend to more pressing concerns.

"Lady Drianna, it's good to have you back." Tullis, castle steward to the Sage of Sare, lifted Drianna's small bag out of the coach and escorted her into the Great Hall. "What with the foul weather we've had, his Grace has been worried about you."

"His Grace shouldn't be," Drianna replied. "He was the one who calmed the waters long enough for me to make a safe crossing. Although I almost froze to death in the process—why he couldn't have seen fit to conjure a warm, southerly wind I'll never know." Drianna tossed back her hood, revealing bits of ice which clung stubbornly to her hair and glittered like a net of diamonds. "I've forgotten how much I hate to travel in winter . . . creeping across the ice to a skiff the size of a bathing tub— I fell three times—and wondering if we'd both make it across the channel in one piece."

Tullis nodded politely, careful to express the proper amount of pity during her lengthy recitation of her trials. "Connor was with you, I take it?" he said, when Drianna had stopped long enough to catch her breath.

"He rode ahead of the coach—probably back in the barracks by now." Drianna let out a short, spiteful laugh. "And good riddance to him, I say—the man has all the charm and eloquence of a weed. I never should have let Brand convince me to take him along."

Tullis tilted his head in gentle rebuke. "Connor is no courtier, my Lady, but he's a fine soldier. You were well protected."

"Oh, I suppose so," she conceded, shrugging carelessly. "But we had to share a room at the princess' camp—did I tell you that? Space was short, and since we told everyone we were married, we got stuck together. Connor slept on the floor, of course," she added hastily, careful to squelch any scandal before it took root.

Ascending to the gallery, Tullis deposited her bag outside a set of doors crowned with an enameled crest. "How is he?" Drianna whispered, as the steward bowed to leave.

"Recovered, for the most part. His scars haven't quite faded, and he gets a pain in his chest when it's damp, but other than that, he's fit enough." Tullis offered her a comforting smile, then retreated down the corridor.

Drianna pushed the door open without a sound and smiled like a giddy child when she saw his familiar form. He was seated in a cushioned chair facing the fireplace, slightly hunched over as if he had just slipped into a light sleep. She crept toward him silent as a breeze and rested her hands on the back of the chair. He didn't move—she didn't even see him draw breath—and gave no sign that he had heard her approach. Quickly, she leaned in to kiss him, but where her lips should have touched the rough skin of his cheek, they touched only air. She drew back with a start, and in the same instant, heard a bellow of laughter erupt behind her.

Feigning disappointment, she turned around slowly and set both hands on her hips. "I wanted to surprise you."

Brandegarth's brows rose only slightly. "When will you learn, my dear, that no one ever surprises *me*."

Drianna flowed across the room and folded herself gracefully into his arms, greeting him with a hungry kiss that spoke of long and lonely months apart. Before releasing him, she hugged him with all her strength and was unpleasantly surprised when he grunted in pain and pulled away.

"Not so hard, Drianna . . . my ribs are still a bit tender."

Drianna pursed her lips, regarding him worriedly. "It's been six months, Brand. You've never taken this long to recover from a Challenge before. Bressel hurt you far more than you led me to believe."

"He was good," the Sage replied simply, rubbing the ache from his abdomen. "Probably the best I've ever faced. But I would suggest to you that *I* dealt the harsher blow," he added with a sly wink, "as Bressel is no longer with us."

He slid her cloak from her shoulders and touched one fingertip to the milky flesh at her throat before tossing the expanse of damp wool over a footstool to dry. Drianna curled up on the hearth to warm herself, then turned to gaze at the nearby chair, still seemingly occupied. "It's a fine illusion," she remarked.

"Of course it is," Brandegarth replied, casting an admiring glance to his insubstantial twin. "I had splendid material to work with." He waved his hand, and his other self promptly dissolved. "Now tell me everything, Drianna. Everything I sent you to find out."

Drianna regarded him dryly. "I've been gone almost five months, Brand, and have a long tale to tell. Won't you at least offer me some wine before I begin?"

Brandegarth cheerfully bowed to her request, and when she had a cup of spiced cherry wine in her hand and her beloved on the hearth at her side, she spent the next hour revealing to him all that she had learned about Princess Athaya's crusade—and more importantly, about the princess herself.

"She wasn't at all what I expected," Drianna told him. "Not spoiled or conceited . . . frankly, she doesn't act much like a princess at all. And as I said, an adept-level wizard."

"As powerful as I, would you say?"

Drianna hesitated and took a thoughtful sip of wine. She didn't dare lie to him, but the truth would have to be carefully presented. "That's difficult to say. I don't know exactly what her magic was like before, but I think that perhaps she is as powerful as you are . . . if not more so.''

The Sage's eyes flashed with envy, and Drianna launched quickly into her explanation. ''I'm certain that her gift was no greater, Brand. But the time she spent under the sealing spell— just over three months, I think—made her power stronger. Nobody knew it would happen. And what does it matter if she has obtained a bit of extra magic, anyway?'' she added negligently. ''She's been a wizard less than two years, while you've been perfecting your spells for over twenty.''

''True,'' he said, somewhat appeased. ''Very true. And no matter what she gained from the seal, it does not mean her gift is the stronger. She falsely extended her power . . . just like her father,'' he added with a touch of spite, ''trying to obtain magic that he wasn't born with.'' The Sage scratched pensively at his chin. ''But it's an intriguing piece of news, this business of sealing spells. I knew that such a spell can shut out the pain of a corbal crystal, but there must be something about the seal itself—the buildup of pressure over time, perhaps—that carves out new paths and makes the magic stronger.''

''Assuming one survives it,'' Drianna warned. ''Athaya was close to death when they found her, but now . . . why, you'd never know she'd been sick! Her preservation spells last longer than anyone else's, she can see farther with her vision sphere, and she never gets dizzy after translocation like she used to.''

Brandegarth jerked his head up. ''Trans—are you certain of this? No wizard has been known to carry that spell since Dameronne himself!''

Drianna smiled. ''I thought that might interest you. It certainly interested the Circle of Masters.'' She leaned in closer. ''Athaya's very close with them, you know.''

''Bah.'' He expelled the word like a belch. ''An elitist gaggle of moralistic geese who forbid any spell that makes them the least bit nervous.''

''As you say,'' she conceded, ''but they've already warned her about you.''

The Sage brushed off the remark with an indifferent wave of his hand. ''Warned her? Of what? They know nothing about my people or my plans for them. If they did,'' he added, indulging in a dark smile, ''they'd have acted against me long ago.''

Shunning the cherry wine that Drianna favored, Brandegarth got up and poured himself a generous serving of whiskey. ''Are there any other surprises you're keeping from me?'' he asked, swirling the amber liquid around in his cup. ''Has our princess also uncovered the ability to turn iron into gold, perhaps?''

''Well . . . the seal *did* give her one new talent,'' Drianna began reluctantly. She licked the wine from her lips, unsure how he would react to her next piece of news. ''Athaya can tell who's going to be a wizard before the *mekahn* comes.''

In all their years together, Drianna had never seen him struck utterly dumb—as he was so fond of telling her, no one ever surprises the Sage. She expected at least a burst of jealous rage, but the significance of the news robbed him of such base emotions. Drianna reached up and plucked the cup of whiskey from his hand, afraid that he would drop it and shatter the fine crystal.

''Are you certain of this?'' he asked for the second time, after a lengthy pause. ''Do you know what you're saying?''

Drianna nodded slowly. ''I heard her talking about it. I'm not sure how she does it . . . but I'm sure.''

''Incredible.'' The Sage was deeply impressed, but Drianna sensed threads of envy starting to tighten their hold on his heart. ''I shall have to ponder this at great length.'' Then he looked directly into her eyes, and beyond them, as if in search. ''Did you ask her if you carried the power?''

''I wasn't supposed to know anything about it—she's keeping her talent a secret. But I wanted to ask so desperately,'' she said, grasping his hand. ''If we knew that magic was in my future, then we could finally make our wedding plans.''

Brandegarth nodded absently, patting her head as if to soothe a troubled child. ''We have waited this long,'' he assured her. ''We can wait a few more years. But my people's time of waiting is almost over,'' he said, offering her a grain of hope amid her sadness. Green eyes glittered by firelight as he looked upon the future now unfolding before him, and the pitch of his voice rose slightly, betraying his excitement. ''Two long centuries of waiting. And to think that *I* will be the Sage when my people come into their true destiny. What an honor the Lord has given me! And the time *has* come, Drianna—everything you've told me confirms it.''

Drianna gazed up at him with unveiled adoration. ''I hope so, Brand. Truly I do.''

Reclaiming his cup, Brandegarth left her side and paced slowly around the chamber. ''So Athaya's crusade is having trouble, is it?'' he said, sipping at the potent island brew. He nodded subtle approval, as if gratified to know that Athaya's new talent was not making her labors any easier. "Dameronne foresaw that as well. Though I'll admit to wondering why it should be so. Perhaps our princess isn't as powerful as she seems. After all, how difficult can it be for an adept-level wizard to defeat the king of Caithe? He knows nothing of magic.''

"More than we may think, Brand. Remember what I told you about the wizard who tried to steal Athaya's magic? Rhodri? King Durek has all of his old magic books, and Athaya told me that he's used them against her in the past.''

"It matters little what the king of Caithe knows or does not know about magic if he has none of his own to wield. Once Athaya has gathered a large enough army, then the king will topple from his throne and—''

Drianna set her wine cup on the hearth and scrambled to her feet. "Brand, no—you don't understand. Athaya isn't forming an army at all. She's not planning to attack anybody . . .'' Drianna's voiced trailed off, and she shrugged helplessly. "She's just teaching magic.''

Brandegarth spun around in disbelief, whiskey sloshing from his cup and onto the rushes. *"What?"* he shouted, loud enough to rattle the windowpanes. "What the hell sort of a rebellion is that?''

"Well, she *is* encouraging them not to be absolved. After that, she teaches them about their magic so they can go on with their lives. She calls it fighting the war one wizard at a time. But that's all.''

"Then she cheats them!'' the Sage cried. He whipped an iron poker from its peg near the hearth and brandished it like a sword. "She *cheats* them!''

Drianna crept back, wary of his temper. "Perhaps, but she often told us that she would never attack her brother directly. Many of the Lorngeld distrusted her at first, thinking she might be plotting something a bit more treasonous than breaking a few laws against magic, but she assured them more than once that she has no designs on the Crown. A few want to fight him, but she's managed to discourage them. She's determined to use her powers ethically.''

Brandegarth snorted loudly. "Ethics are a relative thing, Drianna.''

"That may be so,'' Drianna persisted, "but such a sentiment

may be why she's gaining such a following—she's not the Devil's Child that the Caithans were expecting her to be, and more people are coming to her every day because of it. Most are in a sorry state, though. This new Tribunal is dangerous."

"But not unexpected. The same thing happened two centuries ago. Ironic, when you think of it," he added, chuckling dryly. "You and I wouldn't be here but for Faltil's scourge. In a way, he was the one to whom we owe our place in the world—and our greater one in the future." Suddenly, the Sage's gaze grew more intense. "I think, Drianna, that Princess Athaya needs some enlightenment on the true purpose of her gift."

Drianna lowered her eyes. "You can try to change her mind, Brand, but it won't be easy. I doubt she'll accept your help."

"Then I will wait until a hard winter and a lack of money change her mind for me," he said decisively, returning the poker to its peg. "Even the most 'ethical' of priests will steal bread if he is starving and penniless. But that is a matter for another time." He sat down before the hearth, motioning her to join him, and then curled his arm around her waist. "So you enjoyed being a spy, did you?"

Drianna relaxed, grateful for a less volatile subject. "I enjoy everything you ask me to do, Brand. But I was glad to come back. It was amusing at first, playing the dull-witted peasant girl again, but after a time I started to hate it—it reminded me too much of . . . of what you took me away from." She offered him a quick kiss of gratitude. "Still, it was a useful ploy. People say anything to the servants, thinking it won't matter. I expect that Athaya told me far more than she would have if I were someone closer to her rank."

"It sounds to me as if she has no rank to speak of anymore," he observed wryly. Smiling, he patted Drianna's hair as if she were a favorite spaniel. "I'm proud of you, Drianna. But tell me, how did you manage to leave without raising unneeded questions?"

"I told them I went looking for my brother."

Brandegarth chuckled darkly. "He's easy enough to find. He's been in the same cemetery for eight years."

"Devyn," she said, shaking her head in pity, "what a fool he was to think he ever could have been Sage."

Drianna nestled closer to him, but as she shifted, her foot toppled her wine cup and sent the sticky remains trickling across the hearth. Seeing a swatch of black cloth draped across the nearby table, Drianna picked it up and began to dab the wine from the floor.

"No, my dear—it's not a napkin." Brandegarth plucked the cloth from her hands and shook it out. "You can't see them, but there are bright red runes all over it. It's called—"

"Runecloth." The astonishment is her eyes quickly turned shrewd. "How did you get it?"

"From the new lord marshall. I have a tale of my own to tell, Drianna. It would appear that we are not the only ones engaged in a bit of spying." Briefly, he told her of Nicolas' new post on the island and of their recent encounter, watching with delight as Drianna's eyes went wider with every word.

"She knew it all the time," Drianna said evenly, but with undisguised resentment. "Athaya knew he was coming to Sare and never told me."

"Her friends on the Circle have obviously cautioned her against being overtrusting of Sarians," Brandegarth remarked. "It would seem that the princess suspected you—or all of us— somewhat more than we may have guessed."

Drianna picked up the cloth and brushed it with her fingers, as if by doing so she could make the runes visible to her eyes. "The prince didn't by any chance have a Sarian servant with him, did he? A large man with a red beard—a wizard who used to be a soldier?"

"Not that I know of," Brandegarth replied with a shrug. "Ask the gatehouse captain—he'll know."

"I'll do that," she murmured purposefully. "I suspect that Nicolas brought one of Athaya's friends with him from Caithe— one who doesn't bear us much affection, either. He was always glaring at me as if afraid I'd steal things when he wasn't looking." She folded the runecloth and set it aside. "But as to Prince Nicolas . . . what should we do about him now that he's here?"

"I'm not sure. I was certain that he came to request our aid on his sister's behalf. Odd that he did not . . . it fits so well into Dameronne's prophecy." Brandegarth tapped a finger on his chin, and his eyes took on a mischievous cast. "He seems harmless enough, but his presence on the island offers us quite an opportunity—one that, perhaps, we were not meant to ignore. But I have plenty of time to think on that; Nicolas isn't due to return for another game of dice until after the new year. I have far more pressing concerns at the moment," he said softly, eyes growing heavy with desire. "It's been a long, cold winter thus far."

He gathered her into his arms and let his hands roam over the smooth curves of her body and crushed his demanding mouth against hers, his kisses spiced with whiskey and long-suppressed need.

Drianna pulled back only far enough to gaze bewitchingly into his eyes. "Sometimes I'm glad you've never married me, Brand," she said, turning down the shoulder of her gown. "I suspect if you had, you'd never have stayed so interested in me after all these years."

"I've promised you before, Drianna . . . if the power is in you, then you shall be my wife. But the Sage can never marry beneath him—you know that. Ah, don't look so sad," he said, tilting her chin up. "The *mekahn* has been known to come as late as thirty, and you're but twenty-four. We've a few more years yet. Pray that God sends you the gift," he said, burying his face in the rich expanse of her scented hair, "and in the meantime, let me enjoy you as you are."

CHAPTER 15

✻✻

A THAYA SHIFTED UNDERNEATH THE BLANKETS, FLOATING
in the murky straits between sleep and awareness. While
her body rested, her mind painted vivid pictures of the
forest camp, and in her dreams, she drifted peacefully from one
wizard to another, showing each a new spell or passing on some
bit of wisdom that Master Hedric had once bestowed on her.

But then the scene shifted, and where there had been peace
now there was only horror. The forest was afire, trees crowned
with orange flame like immense candles; the wizards' tents and
shelters burned, branches and ribbons of canvas crisping in the
heat; even the stones burned, giving off clouds of acrid, black
smoke. And instead of practicing their spells under the eye of a
caring tutor, each of the wizards now had his own personal devil
in a black robe—a black robe marked with a blood-red chalice.
To Athaya's left was a man with no limbs, writhing on the ground
and crying out his misery, very much alive. Limbs would grow
again, only to be mercilessly hacked off by the ax-wielding
Justice looming over him. To her right was a woman chained to
a stake, every inch of her afire, but whose skin never blackened,
whose hair never turned to ash. She could do nothing but wail
in pain, wishing she could die, while another Justice looked on,
taking pleasure in her torment. But Athaya herself stood alone
in the center of this madness, unseen, unheard, and unharmed,

yet pained beyond imagining at the suffering of those who had
put their trust in her and had come to these fates because of it.

Athaya's eyes snapped open, at last breaking free of the hell
of her mind's creation. It had not been the first time she had
dreamed such things and would doubtless not be the last. But as
she pulled the heavy blanket tighter around her shoulders, she
realized that the images in her mind had not been conjured
randomly, but had wrapped themselves around reality; the smell
of smoke still lingered, and the shouts and wails of her people
had not been silenced.

No, not the bishop's men, she thought frantically, *they couldn't
possibly have found us here!*

Scrambling out of bed, she braced herself for a blast of January air and threw open the shutters. A cloud of acrid smoke
filled her lungs, thick with the odor of burning bread, and the
back of her head began to throb softly, like the harbinger of a
headache. Beneath her window, tents and makeshift shelters
sprawled across the clearing like a city beneath a castle turret
. . . but it was a city in utter chaos. In the center of the confusion, frightened children wandered aimless and forgotten,
whimpering their fear, while to the right, one knot of people
clustered around the chapel doors—Athaya saw the bouncing
light of a lantern inside—and to the left, a larger group shouted
orders at one another as they battled the columns of flame that
billowed from one of the outlying buildings.

And the smell of burning bread?

Athaya gasped as the facts all locked together, coughing at
the smoke that filled her lungs. It was no raid, but it was almost
as disastrous.

"God help us, the storehouse—"

She slammed the shutters closed and roughly prodded the
snoring bundle of blankets beside her. "Jaren, wake up!" She
shook him harder, obtaining only a muffled grunt in response.
Then she whipped the blankets away, letting the frigid night air
envelop him like a shroud. Squealing his protest, he awoke and
stared up at her with sleep-filled eyes, wondering what he could
have possibly done to deserve such abuse.

"We've got trouble," she told him curtly. She snatched her
cloak from its peg and jammed her feet into a pair of fur-lined
boots, then gathered up a disorderly armful of Jaren's clothes
and dumped them in his lap. "Hurry."

Still groggy, Jaren nodded and groped for a shirt, while Athaya flew down the dormitory stairs and out into the camp compound. It seemed as if she and Jaren were the last ones to awake—the clearing was packed with people, as those who were not involved with dousing the fire emerged from their tents to gawk at the commotion. She bolted toward the storehouse, making no apologies as she bumped and shoved her way through the crowd. One of the newer wizards made a valiant attempt at conjuring rain, but the frosty air interfered with his spell and turned his efforts into a gentle snow, and the fire raged on unabated.

Athaya spotted Tonia in the center of the commotion, shouting caution at the handful of brave souls who ventured inside the storehouse to carry the precious sacks of grain to safety. "How did this happen?" she asked, breathless.

Tonia's lips were pursed tight as she jabbed an angry thumb at a small knot of men to her right. "Ask him."

Athaya turned, groaning inwardly as she recognized the familiar, dark-haired man. *Damn, I should have guessed . . .*

Sutter Dubaye stood in the center of a tight ring of wizards, each of them facing inward and sustaining a shielding spell. Trapped within the ring, Sutter couldn't move more than a yard in any direction without touching one of the shields and sending up a shower of blue sparks and giving himself a nasty sting in the bargain. When his captors saw Athaya approach, they stepped back to loosen the ring of shields to allow her inside. She glared at the prisoner with thinly veiled revulsion, looking much the same way, she mused, as Durek did every time he set eyes on his recalcitrant sister.

"Well?"

Sutter didn't answer, but Nathan—one of those shielding them—did. "He and a bunch of his lowlife friends decided they were hungry. As if the rest of us aren't," he added, sneering at their captive. "They took out the sentry and started to raid the storehouse, but their fearless leader here accidentally set the grain sacks on fire."

"I'm sorry, my Lady," Kale said, shuffling up behind her; his head was bloodied and wrapped with rags. "I tried to stop them, but—"

"It's not your fault," she assured him. "You're good with a sword and a crossbow, but that doesn't help very much if you're attacked with magic." She turned her gaze back to Sutter, silently demanding an explanation.

"I had some small heatstones in my pockets to keep myself warm," Sutter murmured, digging his heel into the snow. "One of them must've fallen out and started to smolder."

Athaya rolled her eyes in exasperation. "And you never thought to put out the flames before they got out of hand?"

"I tried," he protested, "but I couldn't." The admission made him grimace, as if the words turned sour in his mouth. "I tried to counter the spell, but everything I did just made it spread faster."

Athaya knew it wasn't the proper time to berate him for not applying himself to his lessons, but she couldn't help herself. His shiftlessness was going to cause all of them untold hardship. "Any half-trained wizard can smother a small fire with a simple counterspell," she snapped. "I can't believe even *your* skills don't extend that far."

Jaren was at her side just then, cutting off whatever retort Sutter had been about to make. "We caught five others in the chapel," he said. "They were prying up the flagstones and trying to get at our money, but they dug up the strongbox by mistake."

"The—?" Athaya's eyes widened. Suddenly she realized the source of that odd throbbing in the back of her head. Even through the padded strongbox, her adept-level senses could pick up the danger contained within it. "Hold him here," she ordered Sutter's captors and dashed to the chapel.

The strongbox had been partially unearthed from beneath the flagstones, and a shovel and pick were abandoned nearby. Five men had been herded to one corner of the chapel by roughly a dozen others, and one curious young woman was picking absently at the chest's locks.

"Don't touch that box!" Athaya shouted, and the woman lurched back in fright. Sweeping past her, Athaya turned on the five men. "Just what in the hell did you think you were doing?"

One of the men stepped forward with his head bowed—not in chagrin, but in disgust at having been caught. "We thought . . . I mean, there was talk of a treasure buried under one o' the flagstones."

"That's not money, you fools, it's a crown of corbals— corbals powerful enough to kill every wizard in this camp!" She could feel her fingers shaking, unnerved at how close they might have come to unknowingly accomplishing something that the bishop and his soldiers, despite all their efforts, had thus far failed to do. She glanced at one of their captors. "Bring them out with the others," she said, and stalked out of the chapel, her boots making angry, crunching sounds in the snow.

In a matter of minutes, the troublemakers were gathered together underneath the bell tower. By now the fire was mostly subdued, but the smell of burned grain and cloth still hung heavily in the air. To Athaya's dismay, there were far more than she had thought at first. Sutter had always been a problem, but Athaya didn't realize how many allies he'd acquired over the past few months. Although most of the people crowded around the tower were curious onlookers, no fewer than fifty stood by Sutter's side to support him.

Her anger must have been a palpable thing, for as she approached Sutter and the others, the crowd fell eerily silent. "Why?" she asked simply.

"Somebody had to do something."

"Something like stealing our money and food? Just what was it you were hoping to accomplish this evening? Are you hoping to turn everyone here against me?"

"As if I'd need help to do that," he muttered under his breath. Athaya heard a series of muffled snickers from among his compatriots. "Some of us just wanted food and money to go off on our own."

"And you couldn't have simply asked for it?"

Sutter snorted his disdain. "Would you have given it to me?"

Oh, you asked to fall into that trap, Athaya. "To you? No," she admitted. "But to someone who had a commitment to the Lorngeld? To someone who wanted to go off and start another school? Then yes."

Sutter shook his head mockingly. "That's all Caithe needs—more places like this."

"Shut up, Sutter," she said, now truly enraged. "I'm sick and tired of listening to your pathetic whining. I'm doing the best I can. And I haven't heard you make any useful suggestions lately."

"I suggested we take up arms and fight months ago," he shot back, "but you wouldn't listen."

Athaya sighed heavily. Not *that* old argument again. "I told you, we simply can't do that."

"No, you'd rather take the coward's way out and hide from your enemies instead of confronting them."

Athaya had to resist the temptation to slap him for such insolence. "Every single wizard in this camp *has* confronted them by not submitting to absolution. Just because we're not out killing people doesn't mean we aren't waging a war. Sometimes, Sutter, you can accomplish a lot more by *not* fighting."

"Uh-huh," he grunted. "Just look what we have here—starvation and coughing sickness and the stink of too many people living on top of one another. What an accomplishment."

"Would you rather have *this*?" Edging his way to the front of the crowd, Girard angrily thrust his fingerless hand into Sutter's face. "Is this what you want?"

Sutter glared at the half-healed stumps, but said nothing.

"Or perhaps you'd rather be rotting in the grave that Lukin and his priests have reserved for you?" Jaren observed softly. "You'd be there now, but for her."

Sutter threw his arms up dramatically, as if invoking the powers of heaven. "Then let us all praise the ineffable Princess Athaya, savior of her race. But if this is salvation," he added, eyes burning her with their scorn, "then I want no part of it."

Athaya bit her lip, tasting the salty tang of blood. *That* did it.

"Do I look as if I'm getting fat off your misery?" she said, her voice rising almost to a shriek. "Do I look as if I'm enjoying this any more than you are? Go back home if that's what you want. Stay there until the Tribunal comes for you—they will, you know. And when they've broken every one of your limbs with their instruments and branded you with irons and perhaps—only perhaps—decided to grant you the mercy of absolution, maybe then you'll realize how much better off you are here!"

"Better off? For how long? Once we leave, we're as good as dead—just look what happened to Girard! And we're doing nothing to prevent that from happening! Yes, we learn how to control our magic while we're here—"

"Some of us do," Tonia muttered, glaring at the ruined sacks of grain that had been carried from the storehouse.

Sutter returned the glare, but continued. "But what does knowing about magic accomplish unless we *do* something with it? We need to fight back! Why should we sit here waiting for the king and his bishops to give us what we want when we have the means to take it? Why wait, when we can go out and show our enemies how powerful we are and force them to give in to our demands? *Force* them to abolish absolution, and *force* them to allow magic schools to exist somewhere other than out here in these godforsaken woods. I came here because I thought you could do something for me, and now, because of the Tribunal, I've lost everything—and you don't want to help me get any of it back!''

''As if you're the only one who's lost anything!'' she shouted, feeling control over her emotions shred like cobwebs in the wind. ''I know exactly what you're going through and so does everyone else here. What makes your story so much more pitiable than anyone else's?''

''Most of these people never had much to begin with, but *I* could have been Baron of Elsby!''

Instantly, he knew it had been the wrong tack to take. ''Don't try to impress me with what you've lost, Sutter. Because of my magic, I've been expelled from my family, expelled from my home, expelled from the Church—although that's hardly a loss, these days,'' she added bitterly. ''I've lost all my money—God, even the clothes on my back are handouts from the king of Reyka. I've come down farther in this world than you have, Sutter Dubaye, and yes, it's hard . . . but at least I'm trying to make something of my life instead of sitting back and mewling about how unfair it all is. Oh, I did for a while, I'll admit it, but it didn't help anything. Life isn't fair, Sutter. How the king and the Curia treat the Lorngeld isn't fair—but we can't change anything in this life unless we work together. And we can't change the way people think about us if we're going to start acting like the very Devil's Children they think we are!''

It was silent for a time; then Sutter slowly folded his arms over his chest in one last gesture of defiance. ''I just wanted a goddamned loaf of bread and a few coppers.''

Wearily, Athaya rubbed the smoke from her eyes. *God help him, he still can't see it.*

''Get out,'' she said after a pause. ''All of you.'' Her eyes skimmed over the dozens of wizards clustered around him, feeling sharp pangs of regret that she could no longer trust them. But the safety of the entire camp was more important than the safety of a few disgruntled wizards, and for the greater good, the troublemakers had to go.

Solemnly, she turned to Kale and Girard. ''Take a few men and search their tents. Confiscate anything that's not rightfully theirs. Then escort the lot of them to the forest's edge.''

''But where are we supposed to go?'' one of the other captives asked, visibly alarmed. Apparently Sutter hadn't gone into much detail about their glorious future.

"Sutter is a baron's son," she said with dark sarcasm, "as he so often reminds us. In the light of his rank, I'm sure Bishop Lukin would offer all of you a room." She left the rest unsaid. *An interrogation room in the cathedral crypt . . .*

Sutter scowled at her with undiluted hatred, like an inept laborer angry that he couldn't have the satisfaction of quitting his post before he was dismissed.

"Fine," he said. "Throw us out. We know enough spells to protect ourselves." He turned to the crowds of onlookers gathered around them. "And who else is with us? Who wants to do something other than rot here until spring?"

Athaya tensed her muscles, afraid of hearing a chorus of agreement, but the clearing was oddly quiet. Sutter's face twitched, unprepared for such rejection. But now that it came down to choosing between a familiar misery and an unfamiliar one—and especially now that the rebels were being made to depart without any food or money to speak of—Sutter's sympathizers dropped away. Although a handful of people voiced their support and went to collect their belongings, most slipped silently back to their tents, realizing that this was no time to fight among themselves. And realizing, Athaya hoped, that she was far more dedicated to their welfare than were Sutter and his allies.

The worst part about watching Sutter go, Athaya decided, was his genuine surprise at being expelled from the camp. Granted, he was preparing to leave anyway—after pilfering their precious supplies—but being banished openly infuriated him. Within the hour, Sutter and over four dozen others, most of them unmarried men and women with no families to inhibit their departure, were escorted to the forest's edge and deposited there with the forceful suggestion not to return.

By the time Athaya returned to bed it was nearly dawn and she knew sleep was unlikely to find her again. She stared up at the pockmarked ceiling, relieved that Sutter's disruptive presence was finally gone, but worried that, in time, others would follow his lead and desert her, too.

"Damn it all, what did they think this was, a seaside resort?" she cried, pounding the straw mattress with her fist. "I never promised them it would be easy. I had no idea it would get this bad."

Jaren put a comforting arm across her shoulders. "No one's blaming you, Athaya. They're just cold and tired and sick of eating dried fish and pemmican day after day."

"And they're blaming me for all of it—they need a scapegoat, and I'm the natural choice. God, sometimes I hate them. No, not hate," she amended hastily. "Resent, maybe. And not just Sutter and his sort . . . all of them. For needing so much more than I can give them. For *demanding* things of me." Athaya rolled onto her back, staring up at the ceiling. "Now I know how God must feel with all of us down here clamoring for things and never showing our gratitude other than mumbling a few hasty words over our dinner. It's enough to make Him turn away and stop listening to all our yammering, hoping we'll go away for a while and start fending for ourselves."

"But you don't want to turn away, do you?" Jaren said quietly, ever the voice of her conscience.

Athaya sighed. "Oh, of course not."

"It's easy to love someone and hate them all at the same time. Look at you and Kelwyn—you've admitted to me that you loved him, even though the two of you never did anything but fight with each other. I'm sure that's the way most of the people here feel about you. They hate you for bringing all of this hardship into their lives, but love you for giving them an alternative to absolution."

"Maybe. But that kind of responsibility is starting to get awfully intimidating. Changing the destiny of an entire race of people isn't exactly something I was brought up for."

Jaren tugged lightly at a lock of her hair. "If you can't lead them, Athaya, then who can?"

"I don't know," she said, burrowing deep into the bedcovers. "But surely there has to be *someone* in this world crazy enough to want to."

Jaren gave her a quick kiss on the cheek. "As crazy as you?" he said, regarding her dubiously. "I doubt that's possible."

And for the second time that night, Athaya tore the blankets away and subjected him to the cold night air.

The camp was markedly subdued for the next few days, but to her surprise, Athaya found that Sutter's revolt had sparked some much-needed changes. The remaining wizards were noticeably more attentive to their lessons—none of them, perhaps, wanting to be on the receiving end of another of Athaya's tirades—and although there was some grumbling, few bothered to squabble over food, even though it was more severely rationed now. The fire had destroyed nearly half of their grain, and there would be little bread or ale for the rest of the winter.

On a brisk, snowy morning one week after Sutter had gone, Athaya and Jaren were seated in the chapel reading from the *Book of Sages* and leading an informal discussion on the ethical aspects of power. In response to Sutter's determination to use magic against their enemies, Athaya thought it prudent to remind the other wizards at camp that such a thing went against all the ancient Masters' teachings.

"So after hearing what Master Sidra wrote, what can you tell me about using your magic as a weapon to make other people do things you want them to?"

"She says we shouldn't," a fair-haired woman new to the camp replied. "Spells aren't for attacking or intimidating people, but for creating things and protecting ourselves. Doing anything else would be like playing God."

"So, for example, if I want the king to revoke the laws against magic, I can't just use my magic to force him to do it? To change his thoughts and make him believe it's what he wanted to do all along?"

The woman shook her head. "No. That would be taking unfair advantage and taking away his gift of free will. And that's almost as bad as the priests taking away our gift of magic by absolving us. Besides," she added more thoughtfully, "if you cast a spell on him to make him do your bidding, sooner or later the spell would break, and we'd all be right back where we started—if not farther behind."

Athaya nodded her admiration at the woman's keen perceptions. "Very good, Kate. You were listening well—better than I did when I first read this essay," she added wryly.

Just then, the door of the chapel creaked open, letting in a gust of frigid wind. Cameron, who had been on sentry duty at the forest's edge that morning, rushed up to Athaya in a flurry of agitation. "I found Sutter and some of the others," he said breathlessly. "Most of them have split up and gone home—I guess there was some sort of fight about leaving Sutter in charge—but the ones that are left are staying at the sheepfold. I saw smoke from their campfire this morning and went to find out what it was."

"Are they out of their minds?" Jaren said in disbelief. "The bishop's men have been watching that place for months."

"Sutter says it's safe enough," Cameron replied with a shrug. "You've got to admit, the fold's been deserted for a while. Maybe the bishop gave up."

"Maybe," Athaya conceded, although knowing the bishop's persistence as far as wizards were concerned, she highly doubted it. "But how did you know who it was? Did you go and talk to them?"

Cameron nodded, vaguely sad. "I know they're banished, but one of them—Trule—was my friend. Or at least I thought he was," he added sullenly. "I never thought he'd join up with Sutter. I wanted to try and persuade him to come back."

"And did you?"

"No." Cameron's expression shifted, and his eyes reflected grave distress. "They're using their magic to steal, your Highness." A former thief himself, Cameron knew well what trouble such a career could bring. "People in the city know they're doing it, too, and are getting angry at not being able to stop them."

Jaren shook his head at such flagrant stupidity. "Just like Aurel, practically begging the Tribunal to come after them."

"It's even worse than that," Cameron went on. "Yesterday they killed one of the bishop's Justices and had one of his servants tell the bishop that unless the laws are changed, they'll keep on killing."

Athaya slammed her book closed with barely controlled fury. "That does it. They've gone too far this time."

She was too enraged to work an effective translocation, so she worked off her excess agitation by stalking through the snow all the way to the sheepfold. Jaren and Cameron trailed along after her, neither of them thinking it wise for her to face Sutter and his allies alone. By the time they arrived, all three of them were thoroughly warmed by the brisk walk, and Athaya had even cast off her hood, allowing the bracing winds to weave her hair into a mass of ebony tangles.

Sutter and the others weren't even bothering to hide their presence at the fold. Not only had they neglected to ward their camp, but smoke from the cookfires drifted lazily through a hole in the roof, and raucous laughter could be heard over a hundred yards away. Athaya threw back the door of the fold to find nearly two dozen men and women in various stages of drunkenness, stuffing their mouths with eggs, cornbread, and bacon. Athaya's mouth watered at the smell, but she knew that none of this feast had come to them by honest means.

"Careful, boys," Sutter called out mockingly, when he saw Athaya silhouetted in the doorway. "Storm's a-brewing just off the starboard bow. But I suppose we'd better bow to royalty." He got unsteadily to his feet and bent forward, tumbling to the ground again as he lost his balance and spilling his tankard of ale across the sheepfold floor. As much ale, Athaya observed, as Tonia would have rationed him for a week back at the camp.

"I don't suppose I need to ask whether you stole all of this," Athaya said through gritted teeth, motioning to the banquet laid out before her—a banquet to which she was most certainly not invited.

Sutter plucked another slab of bacon from the fire and began to chew on it noisily, knowing that each bite made his guests squirm with envy. "You know, you Highness, it's truly amazing what you can just walk away with when you're hidden under a cloaking spell."

"Look, Sutter. I'm no priest who can threaten you with hell-fire if you steal and I can't make any of you live an honest life. But damn it all, you're going to give the rest of us a bad name and ruin everything we're trying to accomplish. Get out of this shire if this is the way you're going to make your living."

"Far as I know, this land belongs to Cedmond Jarvis, not you," Sutter pointed out. "If he wants us off, he can damned well tell us so himself."

"Can't you see what you're doing? You're playing right into the Tribunal's hands! They expect wizards to be evil and cor-rupt, and you're simply proving their point! Especially when you take the law into your own hands and start killing priests," she added, her gaze going dark.

Sutter threw a quick glance at Cameron. "He told you about that, eh? Well, who cares. They've killed enough of us—I say it's about time we started taking our revenge."

"And lower ourselves to their level? Sutter, didn't you listen to anything we tried to teach you? You can't use your powers to steal from people—or worse, to kill your enemies. It's just not right."

"And absolution *is*? And the Tribunal *is*?"

"I didn't say that. But fighting one evil with a different kind of evil isn't the solution."

Tired of arguing, Sutter scowled and took another long pull of ale. "Quit your preaching, Princess. My friends and I have found a pleasant way of getting by, and none of your self-righteous speeches are going to change our minds." To his right, a drowsy man belched his agreement.

Then Sutter rose unsteadily to his feet again and picked up a stick from the ground. He whispered a few slurred words, and the stick began to glow as green coils of fire wrapped themselves loosely around it, wavering unsteadily at times, seemingly drunk themselves. In moments, the stick had been transformed into a rod of deadly fire, and in an angry burst of strength, Sutter flung it at the doorway with all his might.

Jaren jerked Athaya and Cameron out of the rod's fiery path only an instant before it struck the doorjamb, leaving an ugly, blackened scar. Then the weapon dropped to the ground, hissing as the fire-coils expired against the earthen floor, their energy quickly spent.

"Damn you, Sutter, be careful!" Jaren cried, kicking the stick away. "That's a powerful spell, and you don't know the first thing about controlling it!"

Sutter ignored him and turned an unfocused glare on Athaya. "Get out," he spat. "You don't want us at your camp, and we don't want you at ours." He retrieved the now-harmless stick and waved it menacingly at them, as if it were the finest of swords. "The boy's all right," he added, cocking his head at Cameron. "He's a friend of Trule's, so he can stay and have something to eat. But you two—out."

Athaya pulled her hood up. "Come on, Jaren. We can't do any more good here." And after obtaining Cameron's assurances that he would follow behind them shortly, Athaya headed back toward the forest's edge.

She and Jaren didn't exchange a word on the way, and Athaya was so full of black thoughts that she almost didn't hear the hoofbeats, distant yet growing louder. Hoofbeats like those she had heard in Kilfarnan, heralding the Tribunal.

Wheeling around, Athaya saw a squadron of black-robed men bearing down on the sheepfold, swords drawn; Bishop Lukin, it seemed, had not taken the murder of his Justice well. In their arrogance, Sutter had posted no sentries to guard against such an attack and drunk as he and his friends were, they would never realize their peril until it was too late.

And at the moment, they weren't the only ones in danger.

Three of the black-clad Justices, having spotted two stragglers at the forest's edge, broke apart from the group and rode toward Athaya and Jaren at a furious pace. Athaya didn't have to wonder whether they had corbal crystals; one of the men held his weapon hilt up, catching as much of the sun's winter rays as possible. And even at this distance, she knew that it was a large gem; her adept-level senses already winced at its mind-numbing effect.

"Come on," Jaren said, casting a cloaking spell over them as they lunged into the woods, following the rune trail to safety. "We can't help them now."

Athaya stopped dead in her tracks. "But Cameron—he's still back there!"

"I know," Jaren said solemnly, still pulling her forward. "But it's too late. Now hurry—we may be invisible, but we still leave footprints. We'll be safe once we reach the creek."

They were well ahead of their pursuers and, with the added protection of a cloaking spell, knew that the riders would soon give up their hunt for the easier prey awaiting them back at the sheepfold. She and Jaren traveled a short distance on the ice-covered rocks peppering a shallow creek, then stopped to listen. The woods behind them were silent.

"I think we're safe now."

"*We* are," Athaya replied softly.

"Cam's clever, and the corbals won't bother him," Jaren pointed out, though his optimism sounded forced. "He may find a way to give those soldiers the slip. As for the others . . ." He paused, and the hopefulness died from his eyes. "They'll have to live with the choices they've made."

Athaya lowered her gaze. *Or die for them, as the case may be.*

CHAPTER 16

HEARING THE EXPECTED KNOCK AT HIS STUDY DOOR, Bishop Lukin laid a strip of red velvet across the illuminated pages of his prayer book. "Come," he said, beckoning his young clerk into the chamber.

"Your Grace? We're ready for you on the lower level."

Lukin rose gracefully to his feet. "Excellent, Brother Giles." He pushed the prayer book to one side; it was time to act upon its exquisite scripture, not merely muse upon it.

The bishop's pace was markedly brisk as he and Brother Giles descended the steep, spiral steps that led into the cathedral crypt. Above them, the sanctuary was silent and serene, the air spiced with incense and tinted by the sunlight streaming through the great rose window. But the sunless realm below was thick with death and decay, imbued with the creak of wood and iron, the wails of dying men, the stench of blood and waste, and of rotting straw and flesh. Brother Giles held a scented handkerchief tight against his nose as they proceeded, but the bishop did not so much as wrinkle his nose, not even when two of his brethren carried a corpse from one of the cells, its foulness only slightly dampened by a thin and tattered shroud.

The bishop shooed a rat from his path and then turned to his clerk. "How many of them survived the attack?"

"Five," Giles replied. He led the bishop down a narrow,

smoky corridor and stopped before an iron-banded door. "Their leader is in here."

"Is he one that killed Brother Geoffrey?"

"The others say he is."

Nodding darkly, the bishop signaled for the soldier at the door to admit him. The cell was cold and dim—before the advent of the Tribunal, it had served as a wine cellar—but the bright flare of torches on either side of the door were bright enough to arouse the energies of the corbal crystal resting on a square of velvet in the center of an overturned barrel. Seated before the barrel with his hands bound behind him with iron cuffs, Sutter Dubaye trembled violently from both the chill and the intense pain caused by the walnut-sized gem. On a stool in the corner, a black-robed priest scratched words on a sheet of parchment with a quill, taking down every word that escaped the prisoner's parched lips.

The bishop stepped gingerly over a pile of soiled rushes as he approached his captive, not wishing to sully the embroidered hem of his cassock. "Sutter Dubaye, is it?" he said, taking in the young man's bloodied clothing, matted brown hair, and rancid breath. "My colleagues and I have been looking for you."

Sutter glared up at him with one brown eye; the other was bruised and swollen shut. He made no reply, so the bishop continued. "I've heard of your father, the baron."

"Have you arrested him, too?" Sutter formed each word with deliberate care; the corbal alone might have slurred his speech badly enough, but that, added to his recent excess of ale and his split and bleeding lips, made him difficult to understand.

"Not at all," the bishop replied, quite fluent in the language of suffering prisoners. "In fact, it was he who alerted us that you had evaded your sacred duty by refusing to be absolved. Baron Dubaye is a loyal son of the Church," he added pointedly, "unlike his unfortunate son."

The bishop extended his hand toward the man with the quill and parchment, silently requesting the paper. "Has he been cooperative?" he asked, absently scanning what the priest had already written.

"Mostly he's been sick," the priest replied with a sneer, gesturing to a foul-smelling bucket in the corner. "That is, when he's conscious. Too much ale, it seems."

The bishop snorted his contempt. "Stolen ale, no doubt."

"Look, I told him and now I'm telling you," Sutter cut in,

writhing against the presence of the corbal crystal. "I left her. Don't you see? I'm not one of them anymore!"

Lukin scowled down at him, unconvinced. "Of course you're not. You learned what you needed to know about your wicked powers and then you left—that's a common enough tale. And you were found living as an outlaw because your family disowned you and you had nowhere else to go. Nearly everyone who's allied themselves with the princess can say the same."

"You don't understand—"

"No, it is you who does not understand, wizard," Lukin snapped, looming over the imprisoned man. "You, who does not understand the magnitude of your crimes. But you shall."

The bishop gestured sharply to Brother Giles, who produced a short length of rope with two crude knots in it, roughly four inches apart. Stepping behind the prisoner, he fitted the knots over Sutter's eyes, then took the ends of the rope and wound them around a wooden, cross-shaped lever. Then, when the device was secured, he gave it a twist, like a ship's captain at the helm; the rope tightened, pressing the knots hard against the tender flesh. Sutter jerked against the chains, letting out a piglike squeal of pain.

"You'll see precious little in that vision sphere of yours without any eyes, my friend," Lukin told him. "What good will such magic do you then?"

"Please . . . just tell me what you want from me."

"Information. Cooperation. Simple things."

"But I told you I *left* her—"

"But you have not yet asked for absolution. This leads me to think that you are not truly repentant." A movement of his finger, and Giles gave the lever another turn. "You have far more to explain than your powers, my friend," Lukin went on, his voice low and menacing. "Your thievery alone could lose you your hands, did I wish it. And the murder of a royally appointed Justice? I could hang you for that right now."

Sutter swallowed loudly, making no attempt to deny his guilt for fear the rope would only twist again.

"Is there anything you can tell me to convince me to let you keep your hands or your life . . . or preferably both?" Lukin went on. "Anything at all?"

Then the words spewed out in a frightened stream, and the scribe snatched back his parchment and scrambled to take down everything the prisoner said. "I can take you there," Sutter told

them, his breathing rapid and shallow. "To the princess' camp.
I don't care what happens to her . . . to any of them. They didn't
want me there. They never did. And there's a trail of runes . . .
things only a wizard can see. Please, leave me my eyes," he
begged, licking a trickle of blood from his lips. "Then I can
follow it and lead you through the other protections to the
camp."

The bishop's brows rose in interest, but he kept his voice cool
and dispassionate. "Protections?"

"Wards. Illusions. Things to keep people away."

"Ah, yes. That would explain the failure of my men to locate
this place," the bishop mused. Thanks to his recent involvement
with Father Aldus, Lukin had encountered both sorts of trickery,
but as yet had found no way to combat them. "Tell me . . . how
many people live at this camp?"

"Five hundred perhaps—"

Brother Giles hissed his astonishment. "God defend us," he
said, appalled at such a figure.

"But they're not all wizards," Sutter added hastily. "A little
over half are wizards, but the rest are their husbands, wives,
and children. And most are hungry and weak . . . and they
won't be expecting you. A few dozen men with crystals and me
to show you the way, and you could take them all . . ."

The bishop stepped back, rubbing his chin thoughtfully. "In-
teresting. I'll admit, it's an offer I have not received from any
of your friends."

Sutter, enticed by the bishop's seeming acceptance, quickly
continued. "And I can see to it that you get more than wizards
out of your efforts. I know who stole the king's crown of corbals.
The boy . . . the one you caught at the sheepfold with us. He
did it—he told Trule about it once. There's a strongbox buried
beneath the chapel at the camp. A leather-bound box with three
brass locks . . ."

The bishop's eyes flashed, and had Sutter's eyes not been
blinded by the ropes, he would have realized the success of his
ploy. He had just imparted the precise description of the king's
stolen strongbox, and Lukin knew full well that if he were to
recover it, his Majesty would be grateful. Grateful enough, perhaps, to remember his name when it came time to appoint a
new archbishop of Delfarham.

He plucked the parchment from the scribe's hands and motioned him to the door. "The boy . . . get a signed confession

out of him and then see that he's hanged like the common thief he is. And make certain it's done publicly. I want the people of Kaiburn to see what happens to those who dare steal his Majesty's property.''

''And the others?''

''I have what I need from this one,'' the bishop replied negligently. ''See that they share the boy's fate.''

Nodding, the black-robed scribe scurried from the room like a rat, while Lukin turned his attentions back to Sutter. ''What you have said interests me,'' he remarked, smiling at his captive, though Sutter could not see it. ''Therefore, I propose that tomorrow morning we go on a hunt. You are going to lead my men and me directly to the wizard's camp. And if I am pleased with what I find there, then perhaps we can continue to work together. If not . . .'' He lifted one finger, and Brother Giles gave the lever another half turn, pressing Sutter's already bruised eyes farther into his skull. ''Well, you won't want to think about that.''

Athaya stood before an oblong panel in the chapel, speaking across the miles to Dom DePere in Kilfarnan. She wasn't sure if Sutter's rebellion would remain an isolated problem and thought it wise to alert her other allies to such a danger among their own followers.

''We haven't had a full-fledged revolt yet,'' Mason told her, ''but there are definite factions among the students. I'll be more alert from now on, but I'm hoping that Aurel was our only real malcontent. I'll send word to Jenna and John—the ones who started the southern school,'' he reminded her. ''I doubt they'll run into this kind of thing, though—someone must be funding them, since I rarely hear about food shortages there. Oh, and before I forget—I've sent another bolt of runecloth to Sir Jarvis. It should arrive in another week.''

''Then Drianna finally got there?''

''Who?'' Mason replied, puzzled. ''No one's come from Kaiburn recently. I just thought you might need the extra cloth.''

Athaya bit her lip, worried that something unthinkable had happened to the Sarian woman and her husband, but before she could ask Mason anything further, Kale poked his head into the chapel.

''I'm sorry to interrupt, your Highness, but you asked me to tell you if there was any sign of the bishop's men.''

Athaya nodded and turned back to the mist-edged panel. "I have to go, Mason—we've been expecting some unwelcome guests since yesterday, and they've finally arrived." She touched her finger to the flat stone in her palm, and the panel went black. In another moment, the black faded to white, and the window lost its shape and returned in thin trails of fog to her fingertips, from whence it had come. Pocketing the ward key, she looked to Kale expectantly.

"Soldiers. Fifty or sixty, at a guess. Girard relayed the message from the sentry at the forest's edge." He paused to clear his throat. "Sutter's leading them."

It wasn't good news, but at least Athaya had been expecting it. "Spread the word for everyone to be alert and not to leave the camp for any reason. I don't think the bishop's men will get this far—I just reset all the wards myself this morning—but let's not take chances."

Kale departed to carry out his orders, but Athaya remained in the chapel and curled up in one of the pews. *"Volo videre,"* she whispered, calling her vision sphere to form in her palms. Others would already be monitoring the tense situation in like manner, but Athaya felt compelled to witness it herself.

By the time the image came into focus, Sutter and the bishop's men had come within a hundred yards of the forest's edge, eyeing the line of oaks for a likely entrance. She was surprised to see Sutter alone, without any of those that had been captured with him. Not even Cameron was there, she realized sadly. Close to twenty bodies were strewn about the sheepfold after the bishop's raid—taking prisoners alive clearly wasn't high on the bishop's list of priorities—and Athaya held out little hope for the others. And while he didn't seem to realize it, Sutter was in just as much peril, although his actions revealed that he clearly hoped to buy his freedom from the Tribunal by betraying his own kind. His battered face, however, should have convinced him just how remote a possibility that was.

"Now where is this invisible trail?" she heard the bishop demand, his voice clearly audible through the swirling mists of the sphere.

Sutter picked his way along the forest's edge, looking for the first rune in the trail that led to the camp. Two soldiers followed close behind him, each holding a strip of leather that bound one of the wizard's wrists to the pommel of his saddle. "I—it's here somewhere," he called out. "I just haven't found it yet." He flinched, and Athaya caught sight of the walnut-sized corbal suspended from a leather thong at the bishop's throat—an indication of just how much Lukin trusted him.

"I'd advise you to try harder, my friend. My patience is short, and my men are eager for battle." Behind him, war-horses shifted restlessly in the snow, while fifty grim-faced soldiers gazed into the depths of the forest, hands poised in readiness over their sword hilts.

"The crystal," Sutter said after a time. "I think it's interfering with my sight. If you cover it, maybe I can see the trail."

Lukin was reluctant to comply with this request, but with fifty soldiers to a single wizard, how much damage could he do? He covered the crystal with a gloved hand and motioned sharply for Sutter to continue his work. Sutter stumbled ahead, squinting into the trees for any sign of the blazing red runes.

"Well?" the bishop called out. "You told me the trail began near a dead oak, and we've passed three such trees already."

"No, wait—give me a few more minutes. I'll find it."

Athaya watched closely for the next half hour, as Sutter nervously guided the soldiers along a forest trail—a trail, she knew, that backtracked to the south and came nowhere near the camp. When the bishop and his soldiers emerged from the woods only a short distance from where they had entered them a half hour before, Sutter realized that his ploy was not working.

"There *are* no runes, are there?" Lukin said, halting his mount near a copse of dead brush.

Sutter shook his head in bewilderment, and then in growing dread. "T-they must have erased them."

The bishop's gaze grew dark. "Then they also must have expected that you'd betray them. You can't be trusted by either side, it seems. Just like Aldus," he added under his breath.

Then, realizing his options were quickly becoming scarce, Sutter tried a last, reckless chance at escape. Shouting the words of invocation, he cast whiplike ropes of green fire in each of his hands, slashing backward at his bonds and slicing easily through the leather straps like steel through tender flesh.

But Bishop Lukin had come prepared to battle hundreds of wizards, not just one. At his command, given almost languidly, each of the fifty men uncovered the hilt of a dagger, a ring, a jeweled brooch—all of them containing a corbal crystal. Sutter stopped his flight in midstride, his eyes rolling back into his head as he screamed his agony at the gems' torment. Reeling, he crumpled to the ground, writhing upon the snow as if his flesh were afire.

The bishop turned to his first-in-command. "Finish this," he snapped, and in a matter of seconds, a rope was hurled over the branch of a nearby oak, and a noose was tightly secured around Sutter's throat.

"No, no—I'll help you find them!" he shrieked, but the panic in his voice revealed that he already knew it to be too late.

"And what good is that now? Our main weapon was surprise, you fool. If we don't have that, our crystals won't do much good. And if they've erased the trail, chances are they're watching us right now and already know we're here."

The bishop curled one finger, and Sutter was jerked from the ground and sent aloft. Athaya steeled herself, tempted to banish the sphere, but instead she watched his death throes, morbidly compelled by the eyes, bulging and bloodfilled; the tongue, black and protruding; the limbs, twitching long after he was dead. And despite the gruesomeness of it, Lukin had actually dealt him a mercy; the crystals would have tormented Sutter to insanity, but the rope put an abrupt end to his pain.

Once assured that his victim was dead, Bishop Lukin chewed on his lower lip, deep in thought. Then he turned in his saddle and seemed to gaze directly into Athaya's eyes. "Are you watching us, your Highness? Watching us in that little globe of yours? If so, then know this. I'll flush you out of there one day. This forest is vast and it may take time, but you won't be able to hide from me forever. None of you."

Athaya's sphere wavered in her fingers as she watched the bishop spur his horse and ride off, taking his soldiers with him. Only when she was sure he would not return did she banish the sphere and leave the chapel.

Athaya searched for Kale and found him near the bell tower. He was kneeling beside Master Tonia, who was just banishing her own sphere, her weathered face pale as candle wax.

"Gather a few men and go cut him down," Athaya told the guardsman quietly. "We'll bury him behind the chapel next to Terrence."

Kale departed to do his unpleasant duty, and Athaya helped Tonia to her feet. "I suppose I can go replace the rune trail now," Tonia said, her manner markedly subdued.

"Let's wait a few days. Four others were captured along with Sutter; the bishop may try again." But Athaya doubted that he would try the same tactic twice; predictability was not the bishop's way. He would wait for a less hazardous plan—something not dependent on a single wizard's shifting loyalties.

"It's not your fault, Athaya," Tonia said as she turned to go. "He was a bitter sort and he brought this on himself."

"I know. But Sutter isn't going to be the only Lorngeld in Caithe willing to sell himself to the Tribunal." Athaya shivered at a sudden gust of wind. "We're not going to be able to keep ourselves safe here forever."

Tonia patted her shoulder gently. "You said we'd have to win this war one wizard at a time. We'll just have to survive it one day at a time, too. It's all we can do."

But despite Tonia's comforting words, Athaya was more troubled than ever. For the first time, she was forced to realize that the greatest danger to her crusade might not be the king or his Church, but those of her own kind—those who wanted something other than the knowledge of how their magic worked—those like Aurel and Sutter who wanted to do battle with their enemies and kill before they were killed themselves.

Armed men with swords and corbals were a familiar enemy— an enemy she had dealt with before. But other wizards seeking her downfall? That was another type of battle entirely, and one she had never prepared herself to fight.

favored Mosel with a self-deprecating smile. "I've never been

CHAPTER 17

�֍

"**T**HAT'S ANOTHER TEN CROWNS YOU'VE LOST," Nic- olas said, scooping up the generous pile of silver coins. He grinned at his companion across the enameled game table. "The dice aren't being kind to you today, your Grace."

Brandegarth chuckled, low and soft. "It would appear not." He picked up the pair of ivory dice and dropped them back into the throwing cup, gazing wanly at his greatly diminished hoard of silver.

Although he knew it would be rude to count his winnings at the table, Nicolas calculated there were roughly fifty crowns before him. *About time,* he thought inwardly. This was his third visit to the Sage's palace, but the only time he had managed to win at dice. Strange that his luck had changed so abruptly, but he wasn't about to complain. Perhaps it was the charm of the new year; he'd spent the winter holidays catching up on his duties as lord marshall, and this was the first opportunity he'd had to visit the Sage in weeks.

Why he came, he wasn't exactly sure. For all their lengthy chats—and despite his own subtle prodding—Brandegarth of Crewe rarely said anything on the subject of wizardry, preferring to converse on such benign topics as the island's climate, the construction of his palace, or the latest speculations as to which members of his court were currently being cuckolded. On the topic of Athaya, however, their positions were neatly reversed; Brandegarth posed the seemingly casual questions, and Nicolas answered them as vaguely as possible before deftly changing the subject. He hadn't revealed anything of real significance—or at least he didn't think he had. Brandegarth had an engaging manner—much like his own, Nicolas liked to think—and had an uncanny ability to make him speak of things that he might not have mentioned otherwise, such as his turbulent relationship with Durek, or his lifelong devotion to Athaya. He could only hope that, in time, the Sage would come to interpret his openness as a show of faith and would warm to the subject of his cult's true purpose and his own role among the Sarian Lorngeld.

"The weather looks none too good," Nicolas observed, gazing at the fat flakes of snow now whirling about the casement. "Perhaps I should start back for the manor; I don't relish the thought of riding all the way home in a blizzard." *And neither will Ranulf,* he added to himself, knowing that the mercenary would grow anxious if the prince's dice game ran longer than a few hours. As he had done during each of the prince's three visits, Ranulf waited in the Great Hall, unwilling to let Nicolas journey to the palace alone, but equally unwilling to risk meeting the Sage face-to-face.

"No need to trouble yourself about the weather," Brandegarth assured him. "My wizard's senses will tell me if there's a storm coming." He sauntered to the window and latched the shutters, complaining of a draft. Nicolas thought he heard the Sage mutter something else under his breath and saw him make a subtle gesture with his fingers—perhaps a spell to quell the draft—before returning to the table. "And even if there was a storm," he added amiably, "you would be most welcome to stay the night, as my guest."

Nicolas smiled awkwardly, mentally picturing Ranulf's reaction to such an invitation.

"Besides, it's rude of you to win all my money and then run off," the Sage scolded lightly, though he didn't look in the least disturbed by his losses. In fact, Nicolas found his mood today remarkably cheerful; an undercurrent of mirth brightened his eyes, as if musing upon a long-awaited pleasure that was now only moments away.

"I suppose a few more games won't hurt," Nicolas agreed, rattling the dice in their cup. He was secretly glad for the delay; heatstones made the Sage's chamber far cozier than his room at the manor would be, Nicolas' wine was expertly mulled, and the chestnuts in the pewter bowl at his elbow were roasted to perfection. "And I won't be surprised if you win every coin back from me," he went on. "My sister is quite fond of reminding me how poor my luck is with dice, and to her credit, she's usually right."

"Wizards often are," Brandegarth replied with a grin.

This time, however, Nicolas' prophecy did not come to pass. His winnings increased with every roll of the dice, and within the hour, he found himself nearly one hundred crowns richer.

"A small fortune," Brandegarth mused. He plucked a chestnut from the bowl and cracked it purposefully between his teeth. "A fortune that, as I understand it, your sister could use quite desperately." He paused, waiting for a comment from Nicolas that did not come. "I hear that winter is just as unkind on the mainland as it has been here," he continued, again with well-crafted disinterest. "Bad enough under normal circumstances, but doubly so for the Lorngeld of Caithe. Rumor has it that Princess Athaya is drawing a great number of people to her schools, but that those who come are virtually destitute. The moment their magic is discovered, the Tribunal confiscates their lands and possessions, and with the winter being what it is this year, they're hard-pressed to so much as stay alive."

Nicolas could conceal neither his alarm nor his surprise. "It seems you have more recent information than I do," he admitted. "I haven't received any messages from Caithe since I arrived here two months ago."

"Being brother to a wizard, Nicolas, you know that my people have ways of discovering things outside of normal channels," he said, smiling his pleasure at the air of mystery he conjured about himself. He bit into another chestnut. "Puzzling. Why do Athaya and her people choose to live like beggars in the forest? Surely if they combined their talents, they would have the power to bend the king to their will."

"Athaya thinks that using force will only prove that wizards are as bad as the Caithan people have been led to believe. She hopes that in time, as more and more Lorngeld refuse absolution, Durek will have no choice but to revoke the laws against magic."

"Time may be a commodity she does not have, my friend— not if her people are homeless and starving." Brandegarth leaned closer, and the pounded silver torque circling his throat gleamed like molten moonlight. "But you are the king's brother," he observed matter-of-factly. "Couldn't you persuade him to relent?"

Nicolas laughed mirthlessly. "You overestimate the amount of influence I have with him."

"I'm surprised it does not anger you," the Sage remarked, picking a bit of nut from his teeth. "To be a prince of Caithe and yet be so helpless."

Nicolas hadn't pictured himself exactly that way before and felt a subtle surge of resentment. "Oh, I get angry enough. It baffles me how Durek can be so pigheaded about the Lorngeld, when our father was exactly the opposite."

The Sage offered him an empathetic nod. "If only God had made you the elder brother, eh? Or made Athaya a boy?"

"Believe me, your Grace, I've wondered about that myself. There are times I wish that Durek—" Nicolas broke off, suddenly aware that once again, Brandegarth had lured him into revealing far more than he intended. "Athaya's right, though; force won't solve Caithe's problems. And her teacher, Master Hedric, told her that she was destined to solve them—he knew Athaya was going to lead this crusade long before she did, and since he trained her himself, she must be going about things the right way."

Brandegarth's eyes glittered their private amusement, and Nicolas had an uneasy suspicion that his remarks carried more significance than he realized. But before he could devise a suitably leading question, a crisp knock at the door heralded the arrival of Tullis the steward. He stepped into the chamber and gave Nicolas a cursory, if vaguely pitiable, glance before bowing to his master.

"We've had a slight problem, your Grace. His Highness' servant has attempted to return to the manor without him, and in light of the inclement weather, we thought it best to . . . insist he stay the night."

"Inclement—what?" Nicolas darted to the window and threw back the shutters and was promptly blinded by the shimmering expanse of whiteness before him. The snow fell so thick that he could barely make out the courtyard below, much less distinguish it from the sky above him, and the storm showed no signs of abating.

It's not possible! he thought anxiously. *We haven't been dicing that long . . .*

But did that matter when there was a wizard involved?

Nicolas swallowed back the hot bile inching up his throat. Suddenly, he knew that this was no natural storm—and that he had seen Brandegarth cast the weather-spell himself. The Sage wasn't quelling a draft—he was calling a blizzard to insure that his guest did not leave. And Ranulf must have sensed his trickery and smelled a trap. Why else would Ranulf abandon him like this, if not to warn Josef and the others of his peril?

Nicolas tried to swallow again, but could not; his throat was constricted, as if bound by an invisible noose. The Sage's plans for the day extended far beyond mere games of chance, and Nicolas cursed himself for a fool for not realizing it sooner. No wonder the Sage had let him win at dice; it had proved an effective means of enticing him to linger. Still, he suspected that not everything had progressed according to the Sage's desires. Brandegarth tapped his fingers on the enameled table, betraying a hint of indecision. Clearly, he had not expected Ranulf's attempted escape, but he was doing his best to hide his irritation.

"My senses appear to have misled me," Brandegarth observed with forced languidness, regarding his tempest with idle pride. "Perhaps my forty-two years are starting to weigh upon me more than I care to admit." But the words ran counter to the chilling tone in which he spoke them—he saw the shocked realization on the prince's face and felt no need to dissemble any longer—and as his amiable smile slowly re-formed itself into a sinister one, Nicolas knew that he was well and truly snared.

"Where is he now?" the Sage asked, glancing sidelong at his steward.

"In the Great Hall. Shall I have him brought to you?"

At the Sage's curt nod, Tullis bowed and departed, closing the door soundlessly behind him. Once he was gone, Brandegarth snickered softly to himself. "Such arrogance in thinking he could simply walk away from my palace. It certainly sounds like old Ranulf."

Nicolas' jaw dropped like a stone. "How did you know—" Then, like the frenzied chiming of church bells, fresh alarms began to sound in every corner of his brain. He knew his chances of escape were remote at best, but before he took another breath, Nicolas lurched drunkenly to the door.

Brandegarth didn't trouble himself to get up, but only turned slightly in his chair. "I would not suggest touching the door handle, my Prince."

Nicolas heard the warning too late to halt his arm. His fingers wrapped around the iron handle, and he cried out as shock waves of pain blasted their way from his fingertips to his shoulder. He tried to pull away, but the iron's unearthly coldness had fused his flesh to the handle.

Brandegarth strolled to his side, whispering a hasty phrase, then peeled Nicolas' hand away. He felt little pain, but couldn't fail to notice that a thin layer of skin remained frozen there.

"I'm afraid I must insist," the Sage observed, guiding him back to the gaming table. "Your servant is perceptive; only the most suspicious of wizards would have detected my creation as an unnatural storm. But his perceptions have needlessly complicated matters, and now I fear I must be more forceful than I intended in seeing that the two of you remain here a while longer."

The Sage handed him a silk scarf with which to bandage his hand and within a few minutes—the longest and most agonizing minutes of his life—Nicolas heard several pairs of footsteps in the corridor, growing louder as they approached. Mixed among them was a stream of bellowed curses, a peal of feminine laughter, then the clunking sound of a body being thrust against a paneled wall. Tullis entered a moment later, followed by two guardsmen, both of whom held their halberds at a very short distance from their captive's throat. Ranulf's face was flushed with rage and marred by a darkening bruise below his cheekbone, but—to Nicolas' vast surprise—the mercenary's arms were not bound; his hands clenched and unclenched rapidly at his sides, desperately seeking a Sarian throat to squeeze.

But Nicolas was even more surprised by the satin-draped woman who sauntered into the chamber behind them. He almost didn't recognize her, so altered was she from their first meeting in Caithe. Her auburn hair was beribboned and scented, her snug-fitting gown generously strewn with pearls, and her eyes were sultry, without any trace of a peasant girl's naïveté. Drianna was conscious of his disbelieving stare, but merely tossed back her hair and let her eyes sparkle, as if he were just another man awed by her beauty.

"This is the prince's servant, your Grace," Tullis said, prodding Ranulf forward. He urged the mercenary to bow his respect to the Sage, but Ranulf merely hawked loudly and spat on the rush-covered floor.

Brandegarth smiled broadly, seemingly delighted by the insult. "Ranulf. Ranulf Osgood. Drianna told me it was you, but I didn't think it possible." The Sage favored Nicolas with a sidelong grin. "You appear to have fallen in with some very disreputable characters, my Prince."

"He sure the hell has," Ranulf snapped back, his damning glare falling equally to both the Sage and his lady.

"Still the mercenary, eh, Ranulf?" Brandegarth went on merrily. "Hiring yourself out to the prince of Caithe? It's a step up from the earl of Tusel, but you still do seem to attach yourself to the losing side of any battle, don't you?"

"And now we're your prisoners of war, is that it?"

Brandegarth made a patronizing clucking sound with his tongue. "You insult me. It would have been a far greater cruelty to let you lose your way in the snow and freeze to death. You are a soldier, Ranulf—or at least you were. You know what blizzards can be." Brandegarth indulged in a sigh that spoke of mild annoyance. "You've made this far more unpleasant that it had to be, my friend. I had planned to let both of you stay the night as my guests and send you home in the morning. That is still my intention, but now it seems you will persist in thinking of yourselves as captives."

"What are we supposed to think? Your goon here told me you'd slice Nicolas' throat if I so much as thought about escaping." He jerked an elbow at one of the guardsmen—a man Nicolas found disturbingly familiar.

Brandegarth gave only the mildest glance of rebuke to his guardsman, knowing the threat to be a perfectly valid one, but wishing that his servant had not voiced it so bluntly. "Connor can be a bit tactless at times."

"Then Connor," Nicolas stammered, at last regaining the use of his tongue, "he isn't her husband?" He didn't know why he bothered to ask; the familiar way Drianna rested one hand on the Sage's forearm revealed the true object of her desires.

Brandegarth shook his head. "Only a soldier of my employ. Not a wizard, but worthy enough to serve me in his way."

"And both of them were spying on Athaya . . . for you."

Brandegarth laughed aloud, deep from the belly. "Is that so surprising? Why else did you come to Sare?"

Nicolas thought it best to ignore the question. He stared at Drianna, realizing her as the source of the Sage's information about Caithe. "You told him about everything . . . about Ranulf . . ."

"He and Brand are old friends," Drianna said, casting a coy glance to Ranulf that went thoroughly unappreciated. "It would have been rude of me not to mention it." As she spoke, Nicolas realized that her voice was as altered as her appearance. Gone was the coarse but lyrical speech of the countryside; now her words were polished and somewhat false-sounding—an exactness that Nicolas rarely heard even at court, as if she had studied diligently to overcome her common origins.

"But why send her?" he asked the Sage, trying to forget about his own peril long enough to piece together the scraps of what could be a vitally important puzzle. "Why didn't you go yourself?"

"With three broken ribs, a wrenched knee, and a host of burns, gashes, and bruises? I fear I wasn't up to a long journey at the time. I was Challenged in June of last year, and the man was quite talented." Brandegarth frowned, as if recalling an unpleasant memory. "Quite talented, indeed."

"Too damned bad he didn't kill you," Ranulf growled, but a blow on the ear from one of the guardsmen silenced him again.

"Challenged?" Nicolas asked.

"For my position as Sage. One does not become Sage like one becomes a king, by inheriting the title from one's father. One merits it by defeating a rival in combat—by proving one's magic is stronger and is therefore worthy of the honor. Granted, some kings obtain their thrones through warfare," he added, with what Nicolas regarded as a markedly thoughtful tone, "but it isn't the custom in Sare.

"Drianna's brother, Devyn, Challenged me several years ago. Apparently, he thought that being the Sage would be a more glorious occupation than that of swineherd. He should have stayed with his pigs," Brandegarth added, with a contemptuous wave of his hand. "He was a fool—and an inept magician, as Drianna will gladly tell you. However, if not for Devyn's foolishness, I never would have met his delightful young sister. I was certain she was a wizard herself, her beauty bewitched me so. We're both of us eight years older now, and Drianna is no less lovely than she was at sixteen."

Smiling, Drianna wrapped her arm around the Sage's waist. "Brand offered me a place in his household and saved me from being married off to some witless dullard and playing the dutiful peasant wife the rest of my days."

"At least that would have been an honorable life," Nicolas

observed steadily, as the edges of his fear gradually hardened to anger.

Brandegarth lifted one of his brows. "Meaning?"

"If she was your wife, my Lord, then you would have said so."

Drianna's nostrils flared, but she said nothing.

"Bold words for a man in your position," Brandegarth observed. He detached himself from Drianna and came closer to Nicolas than the prince would have liked. "Surely you realize that I cannot let you scurry back to Caithe and tell your sister all that has transpired here. Such knowledge would prejudice her response. No, I wish to present her with the facts as *I* see them, without undue influence from you."

Again, Nicolas felt bile inch up his throat. "What does Athaya have to do with this?"

Brandegarth reclaimed his chair, motioning Drianna to stand at his side. "Everything, I assure you," he said, with a degree of confidence that Nicolas found unnerving. "I first heard about your sister's crusade last summer, after I'd been injured. Since I couldn't travel myself, I agreed to let Drianna go to Caithe, especially once she convinced me that as a woman, she would be able to befriend your sister more easily. Of course, we had no idea at the time that Athaya had been imprisoned—Drianna only discovered that after arriving on the mainland. But she decided to continue on to Kaiburn, thinking that one of the princes' allies would surely be plotting some sort of rescue. The rest, I gather, you already know. And now that I have compared Drianna's observations to your own thoughts," he concluded, piercing Nicolas with his gaze, "I have a fairly good idea what sort of woman I will be dealing with."

"Dealing with?" Nicolas echoed, feeling the bile reach the back of his tongue. "I thought you were waiting for a sign to tell you when to return to Caithe. Or was that nothing but a ruse?"

"Not a ruse, my Prince. Not at all. The sign," he said simply, "has come." Brandegarth leaned closer, preparing to impart the most precious of secrets. "Or should I say, *she* has come."

Nicolas and Ranulf exchanged horrified glances. "Are you trying to tell me that *Athaya* is the sign?" Nicolas said, aghast. He pulled at a collar suddenly grown too tight, uncomfortably aware that he and Ranulf were caught in a far larger web than they ever imagined. "But that's absurd! She doesn't know anything about you or your followers . . . how can she possibly be the sign you were waiting for?"

The Sage waved his question away as if clearing the air of candle smoke. "You are not of the Lorngeld, my Prince. Such details do not concern you."

"They damned well do if you're going to keep him prisoner here because of them," Ranulf retorted. "And just how long are you supposing to do that, anyway? You can't keep us here forever, you know."

Nicolas nodded rapidly. "That's right. If we don't return to the manor—"

"I didn't say you would not return. I said you would not return *yet*. But even if you did not," he speculated, "do you really think anyone would come for you?" His gaze grew menacing. "Lord marshalls have had a nasty habit of disappearing over the years. You, Prince Nicolas, would simply be added to their unfortunate number."

"Leave him the hell alone!" Ranulf shouted. He took a step forward, but the curved blade of a halberd persuaded him to hold his ground. "It's not fair—he can't even put up a decent fight against you."

"And you can?" Brandegarth replied. "Remember to whom you are speaking, Ranulf. I am the Sage and I have killed many a wizard in my time."

"And a few who weren't," Ranulf grumbled, but without his former brashness. He glared at the Sage, eyes reflecting old hatreds. "Everyone in the squadron knew it was you who poisoned that drill sergeant, Brandegarth. We couldn't prove it, but we knew."

Brandegarth winced slightly, shamed by the exploits of his youth. "I was rather reckless in my younger days, Ranulf, and prone to extreme forms of vengeance for the imagined cruelties of my superiors. But that was before I came into my magic and discovered that I was destined to lead my people. I assure you," he added darkly, "I am far more discerning about my murders now."

Nicolas waited for Ranulf's brazen reply, but to his dismay, it never came. Suddenly, Nicolas felt more helpless than he ever had in his life. Discerning or not, the Sage had the ability to rid himself of anyone he wished with relative ease, and if past wizards had fallen to the Sage's power, then men without magic, be they drill sergeants or princes, did not stand a chance.

"What are you going to do with us?" Nicolas asked, mustering as much dignity as he could.

"Do with you? Nothing, yet. And maybe nothing at all. That is why you'll be staying the night. You see, the time has come for me to speak to your sister face-to-face and discuss the future of the Lorngeld in Caithe. I shall impart to her the legacy of the Sages and reveal her true destiny to her. I only wish you to remain close at hand until I learn whether she will accept or reject it." Brandegarth's eyes narrowed. "Dameronne, the first Sage of my people, foresaw her acceptance—and you had best pray that he was right. Although she does not yet know it, it is her response, Prince Nicolas, that will determine *your* future, as well as mine."

But Nicolas knew Athaya as the Sage did not and knew that Dameronne, however powerful, had seen a false future. "Athaya will never join you—not without hearing from me first. The Circle of Masters has warned her about you."

Brandegarth sighed wearily. "Athaya has heard an abundance of Reykan lies about my people, but she has never been informed of my point of view—a grievous wrong which I intend to put to rights. And despite what Drianna has told me about her lofty sense of ethics," he added with a hint of scorn, "I suspect that Athaya harbors some small desire for the crown, some desire to be something more than the outlawed leader of a persecuted race."

"Never! She's told me so a dozen times."

"And why would she tell you anything else?" the Sage shot back. "For her to take Durek's place, you'd have to be out of the way as well—and the king's young son. Of course, for the Lorngeld to take their proper place in this world," he added with brutal logic, "you'd all have to go eventually. To put it simply, Nicolas, I am going to restore my people to their former grace whether Athaya accepts my aid or not. But Dameronne's prophecy tells me that she will; perhaps, my Prince, he knew more about your sister's true desires than you do."

The Sage's troubling words hung in the air, unrefuted, as he took Drianna's arm and turned to leave. "Bring them food and wine," he instructed his steward, "but see that they do not leave this room."

"And if the wizard tries anything?" Tullis asked.

Brandegarth smiled grimly. "He won't. The prince will suffer for it if he does. But there is little need to look so glum," he added to his guests. "I fully expect you to depart in the morning."

And the only thought in Nicolas' mind as the Sage and his lady departed was that he had discovered more about this island than he had ever expected . . . or desired. The fortune he'd won at dice seemed woefully insignificant; suddenly, the day's stakes had gotten much too high, and Nicolas suspected that he was about to lose everything.

CHAPTER 18

※※

A THAYA SAT CROSS-LEGGED ON THE DIRT INSIDE THE cramped shelter, cradling her vision sphere between her palms, while Emma sat across the shallow pit of heat-stones and rubbed her temples, poised on the verge of fainting. Athaya had been walking past the woman's shelter when she heard a scream and rushed inside to find Emma lying facedown on the dirt, the sticky tendrils of a broken sphere glistening on her palms. Emma had been scrying for a glimpse of Pipewell, but the vision she obtained had shaken her so badly that she lost control of her spell. Once she had recovered her senses and found herself unable to recapture the image, she had begged Athaya to try, hoping to prove that she had glimpsed nothing but a reflection of her own fears.

"I was afraid something like this would happen," she was saying, her eyes rimmed with frantic tears. "I've been scrying the village every day since I left, hoping that no one's found out about me. My brother swore he'd say nothing, but everyone knew you were there. If someone betrayed him . . ." Emma's words trailed off, unable to voice the fear. "No, it can't have been Ethan that I saw."

Within the misty borders of her sphere, Athaya saw Pipewell's familiar village green, the well, and the stocks. But she also saw destruction—far worse destruction than the small-scale riot she had witnessed in September. This was clearly the Tribunal's

253

work—she spied a pair of black-robed men standing in the shadow of the village church, talking to the priest. They had likely been watching the village, since it was the first place Athaya had been seen after her escape from Saint Gillian's, and when Alec's power came and then Emma's, they no doubt felt the village corrupt—a haven for the Devil's Children.

"Oh, please . . . just tell me it wasn't my brother," Emma whimpered softly. "Tell me it wasn't Ethan . . ."

Athaya scried the cottage where she had helped Tonia heal Emma's arm—or rather, she scried the stretch of burned ground and blackened rubble that had once been the cottage. And nearby, dangling from the branch of a hickory tree, was the lifeless form of Emma's brother. It was not the cruelest form of death the Tribunal was capable of inflicting, but the lash marks striping his back gave evidence that he had suffered long before the noose embraced his throat.

Athaya dispersed the sphere, wishing to see no more. "I'm sorry," she said quietly. "Ethan is dead."

"Oh no, no, no . . ." Emma curled her legs tight against her chest and let out a low moan of anguish. "It's all my fault—"

"No, Emma. It's the fault of those who won't let you live in peace. But this is no time for theology—I'll leave you alone now." Athaya crawled through the waist-high entrance to Emma's lodge, her limbs feeling a great deal heavier than they had only moments ago. Had not Ethan once invited her into his cottage, she thought, he might well be alive today. It was scant comfort to know that even if she'd warned Emma about her oncoming magic months ago, it probably would not have saved either her brother or her home.

Shivering against gusts of icy wind that snaked under her cloak, Athaya threaded her way between the dozens of makeshift lodges huddled together in the clearing, seeking a few minutes of solitude in her own stone-warmed room. She had almost reached the sanctuary of the dormitory when she heard the crunch of hasty footsteps behind her and then the sound of Jaren's voice.

"Athaya, thank God," he said breathlessly, spinning her around to face him. He had a startled look on his face, as if someone had just doused him with cold water. "I've been looking everywhere for you."

"Whatever it is, I'm in no mood for it," she said sullenly, the image of Ethan's body still vivid in her mind. That, coming only hours after the news that Cameron and the others arrested with Sutter had been publicly hanged in Kaiburn that very morning, had made for a singularly miserable day.

"There's a summons for you in the chapel."

Athaya sighed wearily and turned away. "Tell Mason I'll contact him later. I need to go lie down for a while."

"But it isn't Mason," Jaren said, staying her with his arm. "It's Drianna. And she's calling with a panel."

Athaya turned back to him very slowly. "But how could she . . . oh, now I understand," she said, relaxing tense shoulders. "Drianna asked me for a ward key the night before she left the camp. She must have found her brother and had him open the panel for her."

They ducked into the chapel, now cleared of the wizards who had been using it as a classroom only minutes before, and there, at the end of the short aisle, was Drianna's panel. It was positioned squarely before the altar, a shimmering oblong bordered by gentle swirls of light and dark, and Drianna herself stood immobile within it, like a perfectly framed portrait. Athaya had been expecting the well-intentioned but unpolished woman who was forever underfoot, but instead she was met with someone who looked more a princess than she herself had in months. Drianna was garbed in green velvet, her throat and fingers were heavy with gold, and a wealth of auburn hair was loosely bound by a luminous string of pearls.

"I never would have recognized her." Athaya kept her voice to a whisper, even though Drianna would not be able to see or hear her until she opened her end of the panel. As yet invisible to Drianna's eyes, Athaya studied every detail of the picture before her, feeling oddly as if she were gazing into a mirror and seeing someone else's reflection. Drianna stood near an enameled table upon which was set a silver bowl of chestnuts, and adorning the wall behind her was a spectacular, gold-threaded tapestry depicting a small group of pilgrims on a journey.

"Let's find out what all this is about," Athaya murmured, and set her fingers to the panel's rim. The oblong flashed white and then Drianna blinked and lifted her chin, informing Athaya that the link had been successfully forged.

"I am contacting you on behalf of his Grace, the honorable Sage of Sare," Drianna announced, in what Athaya regarded as an unnecessarily formal tone. "The Sage wishes to speak with you on a subject of mutual interest."

"The Sage?" Athaya exclaimed. "I don't understand . . . what are you—"

"His Grace shall explain," she said, then promptly stepped out of the panel's boundary. Athaya called to her, but she did not return.

"I don't like this at all," Jaren said, moving off to one side so that the Sage would not see him. "She's up to something."

"I'd say it's 'his Grace' who's up to something," Athaya whispered back. "Or maybe this means that Nicolas has contacted him. If so, there might not be anything sinister about this summons at all." But even as she spoke the words, Athaya knew it wasn't true. If the Sage was calling as a result of speaking with Nicolas, then why had Drianna made the initial contact instead of Nicolas himself?

Athaya waited for what seemed an eternity, although only a few minutes passed. Vaguely, she wished that she were wearing something other than a tired-looking gray cloak and leather boots liberally spattered with mud. If the Sage expected her to look as regal as Drianna, then he was going to be sorely disappointed.

From the time she learned of his existence, Athaya had conjured a mental image of the Sage; but now, when he took Drianna's place in the panel's boundary, filling its entire expanse with his muscled bulk, she realized that her image had been woefully inexact. Instead of an older man clad in costly garments, she found instead a warrior dressed almost as simply as she, his arms riddled with scars. His dark coloring and swaggering gait made her think of Prince Felgin, though the Sage was far more feral-looking in his sheepskin vest and well-worn black leathers. A thin band of silver circled his head, its center marked by a traditional wizard's device overlaid by a golden crown. As she gazed upon the device, Athaya felt a surge of certainty that the rumors about the island's cult had more than a grain of truth to them.

"Your Highness, I am honored to meet you at last. I am Brandegarth of Crewe." His voice filled the chapel like a pipe organ, and though he spoke to her from a great distance, Athaya instinctively took a step back.

"I'm sorry if I seem surprised, your Grace, but Drianna . . . she told me she'd never met you."

"Yes, I know," he said, chuckling softly. "But please do not blame her for deceiving you. It was my idea to send her to Caithe and thus it is I who should ask your forgiveness.''

He paused, and Athaya had the unpleasant sensation that she was being silently appraised. His eyes twinkled their amusement as he scanned her appearance, as if he were secretly delighted by the sorry state of her clothing and the strand of unwashed hair that clung stubbornly to her cheek.

''I remember hearing tales of your father's lack of success in finding you a suitor. The bards sang not of your beauty, but rather of your tongue. Frankly, I expected a plain-looking tomboy of a girl, but here before me is a most lovely young lady full of royal pride and spirit . . . and most important of all,'' he added knowingly, ''magic.''

Athaya forced a smile; she hadn't been so shamelessly flattered in years. ''Thank you.''

I don't trust him, Jaren sent to her. The tone of his thoughts was peevish.

You just don't like the way he's looking at me, she replied, and then realized that from his position, Jaren could not see the Sage. *As if he's wondering if I'm wearing anything under my cloak,* she added, though she sensed that Jaren would have preferred it had she not elaborated. *And no, I don't trust him either.*

The Sage looked past her then, gesturing to someone standing just beyond his panel. ''Drianna, would you leave us now?'' Athaya heard the muffled click of a closing door; then the Sage returned his warm gaze to her. ''She is a dear girl,'' he remarked, his tone instantly conveying the true nature of their relationship, ''and has brought me a great deal of valuable information about your crusade. It is obvious that you and I have a common cause.''

''But why all the secrecy? Why didn't she simply tell me she was your emissary?''

Brandegarth paced in a small circle, tucking his thumbs inside a black leather belt. ''I had no idea how you would respond to such an overture, your Highness. I am aware that there have been rumors about me for quite some time and I did not want them to sway you unnecessarily.''

Athaya shifted her weight uncomfortably. She had already been swayed by them—those rumors were the sole reason for Nicolas' venture to Sare. She was tempted to ask about Nicolas or Ranulf, but the fact that neither the Sage nor Drianna had mentioned either of them made her suspect that they hadn't yet encountered one another. Nicolas had only been on the island for two months, and if there were circumstances—or dangers— that she was unaware of, she didn't want to endanger him by exposing his presence.

"I see." Privately, Athaya thought that Drianna's deception was far worse than the influence of hearsay, but she didn't care to bring this point to the Sage's attention. "Then the rumors aren't true?"

"Not all of them," the Sage replied, smiling enigmatically, "but I shall get to that. In short, I was incensed to learn of this Tribunal and how it threatens your work. Its existence is an insult both to the Lorngeld and to God. And that, your Highness, is the reason I have chosen to contact you. How can I continue to remain here and do nothing, when you are willing to risk such horrors for our people?"

Athaya nodded at the seeming logic of his argument. "What are you offering?"

"Trained wizards, for one. I could have over two hundred there within a month, with more to follow later. And money to aid those who have lost everything to the Tribunal—the island's mines are rich in silver."

Athaya checked her desire to accept immediately. She was still uncertain about his loyalties and reluctant to expose the extent of her desperation. "I won't deny I could use more money—I'm sure Drianna's already told you about the conditions here. But about teaching the Lorngeld their spells . . ." She paused to lick her lips. "With respect, your Grace, what exactly would your people teach them?"

The Sage smiled his understanding. "Yes, it's time we came to that. I am quite concerned about your approach to Caithe's unlearned Lorngeld," he said, tapping his fingertips together. "By following traditional Reykan teachings, you tell them only half a tale. I fear, your Highness, that by fault of omission, you do them all a grave disservice."

At that moment, Jaren decided to step into view. "And how is that?" he asked, his voice tinged with resentment at having his homeland's long-held tenets called into question.

"My husband, Jaren," Athaya supplied. The glimpse of mild disdain that Brandegarth gave him did not escape her notice, but he quickly masked it with a polite nod.

"You promise them life," the Sage continued, focusing on Athaya, "but that is all. You do not tell them what that life is meant to *be* . . . what it is destined for! Why, that would be like the priests telling us there is a heaven, but omitting to mention what we need to do to earn our place in it.''

"And what do you believe we are destined for?'' she asked, although her dialogue with Master Hedric made her quite confident of what his answer would be.

"Greatness,'' the Sage said simply. "It is our due and it is inevitable. Our rise to glory was foreseen centuries ago, by him who revealed to us the true nature of our gift.'' Brandegarth hooked his foot around a stool, pulled it close, and sat down to tell his tale. "Two centuries ago,'' he began, "toward the end of King Faltil's scourge, a small group of wizards escaped from Caithe and came here, to Sare. Their leader was a man called Dameronne. Dameronne of Crewe, whom my people honor as the first Sage of Sare.

"Dameronne had long believed that the Lorngeld were more than the neophyte philosophers and magical craftsmen that most wizards—even today—still think them to be. Dameronne contended that Faltil's scourge never would have happened if the Lorngeld had taken their rightful place in the world. He believed, as do I, that the Lorngeld's gift of magic is a sign that we were meant for greater things; that by having a taste of God's power within us, it is our duty to govern men as God governs us. And the stronger a wizard's magic, the higher a position he was meant to occupy.''

"A position, for example, like the Sage of Sare?''

Brandegarth inclined his head. "Just so.''

"But if you feel that the Lorngeld have always been destined for greater things, then why are you living in Sare? Why haven't you spread your teachings to Caithe? Or Reyka? Or the rest of the world, for that matter?''

"There is a proper time for all things, your Highness. Dameronne knew that. Fewer than a dozen wizards escaped to Sare—and had Dameronne not possessed the spell of translocation, as you do, Athaya, there would have been none at all—and once the rite of absolution spread from Caithe to Sare, there were fewer still to join them. It took decades before Dameronne and his apostles grew powerful enough to draw people away from the Church's grasp. Until then, the wizards' existence was virtually unknown. One thing we do know is that Dameronne was an adept-level wizard and that his ability to glimpse into the future was reputed to be phenomenal. It was said that he used

pastle seed to procure his more far-reaching visions," Brandegarth remarked offhandedly, "but we have no real proof of that.
In any event, Dameronne foresaw the Lorngeld's return to
glory. He glimpsed the precursors of our victory in his vision
sphere. And he promised that one day, we would receive a sign
that our time of waiting had ended."

Athaya and Jaren exchanged wary glances; why else would
the Sage be speaking to them had not the sign already come?

Reverently, Brandegarth retrieved a leather tube from the
enameled table and extracted a frail slip of parchment from it.
"Listen to the words that Dameronne spoke from his trance, as
he scried the future of our race: 'Our time will come when a
woman blessed by both heaven and earth comes forth to lead
the Lorngeld into glory. She will live among the high and the
low and will wield powers unseen since the days of the ancients.
She will obtain aid in her endeavor from an unexpected quarter,
and in so doing will usher in a golden age of a great wizard-
king, and thus restore our people to glory. Until her coming,
we wait in peace for our joyous return from exile.' "

When the Sage rolled up the paper, replaced it in its tube,
and looked up at her, Athaya realized she was shaking. Her first
instinct was to dismiss this prophecy as a mere fabrication—a
ruse designed to insure her acceptance—but something deep
inside of her spoke for its authenticity. Something she could not
yet identify, though it was well within her reach . . .

"Tell me, Athaya," the Sage ventured, "how did you come
to be this leader? Who set you upon this path? I understand you
were not always so enamored of your magical gifts."

"My teacher, Master Hedric. He—"

Athaya felt her heart skip in its rhythm. *He told me it was my
destiny . . . that I was the chosen one.*

He said he saw signs of my coming . . .

The Sage detected the subtle shift in her expression. "So you
see? Your own mentor foresaw your destiny—as did Dameronne, two centuries before."

"But Hedric claimed she was meant to free them," Jaren
pointed out, "not set them up as rulers of Caithe."

Brandegarth raised his brows only slightly. "It is possible
that he glimpsed only a small part of Athaya's role," he replied
coolly. "The future is, as we all know, a notoriously tricky thing
to discern."

Jaren fell silent at that, but Athaya was paying little attention to either of them at the moment. Regardless of her own central role in it, one line of the prophecy disturbed her more than any other. Who was the great wizard-king that Dameronne foresaw? Surely not Durek—at twenty-nine, it would be extremely rare for him to develop the powers of magic. Nicolas, perhaps? He was yet young enough. Or little Mailen? It would be a simple matter to peer into their minds and see if either of them carried the seed, but that, she knew, was a selfish choice no longer open to her.

Or perhaps this king will be some other man, she thought suddenly, staring into the Sage's animated eyes. *One without Trelane blood.* But before she could ponder further on that unsettling possibility and wonder just how far the Sage's ambition extended, Brandegarth spoke again.

"You are the woman of the prophecy, Athaya. 'Blessed by both heaven and earth'? A direct reference to both the adept magic and royal blood flowing through your veins. 'Aid from an unexpected quarter'? The clearest of references to my offer of help, of course—most unexpected. An offer which you are predestined to accept."

"But how can I, when if I do, I must accept your . . . 'philosophy' of magic?"

The Sage chuckled softly. "Do you 'accept' the philosophies of God? No. They simply *are.* You can choose to believe the truth or ignore it . . . but it does not change the truth."

Athaya bowed her head, staring at the muddied toes of her boots. *The irony of this situation is revolting,* she thought sullenly, for after traversing Caithe in desperate search of supporters and being refused at every turn, she was now openly offered help by the one quarter from which she couldn't possibly accept it.

"I'm sorry, your Grace," she said, looking up, "but if that is what you wish them to believe, then I'm afraid I cannot accept your help. If I'm to lead this crusade, then I have to believe wholeheartedly in what I'm doing. And I can't in good conscience tell anyone that their magic gives them the right to dominate other people."

Her words seemed to drift right past him, as if he'd been expecting her to refuse at first—a mere formality. "Do you think God 'dominates' you?" he asked.

"Not exactly," she said cautiously, uncomfortably aware that he was trying to trap her with her own logic.

"Do you think God is above you in the natural order of things? Is He more powerful than you are?"

"Of course, but—"

"And you submit to Him," Brandegarth said, nodding sharply. "You submit to His will. If that is so, your Highness, then why do not those without the awesome powers of magic not submit to us, who possess them and are therefore more powerful?"

"But it's not the same thing—"

"Isn't it? Domination is perhaps the wrong word. Guidance? Our Lord, with His awesome powers, gives us strength and guides us in the ways of wisdom. It is the Lorngeld's duty in this life to give that guidance to other men, since we alone have been touched by the hand of God.

"I know—it is a strange idea to you," he conceded, his tone unpleasantly conciliatory. "But did you not have much the same reaction when you first learned of your magic? In time, you accepted being a Lorngeld. You will accept this."

"Your Grace, you are entitled to believe as you will. But again, I have no choice but to refuse your offer. Ultimately, what you're asking me to do is overthrow my brother and set a wizard on the throne."

This time, her resistance made an impression. The Sage's brows folded inward, betraying inner vexation. Had he truly expected her to acquiesce so quickly? His eyes probed deep into her own, regarding her for the first time as a living, breathing woman and not just the incarnation of an ancient prophecy.

"It will happen eventually, your Highness," the Sage replied with a shrug that was meant to appear more aloof than it was. "It is only a matter of time."

"That may be so," she answered firmly, "but it won't happen by my hand. It was never my intention to topple Durek from his throne. Most of the people who come to me remain here precisely because I've promised them I *won't* do such a thing. It's not about politics, your Grace, it's about allowing people to make choices about their own lives instead of having Bishop Lukin and the Justices of the Tribunal do it for them. I don't want Durek to lose his crown—I just want him to change the law. And the Lorngeld can only do that by showing him through our actions that we're not the evil creatures he and half this country think we are. The moment we start forcing the issue through violence, your Grace, is the moment we start proving our enemies' point for them.''

Her words had a distasteful ring of familiarity to them; she had used much the same argument with Sutter. It hadn't worked then, and judging from Brandegarth's dispassionate expression, it wasn't working now. Her persistent opposition to the Sage's will had sparked a change in his mood; suddenly, it turned dark and quarrelsome.

''Your Highness, I must warn you. If you do not wish to reveal the Lorngeld's true destiny to them, then I will be duty-bound to do so. The time has come for my people's return to Caithe. I urge you to insure that we come as your friends.''

He left the rest unspoken. *And not as your enemies.*

''Is that a threat?'' Jaren asked, instinctively drawing Athaya a few inches back from the panel.

The Sage tossed him a peevish glance, as if he were a child who spoke out of turn at a formal state function. ''It is simply a statement of fact.''

''Your Grace, I implore you,'' Athaya began, extending her arms in a gesture of entreaty, ''believe as you will in your own homeland, but leave Caithe to me.''

''Caithe *is* my homeland, your Highness. It was only Faltil's idiocy that drove my people here. We have much in common, you and I. My people were driven from their homes and hunted by King Faltil, much as yours are now homeless and penniless, hunted by King Durek and his Tribunal. Together, we could heal all the wounds of two centuries and bring Caithe a peace and a place in the world that it has never known!''

His zealousness was compelling—almost hypnotically so. But while she grew increasingly alarmed at what her refusal might cost her, she knew that, prophecy or no, she could never accept the Sage's alliance. ''I'm sorry, your grace. We simply do not agree.''

At her third refusal, he fell into a dangerous spell of silence. Then he gestured curtly. ''Remember this room,'' he snapped. Gone was every trace of his former benevolence. ''Should you wish to reconsider, you may contact me here—there are no wards to hinder you. But do so quickly, Athaya Trelane, for in a matter of days, it will be too late for events set in motion to be stopped.''

And before Athaya could reply, the panel went black.

''I think we've been dismissed,'' Jaren observed.

"Yes," she said quietly, staring at the dark oblong as if trying to scry the future. "But we haven't heard the last of him."

Brandegarth stalked out of the chamber and shoved the ward key back into Drianna's hands. "Apparently her Highness' plight is not quite so desperate as you led me to believe." He threw his weight against the limestone wall of the outer corridor, fuming at his failure.

"I told you she couldn't be easily swayed," Drianna observed. When he did not reply, she touched his arm and added, "I fear not all women succumb to your charm as easily as I did."

It was the wrong thing to have said. She had meant it as a jest, but Brandegarth shot her a look of utter disgust, as if that was exactly what he had thought might happen. Not that Drianna could blame him. Since ascending to the position of Sage eight years ago, Brandegarth of Crewe was rarely refused anything by anyone—and never by women.

"God, those Reykans have made a damned philosopher out of her, not a warrior!" he cried, striking the cold stone with his fist. "She spouts pieties when she should be doing battle with her enemies!"

Drianna leaned against him and stroked his arm, hoping to soothe away his anger. "If you wanted to insure her acceptance, why did you not send Nicolas back to Caithe with glowing report about you first? You could easily have bewitched him to do it and then Athaya would have had no reason to distrust you. Or you simply could have told her you were holding her brother hostage—then she would have accepted you readily enough."

"I thought such meddling would have violated the prophecy. But I don't understand—she has refused, so it is violated nonetheless! And *how* could she have denied me?" he railed on, sincerely baffled by this unexpected turn of events. "The Tribunal searches for Lorngeld under every rock, her people are sick and destitute—oh, they may believe in what she's doing, but that won't put food in their bellies." He rubbed at his pounded silver bracelets as if they were shackles that chafed him. "Dameronne foresaw that she would obtain aid from an unexpected quarter. Who else could that *be* but me?"

"She did get a lot of money once," Drianna said cautiously. "It was from someone in the south that she'd never even met—a man named Adam. That could be what Dameronne saw. And someone else could have joined her since I left. Perhaps you simply misconstrued the prophecy.''

Brandegarth whirled on her in a fury. "Never presume to advise me on such things, Drianna," he said, wrathful enough to prove that he suspected the same thing but did not wish others to bring it to his attention. "You are not of my people and have no cause to criticize my judgments."

Abashed, Drianna hung her head. "I am sorry," she murmured, lips trembling. "You are right, of course."

"No, no, do not cry—that I cannot bear." With a groan of contrition, the Sage reached out to her and gathered her close. "It does not take a wizard to see that I am being foolish. Perhaps I was wrong," he conceded, bestowing a paternal kiss of apology on Drianna's forehead. "It's possible that my offer to aid the princess was premature. Or perhaps her refusal, and what I must do because of it, was meant to occur. Yes, that must be it. And if I was wrong about the meaning of this prophecy, then what I do now cannot be in violation of it. After all, it is *my* destiny to do what I must to insure my people's ascent to power."

Drianna glanced to the pair of guardsmen posted at the far end of the corridor. "Does this mean you'll go ahead with your other plans?"

"Her Highness leaves me no other choice," he replied, though with an air of regret that it should be so. "If Athaya herself won't accept me, then I will have to see to it that her people do. And that, my dear, means that her people must lose faith in her."

"And once they do," Drianna finished for him, "then they will be in desperate need of another leader."

At last, she elicited a tiny smile. "Come, Drianna—we keep our guests waiting."

She followed him down the corridor to a plain oak door bordered on each side by a uniformed sentry. Their presence was merely a formality; Brandegarth had secured his guests inside the chamber with binding spells, though Drianna suspected that he did so simply to irritate Ranulf and not because he feared that the prince and his servant would escape him.

Inside, Prince Nicolas brooded before a roaring fire while Ranulf paced angrily across the hearth, restless from long hours of forced confinement. The Sage strode toward them and loomed menacingly over the edge of Nicolas' chair.

"I'm afraid your sister has disappointed me."

Ranulf snorted his gratification. "Smart girl."

"Perhaps," the Sage conceded, "but one who has made a very foolish decision. But it is of little consequence—Athaya has built the foundation; she has spread the news throughout Caithe that the Lorngeld have an alternative to absolution. Ah, but when they come to be trained! That is when *I* must step in and tell them that there is more to their powers than what Athaya Trelane has revealed."

"They'll never follow you," Nicolas declared. "After all she's done for them, they're loyal to her."

Brandegarth leaned in even closer. "Yes, but will they remain so?" he asked, as if he had every reason to believe they would not. "Only time will tell."

Nicolas shot to his feet. "If you harm her, I'll—"

"You'll what?" Brandegarth replied lazily. "Kill me? I'd very much like to see you try. But in truth, I don't plan to harm her at all. Not directly," he added knowingly. He gazed long and hard into the prince's eyes. "But I make no promises for the actions of others."

The room fell silent but for the crackling of the fire and then Ranulf sucked in a horrified hiss of realization. "No—damn you, you wouldn't *dare*! Not to the prince of Caithe!"

Brandegarth's eyes narrowed slightly. "There are precious few things, Ranulf, that I would not dare to do."

As nothing else could, Ranulf's sustained silence convinced Nicolas that the Sage spoke truth. Then, in a fit of fresh rage, Ranulf's eyes streaked around his prison in search of a weapon— any weapon. Smoothly, he snatched up the iron poker by the fire; his lips moved in swift whispers, and in response, angry bolts of green-edged fire streamed from his fingertips and sheathed the simple weapon, transforming it into a flaming sword.

"Then you'll have to kill me first," he said, and stepped between Nicolas and the Sage.

Brandegarth looked down the length of the weapon, unperturbed. "That would be easier than you seem to think," he observed. "Come now, such theatrics cannot stop me. I am the Sage of Sare, and my will is the law here."

"Then I'll change the law!" Ranulf shouted. He swung his weapon perilously close to the Sage's unflinching face, and the arcane fire left thin streaks of green-tinted mist in its wake. "I'll change the *Sage*. I Challenge you, Brandegarth of Crewe. Right here. Right *now*.''

Nicolas shot to his feet. "Ranulf, don't!"

In counterpoint, Drianna lunged into the Sage's arms. "No, Brand—you're not recovered from the last one yet!"

But the Sage merely chuckled quietly, shaking his head at the wizard's folly. "Really, Ranulf. How very dramatic of you." He glanced down to Drianna. "My dear, go back to my chambers and fetch me the ivory box from the mantel."

Her sculpted brows arched their surprise at the haphazard change of subject and then the fear melted knowingly from her eyes. Nicolas thought he detected a smile on the woman's face as she swept hurriedly from the room.

"You're serious, aren't you?" the Sage went on, assessing the mercenary's stance and technique as if thinking of hiring his services. "Yes, I think you are. But perhaps you have forgotten that I am not obligated to accept a Challenge more than once a year, and while I might enjoy testing you at some later date, I don't have time for this foolishness now."

Ranulf sneered at him and the streaks of fire spat and danced with increased fury, like grease on a hot griddle. "Are you afraid, then? If I win, then *I* become the Sage. And then, not only can I get Nicolas out of this foul palace of yours, but I can command every wizard on Sare to do anything I want them to—I can even order them all to stay here and never go back to Caithe."

Nicolas' eyes went wide. God, what a tempting prize! But like Athaya, the Sage was an adept, and fond as he was of Ranulf, Nicolas knew that the mercenary was no master wizard. A Challenge would be a waste of his time . . . and his life.

Nicolas moved to his friend's side, giving a wide berth to the deadly fire he wielded. "Don't do anything rash, Ranulf. It's me he's after."

Drianna returned a moment later, breathless from her errand, and handed a palm-sized ivory box to the Sage. He did not open it, but merely cradled it in his hand, and ran one finger over the carved lid.

"Nicolas has the gist of things, my friend," Brandegarth replied. "Now do calm down. I refuse your Challenge. And I would advise you not to anger me further."

Ranulf was uninterested in the Sage's advice. "Then forget the damned formalities," he growled. "But as long as there's breath in me, you'll not lay a hand on the prince." He adjusted his grip on the poker and drew it back, preparing to fell a killing blow.

But the Sage had grown weary of delays, and his eyes hardened in decisiveness. As Ranulf edged closer, the Sage took a deep breath, closed his eyes to steady himself and then opened them again very slowly. They bore a milky glaze, the green irises opaque, like a poor grade of emerald.

Calmly, he lifted the lid from the ivory box and extracted a sparkling purple gem. A crystal.

Nicolas' jaw dropped like a stone.

A *corbal* crystal.

Reeling at the sudden blow, Ranulf's magic fire sputtered and died, spiraling back into his fingertips from whence it had come. He staggered back and hurled the now-useless poker aside, clutching his head as he crumpled to his knees. Defiance flared in his eyes, but was quickly overwhelmed by pain.

"Damn you," he cried, recoiling at every lungful of air, as if breathing itself had become a torture. "It's not *possible*!"

"Would you still like to do battle with me, old friend?" the Sage asked, laughing darkly. He drew closer to Ranulf, but his movements were stiff and overly controlled, as if he'd drunk too much wine and had to concentrate on every step, so as to avoid stumbling.

"A clever little parlor trick, is it not?" he said, slightly over-enunciating each word. He held the crystal up, admiring the play of light across its points—a thing Nicolas thought never to see a wizard do. "Do you still think to defeat me, Ranulf? If I can master this, then surely I can master *you*."

Nicolas gaped at the crystal with awestruck eyes; of those scant rumors he had heard about the Sage, none had ever hinted that he possessed such a power—a power that neither Athaya nor the Circle knew existed!

Then, realizing that only he could free Ranulf from his torment, Nicolas shook off his shock and lurched for the crystal. But the Sage's movements were not as sluggish as they first appeared; he swept a muscled arm backward, catching Nicolas squarely on the cheekbone with his silver bracelet. The crystal remained firmly in his grasp.

Nicolas wiped a thin trickle of blood from his cheek as he crept to Ranulf's side; the Sage did not bother to stop him, knowing him helpless to assuage his friend's pain. Odd, but

Brandegarth had opted for a physical blow, not a magical one—not what Nicolas would have expected from a master wizard. He filed the fact away for later.

If there *was* a later.

Brandegarth loomed over them both, proudly cradling his gem as if it were a thing of his own creation. "Surprised, my Prince? Yes, of course you are. But it is a simple trick, really . . . a matter of discipline. Mental discipline, perfected over time. Have you never heard of the wizards in Cruachi who walk on burning sand and feel no pain? But unlike hot sand, the corbal itself does not precisely *cause* pain—it merely deceives a wizard's mind into thinking pain exists. Once wise to the deception, the wizard is free of the pain."

Brandegarth glanced down to the wizard at his feet, his lips forming the faint curl of a smile. "Our friend, it seems, is not so wise."

"You can't cast spells at the same time," Nicolas ventured, and though the Sage did not answer him, an eloquent pause told him he'd guessed right.

"I dabbled with the technique during my training," the Sage went on disjointedly. "Many wizards do, but few stay with it for long—the headaches usually persuade them to give up and there's little enough threat from corbals on Sare. But Dameronne knew that if his people were destined to return to Caithe one day, then the Sage should have this skill, to better protect his flock. A few of my more talented wizards are also studying the technique—Couric is rather good at it, though large crystals like this one still give him trouble. The mind is a powerful tool, my Prince, and those who master its secrets are the mightiest of men."

Brandegarth graced Nicolas with an awful smile. "If corbal crystals are Caithe's only defense against wizardry," he said, pitching his voice low, "then she cannot stand against me."

Reverently, he bestowed a kiss upon the gem, as if it were a sacred amulet that guaranteed his victory in the battle to come. He returned the crystal to its box, then blinked to reorient his senses. The glazed look lifted from his eyes.

Ranulf's taut muscles relaxed as soon as the gem was sheltered from the light, but before he could fully recover, the Sage knelt at his side and extended his arms.

"Stand back and don't interfere," he warned Nicolas, but when the prince showed no signs of retreating, the Sage eyed him darkly and whispered a phrase under his breath. In an in-

stant, Nicolas found himself flat on his back, dazed and breathless, and before he could right himself, he was encircled by a
shimmering web of air, the insubstantial fabric pulsating in time
to his own heartbeat. It blurred his vision like rain-streaked
glass, and when he chanced to touch it, an iron fist of warning
wrapped itself around his heart, and blue sparks shot out their
anger as they seared the flesh from his fingertips.

With Nicolas well secured, the Sage gripped Ranulf's head
between his hands and began to speak. Ranulf recoiled once,
as if from a physical blow, and then fell limp in his captor's
arms. Moments later, Brandegarth set his fingers atop each of
Ranulf's eyes. *"I nunc tu qui mandata mea persequeris."* He
snapped his fingers, and Ranulf jerked his head up and looked
around dazedly, as if rudely jolted from deep sleep. He rose to
his feet, his former pain forgotten.

"Ranulf?" Nicolas cried. "Ranulf, are you all right?"

The mercenary nodded, eerily calm. "Aye, I'm fine."

The Sage beckoned Drianna to bring in the sentries guarding
the door. "Take this one away," he instructed them, gesturing
to Ranulf. "I shall decide what to do with him shortly. He won't
resist you," the Sage added indifferently. "In fact, it won't even
occur to him to try."

The Sage adjusted the binding spell so that his captive could
leave the room, and Ranulf went with the guardsmen peacefully,
his steps balking only once. He glanced back at Nicolas, vaguely
puzzled, then was gone. With a sickly feeling of foreboding,
Nicolas wondered if it would be the last time he ever saw his
loyal friend.

"And now for you," Brandegarth said. The Sage made a
gesture, and Nicolas' shimmering cage promptly vanished. Nicolas felt far safer within it; then, at least, the Sage could not
touch him.

"What are you going to do to me?" Nicolas tried to sound
brave, but even he could hear the fear in his voice.

"You're about to return to Caithe for a visit, my Prince," the
Sage informed him. "But don't bother entertaining the idea of
going to Athaya and warning her about me," he added. "I'm
afraid that in a few moments, you'll not remember that we had
this conversation at all."

Nicolas backed away, but as he edged toward the door, he
knew that he was still bound by the Sage's binding spell; his
bones grew warm and would turn to rods of molten iron were

he to draw any closer. He soon found himself flat against the opposite wall with nowhere left to run. Brandegarth laid a hand on his forehead, and Nicolas' limbs grew heavy, dragging him to the floor with their unspeakable weight. Black clouds crowded his vision, smothering his sight. The weight of the Sage's presence was pressing in on all sides, and alien thoughts suffocated his own, killing them off one by one.

"Now open your mind to me, Prince Nicolas," the Sage told him. "And listen very carefully to the instructions I am about to give you."

CHAPTER 19

✳✳

MOSEL GESSINGER STRUGGLED UP THE NORTH TOWER'S steep, spiral staircase, already puffing with exertion by the time he reached the first landing. Why Prince Nicolas had returned to Delfarham was a puzzle indeed, but why he had come to this particular part of the castle was an even greater mystery. Once, this had been Rhodri's tower; the rooms on the two floors below served as his private chambers, and here, at the top of the tower, was the wizard's long-abandoned library. The air was musty and smelled of rotting wood, and the stairs were generously coated with dust. No one came here now, not even the king—though he had done so many times in the months following Kelwyn's death. What interest could such a place possibly hold for Nicolas?

Catching his breath, Mosel reached for the ancient oak door, only to have it open of its own accord. Nicolas emerged from the library, his shoulders burdened with a leather satchel bursting at its seams with books and tubes of parchment.

"Your Highness—I was told you'd come this way," he wheezed. "This is certainly a surprise, having you in Delfarham again so soon."

"Yes, I suppose it is." Nicolas produced a slender key from his tunic and locked the door. "I wasn't planning to visit so soon, but I had a few ideas about expanding trade between Caithe and Sare and I wanted to get Durek's thoughts on them." He favored Mosel with a self-deprecating smile. "I've never been in charge of anything before, you know."

Mosel glanced curiously at the prince's bulging satchel. "Surely you're not looking for advice in Rhodri's old books."

"No, no. Athaya asked me to look for certain papers the next time I was here, that's all. Notes about Kelwyn, mostly."

Mosel tried not to look wounded, but his weathered face drooped nonetheless. "I would have found a way to get them to her, had I known she wanted them."

"Oh, nothing to worry about. She didn't think of it until you'd already left Halsey. And before you volunteer to take them yourself, I've already arranged for a courier. He'll see this satchel safely to Sir Jarvis in Kaiburn, and Athaya can pick it up there."

"A courier . . . did Ranulf return with you, then?"

"No, he stayed on the island. Business, you know." Then, without so much as a word of farewell, Nicolas brushed past him and descended the staircase, leaving Mosel to trail after him, puzzled by his curtness.

"Wait, please," he called out. He took hold of Nicolas' arm when they reached the landing of the tower's middle floor, just outside the door to Rhodri's old rooms. After a quick glance down the stairwell to insure that no one was on the way up, Mosel leaned close to Nicolas with an air of conspiracy. "Did you find out anything yet?"

Nicolas gazed at him blankly. "About what?"

"About the Sage of Sare." Mosel frowned; it was not like the prince to be forgetful about such important matters.

Nicolas' eyes went vacant for a moment, like a player who has suddenly forgotten his next line. Then, with a blink of recollection, he replied: "Oh yes, the Sage. We've met. A delightful fellow—we play dice together on occasion."

"And?" Mosel prompted, anxiously wringing his hands.

"And he usually wins," Nicolas replied with a shrug, though it was difficult to do with the heavy load of books weighing on his shoulder. "I've been to his palace, but there's nothing particularly unusual about it."

"But what about the cult? Are the Sarian wizards our friends or our enemies?"

Nicolas paused and frowned, as if Mosel spoke in a foreign tongue and he was forced to translate everything before he could respond. "I haven't asked him yet. It's only been two months,

Mosel," he added, with a little-used air of royal condescension. "I can't push things too hard."

"Have you told Athaya that you've contacted him?"

Nicolas sighed his impatience. "No. There's no reason to . . . not until I find out something useful about him. And I've too much to do right now to venture to Kaiburn for no good reason."

Mosel's brow went up in astonishment. No good reason? An odd response from one who had pledged to let Athaya know the instant he unearthed the smallest piece of information about the Sage. "But surely she will want to know—"

"She'll know soon enough. Now if you'll excuse me, Mosel, I have an errand at the cathedral."

Nicolas started down the stairs again, but Mosel stayed him with his hand. "Your Highness, are you feeling well? You seem preoccupied with something. If I can help—"

"I'm fine, Mosel. Just tired from the journey, I suppose. I arrived very late last night and I haven't been sleeping well ever since I left Sare. Now please, do excuse me."

And this time, Nicolas took a such a fast pace down the final flight of stairs that it was impossible for Mosel to stall him again.

Bishop Lukin's footsteps were silent as he strode down the north aisle of Saint Adriel's Cathedral. As was often the case when he visited the capital, he had been invited by Archbishop Ventan to deliver the sermon at evensong, and because a young man was to be absolved during that service as well, the bishop headed to the sacristy to fetch the blessed wine and *kahnil* necessary for the ritual.

Lukin smiled a measure of contentment. Despite the princess' efforts, not all of Caithe's Lorngeld had been seduced by her heresies.

The bishop's smile faded to a frown when he saw the sacristy door slightly ajar and he stepped inside the small chamber to find a hooded man standing in a pool of water, rummaging amongst the items in the cabinet. He was certainly not one of Ventan's priests; instead of a cassock, he was clad in a sodden wool cloak and a pair of muddy, ice-crusted boots.

"You, there!" Lukin shouted, projecting his voice as if to wake a dozing parishioner in the far end of the nave. "What are you doing?"

The man hastily shoved a gloved hand inside his tunic and

whipped around, his cloak sending a shower of icy raindrops into Bishop Lukin's face.

"Prince Nicolas?" the bishop said, wiping the water from incredulous eyes.

Nicolas offered him a winning smile. "Bishop Lukin, how very good to see you again. I didn't know you were here . . . or in Delfarham at all, for that matter."

The prince's breezy openness startled him; rarely had Nicolas been on anything but cautious and distantly polite terms with any of Caithe's bishops, much less Lukin himself. "I'm assisting the archbishop at the service tonight," he said, gesturing in the general direction of Ventan's private study. "I've come to the capital for a few days to consult with his Majesty on a few details relating to the—" He paused to mentally rephrase his reply. "To a project we're working on." He saw no reason to go into detail; not with Nicolas, whose sympathies toward Athaya and her people were well-known.

"Yes, the Tribunal," Nicolas replied. "I hear it's going well. Keep up the good work, Chief Justice."

Having prepared himself for a scathing denunciation, or at least a mild insult, Bishop Lukin found himself reduced to staring like a simpleton, stunned by the prince's anomalous praise. "Thank you, your Highness," he said, close to stammering. "And you? What brings you back to the capital so soon?"

"Oh, much the same . . . a project I'm working on."

"And you've come to Saint Adriel's to offer prayers for its success?"

Nicolas grinned—a secret little grin with a hint of malice that Lukin had rarely seen grace the prince's face. "Something like that," he said. "Actually, I was looking for Archbishop Ventan. I wanted to ask him which bishop has formal jurisdiction over Sare—oddly enough, no one on the island seems to have any idea. I just slipped in here on my way to his study to see if there was any wine to quench my thirst."

Bishop Lukin looked down on him with mild indignation. "The only wine kept in the sacristy is consecrated wine used for absolution and other holy rituals," he explained with a frown; surely the prince knew that perfectly well. "It would be most improper for you to imbibe it merely to relieve your thirst. But I'm sure the archbishop would be glad to offer you something from his private stock."

"Yes, well, I'm sure he will. I'd best see him now." Nicolas swept out of the sacristy, leaving a thin stream of rainwater in his wake. "Good day, your Grace."

Lukin bowed as the prince departed, then crossed to the cabinet containing the ritual supplies. He fetched the wine and *kahnil* that he'd come for, making a mental note to remind the sacristan that he was getting low on both, and then left the chamber. As he closed the door, he saw Nicolas walking swiftly toward the cathedral's west end—the opposite direction from Ventan's study.

The bishop opened his mouth to alert the prince to his error and then reconsidered. He doubted that Nicolas had come to see the archbishop at all—Ventan had never been one of the prince's favorites, and Nicolas' opinions of him had worsened since all this unpleasant business with Athaya had started a year ago. No, knowing the prince's reputation, he had been trysting with a lady—in a church of all places—and had merely ducked into the sacristy to avoid being seen by a jealous rival.

"Ah well, what harm can he do?" Lukin muttered to himself, putting the incident out of his mind and turning his attentions to the sermon he was to deliver that evening, and to the man who was about to die.

That night, in his Majesty's inner chamber, the king and his brother finished the remains of a private supper, shunning the commotion of the Great Hall so that they could converse in peace. A fire burned softly in the fireplace, and the cold rain that had pelted the city for most of the day had moved off, leaving the windows streaked with ice that distorted the view of Delfarham below. The silver platters on the table were mostly empty now, every pigeon bone picked clean, but Durek had done most of the eating that night. The meat on Nicolas' plate had barely been touched, and only a crust of black bread and a few scattered crumbs of cheese proved that he had sampled anything at all.

"Aren't you feeling well?" Durek asked him, as he drained off another goblet of fine Evarshot burgundy. "It's not like you to pass up a meal like this . . . or any meal, for that matter."

"No, I suppose it isn't," Nicolas replied, gazing longingly at his plate like a beggar envying another man's feast. "My head aches, and my stomach's a bit unsettled. I must still be tired from the journey."

"You didn't have to travel in February," Durek scolded

lightly. "Another month or so and the trip from Sare would have been far less arduous."

"I know. I . . . just wanted to."

Durek dismissed his brother's caprice with a shrug and plucked a tart from a silver tray; he had never found much sense in anything Nicolas did, so why should things be any different now? Still, something was different about Nicolas tonight; something he couldn't quite identify. Was it that the two of them were actually having a pleasant conversation, without falling into yet another vicious argument about Athaya? Or was it Nicolas' noticeable lack of buoyancy—he hadn't told a joke all night, nor extolled the beauty of the ladies he'd met thus far on the island. Instead, he avoided meeting Durek's eyes, constantly glancing around the room as if expecting to be pounced upon any moment and was prone to start at every unexpected sound. It was as if he were a spy in a foreign court—and a rather inept one at that—afraid that his true identity was in imminent danger of being uncovered.

"You surprise me, Nicolas. You've been in Delfarham for an entire day and you haven't even asked about Athaya yet." Best to cover that subject straight away, Durek decided, and find out what his brother's thoughts were on that matter now that Caithe was no longer his home.

Nicolas glanced up, seemingly mystified by the observation. "I have a job to do, Durek. That's my only concern right now."

Durek raised his brows as he swallowed the last bit of his pastry. "It's gratifying to know you're taking the marshalcy so seriously." He leaned back and chuckled quietly to himself. "Lord knows no one else ever has."

"I have a few ideas for the island," Nicolas said, suddenly more animated. He leaned forward with his elbows on the table, anxiously kneading his napkin between his fingers. "I'd like to build a new network of roads—the existing ones are in terrible disrepair. And I also think the port could be expanded. The mines north of Crewe are rich with silver, and the people are starved for goods to buy with it."

Durek let him ramble on for the next quarter hour, only half listening to the ideas he was proposing. Instead, he thought of how pleased he was to find Nicolas avoiding all mention of their wayward sister; at long last, it appeared that he had developed some sense—an event long overdue—and put her out of his life for good.

"We could export cloth, I think—especially wool. The land is rocky and not much good for grazing sheep on a large scale. And we might also trade some of our Evarshot wine for some of this," Nicolas said in conclusion as he rose from his chair and went to the sideboard. "I've brought the perfect ending to our meal—spiced cherry wine from Sare. Ideal for a cold night," he said over his shoulder as he poured the wine into two clean goblets. "It's laced with cinnamon and clove . . . you'll adore it."

"On top of the flagon we've already had with dinner? Perhaps not, Nicolas—I'm already feeling drowsy. And I thought your head ached."

"Oh, just take a sip—it's the least you can do after I brought the bottle all the way from Sare without breaking it. As for my poor head, this stuff is worth getting a headache over. Trust me."

Nicolas' hands were trembling as he set the pewter goblets down on the table, and Durek didn't fail to notice it. "You're feverish, brother. You've been distracted all night and now you're chilled . . ."

"Yes, perhaps I am coming down with something," Nicolas conceded, though his words carried the disjointed rhythm of an ill-rehearsed speech. "I'll go straight to bed and sleep it off right after you sample the wine and tell me how many dozen bottles you want me to send you as soon as I get back to Sare."

"Fair enough." Durek picked up his goblet and passed it slowly under his nose. "The scent is magnificent. Is it made in the manor's vineyards?"

"No, this was a gift from—" Nicolas broke off, as if shying back from the borders of a forbidden subject. "From a friend." Nicolas smiled, but his face showed signs of strain, like a wounded soldier desperately trying to hide the seriousness of his injury. He touched the rim of his own goblet to Durek's, and the pewter cups made a delicate chime. "To your Majesty's long life and health."

Again, Durek drank in the scent of the wine before sampling it and then he touched the rim of the cup to his lips, noting that Nicolas' fever had worsened even in these last few seconds—he was sweating profusely and looked on the verge of collapse. And then, just as he went to take an obligatory swallow of the wine so that Nicolas would do as he promised and get himself to bed, his brother let out a strangled gasp and lurched across the table, sending empty dishes clattering to the floor.

"No! No, *don't*!" He swatted the goblet from Durek's lips, sending the wine spattering across the king's silk surcoat and onto the costly Cruachi carpet. "God forgive me . . . oh, God—"

"Nicolas! What the devil has gotten into you?" But even before the question was out of his mouth, Durek realized that something was horribly, desperately wrong with his brother.

Nicolas crumpled to his knees, his limbs racked by spasms, and he clutched his head tight between his hands, twisting it violently as if trying to wrench it from his torso. Then he drew breath and let out a shriek of unholy pain, instantly summoning a half-dozen liveried guardsmen and a flock of alarmed courtiers into the king's chamber.

"Your Majesty? Are you all right?" Berns, a lieutenant under Captain Parr's command, scrambled to the king's side with his sword at the ready.

"*I* am," Durek said, staring down at his brother in stunned disbelief.

Feverish, indeed. This was more than mere sickness . . . the man was mad! He was flat on his back now, wild-eyed and uttering garbled streams of nonsense as he writhed against his pain. But Nicolas was no wizard . . . and what else but magic could cause such a rapid and inexplicable descent into lunacy?

"He was acting strange all night, but I thought it was just a fever," Durek explained, as much to himself as to the others gathered around him. "We were just about to try some wine he brought back with him from the island, and . . . and the next thing I knew he slapped the goblet out of my hand and spilled it all over—"

Durek glanced down to his ruined surcoat, and all the wine he'd drunk that evening seemed to hit him at once; his knees began to shake, and the air suddenly felt too thick to breathe. The spilled wine was eating tiny holes in the silk, and fine threads of smoke were rising from the delicate fabric. He bent down to examine the stained carpet and saw similar holes beginning to form.

"*Kahnil,*" Durek breathed, shifting his horrified gaze to Nicolas. "By God, the wine . . . it was *poisoned.*"

Horrified gasps and exclamations shot through the onlookers like lightning. "A Sarian plot, my Lord?" one man asked, as he pushed his way to the forefront.

"I'm not sure," Durek mumbled, still dazed by the discovery. "But I saw him unseal the bottle and pull out the cork—the poison couldn't have been there beforehand. Nicolas must have added it himself . . . but *why*? And where on earth would he get *kahnil*?"

"He went to the cathedral today," Lukin's baritone came, quelling the others like the voice of doom. He threaded his way through the knot of courtiers and soldiers, then knelt at the prince's side. "I found him in the sacristy . . . where the poison is kept."

Durek's head was spinning wildly. Why on earth would the Sarians want him dead? Why would *Nicolas*? Oh, they'd had their arguments over the years, but Nicolas simply wasn't capable of such a thing! Or rather, Durek had never thought he was. But who else would craft such a plot?

Durek stopped breathing. Who else, indeed . . .

"Oh God," he whispered, and his gaze went black as he looked upon his brother's face. "I don't even have to ask who put you up to this."

It was just the sort of irony he might expect from Athaya; only she would think to slip him a dose of *kahnil* and deal him a wizard's death. To absolve him of his sins, his life, his crown. To take the throne herself . . . God, it was what she'd wanted all along!

Bishop Lukin leaned in closer. "I think your suspicions are correct, sire. He can't have been working alone and he wouldn't have gone through with such a heinous act without being co-erced by someone else . . . someone he holds very dear."

In a fit of rage, Durek pounced on his brother and shook him roughly by the collar. "She's bewitched you, hasn't she? Athaya told you to do this, didn't she?"

Nicolas' eyes were open, but they were thickly glazed with pain and confusion. He yanked out a handful of his hair, as if he could somehow tear out his torment along with it. "—wanted me to," he choked out, "I need to . . . but I *can't*!" His head lolled to one side as he continued to speak, rambling aloud to himself rather than consciously responding to Durek's question. "I only went for her. Only to help Athaya—"

"I knew it!" Durek cried, angrier at his own culpability than at the betrayal itself. "God, I was a fool not to think he was in league with her."

"—help me. Oh God, Athaya, please make it stop—"

"What did she say to you, Nicolas?" Durek persisted. "When did you speak to her? Where?"

Nicolas winced at each question as if recoiling from a physical blow. He looked blindly to his inquisitor, then writhed away, resisting, but no longer certain why he did so, or what valued information he could possibly possess.

"Tell us, my son," the bishop urged, setting a hand on the prince's shoulder. "Perhaps by your confessing the truth, God will relieve your pain."

Nicolas' eyes flashed hope amid his desperation, his tortured mind grasping at the bishop's words as if they bore the promise of an afterlife. "I spoke to her . . . in the woods," he said, every word a labor. "And once . . . once at Halsey."

"What?" Durek rose slowly to his feet and edged back, hurt far more by news of the queen's duplicity than by anything Athaya or Nicolas might have done. "Athaya went to Halsey, and Cecile never *told* me?"

The bishop glanced up, his face grave. "This is grievous news, your Majesty. She is the queen, but she is not above the law. I know it is painful to you, but if she has been sheltering your sister in her home, then for the sake of her very soul, we must find out the extent of her involvement with these wizards. Her Majesty has long been a friend to your sister, and it is possible that she, too, has been bewitched."

Durek was silent for a time, as if inwardly mourning the loss of something he was slowly realizing had never truly been his. Then, channeling the chaos of his thoughts into action, he wheeled around and began firing orders at his guardsmen. "Place my brother under arrest. I want him under heavy guard at all times. And send for Captain Parr. He'll be leaving for Halsey at dawn tomorrow—Cecile has been away from me long enough, I think. And have a coach readied for the queen's return. Oh, never mind about Parr," he countered, rubbing at his temples. "I'll find him myself. I don't want to stay in this room another moment."

The sea of courtiers parted to let the king pass. "I knew something wasn't right when he asked for the Sarian marshalcy, but I saw no reason not to give it to him," he muttered under his breath. Then he whirled back to face Bishop Lukin, a desperate suppliant seeking spiritual counsel. "But if poisoning me was his plan, then why did he go to Sare at all? God, none of this makes any sense!"

Durek had to push his way past Lord Gessinger, who was rooted to the spot in the doorway, staring at the prince. "Out of my way, Mosel. No wait," he said suddenly, grasping the old man by the arm. "What do you know about this? You and Nicolas came back from Halsey together . . . did he or Cecile make any mention of Athaya being there, or what they spoke about?"

Mosel swallowed loudly. "N-no, your Majesty. Why, if either of them had said anything against you, sire, I would have felt it my duty to tell you, of course!" He grimaced, aware that he was a uniquely inept liar, but as he was also a habitually awkward and nervous man, the king sensed nothing amiss in his manner.

"Yes, yes, I thought as much," Durek snapped. "I suppose it was too much to expect for *you* to know anything useful."

Mosel clutched his heart as the king stalked off, shadowed by Bishop Lukin. Inwardly, the councillor offered a prayer of thanks for the king's insult. Were he anyone else, he might have been arrested as well, but his reputation at court served him like a wizard's cloaking spell, deftly shielding him from detection.

He watched in growing despair as Lieutenant Berns and his men carried Nicolas away, futilely trying to quiet the prince's groans and nonsensical appeals for mercy. And then, as he had done but six months before, Mosel hurried to his chambers to fetch his belongings, preparing for yet another unexplained flight to the wizards' camp near Kaiburn.

CHAPTER 20

✶✶

"**S**IR JARVIS DIDN'T LOOK TOO HAPPY TO SEE US,"
Athaya remarked as she stepped over a patch of
melting ice in the cobbled street. Beside her, Jaren
carried a bolt of runecloth under his arm, recently arrived from
Cordry's mill in Kilfarnan. The day was the warmest since the
turning of the year—or the least frigid, Athaya amended inwardly—and that, paired with the brilliant sunshine overhead,
lured the crowds into the streets, eager to escape the confines of
their homes. It was only the first week in February, but Athaya
could sense expectation in the eyes of the cityfolk—spring was
little more than six weeks away. But while both of them would
have liked to throw off their heavy scarves and hoods, Athaya
and Jaren kept their faces well shrouded—they were not here to
preach today and had no desire to be recognized.

"He's got a right to be nervous," Jaren replied. "We used to
contact him through Rupert, but now that the tavern is gone and
the city is crawling with Justices, he can't be too pleased to see
us on his doorstep. He's lucky he hasn't been brought in for
questioning, considering that everyone in Kaiburn knows his son
is a wizard."

"He's even luckier that no one can prove he had anything to
do with Cordry's disappearance. And I'm sure that his generosity to the cathedral over the years has persuaded the bishop to
turn his attentions elsewhere," Athaya pointed out dryly.

The sun glared white on the icicles clinging to the balconies and shopfronts on either side of the narrow street, and Athaya pulled down her hood even farther to shield her eyes. An advisable move in any case, since she and Jaren were nearing the crowded city square. They might have chosen to avoid it—it held a host of unpleasant memories for both of them—but it was the quickest route out of Kaiburn and enough people were out milling in the chilly sunshine that Athaya was confident that she and Jaren would be safely ignored.

The closer they came to the square, however, the more the mood of the people began to shift. Instead of laughter and cheerful remarks about the weather, Athaya began to hear muffled curses and snatches of private quarrels—not the usual spirited haggling and insults exchanged between merchant and buyer, but bitter words that spoke of something far deeper than day-to-day disputes. These folk had more on their minds than anticipating the advent of spring—in front of every shop, people clustered in small groups and talked animatedly to one another, their eyes bright with hostility, ready for a fight. In their hands, Athaya noted, many of them carried heavy stones, and those who did not were actively seeking one. Then, from the direction of the square itself, Athaya heard a swell of wrathful voices, as if a multitude of people were roaring their reply to the words of some unseen speaker.

"The last time there was an angry mob in the square was when you were brought here to recant," Jaren whispered to her, as he shifted the bolt of cloth from his left to his right arm. "What could be as big a draw as that?"

Athaya shook her head worriedly. "I don't know. But if the citizens are this angry, it definitely has something to do with wizards. Come on," she said, pointing to a half-dozen men heading purposefully toward the square, each of them carrying a large stone. "If one of our people is in trouble, we'll need to help somehow."

After two more sharp turns, the street opened onto the city square, and Athaya stopped dead, stunned by the sight before her; it was like an unpleasant step backward in time. The crowd was just as thick as on that fateful day she was brought here—and far more angry, if that was possible—and a bonfire burned hungrily near the base of the cathedral steps. With a sickening lurch of her stomach, Athaya expected to see the remains of some unfortunate wretch chained to a stake, but there was no stake, nor any signs that the fire would be used for such purposes that day. Above the mass of bobbing heads, a fair-haired man shouted from the cathedral steps, waving his arms in quick, jerking motions, like an injured bird trying to fly.

Athaya didn't need to ask who he was; the blood-red chalice device sewn to his black surcoat told her all she needed to know. But since when, she wondered, had Justices of the Tribunal begun to preach in public places, instead of simply arresting those they suspected of heresy and interrogating them in the dark privacy of their jails? After all, the monks of Saint Adriel had never been ones to use words when the cut of a good blade would do their preaching for them.

It was difficult to hear the man speak from the rear of the crowd, so Athaya and Jaren began to thread their way around the perimeter of the square. They had gone only halfway, however, when Athaya lagged back, conscious of the fire kindling inside her skull. "We can't get any closer," she whispered. "Someone nearby has a corbal crystal—probably the Justice."

So they remained where they were, tightly squeezed between a gutter and a pastry cart, and Athaya scanned the faces around her, hoping to see someone wearing a runecloth scarf that she could safely approach. But before she found a potential ally, a pair of old women retreated from the throng, clutching one another for support.

"First our Kelwyn and now this!" the first woman cried. She shook her fist, but the woman was so gaunt and fragile looking that the gesture was far from threatening. "She's the Devil's own child, there's no doubt of it now!"

"And the poor prince," said her companion, a plumper woman who seemed more sad than angry. "The Tribunal won't be able to look the other way simply because he's a Trelane. He'll lose his head for this, you can be sure of it."

Athaya wavered on her feet, suddenly light-headed; the women couldn't possibly be talking about Mailen. And there was only one other prince in Caithe.

"Pardon me, please," Athaya said, keeping her scarf tight against her face. "I can't hear from back here . . . what is the good Brother saying?"

The thin woman's eyes went round. "Haven't you heard?" she exclaimed. "Prince Nicolas tried to poison the king four days ago—and his sister put him up to it!"

Athaya stumbled backward from the shock, and Jaren dropped

the runecloth and wrapped his arms around her waist to keep her from falling. What sort of wild tale was this? Surely Durek would never have started such a foul rumor—it was true that he hated her, Athaya knew, but he had never felt such antipathy for Nicolas.

"Shocking, I know," the woman went on, clicking her tongue. "But what else can one expect from a demon? Brother Giles also said that there's surely more mischief afoot and that we're all to do our duty as good citizens—and obedient children of God—by telling the Tribunal about anyone we think may be involved with the princess and her magicians. The Tribunal will pay half a crown to anyone who turns in someone they find to be guilty. Can you believe it? Half a crown!"

"What about Harold?" the second woman said suddenly, poking her companion sharply in the arm. "His daughter's been away for months—visiting her aunt, he says. But she's with those wizards, I'd bet my life on it!"

"I never thought o' that," the first replied, her eyes turning shrewd as she considered the fact. "And what about Driscol, the goldsmith? His wife said he's gone to buy gems in Selvallen, but she might be lying to protect him. He just turned twenty-three, you know," she added knowingly. "Not too old to be a wizard."

"Let's turn in their names, then—that's half a crown for each of us if they're guilty!"

Stunned by this display of malicious greed, Athaya's jaw dropped as she watched the women hurry toward the cathedral, eager to betray their neighbors for a few pieces of silver. Then a loud cheer erupted as the crowd edged back, allowing room for a prison-cart to rumble into the square. It was surrounded by six black-clad Justices, and packed tightly inside its crudely fashioned bars were no fewer than a dozen prisoners, freshly taken from the Tribunal's prison in the cathedral crypt. Some of the captives were pulling futilely at the bars, struggling wildly to escape, but others sat immobile, their eyes staring blankly at the raging faces around them. These quiet ones, Athaya guessed, were those newly suspected of developing the powers of magic and heavily drugged with looca-smoke so that their burgeoning spells could not save them.

Athaya shot a frantic look at Jaren, silently asking what they could do, but before he could reply, the man who had been speaking from the steps flung open the door of the cart. His brethren pulled the prisoners out and pitched them into the square as if throwing scraps of meat to hungry wolves—human refuse to be disposed of as the mob saw fit. A fresh roar of fury echoed in Athaya's ears as all those who had brought a stone with them pushed to the front and flung it at one of the hapless souls, cheering if their shot drew blood.

My God, Jaren, what can we do?

Nothing, he sent back solemnly. *We can't fight back a whole city by ourselves and one hint of magic right now would be like putting a torch to dry straw.*

Then another frenzied howl erupted, rising up from amid the wizards' death wails and the bloodthirsty cries of their abusers, and Athaya was shoved aside to make way for a group of men carrying a grotesque figure woven of straw and twigs. It was the image of a woman—Athaya didn't have to ask which one—with a demonic grimace painted on its face and holding a lightning bolt made of twigs in one hand and a goblet in the other. It was the fire-bolt that had killed Kelwyn and the cup of poison that had almost killed his son.

"Death to Athaya Trelane!" one of the men shouted, and the crowd parted to let them hasten their crude figure toward the fire. "Heretic and traitor!"

Hundreds of voices echoed his battle cry. "Death to Athaya Trelane!"

I suggest you keep that scarf securely over your face until we're out of the city, Jaren advised her, *or they may not be satisfied to burn you only in effigy.*

The straw figure was thrust into the bonfire, and Athaya watched her own image crackle and burn to ash before her eyes, the painted face peeling back like blackened skin. Jaren tugged hard on her arm and, thoroughly shaken, she mutely followed him out of the square. And as the shrieks and moans of dying men echoed in the caverns of her mind, she imagined that they cursed her for causing their agony, and for not being the savior they expected.

If Athaya had thought to escape Kaiburn's anarchy by fleeing to the forest camp, she was sorely mistaken. The news of her supposed attack on the king had arrived well before her, and the mood of her people crackled with hostility. The compound was thick with wizards who had abandoned their rooms and tents to talk with one another, and not one could be seen tending to a daily chore or lesson. Although no one had yet crafted a straw likeness of Athaya to burn, the accusing eyes of many revealed their opinion that it would be a worthwhile pursuit.

"There she is!" Nathan cried, the moment Athaya and Jaren appeared at the edge of the clearing. He broke off the conversation he was having with his father and stalked toward them, kicking his way through slushy piles of snow. "I knew it," he said, leveling her with an unforgiving gaze, "I knew you wanted more than you were letting on!"

Rupert caught up with his son and clouted him soundly. "Quiet, you oaf! Condemn her without letting her speak and you're as bad as the damned Tribunal."

"Tell us you didn't do it," Emma pleaded, clutching at a handful of Athaya's cloak. "Please, tell us!"

"Of course she didn't," Gilda said sharply, her tone drawing a disgruntled whimper from the infant cradled in her arms. "You know better than that."

Athaya held out her hands, palms up. "Listen, all of you," she began, conscious that she was trembling before the damning stares of her followers, "I just heard about this in Kaiburn not two hours ago and I swear that none of it is true!"

"That's not what your friend from Delfarham said," another man remarked—Darien, the harper who had played at her wedding. Before Athaya could ask what friend he was referring to, Darien continued. "Oh, I knew I should have gone with Sutter—he wanted to fight back, but not like this! By killing Justices, not the king!"

"But I didn't try to—"

Then Tonia stepped through the crowd, and the angry voices quieted as she passed. Whatever they thought Athaya had done, Master Tonia was still trusted, perhaps because she was Reykan and outside the realm of Caithan politics.

"Someone from the capital is here; we found him at the forest's edge, calling for you. He had a strip of runecloth, so we figured he could be trusted. He claims to be the one who told us where you were last summer."

Athaya felt a warm rush of relief surge through her limbs. "Mosel! Thank God, someone who can tell me what's going on. Where is he? I'll talk to him in the chapel."

"Why don't you talk to him out here where we can all hear?" Nathan challenged. "Or are you afraid of what he might say?"

To Athaya's surprise, Tonia nodded. "I think that's best,"

she murmured, and something in her tone made Athaya's blood freeze. Suddenly, Athaya recalled the real reason Tonia had come to Caithe at all—as a watchdog for the Circle of Masters. It had always been the Overlord's fear that Athaya was after more than just freedom for the Lorngeld; at their first meeting, he had all but accused her of plotting for the Crown. God, could Tonia be suspecting the same thing?

"Now, Athaya, don't be looking at me like that," she said, her voice mellowing. "I don't believe a word of this tale—I know you too well by now to think that you'd ever do such a thing—but it is my duty to find out all the facts and relay them back to Basil. And everyone here has a right to know just what's going on."

She sent Emma to fetch the council lord, and within moments, Mosel was seated between Athaya and Jaren on a fallen log near the bell tower, densely surrounded by dozens of curious—and suspicious—wizards.

"I would have arrived yesterday, but my horse took a stone and I had to arrange for another. Unfortunately, I see the news has arrived in this shire ahead of me. His Majesty was doubtless advised to spread the word of your alleged treachery as quickly as possible," he said sourly. "He probably sent messengers out that very night."

"What sort of trick is Durek up to this time?" Athaya asked irritably as she broke up a patch of sun-softened ice with the heel of her boot.

Mosel looked at her, and his eyes were as sorrowful as she had ever seen them—no small feat, considering his many years of friendless solitude at the capital. "It's no trick, my Lady. I was there . . . afterward. Most of what you've heard is true."

A chorus of gasps and impassioned whispers rose up around them, but quickly died down so that the rest of Mosel's tale could be heard.

"True?" Athaya exclaimed, blinking her astonishment. "But that's impossible! Isn't Nicolas still on Sare?"

Mosel shook his head. "No. He returned to speak with the king about the administration of the island—or so he claimed. I saw him the day after he arrived, and something was odd about the way he acted; he was distracted and feverish, but I had to assume it was simply the strain of the journey from Sare. That reminds me," he added offhandedly, "did he send you any books?"

"No. Why would he do that?"

"I saw him coming out of Rhodri's library. He said he was gathering some materials about Kelwyn that you had asked for and that he had a courier waiting to deliver them. Perhaps the messenger was delayed much as I was," he remarked, frowning doubtfully.

"Perhaps," Athaya said, knowing full well that she had never asked Nicolas to send her any such things. But that could wait— a far greater mystery was waiting to be solved. "Go on, please."

"I was passing the king's chambers that night on the way to my own when I heard a horrible scream—myself and half of the court," Mosel added. "There were at least ten witnesses, my Lady. When we got to the king's room, his Majesty was splattered with wine that he claimed had been poisoned. I saw the holes that the acid was eating in his surcoat," Mosel admitted. "I'm certain it was *kahnil*."

From somewhere behind her, Athaya heard soft and bitter laughter. "About time somebody tried to absolve *his* sins," a voice muttered.

Athaya shook her head in disbelief. "I don't believe it . . . it's a lie! A lie Durek is circulating to make people lose faith in me. He's starting to realize we're a real threat to him and this is his way of retaliating!" She got to her feet unsteadily, as if she had drunk poisoned wine herself. "I'll have to go into the city and tell them so myself."

Jaren yanked her back down to her seat. "You set one foot in Kaiburn and they'll burn you the same way they burned your image—that, or stone you to death."

Grudgingly, Athaya had to admit that he was right—at this point, showing her face in Kaiburn would be tantamount to suicide.

"So the tale is true, then!" Nathan cried. "Prince Nicolas *did* try to poison the king . . . and why else would he have done it if not for you?"

Tonia shot him a murderous glare, silencing his complaints until the full tale was told.

"But *how*?" Athaya asked. "If the wine was poisoned, why didn't Durek drink it? Why was it spilled? And why does everyone think *I* had something to do with it?"

Mosel shrugged sadly. "As to what went on in the room before I got there, I'm afraid that only God and your brothers know the truth of things."

"I'll ask Nicolas, then," Athaya decided. "He'll tell me."

"If he can," Mosel replied, putting a steadying hand on her arm. "He was ill, my Lady. Ill and in much pain. Perhaps he's better now . . ." His voice trailed off uncertainly.

"What's wrong with him?"

"No one knows, my Lady. But he was raving that night and except for a few words nothing he said made any sense. He's heavily guarded," Mosel went on sadly, knowing that Athaya would want nothing but to go to his side. "You'd never get close to him without being detected."

"Why go to him now anyway?" Nathan cut in. "So you can kill him, to keep him from telling the king what you've done? The two of you had plenty of time to plot while he was here, and you never bothered to tell us that he was going to Sare. It was just a ruse, wasn't it? A ruse to throw us off the scent?"

Athaya ignored him and buried her face in her hands. "I can't believe any of this. It's got to be an awful mistake." She looked up sharply. "What about Ranulf? Maybe he can tell us what happened."

"He did not return with the prince, my Lady. I think he is still on Sare." His face reflected Athaya's dwindling hopes. "I'm afraid there's more," Mosel added softly. "The queen has fallen under suspicion as well."

"Cecile?" Jaren exclaimed. "That's absurd!"

Mosel conceded the point with a shrug. "Perhaps, but in his confusion, Nicolas admitted that he and Athaya were at Halsey together, and now the king suspects Cecile may be involved in this plot. Bishop Lukin was quick to remind his Majesty that the queen has long been Athaya's friend and that she should be placed in 'protective' custody." Mosel wrung his hands, clearly distressed for the queen's plight. "If the king was angry enough—or the Curia daring enough—she might be turned over to the Tribunal for formal questioning! And even if his Majesty doesn't go that far, Cecile will still have to convince him that she isn't plotting against him. And she can't risk lying to him . . . he's her husband and her king. If he asks her, she'll have to admit that you were there."

"*If* he asks her," Athaya murmured, nurturing the seed of an idea. "But we can see that he never gets the chance."

Mosel nodded quickly. "I already thought of that. He's dispatched his men to fetch Cecile back to camp; they left shortly after I did, but they're bringing a coach and that should slow them by a few days. We can cut them off easily if we leave tonight.''

"I'll go with you," Jaren said. "You may need some extra help, and Cecile is part of my family now."

"So's Durek," Tonia muttered under her breath.

Jaren let the observation pass. "But what if she doesn't want to go back? She admitted that she misses her son. If she goes with us, when would she ever see him again?"

"All we can do is offer her the chance to flee if she wants to," Athaya said. "If she refuses . . . well, then there's nothing more we can do. But if Mailen is the only reason she'd return to Delfarham," she mused, "then perhaps we can bring Mailen to her instead."

"Not a bad idea," Mosel said. "I've seen the boy change these past months . . . and not for the better. The king taints his thoughts against the Lorngeld."

Athaya nodded absently, then set the idea aside to simmer. "We can worry about that later. Nicolas is my real concern right now." She slumped forward, resting forearms against her thighs. "I just don't see how anyone could think Nicolas would do a thing like this simply because I asked him to."

Mosel cleared his throat. "Not because you *asked* him, precisely," he said carefully. "The king says you bewitched him into doing it. And . . . oh, my Lady," Mosel went on, tears of regret forming in his eyes, "with my own ears I heard the prince cry out to you, begging you to relieve his pain . . ."

Whatever loyalty her followers had held for her shattered in that instant. Like the ebbing tide, they backed away from her as if afraid to breathe the same air she did, and instead of looking to her with respect and hope, their eyes now bore disillusionment and despair.

"Can you still deny it?" Nathan said. Unlike the others, he had not retreated and loomed over her like a thundercloud. "The prince himself accuses you!"

"No, it's a mistake . . . he would never . . . someone else must have—"

Then she heard the echo of a voice within her mind—a deep and menacing voice—and suddenly a gruesome picture began to come clear. *Should you wish to reconsider my offer,* Brandegarth had warned her, *do so quickly, for in a matter of days, it will be too late for events set in motion to be stopped.*

Events set in motion . . .

"Mosel," she began slowly, "did Nicolas say anything about the Sage of Sare?"

"Only that they had met . . . but by his manner, I would swear he knew more. Why? Is it important?"

"Very important. I think that the king was right. Nicolas *was* bewitched. But not by me." She turned to Jaren with fire in her eyes. "This is his revenge on us for refusing to join him."

At that, Nathan's temper erupted anew. "Oh, this is rich! If this Sage—whoever that is—is so damned sinister, then why have you never mentioned him to any of us before now? Because he doesn't exist, that's why! It's just an excuse—a lie to cover up your plot's failure! You told us you didn't want to depose the king and then you do this and blame it all on someone far away that we've never even heard of!"

"What can I do to convince you? I had nothing to *do* with this!"

"You can't convince me," Nathan spat. "I'm leaving. I was willing to defy the priests, your Highness—that much of the law I'm glad to break—but I've never been a traitor to my king. Just what are we to you, Princess?" he asked, sweeping his hand over the crowd. "Members of your army—the one you swore to us you weren't forming? Did you save our lives so we'd stay loyal to you once you made your bid for power? Some savior you are!" He shook his head in disgust. "I should have known. You're no holy woman . . . just another scheming blue blood out to get the throne."

"I never claimed to be holy at all!" Athaya shouted, fast coming to the end of her patience. "And I'm sorry if I'm not the sort of messiah you wanted, who speaks in tongues and walks around all day with a halo on her head. But just because I don't make a public spectacle of my faith doesn't mean I don't have any, or that I have ulterior motives for everything I do. Prayer is a fine thing, but it doesn't get the work done. God doesn't do things for us, Nathan, He gives us the strength to do them ourselves. And all *I* want to do is stop people from killing us simply because we have something they don't. I've never wanted anything more."

Her words elicited an approving nod from Tonia and a handful of others, but they did not move Nathan at all. "Very nice," he remarked. "As eloquent as any bishop. But I'm still leaving."

Rupert held him firm. "Nathan—"

"Stay if you want to, Father. But just remember—you lost your tavern because of her."

"Better my tavern than my son. It's because of her you're still alive."

"I know. And I'm still willing to help others like me—I'll teach magic to anyone who wants to learn. But I won't do it under *her* banner. Not after this." And with that, he jerked his arm out of his father's grasp and stormed off to his tent to gather his belongings. Within minutes, he was trudging out of the camp, a hastily packed burlap sack flung over his shoulder.

Nathan's departure initiated one of the most painful afternoons Athaya had ever endured. One by one, those who agreed with him followed in his footsteps; they packed their things, dismantled their shelters, and walked out of the camp, their faces hardened with profound hurt and betrayal. Unlike the vehemence surrounding Sutter's departure, when he and his men had tried to steal money and food, caring little whether those left behind went hungry, these people left with only those things they had brought with them, wanting nothing that Athaya had provided. And looking into their eyes, Athaya thought that if they could give back the knowledge of magic she had given them, many would do so gladly. Few of them spoke to her as they went about their tasks, and those that did said only that they were sorry, but that they could no longer trust her.

"Emma," she pleaded, as the fair-haired girl lifted a cloth bundle and walked away from her wickiup. "Please don't go. Your spells aren't reliable enough yet."

"Then I will learn what I can from one of the others," she said, pointedly avoiding Athaya's gaze. Her voice was hushed, but Athaya heard the hostility in it. "My village was destroyed because you were there. Ethan *died*. And all because of a traitor." Lips trembling, Emma stalked out of the clearing, not once looking back.

Athaya approached dozens just like Emma and received the same cool reception each time. Never before had she felt so helpless, and her heart was ready to break with anguish—she would rather have battled a dozen men like Sutter than watch these good people walk away in quiet rejection, not truly hating her, but utterly bereft of faith.

Hours later, under a cold slice of the waning moon, Athaya closed herself in her room and surveyed an encampment less than half the size it had been that morning. Jaren brought her a bowl of stew for her supper—a greater portion than usual, though the reason for their sudden bounty was scant comfort—and told her the full count of their losses.

"Over half of them are gone. We have about one hundred wizards left, plus another fifty or sixty from their families. But Girard stayed . . . and Marya. We haven't lost them all."

Athaya rested her head on the cold stone sill, thinking back to how hopeful she had been on her first night in this camp last April, listening to her friends sing under the stars.

"Most of them wouldn't even speak to me," she said, poised on the verge of tears. "They just looked at me, disillusioned. God, it was the same way my father used to look at me, knowing I hadn't grown up to be the kind of daughter he wanted. And now I've failed them all."

"Athaya, stop talking like that."

But Athaya wasn't of a mind to be comforted yet. "Sutter's allies hated me because I wasn't fighting back against Durek, now even more hate me because they think I *did*, and those who were my enemies all along—like those people in Kaiburn today—hate me more than ever because they think I've tried to kill Durek just the way I did Kelwyn. It's all falling apart, Jaren. I promised my father I would change everything. I swore I would. If I lose this, I've lost everything."

"Everything?" he said, coming to stand at her side. "You'd still have me, though I'll admit it wouldn't be much consolation for losing a country. But we're not going to lose everything. Have a little faith."

Athaya sniffed, then turned to him. "How can you be so damned optimistic all the time?" It wasn't so much an accusation as a desperate desire to *know*.

"I have to be," he replied matter-of-factly, "since you're so damned pessimistic all the time." He grinned at her, but she could tell that he was only half joking.

Athaya took the admonishment to heart. "Then it looks like we're perfect for each other, aren't we?"

"Obviously," he said, and brought a badly needed smile to her face with a kiss. "I should go soon," he said with regret. "Mosel will be waiting. But I hate to leave you now, after all this . . ." He looked to the makeshift city of tents in the clearing, now half-deserted, and sighed heavily.

"No, you go ahead." She pushed herself away from the sill

and set aside her melancholy for something harder and more useful. "Besides, I have a journey of my own to make."

Jaren regarded her warily. "Don't even think of going to Sare, Athaya," he said, holding her firmly in place by the shoulders as if physical strength alone could thwart her powers of translocation. "It's doubtless what the Sage is expecting you to do, and he probably has a trap ready and waiting. And if you leave now, it will look as if you fled the country once you found out Nicolas' attempt on Durek's life had failed."

A fragile smile formed on Athaya's lips as she listened to his impassioned reasoning. "I never planned to go to Sare," she informed him, once he was done. She reached for her cloak. "I'm going to Delfarham. I have to find out what really happened between Nicolas and Durek that night."

Jaren's expression revealed that he might have been more content had she been going to Sare after all. "But you heard what Mosel said. Nicolas is delirious, not to mention heavily guarded."

"I know," she said. "And that leaves only one other person who can tell me what happened." She wrapped a scarf of runecloth about her neck. "I'm going to talk to Durek."

Jaren's jaw dropped open, and if the subject hadn't been so serious, Athaya might well have laughed aloud at how closely he resembled a codfish. "You can't be serious."

"Do you have a better idea?" She waited, but no better ideas were forthcoming. At the moment, Jaren wasn't capable of saying anything at all. "It's late—I'll go directly to his bedchamber and talk to him there. He's usually alone by this time. And I can pop right out again at the first hint of trouble; I don't need the recovery time like I used to."

"But what if he keeps a corbal in his room?" Jaren said, suddenly finding his tongue. "He might, you know. Then you'd be stuck there."

"That's a chance I'll just have to take."

Jaren pondered that for a while, then reached for his own cloak. "Then take me with you."

"Absolutely not," she replied firmly. "Durek hates you more than he does me—*if* that's possible. Having you along would only antagonize him. Besides, Mosel needs you with him," she added with a smile. "He's not used to stealth."

"No, but he's certainly getting better at it these days." Jaren wrapped her in a tight embrace. "I wish I could think of a good reason why you shouldn't go, but I can't." He waited a long time before he let her go. "Mosel and I will wait until you get back before we leave for Halsey. An hour or two won't matter, and we'll both rest easier once we know you're back safely. Just be careful," he said in gentle admonishment, and bade her farewell with a kiss.

"Right now, I think Durek's the one who should be careful," she said darkly, steeling herself for their encounter. "If I find out that this horrible story was all some plot of his, I just might try to kill him myself. And I doubt I'd use something as painless as *kahnil* to do it."

CHAPTER 21

✵

O NCE JAREN LEFT TO TELL MOSEL OF THE SHORT DELAY
in their departure, Athaya settled on the edge of the
straw-stuffed mattress and cast a vision sphere to insure
that Durek was, like herself, alone in his bedchamber. The mists
of the globe cleared quickly, revealing a deceptively tranquil
picture of the king in repose.

He was nestled in an overstuffed chair near the hearth, snugly
wrapped in a fur blanket, slippers, and dressing gown. A cup
of steaming tea rested at his elbow—not his usual wine, Athaya
noted—and he yawned as he paged through a sheaf of dull-
looking documents peppered with numbers and cryptic nota-
tions. The door leading through the wardrobe closet to the outer
chamber was closed, and casting her vision beyond it, Athaya
found it empty of servants. By this hour, they would have long
finished their work and gone to bed themselves.

And most importantly, she saw no adornment in the king's
bedchamber that resembled a corbal crystal.

Assured that the scene was properly set for her arrival, she
banished the sphere. Then she wished herself luck, promised
herself that she would do her best not to get into an argument
with Durek if she could possibly avoid it, and with a whispered
word, conjured herself from the Forest of Else to the inner sanc-
tum of his Majesty's private bedchamber in Delfar Castle.

Athaya appeared in the bay window, just behind her brother's

298

chair. She waited, watching him, but he gave no sign that he detected her presence.

"Durek?"

Startled, the king bolted to his feet and whipped around, sending the documents flying about him like dry leaves in an autumn breeze. The drooping eyes and sparsely bearded face hardened into a mask of revulsion, appalled that she would have the gall to come to him alone, so confident that her power would insure her safety. But in the space of a heartbeat, abhorrence was replaced by alarm, and his lips twitched vigorously as he calculated how many heartbeats remained to him in this life.

"Don't bother to call the guard," Athaya told him, firmly but without menace. "I can be gone again before you draw your next breath."

Trying—without much success—to veil his fear, Durek backed slowly away. His eyes flickered nervously toward the door to the outer chamber, realizing that to reach it, he would have to pass dangerously close to Athaya.

"So," he began, bolstering his voice with bluster to keep it from wavering. "Come to finish what Nicolas started, have you?"

Athaya shifted her position among the cushions in the bay window. "Durek, if I truly wanted you dead, I certainly wouldn't have needed to use Nicolas as a tool to do it. I could have come in silently, as I did just now, put you to sleep, poisoned your wine—or your tea, as I see you prefer now—and vanished again. I'd have been back in Kaiburn before you awoke to take the fatal sip."

The ease of this plan didn't do much to improve Durek's temper. "I've a right to be suspicious," he snapped. "You do have a history of regicide."

Athaya let the remark pass—she swore to avoid pointless arguments and nothing would be gained by having one now. "There are days when I'm sorely tempted to do just that," she conceded, "and you've proven in the past that you'd be more than glad to get rid of me, given the chance. But however much we may wish each other dead at times, I don't think either of us would ever use Nicolas to do it."

Durek had no rejoinder for that, and rubbed his beard distractedly, piqued that she was right. "So the news has reached you, I take it. Why else would you be here?"

"I came to find out what happened that night." She rose to

her feet and held her hands out in a gesture of entreaty. "We know him better than anyone, Durek. Nicolas simply isn't capable of doing something as heinous as this. I'd ask him about it myself, but I understand that he's ill, so you're the only one who can tell me the truth."

"Ill?" Durek said, laughing mirthlessly as he reclaimed his chair and settled the fur wrap back around his shoulders. "The word hardly does him justice."

Athaya felt bitterly cold underneath her cloak just then—Nicolas' condition was obviously worse than Mosel had revealed, perhaps hoping to spare her undue worry. But she was grateful for his discretion; having half of her followers desert her in the space of a single afternoon had been worry enough.

"But I'll humor you," Durek went on, realizing that she would not leave until he did so and might do something dreadful if he resisted too long. "Will you have some tea while I tell my tale?" he asked, motioning to a small earthenware pot near the hearth. "I assure you there's no *kahnil* in it."

Athaya bit her tongue. "No, thank you. Just the truth, please."

Durek settled back and turned his face toward the fire, and the golden glow of the flames made his creased, pale skin look like old parchment. "We had dinner that night, here in my rooms," he began. He took a sip of tea, grimacing at finding it had gone cold. "We talked about many things—Sare, mostly, and Nicolas' ideas for governing the island. He was preoccupied with something all night, though, and later began to complain of nausea and headaches. He hardly ate a thing and that's damned peculiar for Nicolas."

Agitated by the tale, Durek pushed himself out of his chair and began to pace slowly across the thick Cruachi carpet. "He'd brought me some wine from the island, and we were just about to sample it when his pains got suddenly worse—guilt eating at him, no doubt. He handed me a goblet and offered a toast—to my health, of all things—but just as I was about to drink . . ." Durek stopped in his pacing, struggling for the right phrase. "It was as if something 'snapped' inside of him. He shrieked and swatted the cup out of my hands, spilling the wine everywhere. It ruined one of my best surcoats," Durek remarked petulantly, as if to distract himself from his close brush with death. "He's not been himself ever since. He has constant headaches, and mutters nonsense when he speaks at all. Far worse than Father was in those last days.'' Durek flashed an accusing glance at Athaya, remembering her role in hastening Kelwyn's death, however accidental she claimed it to be. ''We have to keep him sedated most of the time or he wanders from his bed and frightens the servants.''

Athaya felt a sudden surge of sympathy for the nuns in Saint Gillian's who had cared for her day after day, aware that their nerves must have been frayed out of existence by the end of her stay. ''Is he violent?'' she asked, remembering the ugly bruise she, in her own dementia, had unknowingly inflicted on Jaren.

''No,'' Durek replied, surprised that it should be so. ''But he's restless and fearful, as if afraid someone's coming after him. Two nights ago, however, Mailen got into the room somehow—I forbade him to go there, but he heard his uncle was sick and was determined to see him. Strong-willed boy,'' Durek remarked, glowing with pride at his son's disobedience even as he despised his sister for hers. ''When I found him there, Nicolas was surprisingly placid. Something about the boy's presence soothed him—when I arrived, they were playing with Mailen's toys together. Mailen goes there every evening for a few hours, and it calms Nicolas enough so he'll take his posset and sleep through the night. The boy's guarded, of course, but Nicolas hasn't made the slightest move against him. Whoever wanted me dead apparently never realized that Mailen is my heir, or they would have forced Nicolas to go after him, too.'' He gazed at Athaya sardonically, pleased at finding a flaw in what he believed to be her plan.

''And I suppose you told Mailen that I'm to blame for what's happened to Nicolas.''

Durek shrugged mildly. ''Of course. He has to learn what wizards are at a young age, so that he can be wary of them and of the havoc they can wreak upon the country he is to rule. What Nicolas has done has driven Caithe into an uproar,'' Durek went on, as if Athaya needed to be told. ''There have been riots in Delfarham for days, and every prisoner in the Tribunal's jail has been executed by public demand. And if the people are angry here, I can only imagine the hostility you're getting in Kaiburn.'' He drew closer to her, no longer afraid. ''They hate you for what you've done— or think you've done. The truth hardly matters now.''

Bitterly, Athaya knew there was much truth in those words and pitifully little she could do about it . . . other than prove the truth of the matter. But how she would do *that*, she had no idea.

"So what will you do?" she asked, pushing aside her own problems for the moment. "Offer a higher reward for me?"

Athaya didn't care for the brittle laughter than her comment elicited. "Reward?" he replied. "You're sadly mistaken, Athaya. In fact, I may just cancel the bounty altogether. You see, I don't plan to arrest you. After what Nicolas has done, you serve my purposes far too well out among your own people. They hate you so much now that it would only gratify them to see you arrested again." He paused, and his eyes burned with menace. "And I want them to stay angry."

He waited, expecting words of defiance that never came.

"Besides, I tried arresting you once and it didn't work out very well," Durek concluded, strolling away. "No, this is the punishment you deserve, I think, to be spurned—or worse—by those very wizards you sought to corrupt with magic. And if corrupting them, impoverishing them, starving them, and setting the Tribunal on them wasn't enough to make them renounce you, Bishop Lukin is devising some new penalties that will make the Lorngeld despise you all the more."

"But everyone's blaming the wrong person!" she cried, pursuing him across the room. "Nicolas was bewitched, it's true. But not by me. By a man called the Sage of Sare."

Durek cocked a disbelieving eyebrow at her. "The who? Oh, honestly, Athaya. I've never heard of any such person."

"You will," she said softly. "He's the one who wants to kill you, not me."

Durek sighed impatiently. "And why is that?"

"Because you are hostile to the Lorngeld," she replied. "And more importantly, because he wants to rule Caithe." *And everyplace else,* she thought, but left the greater fear unspoken.

"And you don't, I suppose," he said, snorting indelicately.

Athaya felt old rage begin to simmer, but quelled it and remained silent. Durek had accused her of such ambitions long ago; it was only when her own people began to share his suspicions that it truly hurt. But this time, there was a trace of doubt in Durek's eyes—doubt in the truth of the familiar accusation. If the crown was truly what she wanted, the eyes wondered, then surely she could have taken it by now . . . so why hadn't she?

"Why on earth would some Sarian I've never heard of want to rule Caithe?" he snapped.

"Because he thinks it's his destiny—oh, it would take too long to explain—"

"If he wants to overthrow me, then why not just come and do it himself?"

"Why do that when he can accomplish the same end with a fraction of the effort and spare himself the blame at the same time? Think about it, Durek. By trying to force Nicolas to murder you, he would have effectively rid himself of two major obstacles to the throne. You'd have been dead, and the council probably would have seen Nicolas executed for the crime—or at the very least stripped of his claims and locked up somewhere for the rest of his life. And by making everyone think *I'm* responsible, the Sage has discredited me as well. That leaves Mailen, and I don't think the Sage would consider a four-year-old king much of a threat."

Durek scowled at her. "A very intriguing plot, Athaya. Are you sure you didn't invent it yourself?"

"Durek—"

"If this Sage fellow really exists, then how do I know you're not in league with him?"

"He wanted me to be. But I discovered the extent of his ambition and refused the alliance. And everything that's happened since then is his form of vengeance—of getting what he wants the only way he's got left."

Durek tapped his chin thoughtfully. "I'm starting to see a connection here that I don't like, Athaya," he said, glaring at her. "Nicolas has confessed that he met with you months ago . . . it was no coincidence, then, that he returned to Delfarham eager to obtain the Sarian marshalcy, was it? You sent Nicolas there to talk to this wizard—to find out whether he might help you in this absurd crusade of yours."

"No, Durek. It was Nicolas' idea to go to Sare and look for the Sage, not mine. And he wasn't betraying anyone. He was doing it to protect all of us—you, me, and Caithe itself. He was being *loyal*—"

"Really, Athaya—"

"I told him that I'd heard of the Sage and that I'd like to find out more about him. I had no idea what Nicolas was walking into. Who could have known that the Sage and his people had any ill will toward us? Not much news ever comes out of Sare."

"Wait . . . *his* people?"

"There are trained wizards on Sare, Durek. Hundreds of

them. The Sage is their leader. They've been waiting years for a sign to make their move, and now they're preparing to return to Caithe and make a bid for power.''

Never mind that I was the sign they were waiting for, she thought. *Why give Durek yet another reason to hate me?*

Durek expelled his breath in an irritated puff. "That's all I need," he said, clearly not ready to believe in a threat he had not yet seen, "more mind-plagued wizards out to get my throne.''

Before Athaya could explain further, there came a soft rap on the door. Instinctively, she cast a cloaking spell and winked out of sight. Durek blinked at the now-empty patch of space for a moment, but then he cocked an ear at the sound of her breathing and knew she was still present.

A sleepy-eyed servant shuffled into the room, rubbing at one eye. "Your Majesty, the bishop is here to see you, if it's not too late." He peered around the room, puzzled. "I thought I heard voices, and—''

"The bishop? Ah, send him in!'' Durek exclaimed, taking inordinate delight in the idea. He laughed merrily, but tired as he was, there was a touch of hysteria in his mirth. Athaya suspected this was the happiest he had ever been to grant the bishop an audience. "Yes, do send him in.''

A moment later, Bishop Lukin swept into the chamber in a cloud of black wool, as awake now as he would be come the dawn and wholly unconcerned that it was edging toward midnight. "I apologize for the lateness of the hour," he began, his voice needlessly loud in the stillness of the night, "but I require your signature on—''

"Oh, never mind that. Look who's here, Jon!'' Durek swept his hand around the chamber. "Come now, Athaya," he scolded lightly. "Do reappear for the good bishop.''

Warily, Athaya let the cloaking spell disperse. The instant she shimmered into view, the bishop staggered back, sputtering in angry shock. The document in his hand fluttered to the floor, abruptly forgotten.

"Majesty, have you lost your senses?'' He scanned the chamber with wild eyes, seeking a corbal crystal but finding none. "You must leave this place at once—your life is in peril!''

"Oh, I don't think so, Jon,'' Durek replied lazily. "Athaya has already described to me just how she might have murdered me earlier, so I think she has something else in mind tonight.''

"All I want right now is to see Nicolas," she said, keeping a safe distance from the bishop. "He's sick, and if magic had something to do with it, I may be able to help him."

"Preposterous!" Lukin declared. "You only seek to enchant him again, and order him to try his hand at the king a second time."

"You're welcome to go with me to see that I don't," she suggested calmly. Then she turned to Durek, and addressed him as submissively as she could stomach. For Nicolas, it was worth it. "Please, Durek . . . he is my brother, too. May I see him?"

"Sire, you cannot consider—"

"Oh, very well," Durek replied, cutting Lukin off. "I think perhaps you *should* see what your cursed magic has wrought. Or this Sage, if that's the story you persist in using."

Against the bishop's bitter and profuse objections, Durek lit a candle and led the way out of the chamber. Athaya again shrouded herself with a cloaking spell and followed them—it was bad enough that Lukin knew she was here; better that the rest of the castle not be thrown into an uproar as well.

Durek led them down the wainscoted corridor to Nicolas' apartments, whistling in eerie amusement. Two armed sentries were posted on either side of the double door, and Athaya did not miss the look of controlled bewilderment on their faces as the king and bishop stepped past them, holding the door open a moment longer without explanation to let Athaya drift unseeingly into the chamber.

It had been years since Athaya had entered these rooms, and she remembered them as a happy place where she and Nicolas had played as children. The walnut sideboard had once served as an impenetrable fortress, and the low shelves, now used for the mundane purpose of storing plates and goblets, had once played the role of siege engines and their shelves a ladder to be scaled to reach the battlements. Athaya listened for echoes of youthful laughter, but the room was silent. Tonight, the once-merry place held the pall of a sickroom, as childhood memories were brutally shoved aside to make way for adult concerns and tragedies.

Durek led her through the darkened outer room, down the short passageway past the prince's wardrobe, and into the bedchamber. The darkness was lifted here somewhat; the shutters were open to allow the moonlight to spill across the carpet and coverlets, casting the room in silver. Durek set his candle on a low table near the door, adding a touch of gold.

"Your Majesty," the bishop said, this time more softly, in deference to the prince, "I must protest allowing her to—"

"Oh, do be quiet, Jon. You're starting to prattle like Archbishop Ventan."

The comparison effectively silenced the bishop.

Ignoring them, Athaya crept toward the bed with trepidation. The heavy, brocade bed-curtains were open and the quilted coverlets thrown back into an unruly heap at Nicolas' feet. She did not think he slept, nor was he fully awake. He shifted restlessly beneath a sweat-soaked sheet, moaning and whispering under his breath, as if speaking to spirits in half dreams.

"Nicolas?" She lowered herself onto the bed beside him, reaching out to touch the limp, brown hair like a mother offering comfort to a sick child. "Are you awake?"

He responded to her touch, if not her voice. He rolled onto his back and slowly cracked open his eyes to look at her, but his gaze was like winter wind against her flesh. Athaya glimpsed a flicker of recognition in those deep brown pools, but it was quickly gone, as if the part of him that knew her was overwhelmed by something far stronger, leaving him unable to cry for help and unable to remember that he needed any. Then those eyes stopped reflecting internal struggle and went vacant as Nicolas retreated from the pain of his existence into madness—the only shelter from whatever spell was tormenting him—and left only a husk behind.

"Do you know me?" Athaya whispered to him, already certain that she knew the awful answer.

"I can't do it," he said, in response to an entirely different question—one posed within his tortured mind. "The voice says I have to, but I won't."

"Voice . . . whose voice, Nicolas?"

His face twitched with pain; his eyes were those of a young man for a fraction of a breath, then lapsed into those of a child. "These are my men," he said, picking up a pair of carved wooden soldiers from the bedstand. Athaya recognized them— she had given them to Mailen as a birthday present two years ago. "The little boy lets me play with them."

"They're very nice," she choked out, her eyes growing moist. "Nicolas, do you know those men over there?" she asked, moving aside so that he could see Durek and the bishop. Perhaps if she could just jog his memory a bit—like Jaren had tried to do with his incessant questions on their way back from Saint Gillian's—she would be able to loosen the bindings of whatever spell confined him.

"That's the little boy's father," he said, pointing to Durek. Then he lowered his voice to a whisper. "I don't like him, though. He's surly."

Behind her, Durek sniffed his annoyance. "Really—"

Had their situation been less pathetic, Athaya might have laughed aloud through her pain. "And the other man?"

Nicolas screwed up his face in distaste. "He talks too loud." Then, abruptly bored with the subject, Nicolas turned his attention back to the wooden soldiers. Picking one up in each hand, he smashed them together again and again, acting out a mortal combat no less brutal than the one he was waging in the chasm of his mind.

"He doesn't know any of us," Durek said, his voice growing impatient—and surly. "We've tried this sort of thing before."

But Athaya barely heard him, so ravaged was she by her own anguish. She had seen her father's madness, and though it had lanced her to the soul, it was a trifling wound compared to what she suffered now. She had always been at odds with Kelwyn, and her memories of him were not all kind . . . but Nicolas! He was her companion of twenty-one years, with whom she shared every adventure and sorrow of her life; she loved him more than she ever fathomed before and to think of all those happy times he no longer recalled, to think that she was to him now like any other face, broke her heart in a way it had never been rent before.

And in that same moment, Athaya felt the agony that Jaren had endured on the night he found her at the convent—finding her body, but knowing that her *self* was not present, hidden behind a mask of insanity. And then, like a cruel joke, she remembered what he had said to her shortly afterward, hoping to cheer her. It had at the time, but now the words were haunting. *You and Nicolas have been close all your life and nothing terrible has happened to him yet.*

It was a bitter irony. Her life was full of them, it seemed.

You were a child once, in this room, she thought, gazing upon her brother's face. *And now you are all but a child again.*

Her eyes were bloated with tears now, blurring her vision, and she dried them on a corner of the quilt.

"Oh, really, Athaya," Durek scolded behind her. "Such theatricals don't become you."

Athaya was too distraught to acknowledge the insult. "What will happen to him?" she asked, her voice breaking.

"I'm not sure yet. If he recovers, he'll have to be tried. Whatever *you* may think," Durek added scornfully, "trying to kill the king is a rather serious offense, whether one has been bewitched or not. If he doesn't recover, then he may have to be confined somewhere so he doesn't try to kill me again. He hasn't tried yet, but who's to say he might not?"

"Or that she might not in his place," the bishop observed. "Sire, you have granted your sister her wish, although why you have done so I cannot begin to guess. But she is dangerous, and you must not let her linger here any longer, I implore you!"

At long last, Durek saw wisdom in the bishop's protests. Perhaps the late hour helped; his eyelids were heavy, and his tolerance for Athaya's presence, while never extensive, was wearing thin. "You've seen him, as you wished. Now go," he said, turning his back to her. "Go back to the people who despise you."

"And don't dare to return," Lukin added. "I have taken the adjoining chamber during my stay in the capital and will be alert to signs of trouble. If you are seen in Delfarham again, his Majesty may not be so lenient with you."

Athaya wasn't going to argue the point. It would serve no purpose, and her visit with Nicolas had already drained the life and soul out of her; she could not even raise the energy to breathe the mildest of curses at the Sage. Before his Majesty could change his mind, thinking it wise to arrest her after all, Athaya departed the chamber with a whispered word, leaving Nicolas— or what was left of him—behind.

The first thing Athaya did upon arriving back in her room was to release the flood of tears that Durek had chided her for shedding. Then, when her eyes were dry and the sleeve of her gown thoroughly soaked, she sought out Master Tonia, hoping to learn more about Nicolas' affliction. Despite the late hour, she found Tonia in the kitchens, working out the tensions of the day by grinding sunflower seeds into flour with undue force. Mosel and Jaren were seated at the table beside her and both rose to greet Athaya as she slipped into the room, visibly relieved to see her back safely.

Tonia embraced her heartily, leaving creamy spots of flour where her palms touched back and shoulders. "Jaren told me where you'd gone, and I've been worried sick; all I could think of was the time you went off to fetch Aldus and never came back." She drew back, her eyes worried. "Did you see Nicolas? How is he?"

"Not well, Tonia," Athaya replied, lowering her eyes. "Not well at all. I need your help to find out exactly what's wrong with him."

Haltingly, Athaya related all that Durek had told her about Nicolas' condition and what she had herself observed. Out of the long tale, one phrase alone stuck in Tonia's mind. "Something 'snapped inside of him,' " she murmured, lapsing into thought.

"Does that tell you anything?"

"I'm afraid so." Tonia sat beside her and folded Athaya's hands inside her older, more leathery ones. "I think Nicolas has been bound by a spell of compulsion. The Circle considers it a highly unethical spell—dabbling with someone else's free will is unconscionable. It was forbidden long before the rite of assumption."

Athaya's breath coursed out of her, and it was an effort to draw it back into her lungs. No, not *another* forbidden spell. Rhodri had used the rite of assumption in a disastrous attempt to shift magic from one who bore the power to one who did not—in this case, to her father, Kelwyn. But because Rhodri had never acknowledged the dangers of the spell, Kelwyn eventually spiraled into madness—and accidental death, at the untrained hands of his daughter—never to achieve his goal of freedom for the Lorngeld, a race he had hoped to understand by assuming their powers. But Athaya vowed to carry on what he had begun; in a strange way, the rite of assumption was the seed from which her entire crusade had sprouted.

Was the spell of compulsion, then, the seed of its destruction?

"But I don't understand . . . if Nicolas was compelled to murder the king," Jaren asked, "then why didn't he?"

"Because it wasn't in his nature. No, more than that—it violated the very essence of who he is. You see, for the spell to take root, there must be some willingness, however small, for the victim to carry out his task. And I'm sure there's some part of Nicolas—as there is in you," she said, turning to Athaya, "that would be glad to see him dead. The Sage probably got him to admit as much; thus, the spell took hold. But it's virtually impossible to get someone to do a thing utterly abhorrent to them. If, as you've said, Nicolas simply isn't capable of killing—much less killing a brother—then no amount of magic can compel him to do it. But Brandegarth didn't know Nicolas that well and probably misjudged the kind of resentment Nicolas has for Durek and interpreted it as pure hatred. When it came time to carry out the task, something 'snapped,' as you said. That 'snap' was Nicolas' conscious refusal to obey the compulsion, and his sickness is the result. The Sage's magic is still pressing against him, but Nicolas is pressing back just as hard. Thus, his state of madness. And it's my guess that he acts like a child because most of his mind is occupied with resisting the spell.''

Athaya slumped forward, heartsick and exhausted to the point of collapse. *Maybe I'm finally starting to grow up,* Nicolas had told her not four months ago, when he had dedicated himself to her cause. *I never expected it would be my little sister who would inspire me to do such a thing.*

Oh, Nicolas, what a mockery the Sage has made of your desire . . .

''Is there a chance he'll ever give in to the pressure and stop pressing back?''

Tonia furrowed thinning, gray brows. ''I'm not sure—his initial resistance may have been enough to break the brunt of the spell's force, but I can't promise you that. Durek may still be in some danger.''

Mosel glanced from one wizard to another hoping that, in his ignorance of magic, his question was not too absurd. ''Can't you just undo the spell?''

''I wish it were that easy,'' Tonia told him, without a hint of ridicule, ''but the Sage almost certainly has adept-level powers. Trying to unweave his spell might only make it worse—in the way that struggling against certain types of knots only ties them tighter. Freeing Nicolas from such a thing could be far more dangerous than was releasing Athaya from that sealing spell. If the compulsion spell is strong enough, then the only way to release someone from it is to have the victim accomplish the thing he was commanded to do.''

Athaya sat up rigidly. ''Are you saying that Nicolas won't recover until Durek *dies*?'' she asked, aghast. ''Dies by Nicolas' own hand?''

''Not unless we can unweave the compulsion,'' Tonia replied. "Or until the one who set the compulsion is dead. But I don't know that for sure," she added gently. "Hedric is the real expert on spells of this type. We should ask him before we attempt to undo it ourselves."

In a burst of rage and fatigue, Athaya beat her fist against the table, threatening to topple Tonia's bowl of flour. "Damn him, what is the Sage trying to *do* to me?"

"Ruin you," Jaren replied sullenly. "He wants to use what you've accomplished so far for his own ends. I think he saw you succeeding a bit too much and wanted to ruin your good name so he could take over your crusade and bend it to his own will."

"And he sent Drianna to find out how bad our situation was so that he'd know the ripest time to offer us an alliance—an alliance he thought I'd be forced to accept. I'll wager he would have tried to ruin me anyway, even if I hadn't refused his offer. Damn, another Rhodri!"

"More dangerous than Rhodri, I think," Tonia pointed out. "The Sage isn't working for his own selfish ends, but for the glory of an entire race. That tends to give people delusions of grandeur." She picked up her pestle and resumed grinding seeds into flour, gritting her teeth as if wishing the seeds were the bones of the Sage himself.

"Delusions of grandeur aside, the Sage will have to wait. Our first priority right now is Nicolas. And one thing's for certain," Athaya said decisively. "We can't help him if he's stuck in Delfar Castle."

Tonia glanced up warily. "You're going back to get him?"

"I'll have to. But not tonight—the bishop is far too suspicious. I'll wait a few days and then make my move." She turned to Mosel and Jaren. "And tell Cecile that Mailen will be here waiting for her when she arrives. We all know he's the only reason she'd even consider going back to Delfarham instead of leaving Halsey with the two of you."

Mosel's eyes went wide. "You mean to abduct the boy?"

"Not exactly," she said, shrugging her discomfiture at his choice of words, "I'll just be returning him to his mother. Durek is filling his head with lies about us, and it's about time he heard Cecile's point of view. And it won't be so difficult to get them both," she went on, knowing it would be Mosel's next question. "Mailen visits Nicolas nearly every night—Durek told me so himself. I'll bring Mailen here right after I find a safe haven for Nicolas, someplace where the Sage—or Durek, for that matter—

won't find him. I'm not sure where yet,'' she added with a frown, ''but the camp is the first place Brandegarth would look. Once he finds out that his spell didn't work, he may try to bewitch Nicolas again.''

"Or punish him for failing,'' Tonia murmured, and on that gruesome thought, their conversation was done.

Julie Dean Smith   281

"What do she say to you, Nicolas?" Durek persisted. "When
did you speak to her, when?"

CHAPTER 22

✳

TWO DAYS AFTER LEAVING THE FOREST OF ELSE, UNDER dreary skies that promised snow, Jaren and Mosel arrived at the queen's manor. During the journey, they had discussed the best way to break the news of Nicolas' alleged crime, only to learn that, as in Kaiburn, the news had reached Halsey before them. Mosel and his "servant" were escorted to the sunless solar, where Cecile and the infant Lillian received them. Both women were clad in somber gray and both shed tears, though Lillian wept with far more vigor and for vastly different reasons, ceasing only when Cecile dabbed a few drops of cider on her tongue.

"I've already asked my ladies to start packing my things," Cecile told them, casting a brooding gaze out the window at the road which wound its way northward toward Delfarham. "I have to see Nicolas right away."

Mosel went to her side and placed a comforting hand on her shoulder. "I understand your concern, my Lady, but the king may not allow it. And you may wish to reconsider whether you should return at all."

Cecile looked to him in silent alarm, and Mosel drew her into the windowseat and told her all that he had seen and heard that fateful night in Delfarham. He told her of Nicolas' magic-induced illness, of Athaya's certainty that a scheming Sarian wizard was responsible for it, and of more immediate importance, he warned her that Durek had learned of Athaya's autumn visit to Halsey and had dispatched his men to escort her Majesty back to Delfarham.

"Escort me?" she asked, her tone edged with scorn. "As the queen, or as a prisoner of the Tribunal?"

"Truly, I do not know. But they shouldn't arrive for another day or two—his Majesty is sending a coach for you and your trunks." Mosel paused, framing his next words with care; spoken by a less trusted friend, they might be unforgivably presumptuous, but he did not think Cecile would take offense. "I know he is your husband, madam, but as your friend, I would not advise returning to him. Bishop Lukin has the king's ear now and has long resented your friendship with Athaya. He may pressure his Majesty into doing something regrettable."

Cecile sniffed, but delicately. "I have no desire to be packed off to a convent like Athaya was last spring," she declared, though there was a deep pool of sadness behind the spirited words. "I can't trust him anymore, Mosel," she said, bitterness touched with sincere regret. "Sometimes I wonder if I ever could." She rose slowly from the windowseat, still cradling Lillian in her arms. Murmuring endearments, she gently bounced the whimpering princess in hopes of easing her back to sleep. "But my son . . ." she began, her face pinched with concern. "If I do not return, what will become of him?"

Jaren came to stand beside her, glad that he and Mosel had brought good news as well as bad. "Athaya has promised to bring him to our camp, should you wish to leave with us and meet him there—she may be going to the capital this very night. If you do not wish to come," he added, careful not to press the queen into a decision, "then she will return him to Delfarham, of course."

The queen's smile was like a ray of summer sunshine that pierced the leaden skies. "Athaya bears little love for the capital," she told them, her eyes playfully radiant. "She need not make an added journey there on my account. And I'll not ask how she plans to get Mailen out of the castle. I think it best that I not know until afterward; I'll worry myself to death, otherwise." Purposefully, Cecile crossed to the cradle to collect a pair of blankets and a tiny wooden rattle. "I also think it best that we leave immediately. I should like to see this forest retreat, where wizards learn of magic. And more importantly," she added, blond brows folding inward, "I wish to be well away from here when Durek's 'escort' arrives."

Cecile bade them follow her to her private chambers, where she promptly dismissed a pair of young women busily packing her gowns. Ignoring the collection of unwieldy trunks, Cecile selected a small cloth bag and began stuffing it with what little she would need to get her and Lillian safely to Kaiburn—a purse of money, a handful of baby's clothes, and an extra kirtle. "I'm beginning to sense what it is like for Athaya, being a fugitive in her own homeland."

Then Jaren, who had been lingering near the window, jerked back as if to avert a blow. "We've got a problem."

Mosel hurried to his side, and the furrows in his weathered face grew deeper. A problem, indeed. On the rise just north of the manor, four armed men galloped toward the gate, all of them clad in identical crimson cloaks adorned at the shoulder with the royal crest of Trelane. "What are they doing here so soon? They shouldn't have arrived until tomorrow at the earliest."

"Four men, but no coach," Jaren pointed out.

"They must have decided that speed was more important than the queen's comfort. Come, my Lady—and my little Lady," he added, touching Lillian's pink nose, "there's no time to lose."

Cecile tossed a nondescript gray cloak around her shoulders and tucked Lillian snugly beneath it, while Jaren snatched up the queen's traveling bag, abandoning the rest of her belongings. Cautiously, he opened the door and poked his head out, looking both ways to insure that the corridor was empty. "Which way's best?"

"Both ways lead to stairwells, but that one is closer to the stable." She pointed to the left.

"I wouldn't advise taking horses," Jaren whispered, shaking his head. "I can get all of us out of the manor under a cloaking spell, but I doubt I could extend it to cover three horses as well. And once those men find out you're gone, they'll scour the area looking for travelers. It'll be tricky enough just covering our tracks if it starts to snow."

Cecile nodded; though she was accustomed to sumptuous coaches, she was prepared to endure whatever hardships might await her. "Then we'll walk. I have money—if we need them, we can buy horses on the way."

"I suggest you employ that spell of yours," Mosel urged,

tapping Jaren on the shoulder from behind. "I hear them coming
. . . from both directions."

"Not taking any chances, are they?" Jaren took Cecile's hand
in his left and Mosel's in his right. *"Occulta nos,"* he whispered, then led them out into the hall. Cecile held back at first,
slow to believe that the guardsmen would not be able to see her
when she was perfectly visible to herself.

"Not another sound from either of you until we reach the
stairwell," Jaren warned, then began herding his charges down
the lengthy hallway. Mosel felt his skin grow moist with sweat
as they passed within a yard of the two guardsmen that had come
up the stairs they were about to descend, but they slipped by
unnoticed, and the men gave no sign that they saw anything in
the corridor other than the usual tapestries, hunting trophies,
and flagstones.

Captain Parr pounded on the door to the queen's chamber,
scowling darkly when he received no answer to his summons.
"You told me she was here," he accused the frightened-looking
maid who had escorted him.

"B-but she has to be," the girl replied, cowering under the
captain's glare as if expecting him to strike her in punishment
for her mistress' absence. "Her Majesty dismissed me only a
few minutes ago—right after she came back from the solar. She
had two men with her. Visitors, just arrived."

"Visitors," the captain said, his tone transforming the word
into a curse. "Come to warn her, no doubt."

He burst into the queen's chamber, only to burst out again
like a firebrand from a catapult. "She was starting to pack—she
and her 'visitors' must have seen us and fled. They left everything behind."

The fugitives had just reached the top of the staircase when,
frightened by the captain's booming voice, Lillian's agitation
returned in a fit of temper and poor timing and she let out a
disgruntled cry. Cecile hugged her daughter close against her
breast to stifle the noise, but the calming gesture came too late.

"What was that?" the captain said, whirling around on his
heel. His hand flew instinctively to the hilt of his sword.

"It came from that direction," his lieutenant replied.

Mosel turned and felt every joint in his body stiffen; the
guardsman's outstretched finger seemed to point directly between his eyes.

"They're coming this way," Cecile murmured, rocking Lillian rhythmically to soothe her back to silence. "We'll never reach the bottom ahead of them."

"I'll go back and hold them off," Jaren said. "I didn't sense any corbal crystals, and even a few simple spells should keep them at bay long enough. It'll give us away, but they already know you're trying to escape."

But before he could carry out his plan, Mosel moved in front of him to block his path. "No, Jaren. If the captain sees you here, he'll surely tell the king and that will make things look worse for Cecile than they already do. Take the queen and her daughter to safety—they need the protection of your spell more than I do." Then, steeling himself, he let go of Jaren's arm, disengaging himself from the cloaking spell.

"But they'll see you!"

"That's the idea. I'll delay them while you and Cecile make your escape. Now, hurry!" He waved them on, though he could now see nothing but emptiness before him. "I'll catch up with you later—I know my way back to the forest. Don't worry about me."

Quickly, before the lassitudes of a lifetime changed his mind, he retraced his steps, reaching the top of the narrow staircase just as Parr and his men were starting to come down. Captain Parr was not a man often taken by surprise, and Mosel almost chuckled his pleasure at the blatant look of astonishment on the guardsmen's normally stolid face.

"Lord Gessinger?" The owl-like eyes grew even wider and even blinked once. "What are you—"

"Ah, hello Captain," Mosel wheezed in reply. He braced himself squarely in the doorway, blocking their way under the guise of regaining his balance and his breath, as if his aged bones had just mounted the full flight of steps. "What brings you to Halsey?"

The captain was too startled to provide anything but the truth. "I've come to see the queen."

Mosel nodded, and swallowed another lungful of air. "As have I, as have I. I wanted Cecile to hear the terrible news about Prince Nicolas from a friend. As expected, it has upset her greatly. She wishes to be alone now. She even sent me away when I told her . . . me, her closest friend," he added, pretending injury. "Please don't disturb her yet, I implore you. She is simply too distraught."

"But wasn't she just going down those stairs? I thought I

heard a baby's cry, and her chambermaid said that the child was with her.''

"Baby?" Mosel grappled for a remotely plausible explanation—he needed a few more precious minutes before he could be assured that Jaren and Cecile had reached the manor gates. "Oh, no. I was returning from the library when I stumbled over one of her Majesty's cats and stepped on the poor thing's tail. Perhaps that's what you heard." He winced at the feeble excuse, but he had never been an expert liar and lacked Prince Nicolas' well-honed talent for inventing credible tales at a moment's notice.

"That was no cat," the lieutenant snarled. He made to push his way past Mosel, but the old lord refused to yield.

"Sir—her Majesty would be most displeased were you to disturb her rest. She's gone to the solar and—"

Captain Parr glowered at him. "That's curious. Her chambermaid told me that the queen just *left* the solar—with the child—only a few minutes ago."

"Oh? Well, I expect she simply changed her mind and went elsewhere. Women do, you know."

But platitudes weren't enough to satisfy the persistent captain. "Stand aside, sir—we're on the king's business and have no more time for delays."

"And I am on the queen's business," he said stubbornly. "Her Majesty needs her rest." He sat down on the top step like a petulant child, refusing to budge until he was forcibly removed, or the men climbed over him to continue their pursuit.

Then, he knew, he had gone too far.

The captain squatted down before him, slow and deliberate, and the expression in those owlish eyes was altered. No longer was his gaze thick with contempt. Now there was a glint of surprise in it. Not respect—that would be too generous—but a gradual awareness that perhaps there was more to the old lord than he, or the rest of the court, had ever dreamed.

"I've just thought of something, my Lord," he said, and Mosel did not like the knowledge in his tone. "This is the second time you've vanished from the capital without a word. Not that anyone particularly missed you," he remarked with the tilt of a brow, caring little if he gave offense, "but during both absences, something unpleasant has occurred." Slowly, his hand slid down to grasp the pommel of his sword. "During your absence in October, Princess Athaya was unexpectedly set free.

Then you returned—in the company of Prince Nicolas, who has since tried to murder the king. Now you come here, and I find that the queen is being hidden from me. Why these strange coincidences, my Lord?'' he asked, eyes narrowing. ''Can you tell me?''

Sweat began to bead on Mosel's forehead. ''Coincidences, nothing more,'' he said, but Parr could smell deceit as easily as a hound could sniff out a fox, and Mosel realized that he was hopelessly snared.

The captain was on his feet with his sword drawn before Mosel could so much as struggle to his knees. ''Quickly,'' Parr ordered his men, ''find the others and search the grounds—the queen is trying to escape, and this traitor is trying to stall us.'' Then he grasped a handful of Mosel's cloak and hauled the old man to his feet with one hand. ''It seems you're not the doddering fool that everyone takes you for,'' he said, his face only inches from Mosel's own. ''But believe me, my Lord, this is the last day you will ever deceive us.''

With those sinister words, Mosel knew that his days of being dismissed as a useless appendage to the Caithan court were done. But even as Captain Parr led him away with the point of a sword kissing his throat, Mosel felt an odd surge of pride and smiled.

That same night, two days after her first journey to Delfarham, Athaya judged it time to return. She alerted Tonia to her departure and then went to her room and cast a vision sphere to insure that Nicolas was alone in his chamber. Although she sought to bring Mailen back as well, she thought it best to arrive before the boy's nightly visit and speak privately to Nicolas, hoping to prepare him for what was about to happen. In his condition, his mind ravaged by magic, being caught unawares by spell-work a second time might throw him into a panic.

Athaya gazed into the cloudy orb of fog suspended between her palms, commanding it to seek out and reveal her beloved brother. The sphere would know that she did not mean Durek.

The misty vapors swirled, then coalesced into an image; an image of a room, and of the battered soul within it. Nicolas was alone, but he was not at peace.

The prince was agitated and in obvious distress. He pulled at strands of wheat-brown hair, tousling it worse than it already was, and walked in anxious circles, muttering incoherently. The folds of a linen dressing gown flapped and tangled between his legs, robbing him of the natural grace that Athaya knew he possessed—or had, once. The sight brought a veil of tears to her eyes, and the sphere-vision blurred and danced before her, though by no fault of her magic.

She dispersed the sphere, shaking off the last tendrils of sticky white mist from her fingertips, and tossed on a light wool cloak—no need to bundle up in bulky winter garb; she would not be traveling outdoors this night. Then, drawing a deep breath, she journeyed across Caithe by magic roads, by and through a place not found on any map.

Her feet sank into the carpet adorning Nicolas' outer chamber, but to her surprise, her knees soon followed, buckling at an unexpected blow. She fought for balance and braced herself against a low shelf, stifling a cry from the hot blades of pain searing through her skull. Athaya shut her eyes tight against light-headedness . . . God, not even at their worst had the effects of translocation been this bad! And why now, of all times, had they suddenly returned to haunt her?

Thoughts muddied by the pain, it took a moment before she realized that her plight had nothing to do with translocation at all. Bishop Lukin had warned her not to return and had taken steps to keep her away. Somewhere in the prince's bedchambers was a corbal crystal, and Athaya had been so distracted by Nicolas' distress that she never thought to scry for one before leaving the sanctuary of the camp.

It was not too large a gem; she could still think rationally amid the pounding in her skull—at least for now—but she would need to dispose of it quickly before her power was too weakened to spirit Nicolas and Mailen safely away. She may have grown quite good at it, especially since her power had been enhanced by the pressure of the sealing spell, but translocation was still serious business and could not be undertaken lightly.

The Justice from Kilfarnan would testify to that . . . were he still alive to do so.

She struggled unsteadily to her feet, only then realizing that Nicolas had been observing her with detached interest all the while, seemingly undisturbed by her abrupt appearance. "You were here before," he said.

Athaya nodded, though the motion made her head spin afresh. "Yes, I was. Two days ago."

"Are you sick?" he asked with a frown. His voice lacked

concern as well as comprehension; he only asked from childlike curiosity.

"Yes. Tell me," she struggled to say, "is there a purple jewel in your room? Maybe on a chain, or in a ring?"

Nicolas bobbed his head, thinking nothing odd about the question. "On a chain, hanging from my bedpost. It belongs to the little boy's father. I'm not supposed to touch it," he added indifferently. "It's there to keep the Devil away."

Athaya suppressed a scowl. "The crystal is what's making me sick," she explained. "Could you put it somewhere very dark, so I won't be able to see it? Then I'll feel better."

"But I'm not supposed to touch it," Nicolas repeated.

Athaya labored for breath. "I won't tell anyone. It will be our secret. Just make sure it's somewhere very dark."

Nicolas studied her, still skeptical. "Is this a game?"

Athaya bit her tongue and tried to avoid snapping at him out of pain-induced desperation. It had been a long time since she'd had to scrape together enough patience to deal with children—or those who acted like them—and at the moment, she found her dialogue with Nicolas almost as frustrating as trying to talk sense into Durek.

Almost. And far, far more heartbreaking.

"Well, yes . . . yes, it is a game."

He shrugged negligently, as if he didn't care whether he played or not. But whatever his thoughts on the matter, he went into the inner chamber, returning a minute later with a smirk on his face.

"I put it in my chamberpot," he said, punctuating his words with a giggle.

Athaya felt her head already starting to clear, though bits of fuzz still clung to the edges of her awareness. "Thank you, Nicolas. I feel much better now." She paused, assessing him. "How do you feel?"

Nicolas neglected the cushioned chairs and sank down onto the carpeted floor, cross-legged. "My head hurts," he said, hunching over. "It does a lot."

As did mine, she thought, *when there was too much magic bottled up inside of it. But at least it was my own magic that tormented me and not someone else's.*

Athaya squatted down beside him, throwing the folds of her cloak back out of the way. "Do you like staying here?" she asked, encompassing the room around them with a gesture.

Nicolas hung his head and began pulling at his hair again. "They never talk to me . . . only the little boy. And the voice," he added, and the admission made Athaya shiver. The Sage's voice, whispering its seduction and beseeching him to kill. "Most of them are mean and just stare at me."

"Would you like to come away with me? To a place where you can rest and no one will be mean to you?"

He looked up, eyes brightening slowly as the dawn, but before he could reply, there were voices in the outer corridor, growing louder, and then the jangle of iron keys.

"That'll be my friend," he said, jumping to his feet. Athaya's suggestion was abruptly forgotten as he trotted past her to greet his young guest.

Athaya froze; she sensed that her magic was still shaky and wasn't going to place her trust—or her life—in a cloaking spell that might not work. She gathered up her skirts and darted out of the room, turning into the narrow passageway outside the wardrobe closet—a favorite childhood hiding place, in the days when she and Nicolas regularly sought to avoid baths and other atrocities committed against their persons. She burrowed into the folds of countless robes and tunics—mature and princely garb that mocked their owner now—and left the closet door open a crack. Marten's fur tickled at her nose, and she brushed it aside so as not to sneeze.

First she heard a man's gruff voice advising caution and then a female murmur of assent—Mailen's nurse, Mistress Anne. Then came the click of a closing door and a stream of lively chatter as Mailen launched into a description of the deer his father had shot for his dinner that night. Athaya grinned secretly as she eavesdropped; in the boy's youthful opinion, it was by far the largest deer that had ever been seen in the world—almost as large as the castle itself.

Athaya's limbs had begun to cramp by the time she felt safe enough to try her cloaking spell. And she dared not wait much longer, or Mistress Anne might decide that it was time for Mailen to be in bed.

Footsteps neared, and then two figures drifted across the crack in the door, temporarily shutting out the lamplight, one squat and aged, the other tousel-headed and clad in a flowing dressing gown. "Come now, your Highness," Anne's calming murmur came, "time to take your posset."

Athaya heard the rustle of heavy quilts being thrown back and the gentle nattering of an old woman tucking a child in for the night—a child twenty-two years old.

Now.

Casting her cloaking spell, Athaya slipped out of her hiding place. Nicolas was ensconced among the pillows, and Mistress Anne bent over him, tipping a shallow cup of liquid into his mouth. Slowly, Athaya crept up behind her. If she could be seen, Nicolas would give some sign and perhaps she could retreat in time. But the lightness in her bones told her that the spell was working, and as she came to stand just behind Mistress Anne, Nicolas did nothing.

With the lightest touch she could manage, she brushed against the woman's mind and began her silent urgings of how very heavy her eyelids were, then tempting her with the thought of how refreshing a nap would be, and assuring her that Nicolas and Mailen would surely be safe for a few minutes—no need to worry.

Already wearied from the exertions of the day, Mistress Anne succumbed quickly to Athaya's gentle appeals. Yawning, the nurse lowered herself onto a stool near the bedside; a moment later, she lapsed into sleep, snoring contentedly.

That done, Athaya returned to the outer room, where Mailen was quietly playing with a set of wooden soldiers. Still unseen, she glided past him and soundlessly turned the lock in the door leading to the outside hallway. Now it would not matter how many men were guarding the prince's chamber; she would not be unpleasantly surprised before she and the princes could depart safely.

Athaya let the cloaking spell disperse and stepped around so that Mailen could see her. She looked into deep brown eyes— so like Durek's yet more forgiving—framed by a gentle swirl of sandy-blond hair—Cecile's mark. No longer a baby, he was now a young boy and had left off infant's garb for a miniature tunic of black velvet and a shirt of fine white linen.

"Hello, Mailen," she whispered, kneeling down to speak to him eye-to-eye. At first, she worried that the guards would hear her, then reasoned that they would assume her voice was that of Mistress Anne's. Far better that she worry about scaring him— God only knew the tale he'd been told by now. "Do you remember me? I'm your Aunt Athaya. I haven't seen you in a long time."

Mailen's eyes went round, but Athaya didn't think it was from fear. "Papa says you're the Devil," he blurted out. At barely four, he had not yet learned a king's diplomacy. Athaya smiled inwardly. At twenty-nine, neither had Durek.

"I think your papa is wrong."

Mailen thrust out his lower lip. "He's not! He's the king and kings are *never* wrong!"

Athaya's mouth puckered sourly. *You'd best change that attitude before you're king, my little nephew,* she thought. Cecile and Mosel were right . . . the boy had been under Durek's poisonous influence far too long.

"I'm sad that you think so," she told him. "We used to be friends, remember? I gave you those wooden soldiers as a present once."

Mailen paused, considering this evidence. "I guess so."

"And you liked me then, so why wouldn't you like me now?"

Again, a reflective pause; the boy looked as solemn as a grown man reflecting on a subtle point of the law. "Papa says I shouldn't. He says you hurt people and make them do bad things. He says you hurt Uncle Nicolas."

"No, Mailen. I love your uncle." Athaya folded her hands in her lap. "Your mother knows that. She's never told you that I hurt people, has she?"

It was a cruel tactic, but necessary. And it worked. Mailen's lower lip began to tremble as he shook his head. "Mama's been gone a long time."

"I know she has." Athaya leaned forward; now came the real test. "Would you like to go and visit her? She misses you very much."

The boy's face lit up like a witchlight. "Mama's here?"

"No, not here. In another place." The disappointment on that smooth-boned face was heartbreaking. "But I can take you there, if you like. You can see your mother and your new baby sister. Would you like that?"

Mailen nodded vigorously. Then, abruptly, the motion stopped. "But Papa might get mad."

Might? Athaya thought dryly. *You don't know the half of it, little prince.*

"But your mother would be very happy," she went on, using a child's form of logic. "I'll take Nicolas to safe place where he can be taken care of, and then I'll take you to see your mother."

By now, she could hear the sound of Nicolas' rhythmic breathing from the next room—the posset had done its work.

"Let's leave now," she said, and moved into the inner chamber, Mailen trailing a short distance after her. "All you have to do is sit here beside me and hold my hand."

But Mailen stared beyond her, gaping at Mistress Anne slumped on her stool nearby. She slept, but her head had lolled back and her mouth hung open indelicately. The rise and fall of her chest was barely detectable and in the silver-edged darkness of the moonlit bedchamber, the nurse's stillness frightened the boy, as if he feared her dead by Athaya's magic.

"N-no, I don't want to go anymore," Mailen said, clutching the bedpost as if it were his mother's skirts.

"There's nothing to be afraid of—"

He shook his head with vigor, like a pony tossing his mane. "You're going to use magic, aren't you? Papa says magic will hurt me."

"But that's the only way we can go." She folded Nicolas' hand into hers, preparing to leave, but that only made Mailen's fears worse.

"No!" he shrieked, with the earsplitting volume that only a child's lungs can produce. He pulled at her sleeve, trying to make her release Nicolas. "Papa, help! The Devil's stealing Uncle Nicolas!"

Then, from the outer room, Athaya heard the door rattling frantically in its frame. "Mistress Anne, is something wrong?" Another guardsman tested the lock, then spat a curse. "Mistress, open the door!"

This was no time for delicacy; with only seconds remaining, Athaya reached back and grasped Mailen's wrist, making him shriek all the louder. She closed her eyes and delved into her paths, seeking the spell of translocation. But the corbal had fouled her senses more than she'd realized; cloaking spells were one thing, but translocation took far more concentration and skill and the lingering threads of fuzziness were all too evident now.

Briefly, she thought back to her narrow escape from Kilfarnan and wondered why the muddling effects of the Justice's jeweled censer had not lingered thus; she had made an easy escape only minutes after the corbal had been spirited away. But now, long after Nicolas' crystal had been relegated to darkness, she struggled to recall precisely where the elusive translocation spell resided and had already taken two wrong turns within her paths. Judging by the raised voices of the guards, there was precious little time for further mistakes. Even the door to a prince's room had a key; the lock would only hold them for so long.

Especially if there was another way in . . .

As Athaya detected an unpleasantly familiar voice bellowing over all the others, she remembered that Bishop Lukin had taken up temporary residence in the adjoining chamber—a chamber accessible through a servant's door that she had not thought to secure. She heard a string of spirited curses and then the ominous snap of a latch. Athaya's back was to the door as she sheltered the princes in her arms, but she knew that Lukin had at least two guardsmen with him.

"If he sees the Devil you can be damned certain who he's talking about," the bishop was shouting as he burst into the prince's outer chamber. "I thought there was to be a corbal crystal in those rooms at all times!"

"There was!" another man protested. "I put it there myself!"

Athaya was rattled, and Mailen's piercing wails did not help. Another wrong turn. God, where is that *spell*?

It might buy her only seconds, but seconds were precious now. As she heard footsteps racing past the wardrobe closet toward the inner room, she released Nicolas only long enough to flick a finger behind her, drawing a line of waist-high fire across the entranceway. It was a simple illusion, but real enough to give her enemies pause and give her time to locate the elusive spell.

"Fire!" one guardsman screamed. "Someone bring water, quickly!"

"No, it's false!" the bishop countered. "I've seen such tricks before. We can step right through it—" Athaya heard his voice edge closer—he had crossed the mirage of flames. "Just don't touch her," he warned the others. Closer still. "She'll carry us off to perdition right along with them."

The spell is close, I can feel it now . . .

"But how can I—"

"Use your crossbow!"

The guardsman gasped. "But the princes—"

"Fool!" the bishop exploded. "Are you that poor a shot? Give *me* the damned thing!" Footsteps retreated backward, and Athaya heard the creak of straining wood.

There!

Athaya drew a breath. *"Hinc libera me!"*

But as the last syllable escaped her lips, and she stood poised on the edge of the abyss, fire burned through her shoulder and pierced her through the bone. She teetered on the brink of chaos, falling back to Delfarham, then forward into the between-place, reeling between different parts of the world. Ahead, there was the unsettling but familiar chaos; behind it was the bishop's wrathful voice, sometimes fading with distance, sometimes growing with deadly proximity.

''—saving Nicolas from justice and taking Mailen along as a hostage to insure we don't go after them! And I'll wager the prince's lunacy was an elaborate hoax to keep the council from executing him straight away—''

Forward again, dipping her consciousness into the swirl of chaos. The bishop's voice was gone.

And backward again . . . the voice returned.

''—and all this blather about some Sage . . . a lie! The boy isn't in danger from anyone except Athaya herself. Damn, where's that other corbal I asked for?''

Then momentum pushed her through, and she plunged with her royal charges into the abyss of light and sound. Nicolas was placid in her left hand, enveloped by sleep, but in her right, Mailen struggled wildly, sending fresh bolts of fire through her injured shoulder with every move. Her gown grew heavy with dampness as sticky, warm blood flowed freely from the wound, threatening to make her pass out before they could reach their destination.

And that she could *not* do. With gruesome clarity, she remembered the Justice who had clung to her as she escaped from Kilfarnan, only to topple into the maelstrom, shrieking death-cries as his body was rent apart, unable to take the strain of a place not meant for flesh.

She couldn't let the pain overpower her . . . not and leave Nicolas and Mailen to such a fate.

Knowing her strength was waning and that Mailen might well pull free of her grasp if they did not pass through the chaos soon, she descended upon his young mind and spoke to him from within. *Mailen, don't let go of me. I know you're afraid, but we're in a very dangerous place. Don't let go!*

She felt his panic subside a bit, comforted by a voice—any voice—that assured him he was not alone. Remnant whimpers tugged at Athaya's heart. She had never meant to frighten him.

If Basil had been disturbed by the jolt of translocation, poor Mailen would be terrified indeed.

You'll be safe, Mailen. Just hang on tight.

Then, just before she withdrew from his mind, something caught the corner of her eye; something glowing bright and unwavering amid the ever-changing thoughts and memories and fears that made Mailen *Mailen*. A spot of light, bright as sunlight on the sea, yet no larger than a pinprick. It was dimmer than the spot she'd seen in Emma—perhaps because Mailen was so young—but it was unmistakably there.

A seed.

A seed of magic, as yet unborn.

Athaya sucked in a mouthful of air—if there was air, in this not-place—so astonished at the discovery that she nearly forgot the pain that tore through her right shoulder.

Mailen? Destined to wield magic?

Until now, she had assumed that what the great wizard-king Dameronne had foreseen was his successor, Brandegarth. And in light of the man's arrogance, she doubted that Brandegarth had ever considered another possibility.

But now, it seemed, he might be wrong.

Athaya felt as if she had lingered out of the world for hours, but then the spinning stopped, the light died out, and the noises and images ceased their swirling. A flagstone floor rose up beneath her feet, and she crumpled to the ground and released the princes, one asleep and the other sniffling his misery.

She didn't know whether she had reached her chosen haven and through pain and astonishment was barely able to recall just where she had meant to go at all. But then she heard the cry of an old man's voice and knew she had safely arrived. At last, she succumbed to her wound and the strains of the spell and relaxed into the darkness and slept.

reason why you shouldn't go, but I can't.'' He waited a long

CHAPTER 23

❈

ATHAYA AWOKE TO THE GENTLE SOUNDS OF LAPPING WAter and steady breathing, and cracked open an eye to see Mailen curled up in a contented ball on a trundle bed, sleeping soundly. She was resting upon a great feather bed in an unfamiliar room—carried here, no doubt, from the sparsely furnished chamber in which she had appeared. That place she recalled in vivid detail; the emotional jolt of her unplanned meeting with Adam Graylen four months ago had etched it forever in her mind.

Beside her, Adam was washing bloodied bandages in a bowl of warm water. Seeing her awake, he offered her a refreshing cup of ale. She took the goblet with her left hand; her right shoulder was so bound up with bandages that she could barely lift it.

Athaya flicked a glance toward the sleeping child. "He was frantic when we left Delfarham. How did you get him to fall asleep?"

"I raised a boy myself once, you know. I have a few secrets on how to deal with them. Besides," he added with a chuckle, "it's well past midnight—you've been asleep for hours—and the poor lad was exhausted." Adam dried his hands on a clean cloth. "He was none too happy when you arrived—however you managed to do *that*, though I know better than to ask. He was crying that he wanted his father and mother and that you were the Devil taking him away to hell and other such nonsense. But I asked him if this place looked like hell, and he said no, and then I asked if he thought the Devil would bleed if you cut him— as you were certainly doing—and he said no to that, too. Then, while I was binding your wound, I sat him down and spun him a story, and he settled down enough to fall asleep."

Athaya took another sip of ale. "Where is Nicolas?"

"Asleep also." He pointed to a narrow, circular staircase leading to the upper floor. "I have the upper apartment as well. It used to be my wife's, but when she died, God rest her, the earl let me continue to use it."

Returning the now-empty cup back to Adam, Athaya tried to sit up, but a flood of fire enveloped her shoulder and she quickly fell back against the pillows. She must have been hurt far worse than she'd realized, too distracted by the urgent need to get Nicolas and Mailen away from Delfarham.

"You'll not be able to use that arm for a while," Adam cautioned her. "And I know what I'm about—I pulled more than one arrow out of Tyler's flesh when he was a young boy bent on soldiering. Yours is a deep wound, my Lady, and you've lost a great deal of blood."

"I was shot with a crossbow from less than ten yards. Now that I think of it, I'm surprised there's anything left of my shoulder at all. But the arrow might not have hit all of me." She looked away, conjuring the memory of her precarious departure from the capital. "I had already started to fade at the time and then I was vacillating on the border, sometimes there, sometimes not. Maybe the arrow passed through me when I was only half there."

Adam crinkled his brows, utterly bewildered. Athaya could hardly blame him—she didn't completely understand what she was saying herself. To someone unlearned of the ways of magic, she would sound like a lunatic indeed.

"Your Highness," Adam began, growing more serious, "why have you come to me and in such dire straits?"

Gingerly, Athaya inched herself into a sitting position using her left arm. "You told me once that if I needed your aid, I had only to ask. I'm asking now, Adam. I wish I didn't have to, but I couldn't think of anywhere else to go. I need you to take care of Nicolas for a while."

Briefly, she explained that Nicolas was bound by a spell and was no longer himself, but like a child trapped in the body of a man. She didn't go into detail about the Sage—bitterly, she realized she didn't know a great deal about him in the first place—but told Adam enough so that he could be certain that none of her allies had done this heinous thing.

"I knew the tale had to be a lie," he said, breathing a thin sigh of relief. "I knew you would never force Prince Nicolas to do such a thing, no matter what your feelings about the king. I might have thought so once, but not now. Not after what you've tried to do for your people."

Athaya smiled contentedly; such loyalty from a man who had no reason to love her was gratifying indeed. "Will his presence here be troublesome for you?"

"Few but my servants ever come to this tower, and I know which of them can be trusted. And the earl will say nothing. It may make him nervous to learn of the prince's presence, but he has never held any ill will toward you or your mission. And he does not have to know unless I tell him. This is a large castle, my Lady, and even I do not know everyone who resides here. Your brother will be safe."

"I'll come back for him as soon as I'm sure we can keep him safe," Athaya assured him. "The man who did this to him might try again. I'm sorry to impose—"

Adam waved off her concern with a flick of his hand. "He's my prince, and your brother . . . and Tyler's friend. How can it be an imposition to care for him in his time of need? One question, though," he said, brows furrowing, "how can you place such trust in me?" He was visibly honored by her request, yet taken aback by the magnitude of it. "You hardly know me."

"No," she replied, "but I knew the son you raised and that's good enough."

Adam's eye shone with inner warmth, his heart touched by her answer. "What about the boy?"

"I'm taking him to the queen as soon as I'm well enough to travel again. But I'll have to leave soon—if she gets to my camp before I do, she'll be frantic that something's happened to us. Unfortunately, I have a feeling that Mailen might panic if I try to take him home by magic."

"But you certainly cannot ride. You're weak, and that shoulder is going to keep you that way for quite some time. Strain it, and the wound will reopen and become infected." Adam cupped his chin as he thought—a gesture she had seen Tyler employ many times when faced with a particularly pressing problem,

"Let me arrange for a cart," he said after a time. "I know a man I would trust with my life—he will take you home."

Oh Lord, another cart. Athaya let out a wisp of laughter, recalling how she had vowed never to travel in such a conveyance again after the long journey home from Saint Gillian's. This time, however, she welcomed the thought of lying on a bed of warm straw for a few days.

Adam was as good as his word and so was his friend—a groomsman in the earl's stable who had been a childhood friend of Tyler's. The cart was piled with straw, warm blankets, and baskets of food—this time, a haven instead of a cell. Mailen was reluctant to leave Adam's comforting presence at first, but when Athaya promised him that they would not be traveling by magic and that he would be with his mother by the end of the next day, he complied quickly enough. Within a quarter hour of leaving the earl's estate, his fears were forgotten, and he proceeded to ask—with aggravating regularity—whether they had arrived at the camp yet. He was the impatient one during this journey, constantly insisting that he preferred to walk instead of ride, and Athaya couldn't help but laugh at him, much to his princely dismay, as her own words came back to haunt her.

The driver let them off near the Forest of Else with his blessing, and Athaya led her young charge along the rune trail toward the camp. She was forced to walk slowly to avoid jarring her shoulder, and it was a chore to keep Mailen at her heel, eager as he was to scamper off into the woods in search of deer and other absorbing quarries. Their arrival had been foreseen by the sentries who routinely scried the forest's edge for vagrant Lorngeld, and an enthusiastic welcome awaited them when they finally reached the clearing.

"Mailen!" Cecile cried, rushing over the muddy ground in a cloud of gray wool. She scooped the boy up in her arms, hugging him tight. "Oh, my son, I've missed you—how is my brave little boy?" And with a grateful smile to Athaya, Cecile led him to the dormitory to meet his sister, listening with serene contentment as he chattered excitedly about his adventures of the past few days.

Then Jaren was at her side, moving to embrace her, but she winced and pulled back, claiming a bruised shoulder—no need to worry him by revealing the extent of her injury—and settled for a long and lingering kiss. "When we got back before you did, I feared the worst," he said. "I thought Tonia and I were going to have to rescue you again.'' His tone was light, but his eyes revealed that he had been genuinely afraid.

"No, this time I actually managed to get myself out of trouble.'' She scanned the faces in the clearing. "Where's Mosel?''

Jaren's expression changed, and Athaya felt a cold lump of fear settle in her belly. "He's . . . not here,'' Jaren said haltingly. "He stayed behind to stall the guards—Durek's men arrived the same day we did. We waited for him a few miles down the road, but he never came. I scried for him later that night and saw he'd been arrested; they're taking him back to Delfarham.''

Athaya bowed her head; this was an unexpected blow. "And after what I've just done with Nicolas and Mailen, they'll take strong measures to insure I won't be able to spirit him away as well.'' She lifted her head, determined not to brood. "At least we know he's still alive. And being so close to Cecile, I doubt Durek will harm him—if he did, she might keep Mailen from him permanently.''

Jaren nodded, then grinned faintly. "I think my optimistic tendencies are starting to rub off on you.''

"Much as I try to resist them at times,'' she replied. Then she drew him to the edge of the clearing, out of earshot from the others. "I saw something during the translocation. Something important.'' She leaned in close, steadying herself with a deep breath. "Mailen has the seed, Jaren. The boy is one of us.''

Jaren gaped at her, his mind spinning with implications. "But I thought you said you'd never look! That it wasn't fair—''

"It was an accident,'' she protested. "He was struggling to get away from me, and I had to touch his mind and beg him not to let go of me during the translocation. I couldn't help but see the seed . . . it would be like overlooking the rune trail on a dark night.''

Jaren leaned against the trunk of an oak and scratched thoughtfully at his cheek. "Will you tell Cecile?''

"No. I shouldn't even know myself. This should remain between us, I think. It would only cause trouble, especially since we can't prove anything—not for another fifteen years or so. But I may tell her that I have . . . oh, a 'hunch' about him, so she'll be even more vigilant about changing those unflattering ideas he has about wizards. If they got any worse, he'd be in for one hell of a shock one day—and I'd hate to see him decide that absolution is the only answer.''

"Oh, we'll have rid Caithe of absolution by then," Jaren said, thrusting another dose of optimism upon her. Suddenly, he began to laugh. "If you ever decide to tell Durek about this, make certain I'm there to see his face."

"He'd never believe me." Then she frowned—something occurred to her that she had never considered before. "But the Sage would believe it, if he ever found out."

"How could he? No one else can see these seeds and neither you nor I is going to tell him."

"If Brandegarth is an adept like me, then he may be able to see Mailen's future—if he hasn't already. After all, Dameronne was able to see *my* destiny clearly enough. But whether Mailen is destined to be a wizard or not, he's still Durek's heir, and that alone makes him a tempting target."

"He won't be a target for long," Jaren told her. "Cecile's decided to take both of the children to Reyka—I've promised her that Osfonin will take her in, just as he welcomed you last year. Kale and I will escort her . . . if you can spare us for a while."

Athaya acquiesced, though loath to see him go. "I'd offer to take them myself, but I doubt Mailen would willingly submit to another translocation—it gave him a bad scare."

"That's not surprising," he replied. "It gave me quite a start, too. We'll manage well enough traveling the usual way. And the moment I get there, I'll talk with Hedric about the spell of compulsion. Something in his library might give us the key to releasing Nicolas."

Athaya nodded dejectedly, then embraced him with one arm and brushed his lips with a kiss.

"What was that for?"

"Now I know what you went through when you found me at Saint Gillian's," she said. "But now we have the opposite problem. You had the key to my freedom, only you didn't know where I was; I know exactly where Nicolas is, but I don't know how to free him from the spell."

Ironies, she thought. *Bitter ironies.*

"We'll find it, Athaya," he promised her, leading her back toward the center of camp. "Just the way we found you."

Early the next morning, Athaya saw the travelers off on their journey to the Reykan capital of Ath Luaine. She asked Jaren to convey her greetings and love to Prince Felgin and his family, to Lord Ian and Master Hedric—and yes, even to Overlord Basil.

"I'll miss you," she whispered to Jaren, as he hoisted a well-stuffed satchel over his shoulder.

"I'll return as soon as I can. And make sure you're healed of your 'bruises' by then," he said with light accusation. Once they had gone to their bed the previous night, it was impossible for Athaya to hide the layers of bandages swathing her shoulder. "It's difficult sharing a bed with someone who cries out in pain every time you roll over."

The camp was a lonelier place once they'd gone, and Athaya wandered aimlessly through the half-deserted tents and shelters, watching novice wizards go about their lessons. As she went to the kitchens for some breakfast, she mused upon all that had happened since her return from Saint Gillian's. Not all of her friends had been left unscathed by fate—Nicolas had warned her it would happen over a year ago, but the reality was quite a different thing. Tonia and Jaren were well enough, as were Kale and Gilda, and Mason was holding his own in Kilfarnan. But young Cameron was dead, never to know if he carried the powers of magic; Ranulf was still on Sare, dead or prisoner to the Sage; Mosel had been arrested, almost certain to see the inside of the dungeon that Athaya knew so well; Cecile was fleeing in self-imposed exile, along with her children—the heirs to Caithe; and Nicolas—beloved Nicolas—was racked with madness, bearing the burdens of magic though he possessed none of his own and as lost to her as Kelwyn had been in his last days. To make things worse, over half of her followers had left her in the span of a single month, either because she would not take up arms against the king or because they thought she had. And crowning it all, a powerful wizard from a distant land was bent on destroying everything that remained of her creation.

Athaya shuffled into the kitchen and languidly cut herself a slice of day-old bread. Without a word, she sat down next to Master Tonia on a wooden bench near the hearth.

"You going to be all right?" Tonia asked. The older woman regarded her worriedly; the question had nothing to do with her bandaged shoulder, but the somber expression on her face.

"The weight of it all is pressing on me a bit harder today, that's all." Athaya tore off a mouthful of bread and dipped it in honey. "It's spiraling out of my control, Tonia. Right now, I feel as if I'm powerless to do anything but sit back and watch what happens. Why hasn't the Sage come to Caithe yet?'' she asked anxiously. ''What is he waiting for? What's going to be his next move?''

''Who can guess what's going on inside that head of his,'' Tonia replied with a shrug. ''But whatever it is, I can guarantee we're not going to like it.''

The cold weather broke in mid-February, and a warm breeze tasting of spring swept in from the sea and caressed the coast of Sare. The Sage opened the shutters and rested his arms on the windowsill, drinking in the day.

Behind him, Drianna slipped silently into the room, coming to kiss him firmly on the mouth. She clung to him with an air of desperation, as if he were going on a long and dangerous journey. Her once-beguiling eyes were now bloodshot and puffed.

''Tullis is ready,'' she said, sniffling. ''Whenever you are.''

Brandegarth put his arm around her and nodded.

Drianna shifted nervously, picking at the pearls sewn into the neckline of her emerald-colored gown. ''You're not still angry, are you?''

''No,'' he replied, then smiled, as it to assure her that his silence had nothing to do with her, or his former ire. ''I was, when Couric first told me of the prince's failure. Nicolas must have had far more mettle than I'd realized. But perhaps we can do just as well in spite of his failure—he and Durek may not be dead, but Caithe is in an uproar, and Athaya is discredited. Our fundamental task has been accomplished. The Caithan Lorngeld are ripe for a new leader.

''And we have these as some consolation,'' he said, gesturing to the unruly heap of books on the table. ''I will enjoy learning what the wizard Rhodri found so engrossing about King Kelwyn and what Athaya had to do with it all. It's unfortunate that Couric could not send Nicolas back for more; I would have liked him to obtain every book the prince could provide him from that library. From what I've heard,'' the Sage went on, ''Rhodri refused to allow the beliefs of his Reykan teachers to constrain him. He may have developed several magical theories well worth investigating.''

Drianna listened obediently, but she was in no mood for such talk. Her lower lip began to quiver like a rose petal trembling in the breeze. ''I hope you won't forget me,'' she said, kneeling at his feet and resting a tearstained cheek against his soft leather leggings. "Athaya said she didn't recognize anyone after the first few weeks."

He stroked her auburn hair, winding one lock around his finger. "I shall try not to, my dear," he assured her, "but the sealing spell is powerful. I may not be able to help myself. Just console yourself with all that shall occur after I am released and fully recovered."

"Yes, just think!" she cried, pushing away the possibilities that he would neither be released in time nor recover if he were. "You'll be able to see the seeds of magic just the way Athaya can and you can finally tell me whether or not I'm to develop the power! And if I am, then we can marry. At last."

"Of course, Drianna," he replied absently, diverted by far larger rewards. "But the talent would have more use than that. While I remain here, and the seal carves out new paths and spells for me, I shall send some of my people to the mainland to prepare the Caithans for my coming. Then, when I am restored, I shall appear among them, able to give them what no one else ever has—the knowledge of who will be a wizard and who will not. Why, I may even be able to translocate there!" he added exultantly, eyes agleam. "I will be able to make them loyal to me. *Me*, and not Athaya Trelane. For once the people discover that she could have used her talent to tell them what they were, and did not, they will be angry. They will resent that she preferred them to wait for madness and the threat of death to haunt them—crying ethics all the while, no doubt. Wished them to wait until they were so desperate and short of time that they had no choice but to go to her for training and sustenance, rather than flee to Reyka . . . or to us."

Drianna looked up at him with adoration. "They will love you as I do, Brand."

"Aye, they will. Especially when I teach them that their destiny is far greater than Athaya has ever revealed. That they are the true rulers of Caithe, chosen by God. And I shall be God's greatest servant!" He plucked a leather tube from the table and drew out a yellowed piece of parchment—Dameronne's prophecy. "And I shall be a king. Our golden age is coming, Drianna. Almighty God, it is almost upon us!"

"It will be glorious . . . and I will be so proud of you."

The Sage chuckled softly. "But in the meantime, it will amuse me to think that Athaya no doubt expects me to swoop down upon her at any moment—she is probably dreading my coming this very moment—and I will not. Not for months yet. Four months, to be exact. That is how long you said she was sealed, yes? I must remember to tell Tullis the exact date I wish to be released.''

"Three and a half months, to be exact. But—''

"Adept she may be, but I shall be far more so, once I have extended my powers the way she has. And I shall do better and leave the seal on perhaps a few days more, just to be sure.''

Drianna labored to her feet, her face freshly lined with worry. "Brand, are you certain you can trust Tullis to free you?" she asked hesitantly, aware that the Sage disliked her to question him on matters of magic. "You'll be so vulnerable. And what if someone were to Challenge you while you are without your power?''

"Forbidden, Drianna," Brandegarth answered firmly. "The wizards of Sare are not like those clucking hens of the Circle who fall incontinent at the thought of every spell that is the least bit dangerous, but we do forbid certain things as a matter of honor. No wizard may Challenge the Sage while he is ill or wounded; it would not be a true test of God's will. As for Tullis," he went on, "I trust him more than any man on Sare. He is too old to aspire to my position here and too honest to take a bribe from some other ambitious man. Besides," he added darkly, "I've set a compulsion on Connor to tear him to pieces if he disobeys me.''

"And what of Ranulf Osgood?" Drianna pressed on. "He has no respect for your traditions. If he manages to free himself from the binding spells, he would strike you down without bothering to Challenge you first. He tried it once before.''

The Sage tugged absently on an earring. "He does pose a problem. I was only holding him so he wouldn't interfere with Nicolas' actions—he's not such a bad fellow, for all that he was educated by Reykan wizards instead of Sarian ones. But now I think I shall have to keep him here until I am released from the sealing spell. It won't do to have him running about loose while I'm powerless. And I set his binding spells myself, Drianna,'' he chided gently, "so there is no possibility of his escaping them.''

He restored the slip of parchment to its case and motioned Drianna to the door. "Send Tullis to me now. I am ready to be sealed. I could do it myself, I suppose, but I think it prudent that the wizard who is to release me also set the seal. It is difficult to risk insulting the Lord this way . . . to cast off His gift, even for a short time. It will be easier for another man to do. Now go, my dear. Go and do as I ask you.''

She kissed him again, this time in good-bye, and retreated to the door, pausing to watch as the Sage strolled leisurely back to the window—a king surveying his domain. Sea breezes ruffled the shoulder-long locks, and his gaze was glassy as the waters. The day was clear enough to reveal the northern shore of Caithe, waiting within his reach.

"Deliverer of your people," Brandegarth of Crewe said mockingly, his laugh low and rolling like the swells of the sea before him. "Yes, you shall deliver them, Athaya Trelane.

"Directly into *my* hands."

ABOUT THE AUTHOR

Julie Dean Smith was born in 1960 and has been writing since the age of five. Her first published work was a single sentence included in *Bride of Dark and Stormy*—a compilation of entries from the Bulwer-Lytton Fiction Contest.

She studied economics and English at the University of Michigan, during which time she became an avid football fan. She played the trumpet in the marching band, and on New Year's Day of 1981, was fortunate enough to witness Bo's boys actually win a Rose Bowl.

In 1984, she earned her M.A. in English at Western Michigan University, and her interest in computers developed while she was painfully handwriting the rough draft of her research thesis on Charles Dickens. Ms. Smith lives in Ann Arbor, Michigan, and works as a software technical writer, producing reference manuals and user guides (another form of fiction entirely).

Her other interests include Celtic music, medieval history, and pagan spirituality. Repeated viewings of *The Adventures of Robin Hood* and *Star Wars* have also given her a weakness for old-fashioned escapist entertainment, and she hopes one day to fulfill a lifelong dream of being swung by a rope over a gaping chasm, clasped in the arms of an attractive hero wearing a billowing white shirt.